D1141240

die
dancing

JONATHAN GASH

die
dancing

MACMILLAN

First published 2000 by Macmillan
an imprint of Macmillan Publishers Ltd
25 Eccleston Place, London SW1W 9NF
Basingstoke and Oxford
Associated companies throughout the world
www.macmillan.co.uk

ISBN 0 333 90105 3

9 8 7 6 5 4 3 2 1

A CIP catalogue record for this book is available from
the British Library.

Phototypeset by Intype London Ltd
Printed and bound in Great Britain by
Mackays of Chatham plc, Chatham, Kent

For Comets everywhere

Thanks
Susan

1

Goer – a male hired by a female, implicitly for sexual purposes

D r Clare Burtonall stood nervously on the dance floor of the Palais Rocco. Her tweed skirt and pastel blue twinset felt absurdly wrong. To be with Bonn, her hired lover, felt absolutely right. It was really their first time together in public.

She had no compunction about coming dancing after an autopsy. It was a kind of freedom. All doctors survived by closing mind doors. Leaving any clinic, she became a mere individual, untrammelled by memories of bleeding ulcers, sigmoidoscopies, autopsies. Back to humanity, as it were, a return to life.

Unbelievable to be so on edge, though. She stood facing Bonn, many years her junior, among a dozen other couples. So right to be with Bonn, but was the dance lesson a ghastly mistake?

'I'm wondering where to put my feet,' she said, breaking ice.

Bonn said nothing. Serious as ever, as if thinking of Boolean logics. Clare almost smiled, was careful not to.

The instructor, a slim, thirtyish man of fey elegance, clapped his hands.

'A-tten-see-yown!' The thin crowd of spectators seated at

the tables edging the dance floor quietened. The Palais stilled. 'Mogga dance class, beginners only. All rightee? Spread out, tout le monde!'

The pairs edged apart. Clare felt self-conscious. Surely there would be Farnworth General Hospital ex-patients among the spectators? They'd notice her, nudging, whispering wasn't that the lady doctor who admitted young Jessica last month, all that. And, dear God, be tempted to come across afterwards for a stilted chat.

'This dance,' the leader fluted, flashing the sequins striping his velvet body suit, 'is, you dance several different dances in turn, to *one* melodee. Capeesh?'

They waited expectantly. He cupped an ear.

'The phrase you're searching for,' he trilled, 'is, Yes, Bertram!'

'Yes, Bertram,' a few chorused weakly.

Bertram sighed. He wore an exotic matador cape in dazzling colours, high stamper heels, pinpoints of electric lights on every seam.

'As it's your first lesson, we'll all begin with a quick step. Count the bars. On the sixth bar I'll shout to change. You instantly waltz for six bars. Then change. The band will play a tango throughout.'

He cupped an ear, listening.

'Yes, Bertram!' some couples bleated.

'That's all we do. Six bars quick step, six bars waltz. Ferstay-henn-see tout?'

The couples got the idea. Response was everything.

'Yes, Bertram.'

Clare found herself answering obediently, to her embarrassment.

A red-faced girl called, 'Er, Bertram, please. How can we dance a quick step to a tango?'

Bertram smiled, pure sleet.

'With grace, you silly bitch. Heard of grace, have we? Like life, duckie. You pretend one thing while doing another.' He beamed at the couples as the music struck up. Clare saw that his eyes quickly missed Bonn, a slick elision. Bertram was no fool, knew of Bonn, and all about Bonn's stander who would be watching silently from some balcony. 'No more inanities? Then one-*and*-two-*and* . . .'

The pairs began to move, some staring at their feet.

Clare danced stiffly to the music. She had never really been any good, but she didn't care. She was with Bonn. Every minute was costing her a fortune, so she had a perfect right to be here. Bonn, she realized with astonishment, moved with gliding ease. Bertram screeched to change. They all effected a clumsy switch, then lost it entirely as Bertram screamed new orders. She thought of Bertram's vicious crack to the anxious girl. Pretence, like life. Pretend one thing, while doing another.

Less than an hour's walk across the city they were killing Dulsie.

The wallet man, he who paid, stood sourly observing the process. He kept thinking Dulsie had finally gone but the bastard kept regaining consciousness. Endurance was a remarkable thing.

The disused garage could have been Third World, some old Beirut corner made for tragedy. Rusting girders, that terrible stink of dank, tarpaulins crumpled to exotic sculpture under dust. The walls were rimed by sodden grubby white and encrusted with tabular fungi of awesome size groping down from the ceiling.

The wallet was impatient. He'd never seen anyone die

before. The mundanity of the process puzzled him. More pressing was the problem that so far Dulsie had given him nothing.

'It's a question of honesty, Dulsie,' he explained, standing before the nailed man, talking like to a moron. 'You've tellt me fuck all, nothing I didn't know, see?'

The killer liked to be reasonable. It was his way. Politics, after all, was the art of applied reason. Yet he was astonished at how tentative he had felt about this entire business until it actually started. He'd never thought himself squeamish, but now look. Twice he'd had to stare at the floor when the tankers did the hammer bit.

Dulsie came to, croaked, 'I'll do anything, Pens.'

Which only made the killer madder. Now the tankers knew his nickname. It was sheer breathtaking insolence. Squeamishness vanished.

'You think you're in a position to bargain, you frigging germ?'

He began to yell abuse, stalking to and fro. The two tankers watched impassively. Both seemed impossibly gross, heads shaven, necks gleaming with sweat ever since they'd nailed Dulsie with six-inchers to the garage wall. Tankers were cheap, less than the price of a second-hand motor for a night's work. Leeds provided most of the nation's tankers, solvers of disputes by violent moves beyond law.

At first Dulsie had screamed and whimpered in disbelief, until horror took hold. He'd finally surrendered to the welter of pain as they'd hammered the nails through his wrists. He was standing on the floor. The wallet said use the blowtorch, hurry for Christ's sake, get the facts. The two tankers just laughed, scorched Dulsie a bit then resorted to hammers. The wallet left them to it after that. They knew what they were doing.

The only time they showed rage was when the light failed and they had to go outside to their motor to bring a flashlight. They grumbled, blamed the wallet, scaring him. Failure was personal. They took it out on Dulsie.

One tanker spoke. 'Listen. You want him back?'

'Say now if you do.' His mate spat.

Neither looked at the wallet. They eyed Dulsie with dispassion, as inert as their hammers. The wallet considered the question. How did these tankers stay so far from the consequences of their actions? They'd have made good politicians. The fantastic image of the two brutes at some genteel Party fund-raiser was almost laughable. He saw stains seeping down Dulsie's trousers, smelled the stench.

'No,' he said. There were limits after all.

It was the right answer, the only one. Politically correct. Maybe he might work up a pun for a future speech? Worth a thought. Inevitability was the engine that drove political machines, forget design differences.

'I'll wait outside,' he said.

'You'll not,' the lead tanker said back, so the wallet stayed to watch as they walked to the crucified man and put an end to it. The wallet tried to look away but couldn't help himself. Death, as all consequences of a decision, had a certain fascination. Maybe it would be his only time to see the real thing. Politics wasn't usually as easy as this.

Bertram the dance instructor moved into high camp. He was used to a dozen beginner couples but Sol the proprietor was a right fascist drong and always ruled money down. No thought of what fees might do to creativity, stingy pig.

'That,' Bertram crooned while the music stopped and couples froze, 'was atrocious. What was it?'

'Atrocious,' some chorused feebly.

'Correct! Now, mogga dancing is simply the hardest dance form there is. And I'll make you experts in a week.'

'Bertram, please,' a girl in a green woollen dress quavered. 'You didn't actually say *how* we begin.'

Bertram said sweetly, 'With legs like the Pillars of Hercules, dearie, I'd really not bother. If you insist, the music plays one tune, yeah? On my clap you start the quickstep, yeah? Six bars, *change*! Waltz, yeah? Six bars, *change*! Slow foxtrot, yeah?'

Clare was enjoying herself. Being with Bonn in public was entirely original. She'd hardly been able to concentrate in the clinic at the coming excitement of it. It had been a brainwave.

'Please don't worry, darling,' she whispered reassuringly to Bonn. 'It's quite respectable!'

It was her joke. Bonn did not smile back. He stood stiffly waiting for the lesson to continue or to end.

Smiles, Bonn had found, often ended in failure. He had only complied with Clare Three-Nine-Five's request to come dancing because of the unusual circumstances. Sex in a hotel room was the norm, what a client actually paid the Pleases Agency for. This dancing lesson however was a performance, now made into a problem of semantics on account of witnesses. Many spectators here in the Rocco would of course recognize him, but Rack his stander was watching from the balcony. Nobody would dare crack a face, much less call out in derision, which somehow made the whole thing much worse. Bonn had steeled himself to agree. New to the goer game, he must learn to adapt.

Bertram demonstrated, swirling and ending with an elegant pirouette, admiring his own outstretched hands as he moved.

'Ready, toot lay mond? Be-geen!'

The music struck up, Bertram wandering among the couples twittering encouragement or condemnation, shoving elbows and heads into better positions. He never touched or even glanced at Clare or Bonn, merely passed them with a quiet 'T'rific, great, t'rif.'

The session took thirty minutes. By the time they were released the scattered spectators had drifted to the coffee balconies and were paying scant attention. Clare and Bonn together walked off the floor. She was flushed with pleasure, Bonn still silent. People were aware of him, looking away after a quick glance as he passed among the tables.

'We'll leave now, Bonn,' Clare told him quietly when sure she wasn't overheard.

'Very well.'

It was arranged. The Pleases Agency had done the hotel booking, Room 591 at the newly converted Amadar Royale in the city's main square. Aware of Bonn's desperate shyness, she hurried to collect her coat and handbag to avoid keeping him. Hell seemed other people to Bonn, which might raise the question why he was a goer, a hireling whose one function was to provide physical solace to client ladies on command.

Brightly she rejoined him in the foyer. 'There! Shall we go?'

'Separately, please.' Bonn's words were as near silence as a voice could allow. Then more audibly, 'Thank you for the dance.'

Colouring, she searched his face. Few people were about in the foyer. Tea dances attracted only limited numbers.

'Another rule?' she said in quiet anger. After all, *she* was paying *him* for two consecutive hours of his company. She had made that quite plain to the Pleases Agency woman who'd taken her phone booking.

Bonn thought before replying. 'No. I simply do not wish to give rise to scandal, for your sake.'

'I said that doesn't matter!'

She made sure, however, that they left simultaneously to save face, turning away with a smile calculated to show how perfectly casual the dance partnership had been. With restraint she avoided staring after him, and walked briskly towards the Asda shopping mall. Bonn moved steadily towards the Amadar Royale. She did not notice the dark stocky youth who was already drifting along the pavement ahead of Bonn.

Ten minutes later, crossing the hotel lounge towards the lifts, she heard her mobile phone go and paused to answer. Her colleague Dr Ellen Pierre came on to say that she was going out with a dash team, but that it would probably turn out to be a BID. A 'brought in dead' would make Ellen late for her evening clinic, a minor nuisance.

Clare walked on, relieved that her next hour with Bonn would not be ruined. She felt as free as air. Apart from the minor spat about walking together through Victoria Square – she'd imagined this several times, a treat to picture them paired in public – she thought her idea to take Bonn dancing had worked out really well. It was the beginning of possible permanence.

She mustn't do that again, though, she cautioned herself as the lift came. Not to Bonn, especially in public. Showing annoyance could be ruinous with someone like him. On her part it had been nothing more than silly petulance. His agency made the rules after all. She was merely the client. Stupid behaviour might put her, she felt sure, on a par with his other women clients. If it wasn't for that Hippocratic

Oath she could scratch the eyes out of the lot of them and keep Bonn for her own. But she was getting there, getting there. It had been slow so far, yet she felt sure that no other woman could know him as she did. Except, was this conviction felt by all his clients, the bitches? For the next superb hour Bonn would be hers alone in Room 591.

Idly watching the floor numbers click by, she wondered about the BID. Something drug-related perhaps, currency business, or some massive art theft planned by the lifting gangs who dominated the city's necrotic industrial centre.

She erased the problem and concentrated on the image of Bonn. As he, she told herself smiling inwardly, would concentrate on her with that maddening doubtful reticence that made her want him all the more. And now – this was the real pearl – Clifford was gone, her divorce all but finalized and absolute, thank God. She was free, buffered against the evil of loneliness by Bonn.

It would not be long before she would make Bonn all her own. The rest of the world – and that perfidious Pleases Agency he worked for – could take it or leave it. She would find a way. There would be raised eyebrows, of course, but see if she cared!

The doors slid apart. She stepped through, smiling, tempted to swing her handbag with an unladylike jauntiness. She resisted. Unrestrained surrender to temptation would come any moment now. She found Room 591, and tapped on the door, smiling.

2

Key – a goer who controls a group of goers, usually not more than three in number

MARTINA CURSED HER lameness. Posser, her father, blamed himself for it, but she blamed nobody. Her true enemy was the quality of being lame.

Seated quite ten minutes before she summoned the lounge waiter, she was always apprehensive of the eyes of others. They saw her as she simply appeared, a tableau of seated thus-ness, blonde, expensively dressed – and, okay, think it outright – probably scoring her as frankly attractive. Then they might observe that she couldn't walk properly, and instantly their glances became hooded, furtive, with that familiar sneering characteristic she loathed. She still remembered children calling after her in the rougher streets. Now she travelled in physical comfort, in any grand motor she wished to use.

Only Bonn, one of the goers belonging to her Pleases Agency, never noticed her disability. Others saw, then point-edly didn't, showing their modern fairmindedness. Bonn, though, truly didn't see. She swore he actually *never* saw her limp. Certainly he never opened a door or fetched a chair except with that abstracted air of his, a courtesy he would show to anyone, lame or not. She was glad.

Candidly observing in her turn the people around the

hotel foyer, she knew they were less than she. Think of it in any terms – money, power, influence – and she was ahead. Except for the great irony of her deformity.

It was so cruel. Her father Posser was too ill from emphysema to run the Pleases Agency as he used to. She, his only child, had had to take it on and become the sole authority over the goers, plus the strings of street girls Grellie ran for her in Waterloo Street and Victoria Square. She, Martina, alone decided who operated the casino, the snooker halls, who served at the Rum Romeo, who was hired and fired. And who decided how close the whole operation skated to the edge, the ultimate risk of law.

She ordered tea.

Life was becoming more problematic. Posser had begun the Agency with farthings. Now it owned property throughout the city. The Agency was little known except by word of mouth, yet already it was stretched almost beyond capacity as far as goers were concerned.

Sexual liberation was to blame, and Martina blamed it with a fervent hate. Each tide of freedom made more and more women – many young, not even married – book her goers. Already this month Martina had arranged kickback deals with two additional smaller hotels near Victoria Square. And the Agency's shut gelt, paid to ensure silence, already equalled the National Debt. It was sickening. Posser's guidance was still good, but could be relied upon only in lucid intervals when Dr Winnwick had him on an even keel. Otherwise it was all down to her. She was not, however, lonely. To herself she insisted that was not the case.

The waiter brought her tea and set it out. She dismissed him without a word just as the messenger appeared in the hotel's revolving doors. He headed unhesitatingly towards her. She accepted the envelope and opened it. The paper was blank except for four pencilled numbers. Martina returned it to the envelope.

'I'll see Grellie,' she said quietly. 'One hour, at the Shot Pot. Tell Rack to come.'

The messenger left without a word. The waiter came across to ask if everything was all right. Martina inspected him, saw that he was new. He fidgeted, pinned by her cold blue eyes.

'Is anything wrong, miss . . .'

A senior waitress hurried up and quickly drew the waiter away.

Martina's mind raced as she poured tea and leant back, the better to conceal her lame leg by folding it under the chair. Several problems today, each compounding the next.

The Agency was overstretched. One question was whether to establish a new firm of goers. A firm was usually three goers, rarely four, operating under one 'key' who acted as a mentor, just as Bonn despite his newness had been promoted to lead three others. But where would she acquire another goer good and reliable enough to lead such a firm? Good goers were not uncommon, but a key goer must have judgement, and still have that eternal appeal to the discerning client women. They were unbelievably rare.

And a goer like Bonn was the rarest gift of all. That he seemed not to know what was going on around him, that he looked as innocent as any infant, only seemed to add to his extraordinary pulling power. Miss Faith, veteran of the Pleases Agency phone banks, said she could book Bonn out four, five times a day. One booking per goer was the Agency's norm, by Martina's rule, perhaps twice on rare occasions.

There was a further complication and more questions. Grellie, her lieutenant who ran the street girls for the Agency, was possibly hooked on Bonn. Martina saw this as frank subversion, for relationships among the Agency's employees were strictly forbidden. Always had been, ever since Posser started the business.

And now here came another phoned death threat to Zen, one of her keys. She almost rose to leave but thought twice. Give yourself time to feel the problem, she told herself. It was Posser's constant advice.

She considered a biscuit, weakly decided on a Peak Freen and closed her eyes a moment.

Upstairs in 591, just about now Bonn would be entering Clare Three-Nine-Five. There could be no more hateful thought. After the bitch had taken Bonn mogga dancing at the Palais Rocco. Shameless, vulgar bitch of a doctor, dancing with Bonn. When that was something Martina with her lameness would never do.

She tried to calm herself. She had to come to terms with all the difficulties in the goer trade. It was a question of time before everything was exactly as she wished. Central to life, though, was the fact that Bonn deserved release from predators like Clare Three-Nine-Five.

Clare groaned as Bonn almost slid out of her. He was moribund, sleeping, but she managed to keep him within by dextrous movement of her body, gasping at the effort of sustaining his weight. She relaxed, felt him still there, and smiled in self praise at her achievement. It wasn't the kind of advice she had received in medical school, where no – repeat no – instruction was ever given in the enjoyment, practice or manipulation of sex for its own ends. Statistics, of course, figured large in the six undergraduate medical years. Starting to breathe hard under Bonn's crushing mass, she wondered if he, at the seminary where by accident she'd learned he once studied, if any of them for that matter had ever had lectures on the uses and abuses of sex. Or on women, come to that.

Probably no for both answers.

Bonn's breathing slowed and became regular again. This was relish, her own private time in which she took almost as much delight as the act of sexual congress gave. Or was it one and the same process? After all he was *in* her, though now flaccid and at rest, so continuity was there.

She had once interrogated him, rather too directly and perhaps with a little hard edge of cruelty that she now regretted. Her question had been about the way he viewed her. Yet surely she, the hiring woman client, coming through the door to make use of his submission to her purchasing power, had a perfect right to know how he saw the demanding older woman? At her question he had been silent, worried, and was unable to reply as she wanted. Instead her questions had somehow become questions aimed at herself, like one of those missiles that, fired from whatever position or speed, instantly reversed its intended trajectory to attack its origin. The occasion had been, what, her third time with him? It had been the moment she had decided that she and Bonn were for each other.

Immediately afterwards, she remembered bitterly, she had almost suffered apoplexy from the realization that he was already out on the streets heading for some other hotel room, some other bitch who fancied it was time she got herself used.

Used? Some clue in the term there, Dr Burtonall, Clare thought, turning her head for air as Bonn rolled slightly almost crushing her face into the pillow. At their second encounter, she had casually mentioned that a long bolster pillow 'would be nice', and ever since it was somehow always provided for them. Use, though, using, used?

Use was an essential element, she acknowledged to herself. I am being used, though not in the sense of exploited, by this person who is now my lover. I am being made use of, or would that not quite do? Set coldly down on paper, Clare decided she was actually the one doing the using, and possibly abusing, in terms of modern political rectitude, the catchphrase ways everybody spoke these days. It could be that sexual attraction was simply the lure of orgasm, though of course there were other routes to bliss without hiring some street youth this way. So the orgasm could not exactly be the only goal, though it was an appealing one, stronger at some times than others.

Over the past months she had begun to see this time with Bonn as something more than simply a physiological stirring, a series of satisfying lurches with a sweaty release. Relief, surely, was in there too, but that seemed a relatively small part of the gratification when she compared her own reactions to those of Bonn – or her ex-husband Clifford too, come to that. A man reached post-coital relief as a drowning sailor reaches land. The woman, though, doesn't quite dash at it in the same way. That 'use' term lay there in her mind as Bonn stirred and felt for her. He realized that she lay beneath him, and rolled onto his side of the bed with one leg still pressing her down. She was pleased to see his eyes still closed, though she knew he was now awake. She could even ask him these things! Except she knew he would try hard to answer in the vein she wished, not from within himself. She was more likely to reach his truths by asking when he was fully conscious, while he was thinking and looking around the room or at the ceiling, miles away as usual.

Use, though. Therein lay some key.

She was using him, okay, she thought angrily, get the money business out of the way *then* look beyond at what she took from Bonn, what he gave her.

She had had a patient – a girl, given age fifteen – who blithely told Clare in her surgery that no, she never used any kind of contraception. When asked about AIDS or other transmissible infections the girl had said with a cool disregard, 'I never. It'd be like nothing happened, wouldn't it?'

Clare tried hard to understand. After all, the fate of spermatozoa impelled by the male into the woman, the millions of his wild cells flailing in and butting to reach a coitus of their own with the ovum, must have a physiological and emotional response, influencing the woman's own senses afterwards. It was part of the unifying act. The consciousness was the woman's, the oblivion the male's, it seemed to her, now she was becoming an ardent disciple of the process. She reached the worrying conclusion that being used in this way was perhaps even what she most desired. Call it a hired coupling if you like. So?

Which left one serious question unresolved: Why did she and Clifford never agree that the most important part of life was their staying together for ever and ever? She had reached that conclusion quite effortlessly by sleeping with Bonn, quite shamelessly basing her determination on the sickening business of pulling out her purse and counting out the money onto the mantelpiece before leaving.

Did this hiatus come easier to a man who hired a prostitute across the road? Did they simply find the money in a pocket, drop it casually as they left, satisfied, for the girl to pick up and get ready to parade the streets again for the next customer? Try as she might, Clare found it impossible to see herself and Bonn in those terms. There was feeling, some kind of appreciation, an understanding between herself and

Bonn that no quick casual conjoining between a man and one of the Waterloo Road street girls could equal. It just wasn't, couldn't be, the same.

The question of love, what it was and meant to Bonn and herself, could wait until she'd had a chance to make Bonn face the inevitable conclusion that she must have Bonn to herself. It was his destiny, could he but see it, and her own certainty too. She must make sure it came about.

She pulled his leg further over her, grunting with the exertion of it, checked the time, and slept.

'News?' Hassall said bitterly, not just putting on a show. 'What news?'

Sergeant Cockle had introduced himself and got 'More jokes about your name than mine, I'll bet.'

Cockle was short, tubby, a belly-bulger with his stretched coat barely making it. He consulted his notebook, but his eyes were everywhere. For an ageing bloke, Hassall's desk was astonishingly tidy. The paperwork – thirty-eight forms per arrest, since that lunatic Criminal Evidence law came in – seemed done by nocturnal elves. You never saw the old sod writing, yet he was on time with it all. Police clerks on the second floor told him Hassall was 'average everything, no more'. Undistinguished, hardly a career man. Overtaken twice in the promotion leapfrogging. No honours, no com-mendations.

'New brothel opening soon, Mr Hassall.'

'Not an extension?'

'Of the four others? No. Right in the middle. Brad-shawgate.'

'News is supposed to come when things happen. So what,

blokes have a shag on the way home? Wheels of commerce, Mr Cockle.'

The sergeant didn't blink. They'd told him he'd drawn a barbary swine. One sergeant called him Has-Nowt Has-All.

'And there's word of a mill being developed for bare-knuckle fighting, illegal prize fights.'

'Ever seen one?' Hassall asked unexpectedly. 'Goes on all over the north.'

Cockle was disconcerted. 'Er, no.'

'Puts the fear of God in you.' Hassall reflected. 'What worries me is why they keep on scrapping when they're being battered silly. Claret everywhere. They have leagues.'

'I heard it might be in three disused mills.'

'Save your notes. Check the phone companies in case an empty mill suddenly becomes a multi-use subscriber. Electrics, gas, water authority, all that. It's quicker than lurking.'

'Right, Mr Hassall.'

Hassall watched him go, wondering which loitering goojer in Victoria Square had fed him that load of tat. Letting the plod know was just their politeness. Hilarious. Cockle must feel like Hawkeye of the North. He'd learn or, Hassall thought, possibly not. He wondered whether to have some canteen coffee, decided against. He might walk through the city square, innocently show himself by way of saying ta for the news to whatever bint it was.

3

Straightener – an illegal disciplining, by financial or
physical punishment, of one who transgresses

Grellie watched Bonn head for the Butty Bar. She knew all his actions. He would pause there, recover over some tea or merely wait for Rack and hand over his fee. Lovely to go and sit with him for a while, maybe hint how he ought to shack up with her on the sly, at fearsome risk of course, it being contrary to Martina's law. Today Grellie'd checked the girls in Waterloo Street earlier than usual, against all odds finding her first three on beat. Rani however was a cow who ought to be doing the railway station brough by now, and wasn't. If the slut was late again instead of working her arse off she was for it. You could be lenient once too often in this game. Grellie scanned the square, her eyes everywhere.

The central bus station occupied much of the rectangular garden. It looked pleasant from a distance. Close to, you noticed the tatty caff, the shoddy loos with their lopsided Gents and Ladies signs pocked by weather. Lately the city council had tried to do it up, setting paths and garden benches round the flower beds and putting new plants in. The huge squared paving for owd cocks to play walking chess had proved a success. There was power talk of a duck pond.

Traffic roared round, hurling off at the corners named for

ancient city gates. Martina's writ ran here. Rack and his honchos saw to that, enforcing Martina's syndicate. Many of the places that did thriving business were actually owned by the Pleases Agency, Inc. Martina's ailing dad, Posser, had taken possession of the decomposing city's crumbling heart over a decade ago, and made it quite a territory. Grellie strolled the pavement, mentally ticking off Martina's empire. The Butty Bar, the Rum Romeo casino near the north-west corner that was still called Deansgate though no dean or gate remained. Nothing much at Station Brough, for propriety's sake, since the Hotel Vivante stood there and you could give away too much by showy possessiveness. Martina, lovely but lame, was too shrewd for that caper.

Clockwise, Grellie registered, was Greygate. Beyond was the Shot Pot snooker hall, with Martina's day office attached, then the Barn Owl, a converted cotton mill on its last legs lending a show of legitimacy to the syndicate's enterprises. And the Pilot Ship casino plus, on the floor above, Martina's grandly named 'control office'. There, telephonists booked in the lady clients who rang for a session of clandestine sex with one of the Agency's goers. Goers, Grellie thought with a pang, like Bonn. She'd been frank enough to him; she'd have him at any cost. But that was against Martina's rule, and Bonn so far had obeyed the cold, crippled blonde. Martina was inflexible. It would have been easier if Posser had stayed well enough to rule.

'Whatcher thinking, Grell?'

Grellie didn't even turn as she trolled across the top of Waterloo Street. Rack joined her.

'Nothing. Bonn lived here when he first came, right?'

'Yip. At Mrs Corrigan's.' Rack still smouldered over it. 'Thieving cow used to nick next door's coal – I ask yer, Grell, fucking *coal*. I was alwus sorting her out, fucking daft old bat.'

'How long is it since he moved into Bradshawgate?' Though Grellie knew.

Bonn now lodged in Martina's house, after the plod had focused on him. Rack put word about that it was for Bonn's protection, but Grellie knew better. Martina, the deformed cow, was after Bonn, and had got him under her roof. Being boss gave enormous advantage. It was coming close to war, but Grellie dared not fire the first salvo.

'Four weeks, two days,' Rack said, having no real idea.

Still no sign of Rani, the lazy bitch. 'Rack. Why does the syndicate have more places down Rivergate than anywhere else?'

'Eh?' Rack stared, whistled. He bawled a few numbers loudly to a couple of Grellie's stringers trolling languidly down Quaker Street. They joshed back, numbers again. Rack laughed, on song, then sobered. He'd never thought of it.

The shopping mall by the Weavers Hall was muchly in Posser's hands, though Martina didn't bother with details there. The Bouncing Block gym down Moor Lane, plus the new lady doctor's surgery right on the square. Then the ground floor bookie's run by Escho, with syndicate ins at the Worcester Club, the Conquistador Bed and Grill, and some unknowable percentage of the Palais Rocco dance place. An impressive spread. Many bits made much. Grellie was right, plenty there, but what was the plan about Rivergate? She'd never really noticed until now.

'Ah.' Rack was always quick to invent lunatic theories. 'It's because Posser had a dead auntie in the Rivergate corner, see? He liked her, but she had this tumour—'

It was all made up, another Rack daftness. Grellie knew

better than say so. She depended on Rack, as he on her. If they didn't stay pals the whole street series of stringers and businesses would fall apart.

'Pitching the working house next door to Posser is wrong, Rack.'

He gaped at her. This was serious bad. 'Jesus, Grell. Don't say so. Martina'd go ballistic. She's already done it, see? Just like supermarket wheelies—'

'I want it moved down George Street, Rack.'

'*Move* a new fucking brothel, Grellie? You off yer frigging plank?'

Usually Rack would be prancing ahead, a talking walking dervish, explaining crazy notions you'd be mad to listen to. But this opinion made him halt, which was so odd a sight that two of Grellie's stringers, just coming on beat from the street market, actually slowed to see Rack behaving himself for once.

'Don't, fer Chrissakes, Grell. Let it go.'

The problem was, everybody knew Rack had tried pulling Grellie but she'd have none of him, so he'd started wanting Grellie and Bonn to shack up in spite of the fearsome risks they'd run. Grellie craved it too, though crossing between goers and stringers was strictly forbidden. There'd been a stringer called Danielle and a goer called Galahad not long since who'd been caught shagging regular down Haleys Wharf, and they'd paid with being dead, a so-say accident of course. It was a measure of serious because Rack would be the one who'd have to do any straightening. And who could straighten Bonn? There'd be world fucking war. All women's fault, of course, because everything was, but still you didn't need to go ashing a fucking city just for the sake of a fucking rule.

'The meeting's soon, innit?' Grellie was stubborn. 'I want that Rani watched, Rack. She's—'

'There's phone threats, Grell,' Rack said to deflect her, but women were nuisances and Grellie only idly asked who against because she only ever thought of Bonn.

'Zen. Three times, no trace.'

Not Bonn, then, so Grellie lost interest. 'That Rani. If the cow's malarking I'll do her.'

'Keep mum at the meeting, Grell. It were Bonn's idea putting a whore house next to Posser's home.' He tried to end on a good note. 'That Trish you picked to run it looks good, eh?'

He resumed his finger-clicking swagger, trying to talk her round with his fantastic memory. Sometimes he was just frigging brilliant. He wanted a new leather bomber jacket, fronded with slab elbows, which would make him look stupendous.

'It's too much for Bonn,' Grellie said. 'He'll worry.'

Today was becoming a frigging mess, Rack could tell, when minutes ago it had been superb. 'Bonn, worry? Him? About a few fucking tarts?' But Bonn would. Strange how somebody new, puzzled, looking lost, pulled women like a magnet yet knew fuck all about anything. It was well weird.

'I've got to get Beatrice and Patsy,' Grellie said, cutting losses, knowing Rack wouldn't support her when push came to shove under Martina's hard azure eyes. 'See you at the meeting.'

'Don't, Grell,' Rack said after her, but you might as well talk to a frigging lamp-post, women getting ideas in their heads. He wondered if there had ever been a time when women thought straight or if they'd always been off the frigging wall.

He went down Market Street towards the cinema where

he was to meet Coll, best slider in the business if you got him early before he was sloshed out of his mind in the Volunteer. Time to suss these threatening phone calls before Martina got narked. Probably nothing, some nutter. Rack just didn't want to get in Martina's way when she started moving, the absolute truth, one of her silent stares coming at you on a wet Thursday. Fuck that. Rub out the death threats, and all'd be well.

Elora gave Grellie the message as she entered the shopping mall. Grellie saw her reflection in Wardens window among the shoes and handbags and thought Elora dressed too loud by a mile. It was time she reined some of her Rivergate stringers in, got up like Christmas trees. Grellie was a believer in organization and hated loose ends. You had to, ruling strings of working girls as tarty as these.

'Grellie? Martina wants you.'

The girl was a good nineteen – she said that but was a deal older, twenty-four sort of. Stiletto heels a mile tall, three colour zones in her hair, accessories clashing with every flashing shop neon, she was like a spaceship. All sight and no sense. Grellie hadn't been that stupid when she was five, clacking about her granny's kitchen in clogs.

'What for?' It was only token resistance. Elora didn't show she recognized it as that, just said she'd no idea. Martina's summons meant instant yes.

'Dunno. Askey told me, by Fat George's news-stand.'

Askey was the diminutive messenger who lurked among the motorcycle couriers at the Triple Racer facing the Asda supermarket. He was so like the long-dead comedian that the nickname caught on, bottle specs, calf-lick, bulbous head. Reliable, no opinions.

'Where?'

'The snooker place, Askey said. Want me to do anything?'

Bring a message that meant a working girl's absence, you were responsible for taking over and finishing her job if she was on a punter. Grellie shook her head and left Elora to it.

The trouble was Grellie now had too many working girls on the strings to cope. One hand, that idle mare Rani was taking her fucking time doing nothing so the other girls on the station string were already muttering. Other hand, these lasses were dolling themselves up like lighthouses when the tone should be quiet and tasty instead of slamming every pedestrian in the eye with curves, body language, cosmetics, their glitz blitz shrieking that they truly were flashy whores on the street game. The City Watch Committee would only take so much and new girls like Elora were rattling the Watch's cage. Grellie decided she was too thinly stretched especially, she thought, smarting, with Martina interrupting every few seconds with her come-here-do-that.

Martina needed telling. Whatever Rack said, it was time to kick over the traces. Grellie headed back across the square towards the Granadee TV Studios where they made the soap operas about local pub folk. All wrong accents, like any reviewer'd ever notice. She saw Vadne, one of her Greygate string, yakking and strutting among football fans arriving from the moorland village bus routes, and fumed, If I've told Vadne once I've told her a thousand times, no fratting among footer supporters in daylight. Like banging your head on a brick. She'd get Rack to straighten Vadne, only a little routine, this aft, no later. But it was always one more fucking thing then another, never one hour straight.

She looked about for somebody to warn Vadne off, but there was nobody to hand. Why not? Because Rani was still dozing in her sodding pit, that's why not. Blazing, Grellie marched all the faster towards Mawdsley Street and the Phoenix Theatre, turned left into Settle Street and came on the snooker hall. Not all afternoons started trouble and more on the way, but today was a winner all right.

She saw Bonn emerge from the Foundry Street entrance of the Butty Bar into the drizzle and start with meditative slowness across the road towards the Asda supermarket, and guessed where he'd be heading later. Why did he go to stand in churches like that? Her mouth watered. She wished he'd dress fashionable but he didn't seem to understand style. She'd dress him brilliant if he'd let her. She set her face to composure, and went in to see Martina.

Hassall surveyed the scene round the dead man nailed to the garage wall.

'They're always detestable, Cockle,' he told the bloke he'd drawn today. 'Crucifying's new though.'

Cockle was tomorrow's front runner in the police promotion stakes. Hassall knew the desk wallahs had thirteen-to-eight on him for advancement. To Hassall he looked something of a Methodist fresh from Sunday School. Cockle's avowed hobby, though, was forensics. Get trapped in a car with Cockle on the way back to the nick, you got an earful of immunochemistry and electrophoresis. He was a right pest.

'There was a case on Hampstead Heath,' Cockle gave. 'Some years back. A queer got crucified on a beech. I have the details.'

He would have. 'Aye, well.'

Hassall cleared his throat, casting around the dank brickwork of the disused garage. The body had been photographed, everything tabulated from relative humidity to temperature gradients. Some silly sod had scraped dust from every square foot of floor space and taken leachings from each begrimed window-pane. Uniformed stalwarts guarded the mill yard and the surrounding dereliction, tape everywhere. Much good it would do. Gossip, touts, chat among ordinary folk out there, was where crimes got solved. Hassall honestly believed that forensic science was crap. Try telling sergeants like Cockle that, though.

The SOCO came, treading like a kid on pavement cracks.

'Awreet, Hassie?'

'Aye, Ted. You?'

The Scene of Crime Officer was a stout elderly man called Ted Euxton, an old Lancashire name, who remarkably bore nobody ill will, not even crooks or other blokes in the plod. Benignity was just his thing. Hassall remembered him mostly for having once said that being a librarian was probably the best job in the whole world, which was odd even for a copper. He was rightly obsessed with area. Location was everything to Ted Euxton, admit only essential people and compel them to keep their hands in their pockets at all times, film everyone doing anything, time-place-date. He was the bloke who advocated special coverall garb, shoes included, for any crime scene, from a murder site to a littered toffee wrapper.

'Fine thing this, eh?' And Euxton went quickly on as somebody outside started shouting they'd found something, 'I thinks it's tankers, GBH imported across the Pennines.'

Hassall was curious. 'How much you reckon they get paid?' After all, grievous bodily harm implicitly had a purpose, right? Though motive, Hassall knew, was also crap, which was where thinking got you.

'Job like this?' The SOCO pursed his lips. 'Two large

down apiece, then a G each after, summat like that, d'you reckon?'

'There was a police survey,' Cockle intoned to Hassall, 'on this very point, sir. It showed remarkable consistency across the entire country.'

'Aye,' Euxton said cryptically. 'It only means no chance of finding the buggers.'

'ID?'

'Deceased is one Terence Dulsworthy, aka Dulsie. Our bloke Bell out there, said he recognized him.'

'Sir?' Somebody put his head round the door space, eyes on the keep-out tape. 'Found a hammer, blood all over it.'

'Ta. Follow procedure, then.' Euxton raised his eyebrows at Hassall. 'These new uniformed coppers are like a sack of new puppies. Dulsie's a fixer round town. Procures drugs for visiting pillars of society, gets birds for Euro parliamentarians visiting our sordid north, arranges exotic backhanders for Continental mayors junketing on the Twinned Towns exchange programme.'

'Then how'd Dulsie finish up getting nailed to our bricks if he's got connections?'

'Tell you later.' Euxton had a grin like a burned cadaver's. 'Maybe.'

'He's bound to have form, though,' Cockle put in, frowning, because saying otherwise would mean admitting that Forensics might let everybody down.

'Maybe.' Hassall believed nothing.

'Bell says the deceased was into politics.'

'He was tortured, sir.'

Cockle had been listening to the outside chat. Hassall remembered that Cockle and Bell had come through the Silly Circus – the famed police college in London's growth zone – together. 'Burns on his thighs and groin, no blow torch found.'

'What politics?' Hassall and Euxton said together, then felt foolish.

'Shows up at political hustings, it seems.'

'Get as much as you can on that,' Hassall asked after a protracted pause.

They watched Cockle go before Euxton spoke.

'What do you reckon, Hassie? I'm sick of these bizarres. They're getting worse.'

Hassall knew Ted Euxton had had the road rager to cope with the week previous. Three youths had hanged – literally hanged by the neck – a bloke who'd simply transgressed on the 666 trunk road, no satanic significance known. From a flyover. Motorists drove sedately under the dangling figure for over an hour before one, more curious than anxious, phoned in and asked what the hell. Motive for the murder was annoyance, the young blokes having hated being over-taken on an inside lane by a motor judged inferior.

'They keep coming, don't they,' Hassall said. 'Reckon it's purposeful, Ted?'

'Deliberate? Sure as God makes apples.'

Doubtful then, Hassall thought, and decided to go alone for a pint in the Volunteer in Victoria Square where informers tended to get sloshed when they'd something to tell. He told Cockle he'd be among the ponces for the next hour. Cockle had to ask the other police in the mill yard where exactly Hassall meant. They had a good laugh over it.

Hassall instead drove to the Farnworth General looking for a friendly medical face but Dr Clare Burtonall was off duty, some receptionist told him.

'Dancing?' he queried in surprise. 'Dancing where?'

'That's what somebody said. We've no exact information.'

The cocky nurse smiled. 'Can't you find out, you being a bobby and all?'

So Hassall really did find himself drinking in the Volunteer, corner of Deansgate, where the informers tended to get sloshed when they'd something to tell. Among the pros and cons, he punned to himself. He'd tell that quip to Cockle, see if he got a grin. He saw Grellie pass the street window. Twenty-two or so, bonny, the dark-haired girl who heard and saw everything but wouldn't tell you the time if you gave her a gold clock. Boss, some said, of all the street tarts in the city. He wished he had her on the Force instead of these pimply sociology graduates like Cockle. Swap her for a platoon of police any day.

4

BONN LOVED RAIN. The city's necrotic centre always took on a particular sheen in the wet, as if the pavements were nourished rather than washed. He wondered if he had time to go to church. He gazed out of the Asda supermarket doorway at the shoppers thronging Deansgate. Where did crowds come from so quickly in drizzle?

Rack came bouncing up. Bonn's quiet moment was over, his brief anonymity done for. Everybody knew Rack, who scared them all.

'Your next woman's Magdalena Four-Nine-Two, Bonn.'

'Very well, Rack.'

'Hotel Vivante, Room five hundred.'

Rack began singing a song about Mammy. Passers-by smiled, one bloke calling out did he cut any discs today.

'Guess who, Bonn.' Rack was exasperated, Bonn so slow. 'Go *on*! You can't miss this one.' Bonn never knew who.

Pudgy, short, crew-cut, Rack was almost swarthy, trendy in expensive street-smarts, but this last was only Bonn's surmise. He wouldn't know if folks dressed guinea-an-inch or fur-coat-no-knickers, local sayings. He hesitated. Rack's behaviour made him feel apologetic, yet Rack, best stander in the goer business, was almost his friend, sort of but not quite. Friendships, like women, were also unknowable. Bonn thought, have I any friends? Rack had thousands, he would say if he were asked.

'I need a few minutes to myself, Rack.'

'Jolson!' Rack was disgusted, recovering from his dramatic posture. 'You're not frigging real, Bonn.' His knees were soggy from where he'd knelt to do the gestures. 'Al *Jolson*! Y'know?'

'Very passable, Rack,' Bonn said, not knowing.

Passable, Rack thought in disbelief. I sweat blood doing Jolson, Bonn says *passable*? He waved gleeful acknowledgement to the tarts on the Reservoir Street corner who were giving his performance sarcastic applause.

'Grellie's taking on two new bints today, Bonn. She says can she see you in the Volunteer.'

'Thank you, Rack.' The tavern stood opposite. Grellie was in effective control of the street girls so this meant trouble for someone. He hoped it would not end in the usual violence.

'Magdalena Four-Nine-Two's from the Worcester Club and Tea Rooms. I reckon she's SM, so watch it. Know why women like sado-mack? Their hair has special molecules—'

'Thank you, Rack. I take it I am not booked this evening.'

'Why the fuck can't you just *ask*, Bonn?' Rack asked, well narked.

'Language, please, Rack. We're in public.'

For a still moment Bonn observed the crowds, the central bus station, traffic crawling noisily round the square.

'I'll go to church for a minute, Rack.'

Rack thought, church? Jesus. 'I'll be outside the Butty Bar, then. Oh, we had another death threat to Zen. We tellt him. Know why people go crazy? Foreign sand. Blows in from the Far East—'

Bonn cut Rack's mad theories short. 'Thank you, Rack.'

Rack stood there, watched Bonn turn up Bolgate. He couldn't really believe Bonn hadn't taken it in, the seriousness of the news. But Bonn was beyond criticism, an extraterrestrial. Never understood a word anybody said. But the woman clients were barmy for him, so words could fuck off out of it.

It took Bonn ten minutes to reach St Michael's. It was Benediction.

The congregation was sparse. He stood at the back of the church behind a pillar, feeling the sense. Lady Chapel, the Good Friday Chapel to the left, the vestry and confessionals along the right, the Stations of the Cross. All so evocative, but was it religion?

It's nothing but nostalgia, Bonn warned himself, and don't you forget it.

So many candles burned at Benediction that he could feel their heat. They'd reached the *Tantum Ergo*. He almost joined in the Latin, his mind going mechanically along, *Veneremur cernui, et antiquum documentum* . . . until he caught his brain at it and stopped such nonsense. Silence was sanity's friend and falsity's enemy. A restoring subversion existed out there in the city square where the Agency hired him out for sex. It was in here too, where holiness masqueraded as God, that famed usurper.

Candles, though. They bounced light off the celebrant priest's enormous gold cope. The walls gleamed, making the nave a great cavern of lanterns. It raised in him worrying questions of ritual, as opposed to sacramental, service. Of course Benediction was no sacrament, despite the array, the incense, the panoply of ornament.

For a while he stood listening and watching. Lighting a candle was a reflex. After he'd left the seminary it was as if part of his, what, genetic composition was somehow altered. Strange. Did women feel this, when abandoning lovers? The question was relevant, for each woman client had deserted her lover to hire Bonn, hadn't she? And did men too feel this when, in the night hours, they recalled a young wife they'd abandoned years before? He had no means of understanding the complexities of love, and religious love was no criterion.

Zen's death threat, though.

That was new, in Bonn's limited experience. He would have to ask Rack. Odd that Rack hadn't said more about it, when Rack knew everything that happened in the city's maelstrom.

He moved to stand before the statue of St Joseph and Child. Once, he had felt sympathy because Joseph got so few candles. Never a tenth as many as the Virgin's blue votive lights that flickered before her likeness.

Was that nostalgia enough to go and light one, like a football fan supporting a team? Now he had money to buy a thousand candles, votive lights, tapers, for every statue in the place. Maybe sufficient to buy the church as well, were he to ask Evelyn, shrewd bonny accountancy lass in the Rum Romeo, to list his wealth.

Lighting a candle was a moral issue, because the question arose: Would he be lighting a candle for some deep unexcavated guilt? Or to do ritualistic penance for his life as a goer, or perhaps to mark the passing of a lost belief? Or should he simply drop coins into the slot and not light a candle at all? Candles were lowest in the order of physics, as usable energy, so ignoring the brass candle box was an antipollution merit star. He gave up, stood in the shadow of the marble pillar as the congregation knelt and the gong boomed. He had the decency to wait until the vibrations died, then left, ignoring the holy water font, and emerged in the side street by the bakery. Like a lad sneaking from school. To freedom?

Well, to Magdalena Four-Nine-Two. She was his next freedom. He had plenty of time. The *Tantum Ergo* ran in his head. He tried to elide it by pausing to watch students from the City Film & Movie Academy spreading cables and cameras across the Deansgate pavement, but the mental trick didn't quite work.

Dr Clare Burtonall stared out of the upstairs window of her surgery office at the Rivergate corner of Victoria Square. She saw Bonn hesitate, stand to observe the movie makers from the City College. Too far off to see his expression, yet she knew it. His almost smile, she called it. Invariably symmetrical, it began as an apologetic far-off look. With luck, it grew warmer and spread across his features. His blue eyes gave it away as it came into being, taking over his entire face, lifting his mouth into the completest smile—

'Beg pardon, doctor? I couldn't hear because of the printer.'

'Oh, yes, Vannie.' Dear God, Clare thought in alarm, I must have actually *said* something. 'Have you tomorrow's patient lists, please?'

Vannie was a very proper lady of middle years, children now off her hands, a husband who ran transporters near Chequerbent. She did nine-to-five, drove in from her Great Lever bungalow five days a week, and so far had proved utterly reliable. She'd never been a medical secretary before, thank heavens. Clare had had too many run-ins with that breed to hire one for this delicate post. Watch it, though. Vannie's trustworthiness, like everybody else's, could only be warily assumed, not relied upon.

'So soon? Yes, I have them, doctor.' The secretary hurried out.

Clare returned to watch. Bonn walked, hesitating – he'd be apologizing inwardly – when some students, all clip-boards and straggly clothes, angrily gestured him away. She seethed at them as he crossed at the lights, heading for the exit roads near the railway station. She turned aside, now furious for another reason. Moorgate was the north-west corner. The Hotel Vivante stood there. He was going to another woman, some spoiled rich bitch.

At her desk, still ten minutes before the nurse was due in, she accepted the sheets Vannie passed her and stared at them unseeing. Two mistakes, Dr Burtonall, she chided herself, in as many minutes. First, to lust so obviously after Bonn that you have to cover up by making an unusual demand of the secretary. Two, you think 'another woman' when Bonn was a goer for Christ's sake, and therefore on hire to any female with enough money.

And a third error, she ploughed on, scolding herself. Bonn is a decade younger, hardly out of the egg, and you are a professional woman in her twenty-ninth year. The terrible temptation returned despite her anger. Should she reward herself, ring the Pleases Agency, Inc., and book Bonn for an hour tonight? She'd only seen him yesterday at the dance, then the Amadar Royale. Her ache was worse than any sick-ness. Miserably she cancelled that thought, and belled Vannie.

'Check the heating, please,' she said curtly. 'It's freezing in here.' It wasn't. 'And where on earth has that nurse got to?'

'Nurse Torbay isn't due in for some minutes yet, Dr Burtonall.'

'Check that clock, please. I'll be late starting.'

She was conscious of the secretary's hooded glance, but said no more. The afternoon list of patients gave six female, one male. Three vagrants, four of unknown designation. The girls were all below their mid-twenties. She decided to work out some code to record probable prostitutes. Since the Data Protection Act a doctor had to be so careful. Confidentiality was for sale these days.

Bonn would have reached the Hotel Vivante now. She truly hated the idea of what he'd be doing, and with whom. She changed her mind, reached for the handset, and switched to the personal line.

'Pleases Agency. Can I help?' The familiar voice, so prim.

'Yes. This is Clare Three-Nine-Five. I would like to make a booking. Bonn, please.'

'Thank you, Clare Three-Nine-Five. Bonn's earliest next availability is the day after next.'

'Oh.' She hadn't counted on that, and said sulkily, 'Very well.'

'Your time preference?'

'Evening, please. Eight o'clock?'

'That is confirmed. Hold, please . . . The Time and Scythe Hotel, Bolgate Street? Suite one-twenty-one. Is the venue acceptable?'

She had met him there several times. 'Thank you. Two hours.'

The voice went into its routine patter. 'Thank you for calling Pleases Agency. We are always eager to provide the best service for client ladies—'

Clare cradled the receiver and sat back. Less satisfactory than she wanted, but she would still be seeing him soon.

'Did you get through, Dr Burtonall?' Vannie called. She had noticed the red light on the console.

Clare replied evenly, 'Thanks, Vannie. Yes, all's well.'

All would be even better the day after tomorrow.

Women weren't good touts, not for the police. They didn't last. They vanished. For sinister or marvellous reasons, suddenly they were no more and that meant no more use. Also, they let on about this crime, that theft, this drug shaft, and prattled to too many. Women couldn't tell where gossip ended and informing began, so they suffered the mortality. He'd read somewhere that the word for tongue in numerous languages was always female in gender, though what did that prove? The word for poet was often so, and they were the most drunken shagnasties ever.

Sagger was an old sweat, supposedly a much decorated squaddie back when wars were real and not just peacetime interludes. His nickname came from work in the Potteries.

'It's been a swine getting hold of you, Sag,' Hassall told him testily. 'Where've you been?'

They met in the public library. The weather for once cooperated with Hassall's intentions. It was teeming cats and dogs, so a scruff like Sagger could justifiably shuffle in out of the rain. They avoided the baby room, where too many women took their barns and might have blokes who'd be interested, so they met by the financial section's stacks of pink newspapers, talking in slow mutters, hardest to follow if the CCTV picked them up. Sagger kept his head down as if trying to nod off, which Hassall approved of after the endless afternoons he'd spent trying to lip-synch grainy pictures of bludgers in shopping malls.

'Too old. Doing a bit of begging, Bowton market. Safer there.'

'He got nailed, that garage, Sarandons. Know it?'

'Aye, I heard. Serve the bugger right.'

Did it now. 'Why? What'd he do the week previous?'

'What didn't he do, you mean.' Sagger snorted. 'He were owed a wad, for some politico's pals coming through who didn't show. Dulsie took three girls on, had to pay o'course. Rich sod, banker or summert, should've stumped the gelt, but let Dulsie down. Can you believe it?'

Sagger hawked phlegm up, looked about for somewhere to spit. Hassall stopped him by raising a finger in the nick of time. Sagger swallowed.

'This banker bloke. Maybe he's having a bad patch.' Praising the unpraiseworthy often worked, where direct questions failed. It did so now.

'Burton? His missus is a posh doctor, paid in barrowloads so how's he on his welts? No wonder Dulsie got riled.'

'Any dates?'

'Somebody said the Wednesday previous. Dunno.'

'So he got tanked, Sag?'

'You know Dulsie, Mr Hassall. Always a talker. Shoot his mouth off threatening, like as not. I reckon he said like he'd get some pals to claim his wages.'

'That banker should've paid. If he ordered the girls for a political pal, it's his debt, not Dulsie's.'

'Leave off. Life's not fair. Tell you one thing, though, Mr Hassall.'

'What?' Hassall felt a little excitement. He hadn't expected half of this. Already three leads in as many minutes.

'Dulsie were a reet stupid bugger.'

'Ta, Sagger,' Hassall said, stretched as if weary, and left, down the steps into the afternoon rain. 'Ta, for nowt.'

That excitement was still there. Burton wasn't far from Burtonall, whose wife was a well-to-do doctor, soon divorcing. Who had political friends, was often in the papers fund-raising. Hassall felt a warm glow. His copper's instinct was firing today. He'd been right to ask after Dr Clare Burtonall so casually first off. Now, he'd do it in earnest.

For once, plenty.

5 | **Mogga dancing** – that type of ballroom competition dancing where each couple changes their dance rhythm to a different style every few bars – usually four or six – throughout a single melody

MAGDALENA TURNED OUT to have the longest hair Bonn had ever seen. She arrived with it done in some sort of bun, spectacles she didn't need, slim pepper-and-salt tweed skirt and a twinset. It was evidently a disguise. Her raincoat was almost down to her mid-calf. That said, she wasn't at all reticent.

'This is my rehabilitation,' she explained carefully in a prepared speech while Bonn listened. 'I think I have a right.'

'You have, Magdalena.'

The suite was small, a minuscule sitting room with a wall bar, a bedroom through a low ornamental arch, and bathroom. Bonn blamed its excess of flowers.

'Did the telephone lady say?' Magdalena asked, peremptory.

'Ah, in a way,' Bonn said carefully. He'd never gone fast since becoming a goer. One danger was to assume too much too soon. His emotional speed was a definite drawback. 'I only want to please.'

Magdalena gestured at the bar. Bonn hung up her raincoat and went to comply.

'Sweet sherry.' The lady was within reach of forty, slim, crow's feet just in evidence. 'I'm a hotel manager. I've been wondering about taking the plunge for some time. What do you think?'

Plunge? What plunge? Bonn felt alarm. 'You're wise to be circumspect, Magdalena.'

He inspected the bottles, a varied array beyond him. Labels, this vintage, that vintage, four sorts of Indian tonic water alone. Would the lady know if he served something different? In any case, was preference nothing more than affectation? He guessed that Magdalena, manageress of the quaintly named Worcester Club and Tea Rooms at Rivergate, would not suffer fools gladly. She made him feel a fool. Did sherry always say it was sherry on the bottle? Amontillado, Tio Pepe, Cockburn's. Dry, sweet, inbetween? He poured in hope, took it to her.

'There's that saying about on your own doorstep, isn't there?' she said. Bonn thought, *Is there?* She sipped, grimaced, waved him to be seated. 'God, you've given me enough for a bath.'

'I'm so sorry.'

This amused her for some reason. 'You're new.'

'Fairly, I suppose.'

'What, a few months?'

'Yes, about.'

Urbane, that was it. Her manner was urbane, cool. Not quite offhand, but the sort of attitude he always imagined a woman displayed when entering a hairdresser's, in complete charge and knowing what she wanted. She kicked off her shoes, curled her feet up on the couch. He sat facing, obedient.

'Get one for yourself,' she told him.

'Thank you, no.'

She raised her eyebrows, let it go.

'I'll be frank, Bonn – it is Bonn?' And when he nodded,

'I'm not exactly your shrinking violet. I picked you because I'd heard your name.' She eyed him. 'I run the Worcester Club. Simple as that.'

'The new manageress.'

'Things will have to change over there. Altogether too slack. One thing, Bonn.' She was taking him in, eyes moving to register his clothes. 'I expect a certain level of . . . co-operation. This is two-way. I pay. And you play, the way I say.'

'Of course,' Bonn said politely.

'You can start by running me a bath.'

'Certainly.'

He complied, waited until she came out of the bathroom. This Magdalena was experienced, as professional as he'd encountered. Often the lady client was a first-timer to hired sex. He hadn't yet quite worked out if Miss Faith, Miss Charity, or Miss Hope ever received instructions from Martina that such new client ladies were to be channelled Bonn's way rather than passed to TonTon, Fret Dougal, Lonnier, Suntan, Zen, or some other goer lower down the scale. He seemed to have many women who lacked experience. Not today, though, and not Magdalena.

The problem was the assumption some hardened lady clients made. It was as if they needed to keep on extending their horizons, making increasing demands to somehow obviate sexual stasis. Difference is as difference does, maybe? It would be a nice theological problem – taking into account the correct definitions of morality, of course.

'Ready?' She appeared in a white hotel dressing gown, smiling. 'I thought you'd have been in the bedroom by now.'

'No.' He felt she required some explanation. 'That might have seemed presumptuous.'

'A ditherer!' She led the way. He followed, started to

undress as she shelled off her robe and slipped between the sheets. 'I need more from you than uncertainty, Bonn. What kind of a name *is* that?'

He took his time answering. 'I thought I had made it up. Then I remembered somebody calling me that when I was little. Perhaps I reinvented it, or it came to mind unbidden.'

'What does it mean?' She reached out. Her hand felt his flank, pinching the flesh as he peeled aside the bedclothes and lay beside her.

'Something rather crude in French argot, I understand. Good for nothing, worthless, dross. Etymology is uncertain.'

'You talk like you hate words.'

Do I? he asked himself with astonishment, looking at the woman along the pillow. How remarkable women are, he thought, one unending surprise, so clearly seeing in him more than he ever discerned himself.

'What are you thinking?' she asked, sharply. 'I don't think I like being stared at.'

'Forgive me, Magdalena. I was only thinking that you are more prescient than I.'

'You're odd, y'know that?' She took hold of him, making him gasp with the hardness of her grasp. 'Let's see *how* odd.'

He lay in the cool sheets. This lady did not need emotional resuscitation. She needed no encouragement to allow herself to be loved. Hers must be the pace. That was Posser's guidance when first he'd 'come in out of the rain', Posser's words. The client lady's speed is your pace, the old man had wheezed, and her tardiness is your slowness, never forget that.

Rehabilitation, though? She'd said it. From what injury, from what calamity?

He reached for her, and they moved together. He

thought her shining hair dazzlingly beautiful, and for a short while wondered whether he might dare to tell her so. He was still hesitating about that when ecstasy began its rush to oblivion, and the chance to speak was mercifully gone.

It was after they had dressed and come to sit in the suite's living room by the window that Bonn finally realized the extent of Magdalena's error and his own blindness. Did other keys like the kindly Zen, TonTon, or perhaps Fret Dougal, guess brilliantly, ahead of the lady's wishes?

'I'm definite now, Bonn.' She made a peremptory gesture. 'Get me a cigarette.'

He rose and brought a selection from the sofa table. She chose a filter tip. He clicked a light for her, the way Rack had shown him when, ashamed of his ignorance, he had finally got up nerve to ask his stander how to fire a lighter. Magdalena inhaled, looking up at him, eyes narrowed against the smoke. A very practised lady who would not be gainsaid.

'I think you'll do.' She smiled, nodded as if to herself. 'I thought you'd be useless, but you really got me skimming. You're green around the social edges, but that can be mended with a few lessons. I'll settle it with your Agency people.'

'I don't understand.' Bonn thought, Skimming? What on earth is skimming? He hated cigarette smoke. Now he would need to make a complete change. Hair wash, bath, anything to take the stink away.

'I'm taking you on, dear.' She made the reply a studied insult, as to a moron. He coloured.

'I'm rather slow, Magdalena . . .'

'I mean you become my regular man. I shall need you—'

'Excuse me, please.' He drew breath to speak, possibly warn her, but got nowhere.

'No. You listen.' She blew a smoke ring, admired its form. 'I'll want you for social occasions. On call.' She eyed him, amused. 'You understand call?'

'Perhaps it's not possible, Magdalena.'

'Oh it is, dear.' He wished she'd stop calling him that. It was all going awry. 'And on short notice. I can't have you jaunting off with some bimbo when I snap my fingers.'

'No, Magdalena.' He felt so sad. She had been exquisite, the sex superb, and now see what was happening.

'You mean yes, Magdalena.' She smiled, hard and direct. 'I'll match the fees of, what's it called, your Pleases Agency, Inc. Some sort of retainer plus fee-for-service adjustment, that it?'

'I'm afraid you don't understand.'

'Bonn, dear. I'm talking exclusive rights. A walker is a walker is a walker. See?'

'Rights.' The word seemed an imposition. He'd honestly never felt as if he wore a price tag, and here she was making this serious misjudgement. How could you tell a lady who was so sure of herself? 'I'm afraid it might be out of the question.'

'No.' She wagged her head like to a disbelieving infant. It was then that she started to do up her glorious hair into that coiled bun arrangement. Bonn watched, fascinated. 'Don't be more stupid than God made you, Bonn dear. I went into this with your Agency woman.'

Oh, no you didn't, Bonn thought, but did not say. It could become a yes-no pantomime repartee.

'I wonder if you haven't reached a false conclusion, Magdalena,' he said, taking consolation in the fact that Rack would be within call and poised to rescue if this got worse. Rack had never yet let him down.

She seemed to be enjoying herself, sensing a dispute. 'I picked you because I'd heard whispers. One or two other names, certainly, but you they seemed fixated on. They were right!'

'If you were more specific, Magdalena, I'd pass the message on.' It was the best he could do.

Sorrow was too easily come by in matters close to love. Bonn knew the phone ladies at the Pleases Agency were hardly streetwise, being chosen rather for their loyalty. It would be Miss Rose or Miss Faith who had mistakenly assumed some wrong arrangement. He sighed inwardly. Another reason for Martina to find fault.

'From now on you'll be with me, Bonn. Better if you move into the Worcester.' Magdalena smiled, raised her eyebrows. 'You can be discreet, I trust?'

'Of course.' It was time. He rose, extended a hand to assist her. Smilingly she took it. 'How soon will you need a definite reply, Magdalena?'

'I've already had my answer, dear,' she said, stubbing the cigarette out with sharp assertive movements. 'You're it. Get my coat.'

'Very well.'

'Odd style of talk you've got there, lover,' she said, teasing.

Bonn was disappointed at that, because he often tried to change his speech to fit in with other people. He repeated phrases in his room at night, but often fell silent from embarrassing failure when they sounded somehow wrong.

'I shall try to change, Magdalena.'

'No, don't.' She came against him, embraced him as he

helped her on with her raincoat. 'I quite like it. Your fee's on the coffee table.'

'Thank you, Magdalena.'

He held the door, courteously said he hoped to see her again very soon. She left, swinging down the corridor. He waved after her, thinking sadly, Goodbye, Magdalena, and farewell. All that lovely hair. He'd never seen anything like it. Now he'd never be able to tell her that her hair was dazzlingly beautiful. It seemed the way of things, out here among so many unclear, unthought passions. Nothing was orderly where women ruled. Was it simply the brilliant hectic turmoil that was normal life? Sometimes, his thoughts never knew where to start in this desperate, wondrous new existence. He hoped to learn.

GRELLIE HAD TO enter the Shot Pot through the side door. It really narked her off, thinking of the entrance she might make, the lads shouting, whistling, losing their snooker aim and yelling crudities. Some were her girls' regular punters, but it was more than your life was worth to let it be known. Men were odd creatures. Look at Bonn.

She slipped in. The home team was practising trick shots, yelling obscenities, dialects from everywhere, local Lancs tarted up Jamaican, Barbados, God-knows-what, making the talk they called goojer. So far so peaceful, but Grellie knew peace didn't last.

Osmund, the old guardian, was playing his usual patience in his booth by the clothes racks at the rear of the long hall. Grellie stood until he'd done a line, never a mistake, driving the lads mad with his honesty when who'd know if he filched a red nine for a black ten? Thinking about it'd send you crazy.

'She wants me, Osmund,' she said when he'd lost. Did he ever win? 'Quiet today.'

'Hello, chuckie. Aye.' He sighed. Osmund to Grellie seemed wafer thin, paper dry, in his waistcoat. He'd lived local all his life, been in the mills before they vanished and left chunks of the city derelict. 'It'll go bad in an hour. Can't live without scrapping. All you youngsters know best, see?'

Grellie knew that one. Some of the lads noticed her, started up calling, Come here, luv, me cue's bent an' I wants it straight'nin', Grellie len' me a few notes make me 'appy, Who's new out in du beats, luv, cries she heard every minute every day and had to laugh at like they were witty originals.

Bonn, now, would stand on this very spot in the gloaming, looking down the long lines of tables as if at some strange universe. The lads would shout cheery greetings to him, sure, but as from a distance. Not the same with any other bloke, either. She'd once come in with Fret Dougal, also like Bonn a key goer, also entitled to respect as boss of his own click of four, and instantly noticed that the calls had been just that bit more ribald, somehow much freer. The same for Suntan, TonTon, Zen, whoever. The players'd even try a trick shot, accept the ribbing when it went wrong.

But Bonn, that time, had stood in silence for so long that even Osmund got edgy, until Grellie'd asked, What yer staring at, and out it came.

'It's beautiful, Grellie,' Bonn had replied.

Remembering how it startled her, seeing anew the cones of gold light against the umber dark, the green baize fields aligned the length of the place, she still couldn't fathom what he meant. And the snooker players, maniacs all, were only obsessed shabby blokes. So where's beautiful? It was just Bonn. She'd give anything, eat him alive, split herself for him to live on her any way he chose.

'Martina's in, Grellie,' Osmund said, meaning get a move on.

She stepped through the doorway as the racks of musty clothing trundled aside, needed oiling, and left Osmund flipping his cards on his counter for a new game. Inside, silence. A cubicle, begrimed old notices, then the right-hand wall slid away and it was three paces down the non-corridor and into Martina's office.

'Hello, Martina.' No chairs except one for the woman who controlled the syndicate.

'Grellie.' No welcome hello, so it was trouble.

Martina raised her head. Grellie grudgingly evaluated her. Okay, admit the word and think *boss* outright, now Martina's dad Posser was too ill to manage. Boss. And think-admit what was much worse, Martina was strikingly beautiful, the bitch sitting there with her gammy leg. Desk carrying, wait for it, a single sheet of blank paper and one sharpened pencil unchanged and unused ever since Grellie'd taken her knickers off for a feller, taken King Richard's shilling as the street girls joked. An office of tat. Even the lino looked off some council tip. All in all not much, especially as multimillionairess Martina was so lame she couldn't walk straight if you paid her. Single-minded in her own interest, though, which every woman understood but had to hate. Rules she issued at the Barn Owl had to be taken as law, finish.

'This meeting, Grellie. I'm putting in you'll get a twenty-fourth.'

'Me? What for?' Grellie stared.

Takings from working houses, brothels, were traditionally allocated in fractions, twelfths and half-twelfths being commonest.

'You oversee Trish.'

Trish was an older woman, once married, with no street-stringer experience, never even been a working girl, and who was to run the new working house, the syndicate's first. It was due to begin any day now. Bonn had recommended her, which Grellie didn't like either.

'I can't see why she can't be checked on as routine, Martina. The girls'd expect that. Putting me over her tells everybody she's fulham.'

Fulham, from the old name for false dice. It was unfair to the woman. What was she, Grellie strove to remember, thirty-sixish? Not to mention a beginner. Trish was in for a hell of a time if Martina had taken against her like this.

'Her one recommendation is that Bonn says she'll do.' Martina's blue eyes met Grellie's evenly. 'We don't know if she's trustworthy. I'm lodging you so the girls don't all try it on.'

Grellie drew breath, standing there, and went for it. 'I'd do it different, Martina.'

'No, Grellie. You.'

'Right.' She hadn't quite dared to say she wanted the brothel – nobody used that word in the girl trade – wanted the working house moved. It was hard though, and she had to make some sort of protest. 'See, Martina, I'm over-stretched. Out there's got wrinkles.'

'What today?' Martina asked, conscious that the street leader's chance to mention Bonn had come and gone. It was probably just Grellie boxing shrewd. Suspicion was the idiom of women, Martina remembered Bonn saying once, a possible rare witticism.

'Bits and pieces, nothing to shout about. I'll cope, I cope, but I wonder if I'm pulling my weight. I only average one punter a day myself now, what with seeing to the stringers.'

'That's to the good.'

Lovely hair, too, Grellie reluctantly scored. Done twice weekly, Holly O'Berry's natty hair emporium behind the Weavers Hall. Martina was always attended by Holly of the magic hands, queer as a flute and servile by choice, how servile Grellie alone knew. Martina also lacked indecision.

Was she truly hard as nails all the way through? Grellie shelved the question, probably pointless anyhow. Except that Bonn had lodgings in Martina's Bradshawgate home, so not as pointless as all that, if she dared ask outright.

'I'd like it organized different, Martina.'

'Steps or change?'

'Steps, please.'

'That would cost.'

Cost too much, unspoken but meant? Grellie watched Martina's expression for clues. A change among the street girls, the stringers Grellie was responsible for, meant wholesale differences in arrangements. This would breed rancour, every tart still wet behind the ears believing she had a right to mouth off and bicker opinion. 'Step' meant only one or two nominal promotions, some street lasses picked to take responsibility for extra payment, done easy and el cheapo.

'Not cost much, Martina. Something's got to be done.'

Martina didn't quite sigh, but went close. Grellie suddenly realized she'd never ever seen Martina purse her lips, actually heave a sigh, cross her lame leg, drum her fingers, doodle on her fucking blank paper with her inviolate fucking pristine pencil. It was difficult, but Grellie managed to suppress her anger, hoping nothing showed.

'Got to be?' Martina picked up sharply, wary.

'I think the brothel and the street should be considered together, Martina.'

There. It was out and in the air between them. And the b-word spoken, when the street shunned the word. One thing, with Martina you were never left in any doubt. Ask, you got no or go ahead, no inbetween shilly-shallying.

'You mean at the meeting?'

'Yes. The stringers'll be all questions soon as it gets about. Some'll be scared witless, especially the older end.' Older end meant twenty-seven and up. A working girl who stayed active thirty-plus was a miracle of survival. Street law said always to pretend you're younger.

'They've no need to be!' Martina almost spat the words, as she snapped into one of her sudden tempers. 'They all know that. *You* know that.'

Grellie stood her ground, at risk. 'True, Martina. You know the street game. A woman rising thirty can't keep her eyes off the town hall clock. Working girls are worse. They get hating younger girls coming in.'

Martina and Grellie were of an age, barely twenty-two, could have been sisters but for different colouring and neither having Bonn. In another world Grellie might have liked Martina, but that was fantasy. In the way of suppositions, friendship was out of the question, Grellie being wise enough to know that Martina had to keep distance. She'd heard Posser himself say it. 'Distant guns fire best.'

'In spite of the care we take of them?'

'Yes, Martina.' Grellie thought, if only there was somewhere I could sit down in this horrible bare place. Martina must deliberately plan it, a Soviet interrogator's room.

'I hope you at least try to counter it?'

And not above sarcasm when it suited her vicious tongue. Grellie awarded Martina's curt remark a chilly nod. She'd hoped to get through without animosity, but Martina determined how these things went, not her. The cow had probably never even had a man yet, a consoling thought. Or maybe not so consoling as all that, when you thought of Bonn.

'Quite the worst thing, Grellie,' Martina said as if lecturing, 'would be to let our stringers think we'll pick from them to lodge the working house.'

'Stands to reason.' Grellie could be as sharp when she wanted.

The blonde girl's expression did not alter at the barb. Some things she let pass, the head of anything needing the long view. Then for some trivial thing she'd have folk blammed. Grellie knew all the rumours about Martina's silent rages.

'As long as that's known, Grellie.' Martina let the pause lengthen just enough. 'These death threats to Zen. I've put Rack onto it. Have you any ideas?'

Not a shift of direction. Grellie knew Martina too well to assume she'd let the matter of the stringers and the house girls pass, but it had been settled one way or the other. Martina would let her know.

'Only rumours. If they're real . . .' No response, so Grellie was left to make the correct assumption and went on, 'I'd take Zen off duty, let his goers take the slack.'

Which surprised even Martina. 'While Zen does what, swan off to Australia on sabbatical?'

'No, Martina. Does his job as key, sees his goers cope with their usual uppers. The syndicate pays him normally, all that. Meanwhile Rack susses what the hell.'

Martina pondered, gave a nod. Grellie thought, a head beautiful as that should nod more, maybe smile once a fortnight, give the world a fucking treat. Instead she seemed continually at war, always the commissar.

'And if it goes on?'

'Bin Rack and get somebody better. Is it the one person?'

'We think so.'

How Martina winkled out these problems was the syndicate's own business.

'Man or woman?'

It mattered. A jealous husband, discovering that his wife

was clandestinely hiring a goer for illicit shags in a hotel, might reasonably seek vengeance. And a possessive lady client could be at least as vicious from jealousy. Women let things prey. The Agency'd had some instances.

'Woman.'

'Then shouldn't it be easy?'

'The question is what, Grellie. Slap her wrist? Take away her bus pass?'

For the first time Grellie felt astonished. Martina was actually well worried. She suddenly realized, *She's thinking what if it was Bonn being stalked.* So this was now a shared venture. She was astonished, thinking, Christ Almighty, we're allies!

'Have her straightened,' Grellie said bluntly. 'Remember Posser handling the girl who started on her own? Pricey, but worth it.'

Early days, Posser beginning the Agency on marbles, one of his street girls started a franchy, franchise of prostitutes, off her own bat, hoping she would not be discovered. He fitted her up for an arson job. She never did know why, years later and still in prison. This was city folklore.

'She might be doing it for somebody else.'

'I'd say that's for Rack to find out.'

'Thank you,' Martina said unexpectedly as if a weight was taken off her shoulders. 'I'll see you separately about the stringers.'

'Thank you, Martina.' So very formal.

'Tell Rack I'll need him later, Vallance Carvery.'

'Right.'

Grellie left then, dabbing at the moisture that had appeared on her upper lip and temples. With reluctant anger she diagnosed it as fear. But one day, lady, she told herself, furious at having let herself be played upon like that, one day

there'll come a way of shunting you, Martina, and somebody
less lame will fill that tatty chair. A busy girl could do it, with
the right connections. The rightest connection of all, of
course, would be Bonn. If and when. It was becoming a
question of who'd reach Bonn first, herself or Martina.

Cripples don't run as fast, right? She thought the vicious
thought, and even before entering the snooker hall was
herself again. She told Osmund the message for Rack then
cockily, despite the old guardian's disapproving frown, saun-
tered the length of the place amongst the tables, deliberately
nudging Toothie's elbow as he framed up a long pink, top
right pocket in a black ball game. It only caused roars of
laughter, so she'd judged it right. Next time she came in
there'd be ructions of jokey outrage.

Creating an impression is everything, Grellie told herself,
smiling over her shoulder at the grinning, shouting men.
She'd had enough of Martina's laws to last a lifetime. Create
an impression was one of Grellie's own special personal laws
of life, so bugger Martina's.

Stride(s) – the sexual occasion(s) performed by a prostitute

'Wotcher, rack.'

'Coll.'

Rack plonked himself down opposite the little Londoner. He liked Coll because he'd done bad work round Seven Dials, hotel dodging and shovelling tourists. Not a northerner, either, which pleased Rack because you could have too much of a good thing. He'd made that crack to Bonn once, but had only got a glance and 'I understand, Rack.' Bonn's trouble was that conversation never got anywhere. It was time he learned. Rack often wondered how Bonn managed with women, not knowing how to chat proper.

Coll was a slider. Not lean as a whippet or with pianist's fingers like they ought. He was more your stocky bludger, shoulders wide, neck thick, a tanker's build. Truth to tell, Coll was the best robber and susser in the business. You wanted a house done over, or find that incriminating photo took last Sunday shagging some tart, you'd best get Coll. Toss a weirdo diamond buyer off of a Moscow hotel roof like was all the rage these days, you got Coll to do a bit of friend bending so alibis lay thick about the pavement.

Okay, so Coll cost a few more groats. You pay for what you get, was Rack's philosophy. Buy the best, you knew where you stood. Besides, he had something on Coll the slider durstn't forget.

Over a pint they spoke of the rotten progress of London football clubs before Rack got down to it.

'I want somebody sussed, Coll. Dunno who yet.'

''Ere er ver?'

They were both back in Cockney dialect, which pleased Rack. Sometimes he'd just had enough of this guttural crap northerners talked, like they had mouths that were too empty all the bleeding time. It got him down.

'Fuck knows, Coll. It's somebody phones deaf frets. You don't need to know who,' he added before Coll could ask. 'You 'eard of the Agency?'

'Yih. One er them?'

'That's it, Coll. I got a few details, not much. Suss art wotcher can, okay?'

'Wotcher got?'

Rack waited while Coll got another pint. He knew the slider allowed himself two drinks a day, no more. He'd almost died of drink a year back. Now, no problems with Coll. What Rack wanted was an address, then he'd do all the performing Martina wanted. He might even risk doing it before Martina gave the nod, the way he was beginning to feel. Itchy, wanting this untidy fucking threat business stopped. Rack knew it was down to him. Pride was at stake here. A team of forty-three standers, seventeen different places in the city centre, shame and disrespect could spread like a moorland fire. It was just out of fucking order.

Coll returned, bringing Rack a pint, though both knew it would remain untouched.

'Death threats is serious diss.' As if Coll needed telling.

'Leave orf, mate,' Coll said with scorn. 'Juss say what.'

'Threats against a goer. Woman's same voice.'

'He key, then?' Coll was impressed.

'Yih. She give his name.'

'Jesus. She's an upper?' This was interesting: did she hire a goer, maybe even a key like Zen, then grow jealous?

'Dunno. She uses street phones. Maybe it's nuffink, some bint off her nut.'

'Gotter be done, whatever.' Coll understood, thought a second. Rack stayed mute from respect, thinking being half Coll's worth. 'Okay. Give me what yer 'ave, mate. How soon?'

'Fastest.' Rack handed over a folded paper and three audio cassettes in a brown bag. 'How much?'

'Do leave orf,' Coll said as if disgusted at the mention of payment, finished his pint and left without another word.

Rack was proud of Coll. That was real class, taking on a rum job like that and not wanting ackers even mentioned. Took a Cockney to show class like that. Frigging northerners wouldn't know how.

Except Bonn, Rack amended after a bit of think. Bonn would have gone red, looked at the floor, ahemed, said he was sorry, he didn't understand or something barmy like that. Rack sometimes wondered how Bonn asked his women clients for the gelt, but supposed tact must come easy if you'd just shagged their arse off. Maybe it was some theory he'd not thought of? Rack liked theories and knew he was really stupendous at working new ones out, though folk weren't appreciative when he explained them. Not many had the brains.

He left through the pub's rear door, glimpsed Grellie deep in conversation with Rani and walked on leaving them to it.

Grellie was standing to one side of the alley behind a parked forklifter. Rani was almost in tears.

'One last time, Rani,' Grellie was asking. 'Why were you late? You know the rule. Twenty minutes, you send in. Not a fucking word. Why?'

'I was on the toilet, Grellie. Honest to God. Then I dropped my handbag, everything all over the pavement. I couldn't find my purse.'

'Rani. My last ask. Why?'

Somebody emerged from the pub's pantry door, threw steaming liquid across the ginnel and disappeared inside with a clash of metal.

'It was like I said, honest, Grellie, I wouldn't do—'

Grellie's hand lashed the woman's face, knocking her head back against the wall. Rani screamed. Grellie thumped her in the belly, backhanded her head as she doubled.

'Now listen.' Grellie made her breathing regular, waiting for the stringer to straighten. 'Repeat what I say. I want no misunderstanding.'

Rani leant against the pub wall, tears pouring down, sobs shaking her narrow frame.

'You come on beat when I say. What is it?'

'Come on when you say,' Rani wept.

'Late again, I'll have Rack straighten you. Say back.'

'Late, Rack'll straighten me.'

'You're fined a week. No bunce, no sleight-of-handers, you live off borrowings until today week.'

'Today week,' Rani bleated miserably.

'Now a few answers,' Grellie said, low and furious. 'On drugs, are we?'

'No. Honest.'

Lying bitch, Grellie thought. 'You seeing a bloke? It's fine, you're allowed.'

'No, Grellie. Honest. I wouldn't, less I tellt you.'

'Lots of the girls have blokes on the side. There's no comeback as long as he doesn't interfere with your strides.'

'I haven't a bloke, Grellie, honest.'

'Right. Get your strides in today, or else.'

'Thanks, Grellie,' Rani called after her, and made her way to the Ladies in the central gardens to repair some of the damage.

Grellie could hardly see from pure blind rage that took her as she walked to the Butty Bar in hopes of finding Rack. No, Grellie, honest Grellie, no drugs Grellie, no nothing Grellie. One fucking wrong thing after another, this week was. The idle bitch was on drugs, no chance of Rani ever matching the strides needed, keeping her score with Grellie's stringers in Waterloo Street.

Bitch had already passed her street dates, did she but know it. Goodnight, Rani, see if you do better on your own in some gutter, see how you like it out in the cold and wet, dark night falling down on you and old age coming on, and serve you fucking right.

The woman moved across the shopping mall. Plenty of phones there near the playing fountains, the exotic waterfall clock that told uncertain time in menisci. They were possibles, except for the security vids. She judged her moment, when the old men smoking their pipes moved on and the young wives harvested up their kiddies and battled them into pushchairs. She knew the problems with those artefacts of household and young marriage. All done for her, thank heavens. The future was Gordon, her starlight and her guide.

A few lads barrelled down the concourse, charging through the Liverpool Road entrance so boisterously the security guards showed and started talking into their shoulder microphones. Gordon had told her all that, where the arrest-grade CCTV cameras were fixed and what activated them. He'd added details about swivel angles, radio blippers, something called LED signals, but she'd got nervy and almost snapped at him. Too many instructions confused, just say what she had to do.

So far she'd done well. Three calls out of three, and all untraceable. Gordon said so. He was influential and knew these things. She often wondered if Members of Parliament like him received special training, but never dared ask. One day she would, when they were married and he was safely re-elected. In a way she owned him, exactly as he possessed her.

Sitting facing Halford's glittering bicycle shop and Kellon's bakery – how odd, both shops thronged equally at this hour; who'd imagine? – she waited for the precinct to calm down. The rushing lads were evicted shouting joyous football chants, the security men grinning. All serene. Was it time? Gordon said always make certain nothing was amiss, for those were the recorded video sections police wanted to see. Police counted things. Gordon had said it so often she'd begun to count things herself, number of people on a train, women shopping, wheelies in a supermarket line, even tins on her own pantry shelf.

Numbers seemed to worry Gordon.

'They're unable to work things out for themselves, see? So they count. Numbers jog them into seeing things they'd otherwise miss. Be careful, darling. It'll work out.'

Her duty, therefore: never give police reasons to count *you*. She checked the time, smiled at some children on reins clambering up to see the budgerigars in the bird cage. How shopping malls had improved since she was a girl! Almost incredible. Indoors, out of the rain, central heating, cafés where you could get decent tea, that horrid piped music finally quashed.

Time? *Yes!*

She rose, quickly left by the exit facing the Volunteer at Deansgate corner, and crossed at the traffic lights into the central gardens, heading for the bus station. Almost dusk. Dusk was good. Cars were funnelling from Victoria Square towards Warrington, up Bolgate Street, or racing round for the Leeds-Huddersfield motorway that started beyond the railway station. She deliberately avoided glancing across to Greygate, that took traffic to London and the south. One day, not long, that would be her route away, with her Gordon.

It was only justice.

The end phone, of a line of six by the bus station, was free. Crowds were queuing for the moorland buses. Even here, though, there were cameras on metal poles, but fixed, and she'd been given the sweeping arcs of each. Turn away just in case, darling, Gordon'd said. He always called her darling. At first it had seemed somehow mechanical, but she now recognized it as concealment, his way of disguise. It was his canvassing voice, he'd explained, laughing, when she asked him why he said darling to all the women on fund-raiser committees.

Loyalty was their byword, and her creed. She dialled, money in a glove, no cards. She placed the special black disc over the mouthpiece, did the push so its rim gripped, and waited for the woman to answer.

'Pleases Agency, how may I help?'

'This is Zen's last warning.'

'Who is this, please?'

'Zen won't be given any further chance. Tell him.'

'What warning, exactly? About what?'

'It'll be the finish of him. I shall not ring again.'

'Could you please say—?'

'That's all.'

For just a moment she hesitated, as if it would be impolite to ring off without some ritual goodbye phrase. Quickly she thought how silly, hung up the receiver, slipped the voice masker into her handbag and walked briskly away. She had an hour before meeting Gordon.

She felt a warm glow of gratification, almost a kind of pride. Each step was one closer to taking Gordon away from his disloyal wife.

As she made the side near the Phoenix Theatre at Greygate it came on to rain, very like heaven's blessing on her enterprise. Rain was further concealment. Rain, like dusk, was good.

'NOT OBESITY AGAIN,' Clare told the nurse with some asperity, almost meaning it. 'Don't let him in.'

Sister Barraclough left laughing because Hassall always ignored rebukes.

'Your scales were wrong,' Hassall grumbled, almost meaning that too. 'A bloke gets tubby with age. Can't you just give me some leptin?'

Clare sighed. She liked Hassall, but he really did come at the most inconvenient times. She had thirty minutes to complete her review of six patients, four with infectious disease sequelae, and here came the master of the prolonged dawdle.

'I'm honestly harried, Mr Hassall.' He took no notice and seated himself with an apologetic grin. 'I wish the leptin business had never been researched.'

'Mice without leptin get thinner when you give them the hormone,' Hassall remembered, beaming. 'See? You told me so, a fortnight since. That's not Alzheimer's, is it? My memory's still good. Except,' he added gloomily, 'I have to shout down and ask my missus what I've come upstairs for.'

'Leptin has a limited role,' Clare said guardedly. 'Nowadays everything's uncoupling proteins and proton leaks –

and don't quote that back at me! I never should have agreed to do your police medicals. You're all hypochondriacs.'

'Come with me to Forensics. The Terence Dulsworthy post mortem's today.'

Outside some child started screaming, hating the idea of sitting still in a waiting room, his mother desperately trying to shush him.

Clare logged the schedule on her desk screen.

'Four this afternoon? Sorry. I'm elsewhere.'

'Can't they wait? I'd drive you back to Victoria Square.' He wheedled, 'I'd switch the toffee – the rotating light – on as a treat.' He'd done this once before for her, and she had been astonished at the effect it had on traffic. She saw his determination and gave in.

'Thank you, but I'll go in my old motor.'

'Your Humber SuperSnipe? Saw it yesterday at the Palais.' He didn't seem to notice her sudden preoccupation with the screen. 'Maroon's a terrible colour.'

'I had a dancing lesson,' she gave him evenly. It was one of her prepared lines, seeing he must already have checked at the hospital reception. 'And no, nothing to do with my divorce. It's just time I learnt.'

'Good for you.'

He rose stiffly, said he would see her at the post mortem, and left. She'd not even blinked when he mentioned Terence Dulsworthy's name, which maybe meant she didn't link the deceased with her ex-husband, the financier Clifford Burtonall. He went downstairs and out into the coming drizzle, wondering what it was like to be divorced. Some said it was a bereavement, others like a rebirth, but who knew? Even divorcees didn't. His missus said nobody knew what a successful marriage was either. Some folk stayed together, other couples marched apart in a temper, and that's all there was to it.

Clare arrived late. Hassall was already standing there, in the PM rooms of white and green tiles, among new slabs made of stainless steel and old slabs made of some pottery stuff chipped to hell. So much running water, hoses you tripped over, two trolleys bearing dead waiting their turn. Hassall was next to Cockle, like having wandered into a party hoping somebody would hand him a white wine to legitimize his presence. Cockle was silently adding things up, Clare observed while she said hello. Cockle was questing. She could practically see his mind hard at it, so many yards – metres, probably – of hosepipe, so many gallons, litres of water per second, weight of human organs hefted onto scales per diem, so many foot pounds of work, so many joules expended. Endless pointless effort.

'I'm so sorry. Traffic.'

'She'll always be late now she's gone private,' Dr Mantris said. He'd taken over from his old Fife predecessor, but seemed to have similar sardonic views. 'Reneged from the Health Service, for money. Now she brings her sordid friends, thinks we'll supply coffee. What a nerve!'

'Which friends?' Cockle asked quickly.

'Doctor means us,' Hassall explained. 'It's a merry jest.'

'Right.' Cockle nodded, unabashed, registering that pathologists tried jokes out on visitors. Hassall knew he'd ask for further accounting of the exchange on the way back to the nick, so as to classify Dr Mantris's remark among the rest of his mental clutter.

The pathologist was a stocky busy man who walked kicking out his orange-red rubber apron to avoid tripping up on the flap. He eschewed the laminar flow systems unless he was actually performing the work, and consequently dripped sweat. He never lifted a thing.

'Bruno? Please.'

Bruno was the morbid-anatomy technician, displaced from somewhere in East Europe where carnage was the norm and brought in by some visiting medical team. He was elderly, full of wisecracks, a constant smiler.

'Doctors can only lift two ounces, no more.' Bruno hefted the cadaver, slid it without a grunt of effort onto the PM slab. 'They weed out the strong ones in medical school. Pansies, the lot of them. Like police.'

He flicked off the sheet to expose Terence Dulsworthy. Cockle's eyes narrowed at the technician's words.

'Stop it, Bruno,' Dr Mantris said. 'You'll have them believing we're all anti-fascists – or, worse, fascists. Multiple injuries, cerebral haemorrhages galore. The burns you can see, scrotal skin. Pay attention to the symphysis pubis area. Some assailant deflected the penis downwards to flame the region. Seemingly nailed, the wrists you can see well enough.'

They inspected the corpse in silence. It was horribly battered. The skull was stove in, right and left sides. Hassall wasn't prepared for the massive areas of discolouration. Tension sutures, the cobbling thread up the abdomen from the cutting hagedorn needles. Hassall cleared his throat.

'No telling why, Dr Mantris?'

'That's beyond me, I'm afraid. Motives and that are your business.'

'The skull, Dr Mantris,' Bruno prompted.

'I'm coming to that. Note the small mark on the forehead? Dead centre, hardly worth the bother when you look at the rest of the damage.'

'One tap in a million smashes,' Bruno clarified. 'We'll have to ask a policeman why, Dr Mantris. The killer relenting. The killer doing some test. The killer—'

'Bruno,' Dr Mantris admonished. 'Got the sachets?'

'Here. Labelled.' Bruno chanted the locations to a popular song as he ticked off the transparent envelopes of scrapings. 'Heels, fingernails, toenails, burns one, burns two, burns three, skin lesions numbers trauma one to trauma nineteen, dorsum numbers one to eleven.'

'And the charts, Bruno, please.'

'The chart's not heavy, sir,' Bruno reprimanded. 'Not like our little plastic bags. But police can't read, so each number on these charts is a site where Dr Mantris worked himself into a lather taking each specimen.'

'I don't like your tone,' Cockle said stiffly.

'Thanks, Bruno,' Hassall put in. 'How long for the labs to say?'

'They'll be on holiday again,' Bruno said, chuckling. 'They always are. Serology's been empty since last cricket season.'

'Week to ten days if there's a positive,' the pathologist said.

Bruno handed diagrams over in three folders. 'Nothing in his pockets,' he said. 'Police probably cleared them out before they brought him in. Except the tab.'

He indicated a small plastic envelope on the bagged clothes waiting to go upstairs to the laboratories. It contained a yellow paper fragment with a serrated edge, torn away with a number partly revealed. Hassall looked.

'Some hotel, is that.'

He thanked the pathologist and left with Clare and Cockle. Dr Mantris called after them that the PM report would be sent in two days.

'I could get a transcript now,' Cockle said, thin-lipped with anger.

'Maybe that would be worth asking about,' Hassall said to Clare's surprise, as back into the PM suite Cockle hurried. 'Well,' Hassall told her apologetically, 'he gets on my nerves. I think his greatest moment was learning how to say infrared.'

'And I think you're an act, Mr Hassall,' Clare said candidly. They went and stood by her maroon motor in the car park. 'What's your question?'

'Spotted it, have you?' he said gloomily. 'There's me thinking I'm so clever. Did you meet Terence Dulsworthy?'

'Not that I can remember. Why?'

'He's said to have known your ex-husband Clifford. Something to do with politics, fund-raising and that.'

'Clifford could tell you.'

Such skill these doctors have, Hassall marvelled. So hard to chase them into Denial Corner and trap them there.

'Who did Clifford support? I mean,' he put in hurriedly when he saw the same sentence forming in her eyes, 'when you went along, if you ever did.'

'Once or twice to boring parties. I don't remember Mr Dulsworthy at all. Clifford's on some group that helps Mr D'Lindsay. He's still one of our city MPs, isn't he?'

'So he says.' Hassall tried to make a joke of it, not half as good as Bruno's efforts in there. Maybe he was becoming too police careful. An autopsy technician didn't need to be careful at all. 'Here's the rub, though, Doctor. What do you make of the PM?'

'Frightening. Shameful that it can happen here. Terrible. Why would anybody do such a thing?'

'Torture, you'd say? Prolonged or not? I won't call you as witness.'

Because you know I would refuse to attend, Clare thought, but said, 'Over a period of time, yes. More than an hour, maybe two.'

'And why that tiny mark in the middle of the forehead?'

'It looked to me as if somebody suddenly lost heart in what he was doing.' Clare thought a moment. 'But that's insane, because he then killed him with such brutality.'

Hassall thanked her and they parted. For a while Hassall sat in the police car, waved as he saw her drive out of the gate. Her frank opinions were worth a dozen guarded, rephrased and edited, professional medical statements in court.

That hotel docket. And Mr D'Lindsay. And Clifford Burtonall. And Sagger's tale of some birds booked for politicos who never showed up, about which Terence Dulsworthy got narked. He saw Cockle coming, looking sour. They must have refused him. Hassall brightened. Today wasn't all bad news, then.

BREAKFAST HAD LATELY become an ordeal in Posser's home in Bradshaw-gate. Martina clearly recognized the source of her difficulty. It was Bonn, who wasn't quite between herself and Posser her dad, but still a presence that made her guard her tongue. Not that she was given to invective or screaming fits. Posser had ways to cope with all of those. Nor was it that Bonn somehow diluted the sense of comfort, the ease that families developed. He was condign, too hesitant perhaps, too diffident, and reticent to the point of self-effacement.

No, it was things like the coming battle over the working house newly established next door. The housekeeper Mrs Houchin was a blessing, served homely meals briskly then left them to it. She was loyal, yet should she be kept on with a brothel adjacent? Today would decide. And how would a nest full of squabbling girls behave, with Bonn, front runner of all the city's goers, within yards night and day? Today would also decide that little issue.

'Posser,' Bonn said, making her come to. 'Nicknames are strange.'

'The weekly wash,' she heard her dad say. It took three

wheezes for him to manage even that, his face puce, sweat on him.

'I wondered,' Bonn said. He never left a piece of bread, she observed. Something from the seminary? Symbolism in there, was it, after the consecration of a holy mass? She was vague about religious ritual, once felt somehow she should learn more about it, except her convent school days had stopped all that daft business.

'Wondered what?' Too snappy, for mere breakfast. She felt rather than saw Posser's head lift in surprise at her abrupt question.

'Once, Bonn, little lads were put into the washing tub and made to tread the clothes. It was called possing.'

Bonn reddened, sensing he might have transgressed somehow and hurt Martina's feelings. Had he been guilty of impudence?

The old man laughed. His amusement set him coughing, spitting into his serviette. Martina emitted silent reproach.

Bonn attempted to make amends. 'Making your feet feel shiny for the rest of the day.'

'Nice, lad,' Posser managed to get out eventually. He loved to reminisce, was pleased that Bonn too had traces of it in memory.

They finished their meal. Yet the air, Martina felt, was full of new questions. Bonn's hands had moved as he'd made his remark to her father, quite as if about to grip the rim of a large container and hold on. She'd often seen her dad demonstrate it. Children of mill families knew this, did it soon as they could walk. Was Bonn then of a poor local family?

Sitting wheezing and struggling for air, the old man liked to try to converse. Bonn she knew welcomed Dad's company. Martina did too but felt obligation, wanting to talk over practical questions that arose about the Agency. She'd already postponed the inevitable problem of Grellie, stretched too thinly. Those stupid phone threats would have to be left until later.

The meeting at the Barn Owl was for ten-thirty. She had less than two hours. Getting Posser to the near-derelict mill would take time, though it was only a few minutes across Victoria Square.

'You two hark back, then. I've got to get on.' She rose and limped off to speak with Mrs Houchin.

Posser immediately started on bygone days in the city. Bonn stayed to listen, filling in words to help the ailing man. Today would be an ordeal. It had been his idea, the brothel next door. There would be opposition, but from where? It was an essential step, for Posser's sake. The old man would die, without a job to do.

Trish was first to arrive. It hadn't been long since she'd first crept into the Barn Owl on the off chance, braving the 'pickings', as the street girls called their selection. Pickings, like fruit from a grocer's barrow.

She sat in the vast room, remembering how she'd stood shivering on the stone-flagged staircase among a flock of girls half her age. The smell of soot, the echoes in the enormous derelict mill, brought it all back. Not quite so derelict now, for she could hear a machine clacking away below, music from distant radios. What, thirty or forty girls had been there that day, all wanting to become whores? No, she corrected herself quickly, not whores, nor prostitutes. You said *working girls* or got your eyes scratched out. And not *brothel*, but *working house*.

Odd how pride came into it so. Pride! Who would think

they saw themselves as a select band? She wasn't hang slang yet, though she was learning fast. Horrible to risk being made a fool of, your first real day.

Her children were off now, sixteen and seventeen, in Hawick with their dad. Happy, sort of. Her house was sold, all but some quibble over carpets and the heating. She was in lodgings in George Street, the dog-leg thoroughfare that split at this converted mill.

If all went as planned, she would become a successful chatter, part-time madam of the working house in Bradshawgate, next to where Martina herself and Posser lived.

And Bonn.

Quiet, reserved. Drew people's eyes in some way while deflecting the gaze of others. They said, friends' whispers, that he'd been schooled in some seminary. That was priests, wasn't it? Not exactly like convent schools for girls. Plenty of them about still. No, more than that. Definitely odd, for even the roughest blokes in the city halted when Bonn spoke. She'd been in the Shot Pot once when he'd come in and seen all behaviour change. Everybody had still acted coarse, but somehow with an awareness of someone beyond experience.

Grellie would kill for him. Stood out a mile. Martina was distant, terse, almost bitter. You didn't need to look further than her twisted leg to find a cause. Lameness was hard on a woman. Yet it must be so strange, Bonn lodging in her dad's house. What did they say when he got home of a night? What did they talk about? Two Bowton housekeepers came to do for Number Thirteen, Bradshawgate, but the old man was too sick for them to manage him now. Rota nurses came in and did it.

The door flung open and in charged Rack, bouncing, cheerful.

'Wotcher, Trish. Hey, know why these mills don't fall down now they're empty? It's traffic, see, shaking them the other way, geddit?'

And so on. She couldn't help smiling, eventually laughing as he prattled on about nothing. All made up, she guessed. She couldn't imagine Rack anything other than smiling and jokey. She'd been amazed when one of the stringers said they were all scared of Rack. She remembered saying surely not, a teddy bear like him, and the street girl had warned, You wait, just wait, you'll see.

Grellie arrived, dolled up, Trish saw. Maroon the theme today, cocksure beret, black flimsy dress slating below the hem of her tan coat, hair suddenly much longer than Trish remembered from three weeks since. Was it a hair piece from the unbelievably dear Top Lock in Mealhouse Lane? Grellie nodded hello, seeming preoccupied. Trish felt the awkward silence as Grellie crossed to one of the chairs arranged round the central empty stove. The mill's floor space was wide as a football pitch, two maybe, the huge rectangular windows spaced by horrible modern paintings to hide the begrimed walls.

Then, his wheezes ahead of him, came Posser on Osmund's arm with Martina on the other side. Trish went forward to help but Grellie was there ahead of her. They got him seated. He leant forward, knees wide, arms propping up his trunk, sweating, mouth ajar like a door hung wrong.

'Anything I can do?' Trish asked anxiously. He seemed very poorly.

'All right soon,' Posser managed between pauses.

They came then as if on a pre-arranged signal, the young males who were the keys, leaders of the goer teams. Trish felt her throat tighten as they entered and politely said their names. Suntan, TonTon, Fret Dougal, Canter, Angler,

Commer joking he was from Liverpool so watch out, Faul-
kner, Bonn in silence with an apologetic smile that never
reached, and Zen. There was hardly any talk. No coffee was
served, nothing offered. She felt inadequate, worse than a
new girl at school, worrying should she scurry and make tea,
fill the silence. Rack grinned at each, but loafed back behind
Posser.

Late, almost, came an elderly lady they all greeted with
ease. Trish had seen her before at the pickings, prim, very
proper in funereal garb, black court shoes, hands seizing
each other on her black-skirted lap. She terrified Trish just
as when she'd fired questions at that first encounter.

Trish looked about as everybody settled. It was a macabre
scene, something from an ancient sepia movie, refugees
awaiting deportation by steam train from a disused railway
station. Was this it, the mighty syndicate she had nightmares
about? Accidentally her eyes caught Bonn's and she coloured
at the kindness in them. He looked aside. She saw Martina
looking, and lowered her head to examine her hands, Bonn's
gentle glance nothing to do with her, please believe me.

'Right, Dad?' Martina asked. Trish was impressed by the
girl's lovely voice. How marvellous to be in control, lame or
not, everybody hanging on your every word.

'Aye, luv. Get on.'

'We meet about the working house,' Martina began,
not bothering to raise her voice. 'You all know each other,
except this is Trish. She's from the pickings, no experience.
She's been . . . recommended. I've gone along with her
appointment.'

'What?' Suntan asked. He alone had a separate phone
booker to help his firm of five goers in the nearby towns he
covered. He smiled at Trish. 'No hard feelings.'

'Trish is chatter at the working house,' Martina answered

evenly. 'She'll have extra duties, including supervising rota nurses to look after Posser. The working house is Number Eleven, Fifteen, Seventeen.'

'No experience, did you say?'

Zen was more serious than Suntan. He was slightly heavier in build than the others, Trish noticed. She suspected he worked hard to keep in shape.

'That's so,' Martina answered evenly. 'I'm appointing Joan and Nikki on Grellie's say-so. They'll run the house as joint madam. They can do it.'

'Is it too early, too fast, Martina?' Fret Dougal wanted to know. He shrugged when he saw Rack readying one of his glares. All keys were above Rack's displeasure. It would have been different had Fret been a mere goer. Then, he wouldn't have dared to offer Martina an opinion, much less question her decision. 'I'm only asking. Seems bloody fast to me, that's all.'

'Speed's for me, lad.' For Posser it was a prodigious speech. There was a respectful quiet which he filled with bubbly coughs.

'I see.' Fret took in the expressions round the group. 'Fair enough. Bright idea, eh? Congrats, Martina. Means Posser keeps in action, eh, owd un?'

The tension eased. Trish felt herself relax even under scrutiny this intense.

'All Bonn's idea, not mine.' Martina spoke flatly. 'There's one problem. I want the house working by the end of the week.' She waited at the sudden stir of interest. The exclamations almost became a hubbub. 'One week. Alterations are all done. We've moved fast. You must have noticed workmen, architects, if you've gone by. Nine girls are earmarked. Grellie has done wonders, and Miss Charity, Connie, Joan and Nikki. Rewards will be commensurate.'

'How is it advertised?' TonTon wondered, looking at Posser.

'It's done. It will be slow at first, but'll soon be cruising.'

'If I may.' Everyone present looked at Bonn. Trish noticed that Posser started to smile. 'I wonder if everyone here could be shown round the premises. It would be really quite interesting.' Trish saw his shyness as he realized the attention his words were getting. 'Just, well . . .'

'Not bad,' TonTon said to Martina. 'That's on, is it?'

'As you wish,' Martina conceded. 'Any afternoon of the next three. Rack will bring word.'

They said their thanks, Bonn staying mute.

'We have a few problems, I believe. Grellie?'

'There's going to be a bit of feeling between the house girls and the stringers.' The street leader felt TonTon's instant irritation but went firmly on. 'Bound to be. So I'll be asking Martina soon if I can reorganize the street lasses. I haven't worked out the details. Just telling you now in case word gets to you and you start wondering what.' She gave a challenging stare at the keys. 'Frankly I don't care for the way some of my stringers use the goers as confidants. I suggest we puts a stop to it once and for all.'

'Grellie's right.' Martina spoke, knowing such finality would curtail opposition.

'Transfers on, are they?' Fret Dougal asked, curious. 'Your street lasses into the working house, I mean?'

'Out of the question.'

'Do we recommend such a thing, though, if we're asked?' from Zen.

'No, Zen. No phone numbers, no addresses. Hearsay, you just give them hearsay back.'

'Connie and Elora can handle any switchers.' Grellie was

confident. 'AC-DC women clients we already cope with. They're hardly a problem.'

'Posser will advise, I understand,' Bonn put in.

'Yes. Posser is referee.'

'Then,' the old man tried to put in, his voice a whisper, 'give me a bloody whistle.' Nobody smiled.

'That's all, except for Rack and Grellie. Thank you, everyone. Trish, go on ahead to Bradshawgate. I want Grellie to slot you in later.'

That more than anything told Trish she was on permanent duty for the first time. She said flustered thanks and goodbye and almost ran down the stone steps into the mill yard out into America Street and past the Pilot Ship casino. She was frightened yet elated. A new prostitute, heading for forty, and not a clue. All on Bonn's supposition. She had to do right, justify his conviction. Failure? She'd die first, do anything to get her new life right.

What did Gran always say? Next chance is last chance. This was Trish's last chance, take over a brothel and do it brilliantly right.

WATCHING THE CROWDS in Victoria Square, Bonn remembered his first sex.

He found himself wondering what exactly women got from sexual intercourse. Men, Bonn now knew from within the *oppidum* of the male mind, were simplicity. They culled a process complete of itself. But for women there were as many answers as categories thought possessed. Think of the ramifications of contemplation, and you were into hundreds of possibly different answers. Extend it to pure meditation or to blunt recognition, add observation, you leapt to thousands.

Then came technical complexity, the variance of pace, method, the woman's incredible righteousness of demand and her swift conversions from doubt to certainty. Yet still Bonn had to quest on for answer. What *did* a woman get from sexual congress with the male? Very well, with, for bluntness, he thought, reddening slightly in broad day, me?

What did the Americans say (he had read the term in a novel somewhere) 'the whole enchilada', possibly to mean everything of related concern, was it? Some criminals, in the same story, had argued over the proceeds of a robbery and one complained, 'Fuck it, the whole enchilada.' Perhaps it meant dividend on investment, or was it a kind of breakfast? He must look it up.

But, women? A score of travellers alighted at the Affetside-Egerton-Bury terminus and slowly scattered. Bonn loved them for their uncertainties of direction, as his mind raced on.

From sex, a man gained the most profound release imaginable. It had been wholly unexpected, Bonn remembered, that intense pressure smashing behind the eyes, so enormous that it was as if the eyes must surely explode into a morass of sweetness. He reflexively closed his eyes tight shut as when, in that final oblivion of orgasmal rut, his back rigid, his tightening limbs arched his entire body in blissful opisthotonos. An entirety of magic, a sweating, huthering, ecstasy that made all other known sensations mundane. Sex had propelled him into a stupendous new life.

Coming to after his first copulation, still twitching, between brief moments of unconscious absence and transitory shudders, Bonn recalled being astonished that his vision was still there. He could still see, after all that! Therefore his mind couldn't have erupted through his orbital sockets. And he could move his limbs! He felt breathless, yet swollen with a relieving gladness entirely new. Did everyone, he remembered speculating, somehow know this beforehand, or was it always an equal surprise?

It had been a revelation so utter that he knew for the first time the ghastly alarm felt by addicts: Where can the next paradise be found, and how soon? How can I obtain it? Can I bear the cost? Quick! Quick!

But still, women?

Within minutes of coming to afterwards, Bonn realized the male's part, and found it a singularly curious and unique destiny. The encounter however for that first woman seemed to include a strange continuity. She had spoken instantly, not even needing to rouse, flowing into a ready conversation, of this, that, her household duties a terrible pressure, her husband, a child – was he offended that she had a child, it wasn't so terrible was it, seeing that married men got up to all sorts most of the time if you believed half you heard . . . And so on, Bonn adapting, trying to stay out of an enveloping stuporose dream, quickly putting in a murmur here, a nod there while she talked on.

The traffic and pedestrians pleased Bonn, as innocent entertainment pleases seasiders. He tried to pause each day, leaning on the pavement barriers exactly here at the end of Mealhouse Lane within view of the Butty Bar, and for a moment enjoy the hurly-burly of the Square's concourse. Innocence meeting innocence, perhaps? It gave him the opportunity of seeing Grellie's girls, trying to work out their groupings into street stringers, which was not evident as they strolled and trolled, one or two occasionally moving towards some slowing car. He liked them.

During his fifth day as a goer Posser had sent for him. It was a time of questions, all from the ailing old man, and Bonn knew it had to come. Bonn was well aware of his own inability to speak out. This had always been a failure in his character, a flaw to be concealed though his reasons were unclear. They met in a small office at the rear of the Pot Shot snooker hall, the room Bonn quickly came to know so well after Martina took over. Bonn hadn't been apprehensive, merely enveloped in a vague sadness.

'All right, son?'

Posser had had to keep puffing at some hissing gadget, wheezing hard so a powder sprayed in below his tongue.

Bonn felt he ought to bring the old man a drink of water, or was that for ladies who fainted? He had seen a grainy old mystery film on television two days before, where a sip had effected the almost instantaneous recovery of a lady overcome by emotional trauma.

'Thank you, Posser, yes.'

More wheezing, then, 'You're in, Bonn.'

In? The word settled on Bonn's mind, then stretched down into a cortical space. In what? He would have asked it outright if words were easy. He thought to repeat his thanks, but specificity had never been his strongpoint in the seminary's theological debates. Why, only the previous evening a retailer's wife from Chorlton-cum-Hardy had said in wonderment, 'Why don't you talk?' even as she'd knelt astride him, to which he'd only been able to reply, 'I'm sorry.'

'You'll do, is what I mean.' Posser seemed to wait for a reply.

'Thank you' was probably safe.

'I don't know what it is about you,' Posser said kindly, his features becoming puce at the exertion necessary for a sentence so prolonged. He puffed, inhaled, expectorated into a tissue, and got breath enough to manage, 'They're all repeaters, yours.'

Repeaters? Bonn asked himself. Was that good, bad? What was it? And Posser's 'You'll do' had come out as, what, explanation, or was it something more? He was baffled. Over a few minutes, working hard on breathing, Posser took him through the consequences.

'Look, son. All uppers – the lady clients you serve for our Agency – do one of four things. Some simply don't return again, because they've done it, see? They've taken the sex risk, skated on dangerous ice, been thrilled, are satisfied they got away with it, maybe learned the confidence to seduce all and sundry, God knows. That's only some, though. Mostly a woman becomes a drip-feed regular. She comes again. Hiring a goer becomes part of her life, if she can afford it, lashing out on a goer as a treat for herself. Or she becomes a clocker, sort of every Wednesday when she comes to Tansie Laddie's for a perm.'

He did his pharmaceutical magic with the puffer, still not demanding water. Bonn worried where the nearest tap was. Perhaps Osmund, the old gentleman playing patience outside, guarding the door, might know in case Posser collapsed.

'Last, there's the specials,' Posser resumed. 'They book a goer, meet up, have their hour of sexual delight, whatever. But.'

'But.' Bonn quietly repeated the word, recognizing an old trick of philosophical argument, leave a conjunction hanging to invite the unwary to voice a premature supposition. Oddly, he had never fallen into this trap even during the verbal fugues and counterpointing of the formidable Father Tyson.

Disappointed, Posser continued, '*But* a few immediately book the same goer, son. They insist. It must be that goer and nobody else. Whether they're new clients, regulars, or special-interest ladies wanting some sexual oddity, they'll demand an instant re-booking. They're frantic for the same goer. No substitute. They weep, offer double, treble. And we're not cheap.' He shook his head. 'And the fuss they create if they can't have you until next week! I think a madness gets into them.'

Bonn saw. Was this success, in Posser's terms? Was it praise?

'Never seen anything like it, Bonn.'

Bonn felt the old man's rheumy eyes on him, in mere

observation rather than interrogation. He couldn't have borne questions. He might have had to leave.

'New goers like you,' Posser went on, gaining strength, 'I feed different clients for the first few days and nights, see how you cope. Women are all different. You might not believe it, but I was a goer once. Not recently!' He almost chuckled himself into a laughing fit at the quip. 'I give new goers a mixture, duster see? New ladies, regulars, drip-feeders, the lot. The Agency has a corps of specials on a cost list.' The term was on offer to the silent Bonn, but only for a moment. 'Meaning that a few select ladies pay our Agency a retainer. Any new goer, they get priority booking.'

Standing there listening, Bonn had remembered that theology students were, by English liberal education tradition, the only faculty permitted unrestricted access to all ancient library categories of pornography. Applying himself diligently at the seminary, he had once been startled to come across a misplaced volume presenting a detailed analysis of prostitute systems in late Victorian England. He had pored over various pages until he began to suspect his motives, but during that intense few minutes he learned that moneyed gentlemen used to pay enormous fees for the services of a virgin, sometimes from fear of disease but more often for aesthetic reasons. 'Money thus finances gratification,' the Victorian author had written in stern reproof.

Was Posser saying the phenomenon persisted yet among women today, *mutatis mutandis*? But how, Bonn wondered, his face quickly colouring at the week's carnal memories, did one distinguish between client ladies who had such specialist intentions and the rest? And did one have the right to classify women before that breathless exhilaration erased all conscious thought and you entered paradise? It seemed to him a mortal transgression of honesty, an appalling intrusion that was so unfair to the woman. Shockingly, it was a proposition formed of two mutually exclusive blasphemies. Facing Posser that day, he had tried to render his features paler, failed abysmally and reddened all the more. Posser kindly stared into the middle distance.

'You got that mix.' Posser waved away some supposed interruption, though Bonn kept silent. 'I've never known nowt like it. Every one of your clients re-booked, or tried to. Including Vanessa One-One-Four. It doesn't matter, Bonn,' he added as quickly as he could, 'not at all.'

Posser was overcome with coughing, and to Bonn's huge relief took out a small flask from which he eventually sipped himself into quiescence. Anxiously Bonn watched the old millman's purple features settle and the hue slowly improve.

Vanessa had insisted she was thirty-nine, acted coquettishly, and proudly told him she could 'easily afford this sort of thing'. He had done exactly as she said, stood before her as she felt at him, undressed and sat on the bed while she then took off her clothes. They had lain there, he blankly waiting further instructions. Later, conjoined and moving, she had laughed aloud before the orgasm slammed him into that uncontrolled trajectory of amazement where responses were uncharted and thought unable to follow.

The trouble occurred afterwards. It was the fee.

Even the word proved difficult. Did it not stem from the Old English, Bonn vaguely recalled, for cattle? Its meaning 'money' was relatively recent. Waiting for Posser to recover to his usual squeaked breaths (though wasn't the old gent's slowness a little too protracted this time?) Bonn tried to remember the seminary's scrupulous attention to the problems of religious stewardship, where consideration of *fee* was vital. A fee was homage rendered, he remembered with a start, but this was surely not so here, in a goer's life. Paid by a woman to a hired youth for sex? Then a fee was also 'denoting a payment or gift'. He clearly saw again the words, the truly terrible implications of which brought him sharply back to his unanswered question of what the woman *got* from sex with him. With that he could go no further until some lady provided him with an answer. A fee was also a 'prize or reward', intoned the impossible Oxford dictionary, into which interpretation his soul denied him entry, but he easily recognized with a familiar guilt pang his role in the best-remembered definition of all: *A fee is a dog's share of the quarry*, by tradition the neck and belly of a slaughtered prey. Was that any less sickening, though, than the stark *bribe or gratuity, for services rendered*? Fee. Posser had said it, so it must be so.

Vanessa One-One-Four had left no fee. She had dressed, stood teasingly at the door prepared to leave, and exclaimed, 'I *love* it when you're all embarrassed!' And teasingly said was there anything he wanted to ask. He remembered shaking his head and saying, 'No, thank you,' and watching the door close.

She hadn't paid. He didn't know what to do.

There was worse still with another lady. He had actually failed to render the service requested by the plump Pearl Two-Five-Two from Edinburgh, who had insisted on his watching while she made up her face with tons of cosmetics into an incredible mask. She had used several lipsticks, glosses, enormously long false eyelashes, rouge, blues, reds, greens, finally and most sinister of all a blonde wig of Caro-lean dimensions that had quite scared him. Having to sit and observe Pearl's preparations was not the failure, though. He had watched in silence and paid heed while she pointed out the benefits to beauty (her phrase) of overlaying a paler lipstick with a darker, of making sure the eyebrows conformed to the line of the upper eyelid, plus other unknowables equally precise. She had also fetched out a selection of earrings, lip studs, nasal rings, even a pierced-tongue berry made of gold. Having to sit and observe while Pearl inserted them made him queasy, though he had dutifully stuck at it, gazed with what he desperately hoped was an expression of admiration.

His failure was in the rut.

Pearl was considerate, he realized when entering her. She adjusted herself, used her hands and mouth well, initiated the right synchrony, slowed her growing excitement. It was then, starting intercourse fairly quietly and at first hardly moving, that he knew he could not do as she wished. Her thick cosmetics were not the problem, for what during the application had seemed almost gruesome somehow became subtly transformed into exultant beauty when she disposed her limbs about him and the bliss began. No, it was his inability to do what Pearl demanded whisperingly then loudly, finally in a frantic almost panicky shout. 'Mark me, sweetheart,' she'd hissed into his ear, 'mark my body.' He'd wondered, *mark* her? How? What did you have to do? Mark her with what?

It was alarmingly different from the second woman of the week – of life – who had gasped, breathlessly clinging round him as he had seized her harder still a few beats before the final orgasm, 'Please don't mark me! Don't . . .' which afterwards had led to a scared examination of her back, arms, thighs, and throat before she had dressed, almost laughing in relief, on finding herself free of such evidence.

And his failure worsened when, rummaging in Pearl Two-Five-Two, the sex became more complicated, for she banged her fists on his shoulder as he quickened. She began to grunt and told him, 'Talk dirty,' and was soon crying out,

'Talk fucking filth to me, you bastard,' screeching other exhortations with a coarse invective he failed to understand. The sex had been prolonged and debilitating, with Pearl howling for physical hurt and verbal crudities, none of which he knew how to provide, while physical relish shook him into ecstasy and he flailed in her, his only utterance a series of chugging groans as he worked to final stillness.

Pearl had looked at him afterwards, just looked, dressing slowly. She was another who had said, doubt showing in her expression for the first time, 'Why don't you talk?' There was an answer, of course. He could have replied, 'I am ashamed.' And, asked for further reasons, 'I do not know how to mark a woman, Pearl, or what signs of injury you might find desirable. Also, I am afraid I do not know how to talk dirty. I know – please excuse me – "fuck" and "shag" and three words referring to genitalia, but that is all. And the context of their use escapes me. I do apologize, Pearl.'

The truth was, his stander Rack normally translated street speech for Bonn, which was ironic since Rack was a boisterous Cockney unable to pronounce much of the local dialect correctly, while Bonn knew the dialect but practically no street speech. It was a confusion. Bonn had actually wondered for a brief moment if Posser had been about to tell him that Pearl was claiming a rebate because her goer had given her sexual intercourse while being unable to bruise or otherwise mark her, and was untrained in verbal abuse.

Bonn had come to with Posser nodding as if they had enjoyed a full dialogue. It had been a strange encounter.

'Good that you told Rack about Vanessa One-One-Four and the fee, Bonn.'

That word. 'I forgot to ask for it.' Bonn's lies were always hopeless. 'It was not the lady's fault.'

'It's okay. Rack straightened it. You've got the best stander in the business, son. Rack's going to stay with you.'

'I do hope that will not prove troublesome.'

'That's my decision.'

Bonn hesitated. Rack had told him candidly, on his way to his first client, 'I'm the best stander in the fucking world, see, mate? So new goers all get me first week, see? I put yer all straight, see? Then I passes yer on to some other stander, see? Don't worry, I'll give you somebody reliable. I'm head stander, see?'

And had gone on to explain, jigging along the pavement in Victoria Square, between jovial shouts to Grellie's street girls who were eyeing Bonn, the stander's function.

'Any trouble with yer upper, I'm there, see? Any husband or bloke comes in for a screaming match, I sort it, see? You just fuck the arse off yer upper okay, and I'll see to—'

Bonn had halted, Rack waiting to see why. It was then that Bonn had said quietly, the first of many times, 'Please, Rack, moderate your language. We are in public. It might possibly give offence to passers-by.'

Puzzlement from Rack and Grellie's street girls on the one hand, and baffled incomprehension on Bonn's part. That, it seemed to Bonn, was the respective attitude that was making Bonn wonder if he was doing right, except of course for the fact that he was now in thrall to the paradisical wonderment of sex, of women, that sheer ecstasy he knew he must have for ever and ever.

'You're wondering why I'm giving you my boss stander?' Posser eventually got out. 'Safety, son. That's all it is. Nowt else.'

'Thank you, Posser.'

'I want you to stay with the Agency, Bonn.'

'Thank you.' And after a while he said, 'I shall.'

Bonn noticed that Veltie, one of Grellie's girls, was pausing to give Bonn one of her special stares from across the road. Bonn saw Connie, Veltie's street boss, give her a shrewd kick as she strolled by, making Veltie yelp and swear. You see, Bonn warned himself, even obvious actions are a puzzle.

Veltie was a short, shapely girl who dressed slinky. She once said loudly to Edna, who never left the central gardens until daylight, 'Isn't Bonn lovely?' to make him go red and walk faster. Edna had merely said, 'Shhh, you noisy bitch,' but Bonn had answered silently to himself, 'No. I'm nothing of the kind,' and since then kept out of Veltie's way.

Bonn saw Rack approaching, waving and shouting to the girls. His quiet moment was ended. Oddly, his life was now as ordered as his former existence in the seminary. He moved on.

CONFLICT OCCUPIED CLARE'S mind. She was restless, so many routes clamouring to be chosen. Tonight, after supper of fish pie, vegetables, a fruit-and-custard thing she liked to do, all was tranquil on the surface when she settled down. Mrs Kinsale had once done the evening meal, leaving an array of notes, instructions, warnings about the oven's temperamental state when she'd concocted one of her mysterious non-suet creations. Now, divorce chose every evening's pattern and Clare merely walked the dots. This particular evening, this meant for some reason thinking over the divorce, how her evening might have been with Clifford.

He would have talked about City investments, difficulties in aggregating funds for the canal marina, the hopeless Council Ordnances. She'd have nodded, gone 'Mmmh!' or 'Mhhh?' as necessary.

Clifford knew that she had encountered a younger man. She had denied any affair and impropriety, but there was no concealing their estrangement. She knew, from sniping skirmishes of the unrelenting marital sort, that Clifford traced her phone bills. He was not stupid. There were no children. This last thought gave her a pang, but the problem would not go away.

Sister Immaculata at her convent school would have blamed her for the clumsiness with which Clare had engineered the separation; the awkward talks, the ridiculous sense of betraying everything, from religion, parents, future, to possible children. Not to mention Sister Immaculata herself: *Clare, how often must I remind you to formulate thoughts in a sufficiently ordered way before committing yourself to speech? Let's try that a second time, paying strict attention on this occasion to definitions of terms. Clare? Are you listening?*

Clare came to at ten o'clock, some late news programme on and her feet cold as ice. She hadn't even finished her tea. She thought, *Clare? Are you listening?* And went to bed. She resolved to leave the house, let Clifford have the whole place. She had another, newer, life to lead, which meant burning all bridges.

The early part of the day was best, Rack found, really odd seeing how he'd always hated mornings when he was a little lad. Now, twenty thinking years under his belt, he felt life owed him. He wanted it to behave, give the best of order.

To start mornings, he always did the tickets. Hotels, hospitals, student hostels, received complimentary tickets for shows. Every plop – think undeserving cadgers – had to turn in one-for-one to him. Same day, no delay. Rack was proud of it because he'd made it a saying round the city: *Same day, no delay.* It meant he got half of all complimentary tickets. Films, shows, jazz groups, famous stars, got milked soon and late. If some rock star drew, like, twenty thousand in his latest performance, well, he'd papered the house last time round, giving four per cent free tickets, wind the girls up to coming. So for ever and ever they had to stump up that same one-twenty-fifth. Course, Rack himself didn't actually go and collect. He had Erik for that, an honorary local from Belgium who knew fuck all but was brill. Rack only had to walk down to the Volunteer pub some time after eightish, and there'd be Erik with a bundle.

'Got good news,' Rack would joke, saying ta.

'What, Rack?'

'You're safe, Erik.' And Rack would guffaw, leaving Erik grinning amiably because it was true.

That meant giving Cougher Sands the chits to sort into colours, rows, good views or crap, for each show. Then Rack'd estimate value, and chip them on to Reel who worked the ticket agency by George Street. The money came to Rack in a girl's snood as she walked past, no later than sevenish. He'd embrace her, joking, come away with his sleeve fatter than it first went round her. Nothing wrong with money coming in.

Everybody knew the scam. Fat George the newsman facing the Asda supermarket, opposite corner, Askey the messenger from the Triple Racer where couriers convened and lounged. And the girl stringers, more than sixty on a good day, pulling busy, all knew the signal system Rack had invented and changed every day to stay ahead of the game. They muttered, coughed, shouted, screamed the numbers across the swirling traffic with gusto and shrill hilarity, or mumbled them looking nervous as Rack swaggered, strolled, danced by.

'Is things all right, Rack?' Erik asked this morning, doing his bundle.

'Eh? Why?' Rack stared, astonished. This was the most Erik had ever said, extra. In fact Rack'd started to work out a new theory to prove why Belgians were all like mutes. 'I asked why,' he reminded immediately because Erik hadn't jumped to it.

'I'm scared of you,' Erik said.

Rack went on his way mystified. No good asking a mute to explain. But he was so put out, really narked by Erik's answer, that he beckoned Helga. She wasn't German but pretended she was for punters who liked boots. Didn't other nations wear boots? Women were unknowable, so he shelved the boot problem till later and leant on the railings by the Weavers Hall. She'd just alighted from a drab saloon car, pulling down her mini skirt and wiping her mouth with a Kleenex. She came obediently, dropping the soiled tissue in a litter bin.

'Ere, Elga. Erik sez I scare him. Why'd he seh that?'

She weighed Rack up, smiling to show friendliness. Was it a good day, or bad? Good, she could say anything, truth or balls, get away with it. Bad, though, she should run. The things she'd seen Rack do to folk for just nothing made for caution.

'He's timid, Rack. The girls think mebbe something happened when he were on the Contie.'

'Ah.' Rack nodded. Some girls were sage. Helga had hit it. It was because Erik was Belgian and therefore from the Continent, which was well weird. 'Ta, luv. Punter all right? He were early.'

'Night shift worker,' she said, casual. 'Only ever gob jobs, him. Dunno why they bother. Patsy said tell Rack eighteen and forty.'

'Separate, like that?'

'Yih. She's had her hair done new. I hate it.'

He thought, Sod getting into rival hairstyles, wars were fought for less. 'Had your breakfast?'

'Just going, luv. How's Bonn?'

He said his so-long and went on. He collected more muttered numbers from Balan the old busking soldier, then

Glazie Glazebrook, first of the receptionists to report. Then two traffic wardens giving out parking tickets by Bradshawgate. Then he chatted up two stringers who were waiting for early train commuters on Station Brough. He fancied one, a pale lacklustre lass from Preston who, he was sure, fancied him back but wouldn't say so when he tactfully asked if she wanted a shag. She was called Winnie, said she'd been thrown out of her home, except she was from an orphanage Rack knew about. It didn't matter. All the working girls on Grellie's strings wore fake stories, par for the course.

'Tonight, Winnie, after nosh, eh?'

'Yes, Rack.' She gazed at him. He liked her.

'I'll get a motor, come here for you.'

'Right, Rack,' she said. Her mate Lara whispered something and they giggled. Winnie saw Rack wasn't going to wait, so called after him, 'Rack? Christine says tell you eighteen and thirty.'

'Right, Winnie.' He bounced along the pavement, pleased the way the morning was turning out. Lara shouted, 'Rack? How's Bonn?'

'Yeh, Rack,' Winnie called, diffident. 'How's Bonn?'

Jesus, Rack swore to himself. Have a bleedin' newspaper printed, *The Bonn Report*, save a frigging heap of bother. Ask Bonn how he was, though, you only ever got, Very well, thank you Rack, so what was the fucking good of asking? Any more girls asked, he'd get Martina to make a rule, nobody's to fuckin well mention Bonn until noon, let the day at least start.

'Morning,' Fat George said, giving Rack his morning paper. 'Martina, Rack. And how's Bonn?'

'Numbers, George.'

Rack got back nought and thought, Christ, Martina

wanting him this early? He could do with Martina, boss of the known world, but she stared so cold. It wasn't right for a bird. Okay for blokes when they were having a go, fine. But Martina's stare could chill your nape in seconds, and not a clue what the hell she was on about. It wasn't good. She needed shagging, get well rested.

He changed direction heading for the snooker hall behind the Granadee TV Studios. Truth was, it was Bonn ought to be shagging Martina, not just any bloke. He lodged with her and her dad Posser, God's sake. It'd 'save on the hem', locals said, meaning make life easier all round. Tactfully he'd told Bonn this, but with Bonn you might as well talk to the wall.

Leek, a shabby bloke who had the pickpocket franchise at the railway station, was on song, collar turned up to show this. He touched his forehead to Rack, universal sign of police about. Rack repeated the sign to say got it. He saw Mr Hassall at the newspaper stall having a free read, stingy bastard, like the police weren't paid enough to buy one. Much the plod knew. Probably just eyeing up the street bints as usual, never doing nothing. Martina didn't allow pickpocket franchises, but Rack let them stay without pay so they paid their keep in news. Police, news? Christ Almighty. That bad. He chuckled but uneasy, hoping Martina's summons was for nothing.

12

Ammy – a girl who gives sex for paltry gain, as little as a drink

H ASSALL WAS SICK of police drivers. Was there ever a driver, any driver, not given to bad jokes? He could hear the WPC, changing gear and choking laughing, 'This Hollywood actress, Lauren Bacall. Somebody asks, "You like condoms?" and she says, "What's in it for me?" Gerrit?'

'What?' Cockle said, blank. 'Turn right here.'

'What's in it, see?' The WPC fell about, hardly able to concentrate.

'Then second left. Hawthorn Crescent.'

Except wasn't it witty Zsa Zsa Gabor's original crack? Hassall limped out, his right knee giving out from too many toe-punts as a lad hopeless at footer, and gazed up at the boarding house. He already knew what Dulsie's bedsit would be like, tat city, shoddy, that grotty thick smell of under-clothes washed weeks late.

They went up the steps, gained entrance from an anxious landlady, went on up without her.

'Terence Dulsworthy,' Cockle intoned like a court clerk, opening the door and standing there. 'Aged thirty-six, born Northampton. Earned a living messaging, night security, general factotum, driver.'

Driver? Another jester. 'All part-time.'

Nothing in the room took Hassall's eye straight off. No phone, a portable telly. No photos, empty fireplace, no debris. Pretty ordered for a lone bloke. Cockle began searching with maddeningly quiet industry the way he'd been taught, methodically producing a flashlight, squinting along the carpet, kneeling on the floor, weighing up the view from the one window and checking the gas. Hassall envied the man his ability to kneel then spring erect just like that.

'Not much,' Cockle eventually pronounced thirty minutes later. He was irritated by Hassall, who sat on the divan squashing possible evidence.

'Where'd he sleep?' Hassall asked. 'Which way round?'

They worked it out from marks on the carpet. The divan unfolded into a creaky bed. Hassall left Cockle to it, went to stare at the nearby wall. Numbers were crossed out, ticked, some paired with letters. Hassall imagined Dulsie lying there, answering his phone and jotting on the wall.

'Mobile phone. Best find it. Get photographs, please.'

His spectacles were a new embarrassment. First his wonky knee, now eyesight. Staring through his glasses, head at an odd angle in poor light, he found his mouth kept coming open as he peered. What, did a slack jaw help fading vision? It was an old man's trick, peer with an open mouth. 'T/12' might actually signify a date. Terence Dulsworthy had been nailed to a dank garage wall beneath enormous dripping fungi on a Tuesday, which happened to have been the twelfth of the month. It was one of three numbers uncrossed. Hassall said, anticipating Cockle's remark, 'The wall's the only diary Dulsie kept. Let's give it credence. Find out what went on in Dulsie's manor those dates.'

'They might go back donkey's years.'

'They also might not. He did bird, remember.'

'Yes!' Cockle was pleased. 'He was in nick until—'

'Sure we found nothing on him?' Hassall thought of the unfairness of it all.

'And mobiles can be in a duff name. Dulsie used aliases.'

'That's the spirit.' In this mood Cockle could list every obstacle on the planet.

The other two uncrossed numbers were 'T/5' and 'W/6'. Hassall left then, rather face the landlady's prattle and the WPC's jokes than more of Cockle's morose intensity.

Saddest thing was, Hassall's touts in the city weren't as quality nowadays, what with reprisals, money, and new communications. Other career opportunities, Hassall thought bitterly, signs of the times. He found the landlady standing nervously by the stairs and followed her into her ground-floor flat.

'Look, missus,' he said, putting on the we-oldies-together woe. 'About the girl he used to bring in. I know, luv, I know.' He flapped down her protests. 'You have no choice these days, the way folk behave. It's only I've got to ask, see.'

Some days were all messages. Rack got a code number signalled from Vee on the street corner and responded quick, get it out of the way because today was going to be a swine.

'What, Grellie?' He plonked himself down where she was watching the old men play chess in the central gardens. 'These old cocks'll catch their death of bleedin' cold.'

'There's ammies around.'

Rack tried to spit on an old bus ticket on the grass. He missed, swore. Say two strides off. Grellie tutted.

'I wish you'd stop doing that. It's disgusting.'

He sighed. That was women for you. Shag anybody, do anything for a fistful of zlotniks, was okay, but spit on clean grass you were horrible. He'd work out why in a minute.

'Rhona and three of our stringers reported ammies on the Station Brough again last night. I'm sick of it.'

Grellie waited for Rack to explode, but he listened in silence. She eyed him, wondering what.

'They were a team, Rack. One, trying for a fare home, I can stomach.'

'Who've you got can finger them?'

'Rhona. Don't heed what Vee says. She's out for trouble, that one. She'll have you dicing commuters given half a chance.'

'Thought of having Bonn, Grellie?' She listened warily. So this was what preoccupied him. 'I keep telling you, it's time Bonn got himself a private bird. You're it.'

'Crossing's dangerous, Rack. I wouldn't want you calling with the lads some dark night, giving me the wet walk home.'

He urged, 'It wouldn't come to that, Grellie. Promise. Hand on my heart. And nobody could do anything to Bonn. Can you imagine Martina telling me to carnie him? Jesus!' It didn't bear thinking about.

'No good, Rack. I couldn't put him in risk.'

'The poor bugger's desperate. I just know. A bloke's got to have his own bint. He'd jump at you. Ask him.'

'Rack. You know her rules. There'd be no second chance for either of us.'

'Leave the game, Grell. Then nobody could say anyfink.'

But she'd already risen, and strolled off among the flower beds. He watched her. It was a crying shame, the two of them naturals. He wondered if he should talk it over with Martina, see if she thought it a good idea. Some days, folk were beyond him. Barmy. He'd asked Grellie to be his own bird months back. She'd told him no straight off. So it was only right she should service Bonn. But maybe if Bonn took to using Martina, Grellie'd be disappointed and ask Rack to be her bloke! Things would be straightforward, if only women'd think. He just couldn't see the problem. Women were well odd. He'd work out a theory to see why.

Hassall met Grellie as if by accident near the grass rectangle's seats between Bradshawgate and the Volunteer pub.

'Miss Grellie? Half a sec, if you could.'

'Mr Hassall.' Grellie knew he'd been waiting for her to pass by. She'd engineered the meeting as much as he, in the way of peaceful coexistence.

'Something's awry, you see.' Hassall made sure he appeared to be waiting for Victoria Square's traffic to lessen so as to cross, for the girl's sake. 'Did Dulsie – you saw the news – list three girls for him, some time before the Tuesday he got topped?' He watched her expressions sequencing. She was too bright to muck him about, so waited patiently.

'I got asked, Mr Hassall. He was touting for some visitors, don't know who.'

'All nighters?'

'They're the only sort he ever booked. I made him pay up front in case he backed out.' She eyed Hassall belligerently. 'It's only fair.'

'Course it is, luv, course it is.'

'That's all.'

'Thanks. Good day, Miss Grellie.'

'Bye-bye.'

He took the opposite direction, and headed for Mealhouse Lane. It wouldn't do any harm now – and do Grellie a power of good – if he had an idle cuppa in the Butty Bar, making pretend he was sussing out the entire city centre. That would leave Grellie untouched by suspicion. Not that she'd ever been a police grass. She was simply too brain-bright to bugger him about. But he was happier. A political meeting for D'Lindsay's support committee had been slated then cancelled that Monday. Among many others, sure, but it was a definite contender. He wondered if things were looking up, except they never did in police work.

13

Truth – retribution

'THAT'S IT, VANNIE. Thank you.'

'Thank you, Dr Burtonall.'

The surgery and office closed for the evening, Clare felt she could relax. If she could, when she was going to have Bonn so soon, at the Time and Scythe in Bolgate Street.

She heard the outer door click shut and the small lift whirr as Vannie went down. Odd, but Clare had never known a medical secretary use stairs, however short the journey. Always they pressed the button, waited complainingly for the lift that would eventually carry them grandly one floor down. Was it their training, moving legs an affront to status?

Six o'clock, the nights drawing in now. In Victoria Square traffic swirled in streams, rear lights showing as the Warrington exit lights held on red. The vehicles would career up Bolgate Street. She could see it from the window, but not as far as the hotel where she would lie with Bonn. With, or under? On? Around? Her tongue became tight in her mouth.

The one hazard – all right, fine, the one indecision – was Bonn's reticence. By now she felt entitled to know more of him. 'Knowing' another was a risk in love. She'd seen enough of that in her doctoral days.

'Love affair' too was a stretchable term. Nowadays it meant whatever you liked. Check any magazine. Stars shifted their partners after anything from a transient marriage to a weekend's unexpected passion, and rushed to tell tabloids. Wiser to hire a lover, if that encounter suited. And Bonn definitely suited her. It was her one certainty. No problems, now that Clifford and she, after an agonizing sexual armistice, were parted. Clifford had wanted to 'remain good friends', in his trite phrase, but divorce was departure, an ending. Friends should never have been enemies. She knew she was rationalizing, but wasn't this arrangement far more sensible for herself as a professional woman employed by a respectable registered charity doing excellent medical work for the disadvantaged in a grim post-industrial city?

Another exception came to mind. It wasn't quite a love affair, not even as the glossies defined it. She hired. Bonn was her hireling. She paid, Bonn received payment. In a way, an ugly thought. A few months ago she couldn't have imagined being involved this way. The expense, not negligible, she could live with. Had to live with, in fact. She blocked thoughts of transience but they pushed through. How long could she go on without wanting something permanent? She'd already almost blurted out her intentions to Bonn, but love – all right, bring it down, *sex* – had intervened and mercifully they'd both been saved the embarrassment. Yet what would he have said, if pressed?

She glanced at the file bank. Already nearly thirty girls had registered with her, some of them admitting to regular prostitution, and signed up for regular attendance. Odd that their addresses were spread so. Had the charity some advertising campaign she didn't know about? She made a note to check on that.

Vagrants too. At least three shiftless youngsters, drug addicts wanting to be recorded as permitted addicts. She suspected they lived under Station Brough. Each had the patter off, one grinning bad teeth and saying blithely, 'See, Doc, I wants fert be a reg'ler scrip fusileer,' cackling in merriment. Clare had explained that you couldn't simply walk into a doctor's surgery and demand to be given a 'scrip', prescription, for free drugs listed as Schedule DDA, under the Dangerous Drugs Act. One lad – filthy, emaciated, stinking – had become indignant. His mates were scripped so why couldn't he? Etc, etc.

She looked at the time. Ten past six, time going slower. Should she go home? But to what? Clifford was no longer there. Mrs Kinsale would have left the house tidy – still her domain, not Clare's, seeing she'd been there since the year dot. No. Better to have a light meal at one of the local places in Victoria Square. Wasn't there somewhere reasonable at the Granadee TV Studio? She'd had lunch there once with Clifford. Failing that, the Vallance Carvery in Rossini Street would suffice.

This was one niggle, not being able to meet Bonn for supper. Or anywhere else, not even over a casual drink. The mogga dancing had been a disturbing miracle, but one she wanted repeated. She checked herself in the mirror.

Throw a lipstick across her mouth, ruin two tissues getting it right for the short walk across Victoria Square in the dusk. Her eyes would do, and she'd have time after having a bite. Defiantly she ignored the lift and walked down, no mere typist she. She saw a group of girls standing by the Rivergate shopping mall move out of the bright lights cast from the Weavers Hall entrance, and smiled. Quite like a shoal of minnows. The image disturbed her, she wasn't sure why. She turned right, trying not to move briskly. No good rushing, reach Bonn worn out. Exhaustion was for afterwards. She caught herself smiling openly, and carefully adjusted her features.

Take any two from three, what do you get? Answer, three, possibly four, for this was politics. Political groupies bred like flies.

Gordon D'Lindsay, MP, hated, deeply hated, party agents. He especially hated his own, this man he was chatting so amiably to. Listening to, more like. You couldn't get a word in edgewise with political agents. Paid by the word.

'Skinhead's taking up the Birmingham offer,' Alan Pennington was saying. 'Which isn't bad news.'

It happened to be catastrophic fucking news, D'Lindsay thought irritably. And was it actually news? Skinhead was Pennington's nickname for the Shadow Education Minister, once a local political rival. It could mean anything.

'Sure, are we, Pens?'

'Don't hold me to it, Gordon,' the agent said urbanely, waving to somebody across the gathering. Smoking had begun, the thronging ladies competing for eyes and ears.

Oh, but I shall, D'Lindsay told himself grimly. Loss of a moneyed political supporter was an insult. He didn't take insults from an agent. Do that, you're dead in the water.

'Soon?' he asked, nodding to people who crossed his gaze.

A burst of laughter attracted his attention. Clifford Burtonall was at the centre of a business group. Lately divorced from his doctor wife Clare, the investment man was quite the popular raconteur. D'Lindsay wondered uneasily if the bloke – youngish, presentable, wealthy – harboured political ambitions. A moneyed Party supporter immersed in inner city development was an ally, sure, but the type could easily become a rival. Gordon raised his glass, smiling, and Clifford gave a hearty grin in return, miming a golf stroke. Gordon gave a thumbs-up to agree a match, tapping his watch to say soon.

'Next week, if word's right. I decided no action as yet, eh?'

You decide? D'Lindsay could have clobbered the oaf, with his lapel badges that meant nothing except expenses-paid trips to yak with others of his kind in Blackpool hotels. Pennington was going on forty, like all political agents. Loud, assertive, never short of ballpoint scribers, given to using nicknames. And unpleasantly sweaty. Christ, the dolt would sweat on ice. But that was the way of the agent, never a real day's work, hunting the sinecure. At least D'Lindsay, for all his name, had honestly dirtied his hands in real labour. Rotten time it had been, too, back then. He made no bones about it. He'd thought fuck this for a game, and made sure he'd climbed the political ladder. He wasn't going to give it up, either.

'Any grief, Pens?'

The agent's expression did not alter. 'Not really. Somebody called Dulsworthy was killed. In all the papers. A drugs thing, most likely.'

'He wasn't anything . . .?'

'To do with us? No. A general city dogsbody. He once did us a couple of bookings, cars-and-theatre things. I've notified the investigating officer, done the honest citizen act.'

'Good. Bookings directly through the Party?'

'God, no. It was Clifford Burtonall, I think. Dulsworthy started as one of his office gofers, far as I know.'

'Keep me abreast, Pens.'

'Right, Gordon. Politically, the constituency needs a serious boost at Drakeshaw.'

The agent whipped out an electronic gadget. It clicked, reflecting green incandescence onto his sweaty jowls. The MP wondered how agents never died of gluttony. It was bizarre. Did God spare them, as a reminder to the rest of us? There was a joke in there, work it up for after dinner on the rubber chicken circuit.

'Will a shout do?'

Local parlance had three grades of political hustings. Election supporters were cheered more by a visit from their Member of Parliament than any other response. There were, however, visits and visits. The 'shout' was a quick series of phone calls, maybe with some scribble issued by a devoted underling on a topic. Pollution, health risks, education and such dross usually deserved a mere shout. Most of the verbiage was crap, plagiarized Party prattle, but did the trick and shut people up for a week or two.

'Doubt it, Gordon.' Pennington consulted his button panel. The MP wondered if it was all meaningless nonsense coined on the spur of the moment to convince others of his unflagging industry. 'Maybe a DB?'

'Does Drakeshaw deserve that?' Drakeshaw had once been rock solid.

Drive-by, DB, was a term borrowed from the spreading practice of shooting from cars, thank you America. Politically it was a swift actual visit to assembled Party faithfuls. You rushed in, sipped their crappy tea, nibbled cakes, praising, praising, Christ Almighty how you had to praise. You remembered names, shook hands, patted shoulders, looked longingly into eyes, expressed grief at having to leave so soon. And you promised, promised, Christ how you promised! You hinted at deep desires for personal meetings with this elderly cow who had influence, or with that pushy git who wanted some trivial award in the New Year's Honours List, and you left exhausted.

Success was measured by how ephemeral you'd been. If you escaped without having actually truly promised a single bloody quotable thing. If your hints were unremembered vaguenesses. If your clumsy grin at some old dear in her seventies was recalled by her as genuine personal interest or even, Jesus, lust. If and if, then you'd done well. Especially if it took less than an hour so you could squeeze in another DB and a couple or three 'shouts' in the same afternoon.

Be busy enough, you could then get the hell out of this decaying city.

'You see, Gordon, Shacklan's got a team in Drakeshaw Saturday.'

'Bastard,' D'Lindsay muttered, smiling beatifically at somebody who wanted to shake his hand. He managed his glass successfully, beamed, quipped about local city developments, nearly promised, hinted, turned aside with a vague suggestion of meeting the boring old fart in private somewhere, some time soon, eh?

Shacklan was the prospective candidate for the constituency. Shacklan was the enemy. Leader in the polls, up and coming, got tabloid attention lately by beating the drink-driving drum and food hygiene balderdash nobody in their right senses would ever worry about. But it would be solved soon, thank God. By a fluke, Pens Pennington had learned from Fern, D'Lindsay's helper, that Ellot Shacklan's wife was seeing some hired youth. D'Lindsay could remember feeling perspiration start on his back, actually prickle his spine, hearing the marvellous news. Shacklan's missus, hiring a shag. Hiring, meaning actually going out and *buying* somebody who'd dick her! Who'd have thought it? It was truly marvellous news, conclusive proof that God lived and was in Gordon's corner.

The higher Ellot Shacklan got, the harder his fall would be. Gordon envied Shacklan his ease of manner. And his Party organization wasn't full of stingy bastards like this load of parsimonious ingrates. Shacklan's cretins shelled out for a decent limo – never mind the serfs trudging out there. *And* they paid for decent overnights, proper hotels with cuisines to match. D'Lindsay felt aggrieved. He'd bed-and-break-fasted in back streets before now, aye, two nights before by-elections too. Thanks to these mean sods all around him, basking in minutiae. He eyed Clifford Burtonall. That game of golf might bring him in a bigger donation.

'Drakeshaw,' he mused to Pennington. 'Anything at all going for us there?'

'You did their football draw, Gordon.'

The worst thing about Pennington was his reproachful whine. Don't forget you opened the ward at Breightmet General Hospital, Gordon. Remember you sent to that fireman's memorial service, Gordon. Unspoken, but defi-nitely in there, was Agent Pennington's whimper, *But that's all you did, Gordon*. One long whinge.

'Football?' The bloody sport was like flu, never went away.

'They've reached some minor league cup thing.'

'Jesus.' Stand in the rain for two hours?

'Arrive ten minutes before the whistle, Gordon,' Pen-nington wheedled. 'If they're winning, exuberance. Losing, ask what happened. I could make sure a photographer from the Rottenstall *Guardian* was there.'

Stealing Shacklan's thunder. 'Pencil it in,' D'Lindsay con-ceded grudgingly.

'Next is the city freemen, Gordon.' Pens flicking in his tome. 'They're worth a TJ.'

From bad to worse. The TJ, tie job, was the third order of magnitude in political canvassing. It meant a full evening wasted. You yapped at bloated bellies and flabby shoulders for an hour while the fat bastards nodded off. They wanted jokes. They wanted praise. They wanted promises of affluence, every political whim satisfied, the ungrateful swine. Cheap acidy wine, whinnying snoring audiences, stodgy food you wouldn't shake a stick at. Was life worth it? Politically, no question. The answer was yes.

'How soon?'

'Next month. Think positive, Gordon.'

'I always do, Pens.'

'I know, I know.' Nobody could agree like a paid Party creep. 'What I actually meant was . . .'

D'Lindsay saw Fern. She entered with two other women who were dolled up to the nines. Fern didn't stand out, which was all to the good. This encounter legitimized their meeting. What could be more harmless? Mousy hair, average height, neat, a regular helper down at Party, did meals-on-wheels for the elderly was it? Something holy anyway. All in all, an innocent supporter. That was Fern. Husband a shrimp, completely non-political. So was Fern, truth to tell. But she was dazzled by the glamour of associating with a Member of Parliament. And promises, of course, but what were they?

Clever woman, she didn't catch his eye, just talked, smiled, said her hellos. She never talked as such. She simply responded, smiled complacently. See, Gordon explained with complacence of his own as if to some fawning devotee, you need obedience in others to get on in politics. Astuteness turned loyalty into devotion.

It was Fern who had brought the great gift of gossip about Shacklan's dim wife. He'd made Fern promises – some very personal, one or two even fulfilled! Meanwhile, Fern stayed vaguely around, there, one of the many. Harmless, she was that pleasant unnoticeable lady, whatsername, Fern something, does meals-on-wheels, you know the one. In other words, ideal.

'Bit short notice, isn't it?'

'Time, Gordon.' The agent grimaced, going for it. 'It's a let-down. That Yorkshire cricketer. Loudmouth, always on TV. He's going in for his hernia soon and can't make it.'

'Bloody fine,' D'Lindsay groused. 'Member of Parliament for a great northern city, I'm stand-in comic for that gabby sod?'

Pennington shoved his face into maximum grin and said quietly through teeth, 'Ears, Gordon, ears.'

'I'm quoting, Pens. It's what somebody else called him.' The MP always had been slick. 'I admire the man for that fine innings he did. Isn't it in the record books?'

'That's the one,' the agent said with relief. 'Wish you had more time to support regional sports.'

'I'll do it. Announce it as a tribute to him. Handle it, Pens?'

'Pleased to.'

Fern was drifting through the press, gently smiling. His arrangement with Fern was to meet exactly an hour after he did his usual loud exit from this mob of sycophants. She knew where. From the Free Trade Hall, here, it was the nearby Worcester Club and Tea Rooms. Which was sensible, allowable, and offended nobody. Scandal was too vigilant for him to take risks at this stage, Government majority falling.

Pens Pennington made sure he intercepted Fern,

greeting her with a political agent's effusiveness. He managed to breath into her ear, 'All go okay?'

'As ever, Pens,' she said, looking across to where Gordon was, and colouring with pleasure when he waved to her.

Gordon noticed how pleased Fern and the agent seemed, and perked up. He felt like it tonight. Trouble was, he did too much for too many other people. Thank God it was time for some personal recreation, even if it was only the drab self-effacing Fern. Though tonight he rather liked the notion of servility without ambition, and she wasn't at all bad once he got her going.

He decided to have a word with that Burtonall chap on the way out. Moneyed supporters could make sure that politics wasn't all muck and bullets.

14 |

T WO OF THE girl stringers found Grellie disembarking from a saloon by the textile museum in George Street. They waited, speculatively eyeing the driver as the motor left for the London road.

'Got a problem, Grellie. A minute?'

Grellie sighed. She felt worn out, always needed a while to recover from a car session. Some punters were unreasonable, finished with a row over money, how a girl'd shagged, too slow, too fast, anything. Others could be no trouble, wankee, hankee, thankee. This pair of girls were a right caution, always laughing, jokers both. Now they looked sombre.

'Keep moving,' she said. 'Coffee bar in there.'

They separated, met quickly at the counter, moved along with their trays. A score or so visitors were in, schoolchildren among them. Grellie thought, Christ, were we that noisy when we were kids? Maybe. She could always remember being told to shut up.

Her two stringers approached across the self-service. Not bad girls, these. Jokers but not comedians, as the city dubbed such carefree souls. A street girl who got herself called a comedian wouldn't last an hour. It meant liar, untrustworthy, a lass to get rid of.

'What?' she asked, sitting down, her feet throbbing. She badly needed a fag, but had given up cigarettes because Bonn never smoked. 'One at a time. Patsy?'

'Balan told us, Grellie. Rani's on the clag. Gets drugs from her bloke, some goojer plays at the Palais Rocco.'

Patsy was as youthful and compact as a working girl ever could be. Tiny, with big innocent eyes any lass would die for. She had everything, including the most horrible dress sense that was the despair of her pal Emma here. They had terrible rows about Patsy's naff working clothes, always finished up in hugs and helpless laughter, thank God. Some working friendships could end in blood.

'Right. Emma?'

The other girl was older, so discreet you'd miss her in a crowd of school-marms. Despite her brash manner she dressed hazy, muted colours so disarmingly prim no plod ever doubted her propriety. Her demure appearance had got her out of many a scrape, and curiously attracted the punters. Patsy, though, was the first girl a raw copper would collar for soliciting.

'Balan can be trusted, Grellie.'

Grellie made her get on with it. 'Don't give me the fucking obvious, Emma. If the old soldier wasn't on proud for trust, Rack wouldn't let him stay busking outside the mall.'

'Balan's seen Rani paying for satches. He said she was too stoned to realize she dropped one.'

'You've not still—?' The plod would go mental, catching a working girl with drugs on her. As for cold-eyed Martina . . . Grellie shivered.

'No. I got the satch, thought you'd want to make sure it

was what Balan said. It's near the garden chess place among the flowers. I put Shar watching, see nobody nicks it.'

'Good girls, both of you. Thanks, Emma.'

They left, swaggering too much for this sedate crowd. Grellie wanted to stay, have a decent blow for a minute while she sipped her coffee, but hurried out before she was quite recovered. She'd suspected Rani for weeks. Now she had proof, though a mere suspicion would do.

She walked round the square, making sure she passed Balan. The old soldier was playing his mouth organ, his cap on the paving holding a few coins. He wore an old greatcoat, seven or eight medals clanking as he moved. He was called Balan after some ancient desert battle called Barani, the approximation the best the girls could pronounce. If you weren't quick, he'd tell you all about it, guns, troop movements, drawing outlines of forgotten tank units on flagstones. She paused long enough to drop coins in his hat.

'Ta, Balan,' she told him. 'See Rack, get paid.'

The old man interrupted his playing. 'Ta, miss.'

Grellie walked on. She'd go for a quiet lie down, then eliminate Rani from her – and the city's – consciousness. That unbelievable Rani. The stupidity of some girls took your fucking breath away.

'It's getting marvellous, Dad,' Martina said. She held a booking sheet.

Posser craved a smoke. He still had one pipe, and a secret cache of tobacco that Martina and Mrs Houchin the housekeeper hadn't yet found. Dr Winnwick was a cruel swine, and would shoot him if he found out.

'Glad, luv.' His breathing hadn't been too bad today.

Colder weather always helped. It was damp did him. 'What?' He'd not the breath to ask for details.

'Somebody wants girls for a party.'

'Aye?'

'We can do it, Dad. We've done similar before, using Grellie's stringers. Now we've the working house coming on, should it be them?'

'We got enough?'

'I'll draw some from the casino, fixed places. We'll need a minimum of five or six to start.'

'Careful, luv.'

She wanted to know why so, but it would have been cruel to question him until his breathing eased. After a few minutes his colour returned.

'Our street girls, luv,' he managed after coughing, raising his hand to show he was still with her. 'Some fancy theirselves.'

Martina nodded, having foreseen this.

'I'm putting embargo on them, Dad. Street girls are separate. I think we recruit from indoors and stick to it.'

'Me too, luv.'

Together they thought over the territory. The Rum Romeo, the syndicate's casino in Mealhouse Lane. Plus a couple of decent girls working in the three hairdressing places Posser had bought as fling bids some months since and not known what to do with since.

'The Bouncing Block?' Martina asked. Posser nodded at her good thinking. 'We've seven girls in the gym. Two work the saunas, apart from show days when they need to be on best behaviour. I'm sure those two'd jump at the chance.'

'Beth?' Posser got out. He had to put his head back on the chair rest, mouth like catching raindrops, breath rasping slow.

'Good idea, Dad.'

Martina frowned, though, for Beth was the waiting-on girl at the Shot Pot, the syndicate's snooker hall in Settle Street, and Beth was her own worst enemy.

'She still shacks up with that antique dealer in Hulme. Can't see that we'd allow her to keep him on. She does occasionals in the alleys with the snooker lads, not much more. Clean. Sensible. She's not got the nerve to push off from the side.'

'Her'll swim all right!'

Martina's father creased in semi-laughter, only coming to after Martina limped across the carpet and banged his back. He began breaths with relief. She wiped his mouth free of spittle and eased him back into his chair.

'Beth knows what it's all about. I'd like her to move in now, not wait until the working house is a success and then come whingeing.'

Posser thought Martina ought to be with Bonn but couldn't say outright even if he'd the wind. Bonn had now lodged with them several weeks, and remained the soul of propriety. He'd dined out with Posser's daughter once or twice, but Posser suspected that had been when they were planning to establish the brothel next door. The alternative would have been to send Posser away to an old folks' residential nursing home.

The brothel, with all its ancillary care, was all Bonn's idea. It had saved Posser's bacon. He needed to be near Martina until he saw her settled or until he popped his clogs. He'd privately fixed on Bonn for a son-in-law and wanted it now, not when he was long dead from this flaming chest ailment.

'Any progress with Bonn, luv?' All that, in two breaths only, a measure of his urgency.

'Don't keep asking,' she reprimanded primly.

'But it will come, won't it?'

'I don't know.' She hated this.

'Has Bonn said anything?'

'Dad! How many times do I have to tell you?'

Martina limped to the bureau and brought out his whisky. Posser watched her measure it out, and glumly noted that she diluted it. He was allowed one tot a night, Dr Winnwick being a right bastard. The quicker the two women arrived to housekeep for the brothel next door, the better chance he'd have of getting a decent drink now and then. He told his beautiful daughter ta, wondering if she knew about his secret cache of tobacco.

15

THE MICROSCOPE SLIDE responded to the old laboratory trick. Clare clouded it over with a sharp breath then wiped it firmly on her white coat. Nothing worse than a spot of grease to ruin a slide preparation.

The patient, a sullen teenage girl, had begun itching soon after having sex, or so she claimed.

Clare explained the cause, taking her time. Bedclothes, skin contact with an infested sex partner, could transfer the parasites. New cases would acquire the scabies mite only slowly, sometimes even after a prolonged incubation of weeks. Patients who'd been previously exposed, though cured long since, would pick up the *Sarcoptes* mite with appalling speed. Clare had known cases who started excoriating themselves within minutes, clawing frantically at their skin in a forlorn attempt to relieve the fiery itching as the mite speedily burrowed its head into the dermis and there began sucking nutrients from the warm-blooded human host.

'Is this inky stuff necessary?' the sulky girl asked.

Clare answered evenly, 'It helps me to see the spots better.'

'Bad eyes, have yer?'

'Not yet.' Clare smiled to maintain patience. 'It shows me where best to take this specimen.'

The old doctoral tricks always worked; in this case ordinary writing ink dabbed on the skin and quickly washed off revealed pinpoint black dots showing the mites.

She avoided the parasite's burrows, visible with the aid of a small times-ten magnifying loupe, and took a sample from skin that had not yet been scratched. Using the microscope's coarse adjustment she racked the objective down, peering sideways to judge the lens distance as it approached the fragile coverslip, then looked through the eyepiece and racked the Abbé condenser to adjust light intensity. She then slowly racked the microscope nosepiece up until the mite came clearly into view. After that, it was a moment to refine the clarity by the fine screw, taking care always to rack up rather than down. As a medical student she had broken too many wafer thin coverslips by making careless downward turns without thought, shattering slides and ruining valuable specimens. Shortcuts had always seemed quicker when she had been learning clinical pathology. Only experience had taught her the obvious, that a few moments of painstakingly correct procedure saved endless time and resulted in fewer hopelessly damaged specimens.

It was plainly the *Sarcoptes scabei* mite, 'scabs' in popular language. The girl had red areas at the lower parts of her buttocks, her girdle zone, and the anterior areas of her axillae, antecubital fossae and wrists.

'This is simply a small parasite, Deirdre.'

'It's scabs, innit?'

'Yes. It comes from contact with bedclothes, people, garments. It's quite easily treated.'

'Will it go?' The girl paused as Clare indicated that she should get down from the couch and dress.

'There's a very effective treatment. It's quick and painless.'

Clare went to wash, disposing of the coverslip and marking the surgical instrument tray for sterilization as she did. The girl was new to Clare's panel of patients, having been brought in by a friend she described as her room-mate.

'I shall give you a prescription, Deirdre. You'll use the cream rinse then return here the day after next for another examination. Use the rinse after a non-conditioning shampoo. Do your hair, but don't dry it absolutely. Then use the prescribed rinse. Leave it on for ten full minutes, and simply wash off. No conditioners. Have you got that?'

'I'm not a kid,' Deirdre said, truculent as ever.

'Fine.' Clare wrote the scrip and handed it to the girl. 'Please wash your clothes completely and separate from other people's. Changes of clothes, remember. You might have some residual itching afterwards for a couple of days, but that's normal. I might have to give you another go of the miticide, but you will be free by the weekend.'

'How soon can I go back to work?'

'What work do you do?'

'I'm an escort.'

'Escort?' Clare asked, blank.

'I check people in at hotels and boarding houses.' The girl eyed the doctor's desk as if looking for something. 'I'm a kind of receptionist. I see lots of people, all sorts.'

'Oh. Well.' Clare was at a loss. It seemed terribly vague. 'You should avoid close contact. Think of the mite as a germ passed from skin to skin or from bedclothes recently vacated by someone infested. Normal encounters aren't a problem.'

'Ta, then.' Deirdre tried to read the prescription. 'Where do I pay?'

'No payment is required, Deirdre.'

'National Health, are yer?'

'No. It's a . . .' Clare had been about to say a charity, but that word was still a stigma among northern folk. 'It's a sort of private adjunct to the NHS.'

'Right.' Deirdre left, cheekily asking the receptionist for a light for her cigarette as she departed, and letting the door slam behind her in annoyance at the inevitable refusal.

Clare thought over the day's cases. Seven patients, four of them prior bookings for routine medical assessments, three calling in unannounced. One a girl suffering severe bruising from 'a fall on the railway station steps' – except there were no steps there, Clare remembered. One seemed to be suffering withdrawal symptoms from drug abuse, probably Ecstasy or some combination. Clare felt despondent. Irreversible damage to the serotonin sources and biochemical pathways, with the hopeless loss of effective memory in later life, was a terrible price to pay for a few moments' synthetic drug-induced bliss.

And Deirdre, with her sorry ailment. Was she the simplest of the girl patients, or merely one feature of a social tribe?

'Who is that shouting?'

'Dr Burtonall!' A man's voice called her name up the stairwell. 'Could the doc come, please?'

Not even taken my coat off in this practice, Clare thought, but was out of the door carrying her emergency case without hesitation. Downstairs there was a small bookmaker's enterprise, all cigarette smoke and muted TV screens, walls covered with newspapers showing racing lists. There was a rear entrance. As she ran down she saw a face.

'What is it?'

'There's a man dumped in my van. Hurt badly.'

He seemed scared, not putting it on. His hands were bloodstained. She followed him into the daylight. Behind the building was a small yard. Her own old maroon Humber SuperSnipe stood there with two other motors, presumably belonging to the bookie's people. A trader's van was positioned between the back doorway and the pavement.

'Dumped?' Clare was saying, when he opened the vehicle's rear door. She almost cried out.

A man lolled inside. He wore only black tights. Blood was smeared around the van's interior. One side of his body was criss-crossed with cuts, bleeding profusely. Several slashes were on one side of his face, the other seeming relatively spared. His left arm was almost sectioned, pale tendons glistening at their insertions into bone. She could see the bellies of muscles in his left forearm bulging through the cuts. A small artery pumped listlessly.

She moved in. The vehicle was some sort of refrigerated butcher's van, the smooth walls frosted. Her emergency bag held only one unit of intravenous saline. In seconds she had it out and quickly wiped the encrusting blood from his right wrist. Oddly the veins seemed relatively spared there.

'Hold the forearm,' she asked the witness. 'Hard as you can, please.'

'We've phoned for an ambulance—'

'Now!' she almost yelled, kneeling.

No time to examine the injured man in detail. He appeared a good physical specimen, muscular and slender, what, thirty-four, say? He was in surgical shock. Well-nigh impossible to estimate his blood loss. From experience she knew how misleading spilled blood could be. A spoonful spread round a sitting room looked like a bloodbath. But this man had bled and bled. Blood was already congealing in pools on the floor of the van.

Uncapping the IV giving line, she passed the van driver the plastic container, telling him to raise it. She speared the needle into the man's vein.

'Relax your grip, but keep his wrist still.'

'Yes, Dr Burtonall.' The butcher was shaking.

The intravenous saline made its first faint distension as she undid the clip. Hurriedly she found strapping and stuck plaster across the needle's position. She looped the tube to make an oxbow, strapped it firmly into position.

'You can relax. Keep that bag up, please.'

The flow she regulated one-handed with the milled wheel control as she made a swift examination of the knifed man. He seemed encrusted with sweat. His breathing was rapid, shallow. She took his blood pressure, thanking heaven for the miniature electronic sphygmomanometer. He was so pale. She glanced round. Her receptionist had followed.

'Mrs Vanston? Get me the E container, please.'

'Yes, Dr Burtonall.'

With the assistance of the trader Clare was able to inspect the injuries. Strange. All seemed to be superficial cuts, almost as if he had stood aslant in front of attackers who had slashed at him. Except his groin was heavily bloodstained. She cut away his trousers, undid the tight belt and immediately began classifying the injury in anatomical terms. His penis was squirting bright blood from a severed artery. The dorsal artery, deep dorsal vein and dorsal nerve of the penis had been severed by a clean cut that had incised, actually transected, the external spermatic fascia and the left spermatic cord. A second cut, so unbelievably precise that it might have been done by a surgical scalpel, severed the bulbospongiosus and the corpus cavernosum penis. Urine leaked into the soaking blood from the severed urethra. The membranous layer of superficial fascia over the penis was badly cut, she observed irritably. Nothing she could do here except arrest the bleeding and get the man speedily to Casualty. The plastic surgeons would grumble for a week over this, have a field day trying to restore the patient's erectile function if he survived. Plastic surgeons groused even worse than orthopaedic. Quickly she examined the scrotum. Apart from a small clean nick into the dartos tunic the man's scrotal sac and testes were intact. She turned to the rest of him.

One ear was almost cut away. It hung only by a tag of skin near the ear lobe. Three cuts had gone dangerously close to his left eye, removing the eyelid so the orb stared up unblinking. He had lapsed into unconsciousness. The pulse did not improve. His hands were clammy in the interior of the cold van.

'I found him inside when I drove in here, Dr Burtonall,' the driver said.

For the first time she noticed the witness wore a blood-soiled white coat, greasy on the left shoulder and arms.

'Who brought him here? Did you see anyone?'

'I don't know.' The man seemed terrified of the saline bag he was holding aloft. He stared intently at it. 'I heard a moan as I switched the engine off. I was just going to put a bet on. In Escho's, the bookie's. I've finished all my deliveries, see.'

'Give me that. Go and flag the crash ambulance in, please.'

The butcher thankfully relinquished the infusion and jumped down. Clare noticed a few gaping spectators in the small forecourt. Only then did she appraise the injured man with any detachment.

Precisely a minute later later the patient was being loaded into the crash ambulance. Clare took her case with blooded hands and made her way inside. The butcher was standing beside his refrigerated vehicle narrating his involvement to two young newspaper reporters.

She was glad to wash away all signs of blood caking on her fingers. It took almost an hour to remove all traces of the encounter. The oddities however stayed in her mind. This new GP post was going to be livelier than she'd thought.

The police came back for a statement just as she'd got herself organized.

A SEPARATE TALK with Martina was unusual. Stranger still, Rack and Grellie were treated to cakes and tea in Posser's terraced house at Bradshawgate.

'Hey, Martina! These places are bigger than you think. Where's Bonn's room, then?'

Nervously Grellie tried to intervene but Martina calmly took it up, knowing Rack.

'Bonn has a mini flat here,' she said smoothly. 'Living in each other's pockets does no good.'

Neatly done, Grellie thought. But one roof one folk, the old Lancashire saying went. It was time she sprung Bonn from here before anything of that sort actually happened, and what better time than when all these changes were going on?

Rack guffawed, almost bouncing off the couch. 'Charge much rent, do yer?' and rolled in the aisles as if he'd made the subtlest of quips.

'Death threats, Rack. Please help yourselves.'

Grellie was careful. The sweetmeats on the cake stand would have fed a regiment. Rack fell on them, wolfing three at a time, speaking with his cheeks bulging, spattering fragments.

'I got a slider on it, Martina. Best in the business. I tellt him come up with sumfin.'

'Zen's suspended,' Martina reminded them. 'I'm thinking of reinstating him.'

'To be a decoy?' Grellie asked. Decoys got killed simply because they were expendable. Thinking crumbs, she selected the smallest cake, but immediately began to doubt her choice. Battenbergs were spendthrifts of elegance. She'd read that, some cookery glossy in a waiting room. 'Is that wise, Martina?'

'Something has to give, Grellie.'

Odd, Grellie observed, how locations altered attitudes. In the Barn Owl everyone had been taut, on best behaviour, into plots. Friendship was out, war in the old mill's air. Here, it was soirée time, pass the silver sugar tongs, please, and careful with the marmalade. Look at the way Martina spoke just then, showing tiredness, relaxed as if with a friend. Rack didn't count, a male between warring women.

'What, though, Martina?' she asked soothingly. 'I'd think it best to let Rack do the delving, and think possibilities.'

'Which are?'

She's worried, Grellie clocked, because she's got Bonn in mind. She wants Bonn. It's why she's panicking. Suspending Zen was sensible, keep him out of harm's way while Rack did the business about all these death threats. Then reinstate Zen when it was all safe again. What could be more obvious?

'Loons.' Rack sprayed the room and reached for more. 'Some loon.'

'I have Miss Faith doing tabulations,' Martina explained. 'Our confidentiality rule goes against us, times like these. We've only pen names. Client ladies choose those them-selves.'

'Women're forever bleedin' yakking,' Rack said through

a new mouthful. 'Gossip wiv their barber, talk in shops. Never get a bloody move on when yer try ter buy summink.'

'I agree. It could be hearsay picked up anywhere.'

'How many threats so far?' Grellie asked.

'Four. The last was from a public call box.' Martina poured to replenish Rack's cup, offered more to Grellie who declined. 'You said possibilities?'

'Yes.' Grellie readied herself. This was why they'd been summoned. 'It's only centred on Zen, right?'

'Every call mentioned him.'

'Alone, see?' Rack spluttered, working up to rage. 'It's bastards out there buggering us up. When I catch the sods—'

'Rack.' Martina's curt admonition shut him up. He grabbed the cake stand across Grellie, almost elbowing her face, well into a sulk.

'We let Zen resume work?' Grellie's eyes locked Martina's. Both understood the issue in plain view. If a key like the inoffensive Zen got threatened this way, it could easily happen to any of the others. Bonn, for instance.

'Whaffor?' Rack burst out. 'Jesus, Grell, wotcher want?'

'It's sensible, Rack,' when it clearly wasn't. 'I want her fetched into the open.'

'Look.' Rack was fuming, things getting ugly, starting to feel under criticism that he'd not solved it and done whatever straightening was wanted. 'Zen gets blammed it's down to me, not a load of tarts doing knee-tremblers in Waterloo Street.'

'My lasses'd do anything to stop this kind of thing,' Grellie said, feeling the heat in her face. 'And you know it, Rack, so shut—'

'That will do, the pair of you. Bonn . . .' Martina closed her face somehow, her trick to mask feelings.

Quite a knack, Grellie thought grudgingly. She wished she had the same skill. She searched for words to complete Martina's sentence for her and came up with, *Bonn could walk in here any second*. Martina left clues if you knew where to look.

'You were saying about possibilities, Grellie?'

'Some loon, like Rack mentioned, but what if she's not? I don't like it. It's too regular. So it must be something to do with Zen. Not,' she added hurriedly, 'Zen himself. He's straight. No drugs, no salts. And, besides . . .'

Whoops, same mistake. She'd almost said, *And besides, Bonn likes Zen*. Bonn himself had told her how Zen had shown him kindness when he'd first been promoted to key.

'Is it safe, Rack? For Zen to keep working his goes?'

Rack stopped masticating, decanted tea into his saucer and blew vigorously. Small waves dripped over the rim onto the carpet. The girls waited as he slurped noisily. It was all for thinking. He gulped, exhaled with relish.

'We might get lucky if Zen did,' Grellie encouraged, wanting him to say yes. 'Resolve it in a single day.'

'How?' He was truculent.

The head stringer answered before Martina could cut in. 'Whoever books Zen is a cause. Has to be. One of her friends is the threatener.'

'Yer oughter've got me in straight orf, Martina,' Rack accused. 'I'd have it sussed by now.'

'I know, Rack, but we get all sorts of calls. Our phone ladies do well, considering how the Agency is placed.'

'She *says* Zen, see? Two weeks the calls bin coming. How long since you lifted Zen, Martina?'

'Five days.'

'See?' Rack forgot the food, stood and paced across the room, spat once into the fire, and returned to pose on the carpet before Martina. 'The 'orrors are still coming. And it's all city.'

'Zen's clean, Rack.' Martina spoke almost with regret. 'That's the trouble. If Zen was one of the goers with a background of, what, gambling, maybe past drugs, it would be simpler.'

'See, Martina,' Rack said with unexpected gentleness, 'it'll risk Zen putting him back to work.'

'What if we ask him?' Martina asked Grellie.

'He'll agree. But I think it's for Rack to decide, not Zen.'

'I fink no, boss.'

That was the measure of the problem's gravity. Rack called Martina boss, nobody else, not even Posser, and never in jest.

'So we're back where we started?' Martina demanded. Grellie thought, She wants me to answer, but I won't give the bitch the satisfaction. She's already decided what she's going to do. She'll send Zen back on, risk him getting topped.

'I wonder if we'd better ask Zen, Rack, and play it off the cuff. All right?'

'Yih, boss.'

'All right with you, Grellie?'

'You know what I think,' Grellie said, trying not to sound abrupt. 'Folk don't call death threats horrors for nothing. This is creepy.'

'Will you want extra people, Rack?'

'I'll pull honchos from the Rum Romeo.'

'No, Rack,' Martina said quickly. 'I've carded three of the casino girls for the working house starting tomorrow. They'll be numbers down.'

'Jesus, Martina, you might've tellt me! I use your blower?'

'No. Get your mobile. Grellie, I'll want you in the house

tomorrow, please. Talk the girls on. And bring Trish in on everything.'

They left then, Rack grumbling about telephones. By the time he and Grellie reached Victoria Square, less than a furlong, he was into theories.

'Phones, see, oughter be all wood, Grellie. Know why?'

A girl caught them as they turned right towards Turton Street. The tall dark girl was shivering from the cold. She had been waiting some time.

'Grellie? A message.'

'See you later, Rack. Tara.' Grellie let Rack swagger on before she gave the nod. 'What, Meeya?'

'The girls are a bit off, Grellie. Connie says it's having that doctor so near and can't her place go somewhere else.'

'Tell Connie ta, leave it with me. Go back on, Meeya.'

'Butty Bar, have a warm?' Meeya wheedled.

Grellie smiled to herself. Meeya's private lad was a biker at the Triple Racer, a nosh bar where all the bike couriers loafed between sprints. Going across the square would give Meeya the chance of seeing him.

'No, Meeya. Spell yourself in the Volunteer. Go no further.'

'Oh, Grellie, you're a rotten cow.'

Meeya stalked up the pavement, deliberately ignoring a motorist who sounded his horn as he passed. Grellie almost laughed out loud at the girl's petulance. The cocky bitch would get some salt on her tail before long, behaviour like that. To a girl out on her beat, though, a spell in a fug-warmed caff was heaven, off her pins a few minutes and a hot drink. Grellie could remember being that saucy herself before she was promoted.

She wanted to find Bonn but guessed Martina had chosen a clever moment to summon them in for that serious talk. It meant that Bonn was probably on a go with a client. Martina hadn't wanted Bonn arriving to hear what was said, as he was entitled. Which meant that Martina intended all along to get Zen out doing his goes again. Grellie noted the time. Work it out. A lady client hires a goer, which was one hour. Punter who hires a street stringer gets ten minutes max to shag her and get gone.

So Bonn would be free soon. Grellie wanted Bonn to send urgent word to Zen, tell Zen to say no when Martina suggested he went back on. A horror – any phone threat, uttered or simply heavy breathing – was eerie bad. From the nature of things, working girls in the streets were more at risk than goers, seeing men did most of the bludging, though times were fast a-changing. For a goer to be at hazard was truly weird. It went against the natural order of things, so was odd. And Martina's attitude seemed to be that it'd be only a small risk, with Rack on the suss. But how could she – or anyone – know that for certain?

Small risk, sure, but why take it? Martina should have put it all in Rack's hands from the start, first phone threat and off to the races, let Rack do whatever. The Cockney was loud, violent, but hundred per cent. Grellie deliberately went close to two of her Rivergate girls loitering by the Weavers Hall, and said quietly, 'Bonn.'

Prissy, a tubby Atherton lass, nodded and immediately took off across the square, darting through the traffic heading for the central gardens. From there you could see the end of Bolgate Street, where the Time and Scythe Hotel was. Grellie took station on her beat, lolling against the Weavers wall and thought, Come out Bonn, look sharp. I've an urgent warning, before something happens.

THE TIME AND Scythe was smaller than the Victoria Square hotels. Clare would have found it charming, had she happened on it by accident or alone. As it was, it served her one function. That meant Bonn.

'Do you associate places with people?' she asked him as they lay.

It seemed so natural to speak into his face along the pillow, use her valuable purchased minutes to learn about him. Once, she'd have insisted on this process first. Love, sex, whatever it was, had an intrinsic progression. Meet a person, get to know, reach some kind of understanding, move gradually into companionship, attraction, then the whole physical assimilation. With Bonn it had been the reverse. If either was the predator, it was she. Under normal circumstances it would have shamed her, but what circumstances were normal now?

He took some time answering, one hand behind his head, looking at the ceiling.

'I sometimes think places do their own associating.'

It seemed a weightier judgement than her question warranted.

'That's the wrong answer, darling.' She didn't quite

pause, but thought, *Darling*. Too revealing? 'I expected you to say yes.' She raised herself on an elbow, looking down at him. 'You can't mean that buildings have feelings.'

She had to wait before he said slowly, 'It's the way I feel about a country. It imposes a character on its people. Buildings do the same.'

'Where do you live? I know it's somewhere near.'

'I was in church recently,' he told her after a protracted pause. 'I left baffled.'

Accidentally, she had learned that he'd been in a seminary, but of his home, his origins, nothing. She felt riled. It was time she knew more. It was due her. God above, hadn't she begun to think of asking him for more than occasional bought sex? Her own rights were in there somewhere. Church, though? Why, when he'd reneged?

'You still go, then, Bonn?' She was pleased with herself, remembering to say his name instead of some endearment. Nerves of steel, this lady.

'I went into St Michael's. I couldn't get further in than the rear pillars, worrying about candles.'

She had serious issues on her mind. Candles weren't included. She asked, and he quietly began to explain his dilemma.

To light a candle or not, St Joseph's statue with the Child, usually so disfavoured. Then doubts surfacing, seeing he could afford the candle, a thousand dozen, all the candles the church possessed.

'You didn't light a candle because you could afford to?' Clare couldn't see the problem. 'Why not simply put a donation in the box?'

'That church, though,' he mused. 'Not the Quakers or some Episcopalian. And how much is show, how much nostalgia, is only part of it. The question becomes, is a person entitled to display his own need of comfort from such a source?'

She waited for a punch line. None came. 'Well?'

He budged over so she was more directly above him. He reached for her breast, moved his knee between her thighs.

'I don't know where to go from here,' he said quietly, giving her his almost smile. Moments like this, he seemed hidden beneath diffidence.

Had he fallen right into her scheme of things, saying that? Except now that she knew him a little, it might be his queer knack of guessing where the whole thing had been leading all along.

'With me, Bonn,' she said, making light of it so as not to alarm. 'You go with me. Any distance, anywhere.'

He didn't smile, just stroked her breast, sucked the nipple, pressed his flexed knee to her. She moved to accommodate him, angry at having to glance at the clock just visible from the bedroom. That was another thing, she thought in sudden temper. Was the bloody timepiece positioned there so Bonn could keep an eye on it? How much of all this was planning of others, and how little was himself, or love? She might never know. And it was becoming important, daily more vital.

'That's hard to understand, Clare.'

'Why?' Right, she told herself, abruptly shedding caution, let's get down to it. 'Healthy woman meets healthy male. The plot's hardly original. Men and women have been known to pair off, however it happens.'

'Me,' he said, his hands round her now, crushing her to him. 'And you.'

'The Agency could find somebody else, Bonn, if that's what's worrying you. I'd pay them to.'

Here again, she lectured herself in fury. Is he hardening as a distraction? She felt resolve go.

'There are recruits,' he answered gravely. 'The pressure from hopeful goer candidates is extremely heavy.'

Twenty years old, she thought, almost laughing aloud in exasperation, and he talks like a UN delegate confronting global mayhem. Is it just me, going off my head because my husband was a criminal and my marriage came unstitched?

'There, then!' She put her mouth on his, talking into him. 'Come with me, you wouldn't be letting anyone down.'

'I let everyone down, Clare.'

She jerked away to stare. 'How?'

'All those TV talkshow fudge words – commitment, declaration, relationship – I match up to none. Perhaps that's my part to play, what I intend to have been all along. Stay with the moment, each lady a *now* proposition.'

'Then what, Bonn?' She felt compassion grow but quickly quelled it because she was in there with him. 'Eventually, I mean, what do prostitutes do when they're, well, of a certain age and have to move on? Presumably they look for a new life?'

'Stringers retire, if they want, go off with some punter for supposed ever. Not many do, though.' He seemed easier talking about the street girls. She felt intrigued. He must know a great deal about the other side of the gender coin. 'Retire, I mean. It'd be a statement that they are finished, no longer attractive. Giving in.'

'Where on earth do they go?' Clare wanted to know. 'I asked a patient – I'm sure she's a prostitute – what she will eventually do. She wouldn't say.'

'It's competition as much as anything.' He had found her, was stirring her with his fingers, his body moving gently as they spoke. 'They see younger girls coming in, constantly seeing their own takings diminish. Fashions change. Their street lives become less profitable. They become frightened.'

'Do they?' Clare said, trying to push him round so she could edge beneath him. Her voice grew husky. 'Do they?'

His answer could wait. She forgot why she'd experienced that start of compassion, and reached and welcomed the loss as the event took her over.

'Stay, Trish, while I bag a stringer.'

Trish asked nervously, 'Will it be all right?'

Grellie gestured to Rack to stay calm as he moved in sudden irritation.

'If I say it's all right, then it is. Understand?'

'Yes, Grellie.'

But it couldn't be, Trish worried. Martina'd said the two activities were distinct, the stringers out there working the punters in Waterloo Street and Raglan Road, wherever, and the working house Trish herself was to help manage.

They were near the Lagoon, a small place for card playing and slow drinking. No money changed hands there. Tatty posters blocked its broad windows, and few men entered or left. Even the hallway was unkempt. It held a rusting bicycle and a soiled pram. Bare wooden stairs climbed to nowhere.

'Rani's here, Grell,' Rack told them. 'I'll wait.'

Grellie went ahead. Trish followed to the second storey landing, peering after as Grellie knocked and went in. Rani was sitting nervously on a narrow bed. There was no other furniture, just a mantelpiece and a small portable television set on the pocked linoleum. Rani tried to smile.

'Grellie, look—'

'Shut it, Rani. Get up.'

Rani stood, pale. Trish wondered whether to say something, offer to mediate. Grellie shot her a look that stopped the thought.

'Rani, you're out.'

The girl's features crumpled. She began to wail. Grellie smacked her across the face with such savagery that Trish exclaimed aloud. The head stringer turned, venomous, and raised a forefinger. Trish backed to the wall by the door, scared.

'You'll draw three notes from Connie. She's waiting at the corner of Moor Lane. Hand over everything. Address book, handbag, suitcase, clothes, jewellery, rings. Any satches of drugs, money, bankbook, savings accounts, the lot.'

Rani slumped to the bed, sobbing. 'Grellie, as God's my witness I never did anything you said not to. I only see my feller—'

'You want me to send for Connie? Set her on to you, you lying bitch? Think I can't smell this stink?' Grellie hauled up the pillow, shoved Rani aside and ripped off the bedclothes. She lifted up a packet covered in silver foil. 'Think I'm stupid?'

She waited until Rani could listen.

'You had a good straight stringer life, you ignorant whore.'

'It wasn't like that, Grellie!'

Grellie slapped her head. 'I said shut it. We gave you honest profit for tarting your arse round the city. You had sweet fuck all when you stood in line at the pickings, and what thanks do we get? You, late on troll four times a fucking week!' By now Grellie was yelling, repeatedly cuffing the girl's head so her hair flew up in brush strokes. 'My other girls have to take up your fucking slack. Is that fair?'

She glared at the weeping girl, breathless.

'I ought to get Connie, send you the wet walk home, you silly whore. Throw everything away for a tuppenny satch of powder?'

'What can I do to make it up, Grellie?' Rani begged, plucking at the other's skirt. 'I'll do anything.'

'You're done.' Grellie pulled away. 'None of the girls, none of Rack's folk. Nobody belonging will speak to you, stand you a cuppa, lend you a fucking comb. You're out. Leave the city.'

Grellie jerked her head at Trish, who stepped outside trembling almost uncontrollably. She heard the head stringer speak to the dishevelled girl from the doorway.

'You've got to tonight, Rani.'

'Please, Grellie. I'll do—'

'Do anything you fucking well like. Get gone before dark. Stay in the city, you know what happens.'

'Please! Please!'

Trish was alarmed at Grellie's swift exit. Quickly she followed downstairs, where Rack was talking to a dark-skinned man.

'No question,' Rack was giving it. 'Footballers are failed carpenters. It's to do with school, see?'

The other was laughing, nodded casually to Grellie and ignored Trish as they passed.

Grellie slowed as they reached the pavement. She said conversationally, 'Any questions, Trish?'

Trish was shaken, never having seen such utter violence.

'Can you do that, Grellie?' she said with timidity. 'I mean, where will the poor girl go? And drugs, I mean can't she be helped some way? I didn't understand. What is the wet walk home?'

'Wrong, Trish.'

'What?' Trish was relieved to see Grellie smiling.

'When I say, any questions, you give me the wrong answer. You must say, No questions, Grellie. *That's* lesson one, see?'

Grellie halted, checking her hair in a shop window.

'I didn't hear you, Trish. I said, see? You didn't say yes. Let's try it once more.' Grellie repeated as if to a schoolchild, smiling at her reflection, 'That's lesson one, see?' and waited. Her smile was not at all malicious, simply pure amusement.

Trish said, chilled to her nape, 'Yes, Grellie.'

'There!' the other said brightly. 'Now we can get on.'

'Do we have to wait for Rack, Grellie?' Trish asked.

'There you go again,' Grellie chided. 'Asking.'

'Sorry, Grellie,' Trish said.

Now she felt truly frightened, but her fear gradually allayed as the stringers started calling hello and smiling across to Grellie. They eyed Trish with curiosity, but seemed quite friendly. Her spirit eased as they walked. Once, she almost drew breath to ask Grellie where they were going but wisely she asked nothing. Lesson one, then, meant obey in silence, never ask. And an invitation to raise questions meant raise none. She would have to get used to it. She put Rani from her thoughts and tentatively made an attempt to return the smiles of the other girls. They both walked into the square and towards Bradshawgate.

Pandle, panny – a female who supervises the reception
lounge of a brothel

M ISS HOPE WAS almost in a state of
surgical shock. She felt quite giddy,
and had to sniff her sal volatile before
she could tell Miss Faith all about the really fantastic phone
call she'd just had.

'It's that Magdalena Four-Nine-Two!'

'What did she say?' Miss Faith was less responsive than
Miss Hope thought she should be. It was almost a slur. For
two pins Miss Hope felt inclined not to tell her a single
word, which would really put her eye out. But then she
would never know how Miss Faith might have responded.
Anyway the temptation was too great. Temptation, Miss
Hope found, was always a nuisance.

'It was astonishing!'

'Not another cruise request?'

Miss Faith eyed her opposite number with suspicion.
Miss Hope was inclined to theatrics, forever claiming to
have logged exotic requests from the lady clients who rang
in to book passionate encounters. Half of Miss Hope's
stories were quite made up, Miss Faith had long since concluded. Either that, or they were so heavily tinged with Miss
Hope's emotional colouring-in that the thread of whatever
she was wittering about became quite lost.

'Nothing so simple!' Miss Hope inhaled from her sal volatile phial and rummaged for a tissue to dab her rheumy eyes. 'I for one wish it were!'

Miss Faith took off her headset. This began to look promising.

'To whom does it refer?' she asked, guarded but intrigued.

'To Bonn.'

'Oh, dear.'

'Why did you say "Oh, dear" like that?' Miss Hope demanded, suddenly on the defensive.

'More fibs positively *litter* the city about Bonn than all the other keys put together, that's all.'

'Are you suggesting I'm fibbing?'

Miss Faith considered calling Miss Hope's bluff for once, but decided on prudence. Martina might just ask, with her poisonous sweetness that boded so ill, why Miss Faith had stopped paying attention to what went on in the control office. Martina was a terrible force when she wanted to be, which was becoming really far too often lately.

'Not at all,' Miss Faith said, compromising. 'I'm merely implying that Bonn suffers in that regard.'

Miss Hope judged Miss Faith's exasperation and finally spoke.

'Magdalena Four-Nine-Two wants to buy Bonn,' she said.

Miss Faith gaped, almost fell from her swivel chair.

Coll the slider found Rack by telling Fat George. Fat George sold newspapers on the Bolgate Street corner facing the Asda supermarket. Everybody knew he was really there to tell Rack what went on, which meant telling Martina.

'You better have news, Coll,' Rack said. He'd been pulled out of the roulette finals, best of ten games and doing not bad on the third. He was proving theories one after another.

'I need more, Rack,' Coll said. 'You gotter tell me who the horrors were for.'

Rack couldn't believe his ears. 'You interrupted me for a moan?'

'Nar, Rack. I got vid cassettes copied.'

Which astonished even Rack. 'The plod's?'

'Straight up.' Coll was proud. 'Seventeen.'

'Jesus, mate. You done good. Where are they?' Rack bawled numbers across to Beatie and Rice, two stringers heading back to Rivergate from car jobs down Raglan Road where the recreation grounds offered doubtful seclusion. They shouted back with scornful gestures.

Coll held a massive shopping bag. 'I feel a right prat carrying them round like this. I seen one, to check I'd nicked the right vids. Sorry, wack, but it's only shoppers and car parks.'

'That'll do. Where, when?'

'They're labelled,' Coll said, now well narked. 'Fink I'm frigging green or summink? Jeez, mate.'

'No, great,' Rack appeased. 'You're in bunce.'

The slider handed them over. 'I can't see what you want them fer. 'Nless I knows what we're looking fer, see.'

Rack hadn't even to think. 'Pilot Ship, sevenish. Know it, Waterloo Street, left-hand side?'

'That casino?' Coll marvelled. 'You know some right frigging dumps, Rack.'

Rack cackled, falling about the pavement laughing. 'It comes of being an Arsenal supporter, mate.'

He went to phone Martina on her reserve mobile. Only he and Posser knew its number. She answered instantly, heard him out in silence then thought a while. Finally she asked could Coll be trusted. He assured her. She said go ahead, unless she called to put the kibosh on it beforehand. That meant, Rack knew, she'd be seeing Zen, would ask him if he minded. It was arse-about-face wrong, but if Martina said a definite go ahead what could he do? He wondered about theories that would explain women's ways. There ought to be one.

Martina, Rack knew, needed a bloke, get her serviced regular and stop all this fucking wrong guessing overnight. It wasn't rational. He'd asked Bonn to dick her but Bonn only looked at him like he was sad-sorry for summat. What sort of a fucking answer was that?

He went back in to the roulette finals knowing he'd lose now. He reckoned luck depended on the size of your feet, which felt bigger than usual. He toted the shopping bag of police videos with him.

Martina put her phone away and went through to where Zen and TonTon were talking with Connie in the lounge room of the working house.

'Sorry about that,' she said. They waited, expectant. It wasn't every day that Martina's mystery mobile rang in her handbag making her start like a deer and limp-rush to find seclusion enough to answer. 'The architects have done a fairly decent job, don't you think?'

They all started speaking together, nodding and inspecting the fireplace, the angled windows the city council had infarcted over. Connie would have chosen different furnishings, but Carol from the Café Phryne had okayed them so that was that. Nobody better than Carol on design.

Connie was still a bit huffy about it, knowing her own ideas of decor were better than Carol's by a mile.

'The bar, though, Martina,' Zen said after more praise.

'Pull the bell, Zen.'

The key gave the hanging Victorian fronds a slow yank. Part of the wall slowly everted as a bar slid silently into view. It was arrayed with bottles, optics, refrigerators, velvet-covered stools, and was already well lit. The room's lighting instantly dimmed.

Zen laughed. 'Marvellous! Who thought of that?'

'Carol. The architects do as they're encouraged.' She smiled at the innocence of her remark, knowing it would rile Connie more, and gestured them to go ahead. Connie, a heavy droop-breasted girl with a mannish hairstyle, fancied her chances at being made Martina's chief lieutenant and wanted to prove herself capable at everything, so detested Carol the designer whizz-girl who ran the Café Phryne.

They went on to tour the bathrooms, the second and third storeys, the bedrooms. Two electronic safety systems had them all interested.

'Fret was doubtful about them,' Martina said candidly. 'He wondered if there should be any at all. People's rights, you see.'

Fret Dougal had said no such thing, but it was the in that Martina wanted.

'It's got to be, Martina,' TonTon said, frowning. 'I mean, what's the point of not having them? One slip, the Watch Committee'd hit the fan. Then it would be all up for the house and everything else.'

'That's why I overruled him,' Martina lied suavely, moving to it. 'What do you think, Zen?'

Connie and TonTon went across the landing to inspect the saunas. Zen from politeness stayed back, for Martina seemed to be having momentary difficulty with her lameness.

'I agree with TonTon, Martina. I mean, why not have each punter routinely filmed, then wipe the tape once he's left? It'd give Trish a chance to check all was well, the girl unharmed, no wars started.'

'Good idea, Zen.' Martina checked they were out of earshot of the others. 'Incidentally, Zen, would you mind going back on? I've had your client ladies told you were temporarily unavailable.'

'Not at all, Martina.' He smiled. 'Decoy, eh? I hope Rack's honchos've got their skates on.'

Martina treated him to a smile of dazzling radiance, knowing the effect.

'Thank you, Zen. You will take care?'

'Believe me,' Zen said, moved by her exquisite beauty. 'Anything to make life safe again. Since when did you guide us wrong?'

TRISH WAS SCARED of her newness, which was absurd for somebody in her fourth decade, and durstn't ask, so she listened to the girls. One called Lovee was delightedly rabbiting on about how to actually do it.

'You've no right taking it up, your age,' Lovee kept on saying. 'Fucking geriatric, you are.'

Despite her everlasting tirades, Trish liked the Clitheroe lass. Nothing fazed Lovee.

'I can't help how old I am.'

'There's two things, Trish. Your gob's not for whistling with. Never kiss, either, you get germs, see? Fastest way to clear him of it and get rid is your gob, but don't kneel or you choke. Everybody knows that. And whether you let him soddery's up to you. Like I don't take bareback coz that gets you that AIDS, dunnit? An' the money's got to come up front or you get Grellie on you and she's fucking trouble.'

Lovee had put in to Connie asking could she get taken on in the working house, which was why she kept coming to see Trish but Connie'd given her a flat no. It wasn't any good keeping on but she kept on. Lovee was always cheerful.

'I think Grellie's nice.' And clever, Trish thought, but didn't say. 'Clever' was a troubled word among the street girls. She'd already learned that calling somebody clever could get your eye blacked and your face marked for life, she still wasn't sure why.

'You've never seen her really motoring.' Lovee laughed. 'I had a punter two nights since wanted round the houses and said he'd pay after, fucking cheek. Turned right nasty. I signed up Donny, that stander, you don't know him, Accrington halfie not got crinkly hair but nice teeth, and he seed him off.'

She cackled a laugh that sounded inane. Trish wished Lovee wouldn't smoke, and that started her worrying what the smoking rules would be for the working house once the girls got under way. Was it up to herself to lay down about it, or had she to ask Grellie or, with a gulp, Martina? She drew breath to ask Lovee what she meant.

'What does round the houses—?'

'Think fifteen minutes, max, whatever the punter wants, see? Ten's best. Unless it's Derby Day or the Cup Final. Grellie gives special rules for them, always fucking trouble because you've to do them quicker or Grellie does her nut.'

Lovee threw back her head and did her cackle through nicotine stained teeth. Trish wished she wouldn't smoke. 'Get him milked quick then ta-ra, wack.'

'How do you get rid of them, though, if—?'

'No fucking ifs is how, luv,' Lovee said and, suddenly filling with glee, 'Listen this: Last Saturday neet this goojer, ever so nice in one of them long motors, wants me for a shag in the fountain, Queens Park, all them fucking lights, can y'imagine? Like, fucking *in* the water?'

'A punter actually wanted—?' Trish was lost.

'It were some goojer holy day, had to be in the fucking cold water or it didn't count, see?' Lovee hated being interrupted by a listener's ignorance. 'I says yih on condition I'm in his fur overcoat, see, and two of our girls come and stand watch or nobody'd believe it.'

Lovee set herself coughing from laughing, lit another fag from a lighter shaped like a red heart.

Trish really wished Lovee would stop smoking. A lovely girl, merry as a cricket and talked up by the others at Bolgate Corner, but a born chain smoker. Seriously, she needed someone to ask about all this, what to do. These girls were too concerned with doing their own thing, all engaging in their different madnesses. Trish needed somebody who would listen to her question, think a little, then answer clearly so she could understand. She realized she needed to ask Bonn.

Chance'd be a fine thing. She'd seen Grellie's face light up when Bonn's name was mentioned. Trish knew to steer clear. She was getting educated.

Hassall was worried sick. He hated having Cockle along when he went to interview Burtonall, but there was no way out. Letting Clare know that he would be visiting at Clifford's office that Wednesday afternoon – she finished early that day, he learnt from her receptionist – was his only buffer against Cockle's tight-lipped tactlessness. Hassall only progressed by plotting against the help offered by subordinates. You can't trust a policeman, his perennial joke.

In spite of his anxiety, Hassall tried his quips as they ascended the stairs of Burtonall's office. 'Now, Sergeant Cockle, no eyeing the secretaries. Let's concentrate, eh?'

'Right.'

Not a glimmer of humour. Hassall decided he'd keep low, seeing Dr Burtonall hadn't seen fit to arrive and support her

ex. Hassall almost snorted. Ordeal by marshmallow, interviewed by the oldest dud in the Force and the youngest prat.

He didn't knock, according to custom, wanted just to
stand there immobile and silent until some typist came. It
was always better to compel them to announce you. Cockle,
though, was on hand to ruin it by saying a loud, terse
'Police'. The tact of an axe.

'That way.' The girl chewing gum pointed at a glass door.
Not another soul took notice.

Clifford Burtonall jumped up, positively glad to see them,
his hand outstretched, his grip firm. 'Anything I can do, Mr
Hassall, anything I can help you with. Coffee's on the go, tea
if you prefer.'

Which made Hassall even more irate, having to decline
the offer. And the financier was smooth enough to pooh-
pooh the notion of having some himself. The little charade
made Hassall a guest, the element of threat lost. He blamed
Cockle for having to accept the seats Burtonall waved them
to. Maybe all money men were this cunning?

'Terence Dulsworthy,' he began. 'It's come to my know-
ledge that you knew the deceased.'

'Poor chap.' Burtonall was quite at ease, heels on the desk
and leaning back, ready to dispense largesse. 'I heard of it.'
As if he'd had hordes of lurkers getting him secrets, when
it was all over the city papers. Hassall honestly didn't like the
man. He'd nearly got him once. All he needed was half a
chance.

'You knew Dulsworthy how?'

Burtonall went into sombre mode, tipping his fingers,
staring at the middle distance, the thoughtful contributor
any copper would respect.

'As far as I can recall, he was some kind of floating agent.
You know the sort of thing, tickets for football, shows, hotel

bookings.' Burtonall shrugged, derogatory. 'Actually the sort of things anybody can do.'

'But Dulsworthy did them for you?'

'Not *for* me, Mr Hassall. For occasional visitors. Sort of gofer, really.'

'Was he paid?'

'Haven't a clue. Commission, I suppose.'

'You contribute to Mr D'Lindsay's fund?'

Burtonall treated the world to a wide smile, ever the willing citizen with humour never far off.

'That's confidential, Mr Hassall. So I'll tell you!' He brought out a list, a single sheet in transparent plastic. 'My contributions over the past two years. Travel on the left, monetary contributions on the right. With dates.'

'What are those in red?'

'Parties. Sort of gatherings where Party officials attend, wives and partners. A throng.'

Which defused Hassall's concealed firework, the hotel stub from Dulsie's pocket. Three hotels were named here.

'You had it all ready, Mr Burtonall,' was the best Hassall could manage.

The financier sighed. 'I wish I could think so far ahead with money matters, the state of the market.'

'How is the market, sir?' Cockle asked, his quietness startling Hassall. Had the bastard some hidden tact after all?

'On the wobble, Mr Cockle, but different. Local quotations have gone astray. We have these comparative measures, you see . . .'

And he was off into safe, boring data. Hassall felt defeated on every count. A wasted visit.

'Zen's back on, Bonn.' Rack bawled along the balcony for coffee so loudly that even the Palais Rocco's band faltered, the dancing couples looking up in annoyance.

'A poor decision, Rack,' Bonn said after a moment. 'I should like to leave.'

'Don't, mate.' Rack checked that Bonn made no move to rise, which was good. 'Martina decided.'

'I trust you are closing in on the threatener, Rack. I regret the judgement.' Rack knew that Bonn would tell her, too. Nobody else'd dare. Bonn had a knack with sorrow.

The music crashed to a crescendo. People at the tables round the dance hall cheered as more dancers took to the floor. The MC started his introduction, semi-finals of the mogga dancing North-West Championship.

Rack was thinking, Jesus H, don't go telling Martina she's wrong, not just yet. Let it cool. The world was in enough fucking trouble without poking Martina awake, send her kong.

'It's not worth it, Bonn. Don't say a fucking word.'

'Language, please. We are in public.'

Rack controlled his exasperation thinking, Then how can you talk normal? Say tut-fucking-tut, or what? He opted for gentle tact. 'Look, Bonn. Innit time you got shagging Grellie? I'll talk to her, if yer shy.'

'Thank you, Rack.' Bonn looked over the edge of the balcony. 'I can't see Lancelot.'

'He'll be milking the clapping.'

'Milking the clapping,' Bonn repeated. 'I, ah, don't—'

Rack sighed. 'I could fucking do with you, Bonn. Whyn't yer just ask outright what fer? Instead, yer go, I, ah, don't. You got ter learn ter talk natural.'

Bonn tried to see what was happening. A spotlight searched the crowd of spectators. Lancelot emerged, sprang onto the dance floor with a flourish, drawing a pretty girl after him to rapturous applause.

'See?' Rack shook his head. Bonn was the city's greatest goer, and here he was, surprised by ordinariness, like everything was new and him just in from some frigging planet. Weird.

'I don't understand.'

Rack swallowed, stayed calm. 'Because the other fucking competitors hate it, see? Riles them. They'll make mistakes, get marked down, see?' Rack heaved a sigh. 'Give me fucking strength, Bonn. You're like a frigging kid.'

'Language, please, Rack.'

Like anybody in this roaring mayhem'd notice that Rack'd used a naughty word? He saw Bonn's glance and mumbled a sorry. Last thing he wanted, with the news he had to pass on, was one of Bonn's silences that made you feel rotten. Bonn's fucking forgiveness was even worse. The George Street girls were whispering Bonn was touched, like thick or holy. But they were only birds, and women never could tell who was a prat and who wasn't. Also, women couldn't see that holiness was gunge. Holiness could ruin a bloke, if you let it.

'It seems rather unfair, Rack.'

'It's routine, Bonn.' Jesus, like pulling logs through water. Rack had had to do that as punishment at the reform camp, slog hours and get nowhere dragging a fucking dead tree. 'Lancelot pays ten notes for the spotlight and the band to do it.'

'I do wish he wouldn't.'

Rack went for it, before Bonn's unhappiness at Lancelot's cheating became an order for Rack to stop Lancelot doing what was virtually flaming normal and all the entire world expected.

'That Magdalena bird's made an offer, Bonn.' He said the words quietly, clearing his throat to get it right. It still came out terrible.

'An offer.' Bonn considered, didn't add anything.

'For you, mate. I'm sorry.'

Then Rack thought indignantly, What the fuck am I saying sorry for? I done nothing except bring Martina's message. Fucking Nora, I'm worse than Bonn. Rack reckoned it was something they were putting in the coffee nowadays. He'd work out why. It was a good theory. He should have thought of it before.

'Magdalena Four-Nine-Two.'

'Yip. Sorry.' There again, sorry for fuck all.

'Thank you, Rack.' Bonn gazed at him levelly. 'I appreciate your sympathy.'

Rack brightened. He'd got a straight ta from Bonn. That was major good. Maybe Bonn was learning at last. Maybe Bonn wasn't as dim as Rack thought after all.

'She's offered a load of gelt.' Rack clapped and whistled as the music started, the ten teams of dancers sweeping instantly into action. 'Clap, Bonn. Lancelot's on.'

Obediently Bonn applauded. The idea in mogga dancing

was to adapt your dancing style to the music, while changing the dance every six bars. He could keep time, but with Clare Three-Nine-Five the changes had proved rather awkward. Do it swimmingly, get in more and better dance-style changes than your rivals, you won. Lancelot was one of Bonn's team of three goers, and was as exotic as his name. Tonight he wore diamanté down to his shoes. His partner was petite, shimmering in electric blue.

Some spectators were booing, though, as opponents passed their tables, causing Rack to lean to see who. He started yelling insults. Bonn touched his arm.

'But they're dissing Lancelot, Bonn,' Rack fumed, sitting back.

'They are merely supporting their friends.'

'Same thing.'

'She is manageress of the Worcester Club and Tea Rooms, I believe.'

'Yih. Wants you to move in. You tellt Martina, right? Four-Nine-Two sez she'll lodge you in a flat. She owns two hotels, one in Fife, one Cheshire.'

'She is fairly wealthy, then.'

'Thinking of buying the Worcester. Tough tanners, her, Bonn. Bin about.'

'Yet still she works as a manageress.'

'It's her mod, Bonn.' Rack had to raise his voice over the roars and music below. 'Takes a job running some place, susses it out. Fiddles the books to down the takings. It lowers, then she buys it.'

Bonn wondered how Rack knew all this, but felt it might be impolite to ask.

'I trust Martina has given a reply.'

See? Rack marvelled. Not even asking straight out if he

was going to be sold to some bint. Bonn could wear a bloke out.

'Not yet. She wants to see this Magdalena.'

Bonn said nothing. Below, the crowd was becoming fevered. Somebody threw a glass. It skittered across the dance hall causing a couple to lose their step. Boos rose. A squabble started directly beneath the balcony. A spectator rushed onto the floor, was restrained by the Palais honchos. Rack guffawed.

'It's okay, Bonn. It's only Donk.' He grinned at Bonn over his shoulder. 'I tellt him to chuck three when time's right. They don't stop, see, except for fires or summink. Now Lancelot's a cert.'

It was beyond Bonn. Rack seemed to be involved in everything. Three days back he had traffic wardens paying for something in Victoria Square.

'I fail to see why.'

Rack stared. 'Give me strength.' Bonn wasn't learning at all. In fact he was getting worse. 'Because Lancelot's eleven-to-eight on.'

Bonn considered that, still baffled. Lancelot had been quiescent lately, just doing his goes, everything peaceful. Was it a good or a bad sign?

'I hope Martina can be dissuaded from meeting Magdalena,' he said. Rack didn't seem to hear, just hung over the balcony yelling obscenities at Lancelot's opponents.

Bonn thought of women. Clare Three-Nine-Five, Grellie, Martina, and now this Magdalena. He felt so tired.

Zen was in a position of danger that might be no danger at all. But might, as philosophy taught, only means might not. Need he remind Rack of the serious need for possibly an extra stander for Zen? Anybody can make a threat. Jokers can, for instance. Killers too.

'Yer got two goes, Bonn. One's Candice One-Two-Five, she's new. The other's Amarice Four-One-Seven. You done her before.'

'Very well.'

Rack yelled for the coffee. Bonn could tell he was on edge over something. What, though?

'The coffee is already here, Rack.'

It had arrived while the stander was howling with rage over incomprehensible tactics on the dance floor. Bonn withdrew within himself, thinking of Clare Three-Nine-Five. Some events were beyond him. In fact, practically everything he could think of was beyond him, out here where things happened. Such as this: If, as Rack implied, the mogga dance judging was rigged and the dancers all knew, why then did anyone dance at all? God must wonder similarly about life as lived by individuals with free will. He wondered then about free will, as in buying and selling. And as in Magdalena's tactics of buying hotel businesses. Could she be Zen's threatener? But if so, why? No. There was a reason beyond the streets, somewhere out of normal reach, up there among city councils and politics.

Fern spent the evening supporting a Party Political Broadcast session at one of the outlying town halls. The audience numbered fewer than seventy, poor even for the time of year. Gordon was bound to be disappointed. He was absent, having to attend a division in the House. Loyally, Fern sat through the video cast onto an enlarging screen. Fewer than a dozen of the diehard Party faithfuls attended.

She left in a mood of dejection. Surely something more positive could be done than making hinty phone calls to some anonymous woman, an invented death threat to a youth she'd never met?

The BBC broadcast had been less than ten minutes, even counting the introductory words. A feeble question session followed, with primed queries parroted from the hall to seasoned Party men, candidates or would-bes embarking on early electoral careers.

Fern knew that Gordon had everything going for him, yet his support was inexplicably draining away. Couldn't people *see*, for heaven's sake? It was all wrong. It was bound to be his last term – he'd sworn that before, though. He could then rise, maybe even make the Upper House. Final terms were notorious, she knew, for retiring MPs often lashed out and declared their independence from family trammels. Too long Gordon had been kept on a leash of social propriety by his cow of a wife. It must end, and soon.

He'd explained it all to her, she remembered as she drove from the town hall heading for her lonely flat. He would definitely strike soon, though, when the time was right. It would naturally be with heartfelt regret, his announcement to the media about the Opposition candidate's sordid wife's secret perversion. And of course he would clear it with Party Office, but swiftly rush into a sad denunciation of Ellot Shacklan. The public wouldn't stand for it. They'd never elect a politician whose wife paid for sex. Goodness, it was *worse* than prostitution!

There'd have to be a trial, Gordon had told her. Shacklan couldn't let it pass, would brazen it out until the facts emerged. Gordon said he was already collecting evidence, and all at his own expense. Which was most unfair. The Party should fund an investigation. If the Party wasn't bene-fiting, who was, for heaven's sake?

They'd laughed about it all that lovely evening in the

small cottage she rented for them at Lostock. Gordon had been in the best of moods, joking and getting tipsy. He'd acted out Shacklan's surprise when he heard of the scandal breaking, most amusingly. Twice Gordon had had her in fits about Shacklan's wife eagerly making her way to meeting her hired man. The image had been quite obscene, yet Gordon's light-heartedness made it seem extraordinarily entertaining.

Only at first. Now, a day later, it didn't seem all that strange, less so as she thought it over. Men hired girls, didn't they? Of course there was the social stigma. It wasn't the sort of thing a, well, politician or somebody in the professions would do, though there had been the occasional parliamentary scandal or two. And presumably something must have driven Mrs Shacklan to it, one must suppose. Her husband's horrible behaviour perhaps? Fern had heard rumours.

That was troubling her. She took the city road, slowing as rain started again and folk emerged from cinemas along the High Street. Evidence. You needed evidence.

Shacklan would make a formal denial, but in the way of these things the newspapers would start ferreting away. It would all come out, in time. The trial would become an accusation of scandal, Gordon said. It was up to him to provide evidence as to the truth of his news release. That would damn Shacklan. Gordon would sweep in with an overwhelming majority. He would divorce, and marry Fern.

But would there be *enough* evidence? She wasn't sure if Pennington was in on Gordon's search. Ever since she'd told him what she'd overheard in the hairdresser's about Dawn Shacklan – only obliquely, but gossip is often enough – he'd told her to leave it with him, not to go on about it.

It had been enough, until tonight.

Tonight, the lowest attendance on record for something so important as a Party Political Broadcast and a question-answer discussion? It was outrageous. After all Gordon had done for the city. Look at his record!

Clearly she needed to do something herself, collect evidence on her own. It would be expensive, she supposed, but worth it. Imagine Gordon's face when she turned up at a crucial moment with tons of new and utterly damning evidence!

At the central library where she called to change her book, last minute before it closed, she phoned the Pleases Agency, Inc., and asked to book someone for a quiet hour. That was the expression she used, 'a quiet hour'. It was the one she'd overheard in the hairdresser's that time. It was what Dawn Shacklan did. Fern was the huntress, poor Mrs Shacklan the surrogate prey.

'How did you hear of our services, madam?' the woman asked. Fern was not using her voice-masking device.

'In the hairdresser's,' she answered, her heart thudding, staying calm. 'I found your number in the phone book.'

'Do you have anyone in mind, madam?' The voice was not guarded, but you could never tell.

'I heard the name Zen, but I don't know if . . .' Deliberately she let her voice trail away, as one would when doubting if she'd heard rightly, head under the drying hood.

'Zen? Yes, that would be quite in order, madam. Can I ask for identification, please?'

'I thought you said—'

'Any first name of your choice will suffice, not necessarily your own, and three digits of your own choosing. Just like in your bank card, a special one only known to yourself.'

'Seven-One-Two, please,' Fern said, struggling to keep her voice level. 'And Christina. Like that?'

'Very well, Christina Seven-One-Two. Would you prefer any particular time?'

They fixed on a small place she didn't know, the Swan and Bard Hotel along the Liverpool Road that led out of the city from Deansgate. For the evening following.

She replaced the receiver, her hand trembling, and stared at it until the librarians announced closing time. Leaving moments later, an assistant came running after her. Fern almost fainted from fright at possible discovery but it was nothing. Forgetful under the stress of it all, she'd left her handbag by the public phone in the foyer. She thanked the girl in a welter of relief, and walked to her car. The Swan and Bard, Liverpool Road, to harvest evidence. She would be Christina Seven-One-Two, otherwise anonymous and untraceable, calm as a huntress must be.

21 | Fit up – to have an innocent blamed

CLARE HAD A light meal at the Vallance
Carvery, a place across Victoria Square.
The policewoman joined her there on
Mrs Vanston's suggestion and had been lucky enough to
catch her before she left. Clare was relieved, for Clifford had
just walked in. He'd waved, and been about to come over
until he'd seen the stranger joining her.

He was undoubtedly handsome, this currency financier
she'd just divorced, but Clare felt quite cool, even distant,
able to appraise him without significant emotion. The last
thing she wanted just now was a spell of false heartiness from
Clifford.

The woman's name was Payne. She was compact, firm
and unsmiling under close-cropped hair. She wore plain
clothes, sensible everything, and carried a small leather
folder. Her spectacles surprised Clare for some reason.
Wasn't there some quip about police being too young these
days? Same age as me, Clare thought, different jobs.

Payne scanned the clientele, and quickly got down to the
injured man without apology. Clare narrated the bald
details, just as she had to the worried police constable at her
surgery.

'You have an assistant doctor, Dr Burtonall?' Payne asked.

'Hardly need one. I've two nurses, and a receptionist, Mrs Vanston. The work so far is well within my scope. Extraordinary events throw me, like last week. Two girls had fought. One was a patient, punctured her lung with a broken bottle. I did the necessary, fired her over to the District and General. I'm not running an emergency unit.'

'Why do they bring the cases to you?' Payne was candid. 'Isn't that rather odd? Best to send them straight to Casualty, isn't it?'

'I'd have thought so. That cut man was a fluke. The driver parked in the courtyard to place a bet with the bookie. No parking in Victoria Square.'

The woman's manner was almost reprimanding. She took out photocopies. Clare recognized her own handwriting, and felt a spurt of anger. The police had no right obtaining clinical notes from hospitals – or anywhere else for that matter – without a patient's agreement.

'Dr Burtonall, are these your notes and reports made to the Casualty doctor at the District General today?'

'Can I see the patient's consent form, please?'

The policewoman's lips thinned. 'Is that necessary?'

'Yes,' Clare said coldly, no concessions.

She simply waited for the single release form, scanned and returned it.

'Yes, they do seem to be my notes. Rather hurried, I'm afraid.'

Payne said drily, 'Now that you've ascertained that we're probably speaking of the same instance, Dr Burtonall, might I ask your opinion of the man's injuries?'

'He was seriously hurt. Multiple cuts, profound loss of blood, in surgical shock.'

'The distribution of the cuts, Doctor?'

'I thought them odd. Explicable only if the patient

somehow tried to protect himself from some armed assailant. The oddest thing was his right hand and forearm.'

'What about them?'

'Hardly any injury at all. As if he'd used mainly his left arm to ward off a knife attack.'

'He might be left-handed.'

'I'm certain he's right-handed.' Clare pointed to her own right hand. 'His right palm and middle finger had segs, hard excrescences of skin. They are usually occupational. Tailors, miners, manual workers.'

'Are you sure?'

'No,' Clare admitted frankly. 'I was more concerned with keeping him alive.'

'How do you think it came about, Dr Burtonall?'

'I don't know. Perhaps he was trying to hold somebody away – a child maybe? – as the attackers struck. Or keeping something tight in his right hand?'

Payne made a note. Clare poured herself more tea, her movements deliberately casual. She was becoming conscious of the dwindling number of customers, far fewer now than when Payne had arrived.

'Have you any idea how he came to be in the refrigerator van?'

'None.'

Clare refused to be drawn even when the other added, 'It would be of the greatest assistance to us if you could throw some light on the incident, Dr Burtonall.'

'It wouldn't, Inspector,' Clare said calmly. 'Your expert speculations would be far more use than guesses from me. I'd never seen the van before. I didn't recognize the patient. I don't know Mr Hordern the butcher or his route.'

'Would you be willing to come to the police station and

make a statement concerning your involvement, Dr Burtonall?'

'No,' Clare said evenly, furious now. 'It would serve no
purpose.' She finished her cup with finality. 'I must get on,
Ms Payne. I have things to do.'

'I understand.'

Payne assembled her notes. Clare thought, masking her
dislike in a smile, *I don't like you one bit, lady.*

'If there's anything useful you think I could contribute,
do please ask.'

Clare casually remarked, paying the bill, 'How is your Mr
Hassall? Well, I trust? I encountered him on one or two
former cases.'

'Hassall? Yes, I know him,' was all Clare got in reply, as
they separated. The Vallance Carvery now seemed almost
empty, surprising at this time of day. Clare supposed
numbers fluctuated.

Half an hour later, Plunt caught Rack at the Volunteer.

The lead stander was sulking. Bonn seemed withdrawn
today, and had asked for a go to be postponed to the afternoon, which Bonn never did and which buggered up Rack's
time with Stacey, a lass trying out for the new brothel in
Bradshawgate, which Grellie would now learn about but
wasn't supposed to ever get wind of.

So Rack observed Plunt morosely, wondering what the
fuck was in Bonn's mind. Maybe that was Bonn's secret,
women always having to guess what Bonn was thinking?

'What?' he growled at Plunt.

The youth was a scrubber at the Vallance Carvery. He
shook visibly as he stood by the pub counter, not daring to
seat himself without Rack's say-so.

'That filth, Payne's her name, talked about Stir with that doctor bird. You know her, Rack, has a surgery over Escho's the bookie's. Got nowhere. The doc said she knew fuck all.'

That was good. Stir was the knife fighter, five-to-four on and still the bastard goes and loses in a bag-and-ladder bout. 'And Stir? How is he?'

'Eh?' Plunt looked blank. 'Dunno.'

'Then fucking find out.' Rack thought a moment. 'Pals, were they, Payne and the crocus?'

'Nar.' Plunt grinned. 'Looked like they hated each other.'

This was even better. Rack cheered up.

'The plod woman came back in. She talked to the doc's ex-husband, Clifford Burtonall. He were in having his dinner.'

This was bad. 'What they talk about?'

'Politics.'

'Hop it,' Rack said, souring. This was multo grief. What a fucking day. Now he'd have to go and see Martina. How bad could an afternoon get?

Martina composed herself well enough before eleven o'clock. She did not quite hold court as she waited in the ante-lounge of the Worcester Club and Tea Rooms, but she had at least six formal acolytes in close attendance. All had been hired by the fussy Margaret. The three females were slickly attractive, all public relations presenters, one with features vaguely recognizable from once having been a failed Granadee TV newscaster. The three males were all motor-caders from trade shows, all educated at eminent schools. They stood in silence about Martina's couch impressing the club members while Margaret repeatedly checked her watch.

Magdalena Four-Nine-Two appeared as if from a head-long sprint, calling apologies ahead of herself like an appeasing gale, taking Martina's hands in hers and gazing soulfully into her face for a moment before releasing them and sitting beside her.

'How lovely of you to come, Miss Martina!'

The six aides faded. It was well done. Martina noticed her secretary's sleight-of-hand tap on the wrist, the universal sign to listen for quickly phoned messages.

'Now, what can I do for you? Property investments, I believe!'

Martina noted the irritating coyness, hating the brisk stride with which the cow had crossed the carpet.

'Your technique works quite well,' she said, unsmiling. 'Until now.'

Magdalena's bright smile hardened. 'Technique?'

'Falsifying records, overbidding on a price for leisure properties, then making disclosures followed by under-bidding. Followed,' Martina added, 'by outright purchase.'

'Are you trying to say what I think you're saying?'

The woman's face became a mask. Martina was delighted to see her visibly age. In a second the neck became vertically ridged, her cheeks tightening. She must have had two, maybe three, episodes of facial surgery. Her spirits rose higher still. Why on earth had she been alarmed by this scarecrow of a creature?

'Yes.' Martina brought out of her handbag a list, showing it to the woman but not letting her take the piece of paper. 'Numbers of accounts you'll recognize. I have access to two. By nine this evening I shall have access to them all. I shall transfer the funds from them to my private account unless you are gone from this city by then.'

'What . . .? Who are you?' The woman showed a little bravura in defiance. 'Trade and Industry?'

'Certainly not.' Martina replaced the list and closed her handbag with a snap. 'I have no interests other than your departure.'

Magdalena's eyes took in the younger woman, studying her slowly. Her expression cleared.

'It's to do with that Bonn, isn't it?'

'It's to do with fraud, and your accumulated properties.'

The choice had been to torch one of the hotels – Rack's solution – or grievous bodily harm. Martina reserved the options.

'I see. You want to buy Bonn for yourself?'

'One more remark like that, I shall reduce your financial holdings by twenty per cent. Understood?'

'I . . .'

The six presentable young assistants appeared on Martina's signal, of reaching for her gloves. They came slowly and stood about the couch.

'That will be all,' Martina told the older woman. 'Mind what I say.'

The manageress left, her movements less fluid and her air less jaunty. Martina observed the change with pleasure. She sent the secretary and her assistants ahead so she could take her time and leave as unobtrusively as possible. She regretted not having made Rack disable the security videos beforehand. The evil cow would probably watch her limp from the ante-lounge and have a private gloat.

In temper, she boarded her waiting saloon and rang in before the motor had even drawn away from the kerb.

'Dad?' she said quietly into the mobile. 'Bubble the woman anyway. Yes, I know I said we needn't as long as she left by tonight, but I want her penniless.'

'You sure of this, love?' Posser's thick voice wheezed from the receiver. 'We don't normally.'

'She needs it, Dad.'

'Awreet, luv. Straight away.'

Martina sat back in the leather upholstery. She felt replete. Forget the oncoming headache, she felt she had had a truly excellent day. Magdalena Four-Nine-Two would be under arrest within the hour, and Bonn need never know. He never read newspapers. She wished she had the emotional means to celebrate this evening.

MUTED VOICES OF the card players wafted through on the fag smoke. Coll sat as Rack played the video recordings stolen from the police cameras.

'All maps are wrong,' Rack was giving it. 'Know why?'

'Leave it aht, Rack.'

Coll was fed up with Rack's loony theories. They'd been in the shoddy little casino four hours now without letting up. Rack hadn't even let Coll send for an ale, insisting on water, another dumb theory. He thumbed the remote, people in the Asda entrance jerking like ants, slowed it as the marker time showed.

'Wind.' Rack was undaunted. 'They map places when the wind's wrong. Know why?'

'Tuesday.' Coll wanted to write things down, but Rack had forbidden that. 'What time was it again?'

'Two minutes, twenty past seven.'

'Got it.' Coll saw the woman walk through the mall, out into the street at Deansgate, cross into the gardens. 'Same woman.'

'Is it fuck!' Rack showed disgust. 'Different clothes, mate.'

'Same woman,' Coll insisted. 'Copy it, Rack.'

Against Rack's arguments the slider set it to copy. What-ever the chief stander said, Coll didn't have to dodge and duck every time Rack said. Coll'd learned that first impressions were everything in his game. Easy for Rack, chat up tarts and stringers day and night, ale and cunt on the house.

'Two out of four means it's her, mate.'

'Can't be.' They were on their fifteenth tape.

'I'm bog-eyed. Can I have a beer?'

'No. Thirsty's all in yer mind, Coll. Know why?'

Mattie came hurrying with a message for Rack. There'd been two bookings for Zen since he'd gone back on. Miss Faith had reported in about one of them to Martina, who'd sent for Grellie to find Rack and bring him in to listen.

'Finish the rest, Coll,' Rack said. 'Good girl, Mattie.'

The slider groaned, thumbed the remote. 'Same bird,' he grumbled. 'Bet you twenty she got out of that big blue Jag. Get its number, eh?'

'Don't you dare fucking write it.'

They watched the screen fast forward then slow, with a washout. The shopping precincts resumed action.

'You gamblers keep risking winnings, Coll. Know why? Different ear lobes. Know why?'

Coll thought, Is this fucking worth it? One more crackpot theory he'd go frigging mental. It was the same woman, as God judged dead. Once, chance. Twice, coinci-dence. Thrice, it was Spring-heeled Jack. He wasn't taken in by Rack's barminess. He just hoped he wasn't called in when Rack went to top the silly bint. Asking for it, not knowing what she was playing at. Or who with.

He'd kill for a pint. Same woman twice meant same woman always. Where was the problem? Get Akker to do the stupid bint over, finish. Then Coll would be able to suss the big house down the Wirral he had his eye on.

Newness was less a description than an ascription, Bonn reminded himself. Candice One-Two-Five was a plain girl, tubby and bespectacled, dressed as she thought fashionable. She entered dead on the hour, dropping her handbag, not knowing quite what to do when Bonn came to take her coat.

'Candice!' He smiled in relief. 'I worried you might not make it!'

'I was on time!' she said, defensive.

'The traffic has been terrible. I hope you didn't have too much of a journey.'

'No!' she almost shouted the denial, repeated it quieter. 'No. I hadn't far to come.'

She was terrified of revealing any details. Schoolteacher? Clerk? No job worth speaking about? Her perfume was fairly mundane, but almost pushed him back. She must have drenched herself in it. Bonn wondered about Candice One-Two-Five, then caught himself. It was unfair to speculate about the lady client. No investigation, no interrogating. An upper was simply the lady, anonymous, here to use him as she wanted. It was her hour.

'I'm so sorry,' he said contritely.

She looked about in alarm. 'What for?'

'Sounding as if I wanted details about you,' he admitted, hanging her coat and leading her to the couch. 'It was wrong of me.'

'Not at all!' Another shout.

She was desperate. Who on earth had criticized her so remorselessly, programming inadequacies into her? Her anxiety communicated itself to him.

He tried not to notice that she was seated as if on guard, knees together, hands clutching her handbag, knuckles white. She had tried mascara, then eliminated much of it leaving inexpert traces. Her hair was freshly done. Bonn chided himself for sly investigation. Yet wasn't it one of Posser's lady rules, as Bonn called the old man's dictates, that observation gave important clues to how you must proceed? They determined a lady's eventual pleasure. There was a worrisome corollary, though; how did pleasure become satisfaction? Bonn suppressed the thought. Leave torment for night, for solitude when he lay awake alone.

'Can I offer you tea, Candice? Coffee?'

'Tea, please.'

It was already brewed. There was a selection of biscuits. He went to the suite's minuscule kitchen. 'You won't criticize me if I drop them. I'm too clumsy for words.'

She managed a smile at that, but the words she wanted to say wouldn't come. Bonn's heart ached for the woman. What, twenty-six?

The more matter-of-fact the lady client was – actually *was*, not merely seemed to be – the surer a goer could feel. The more hesitant she was, the more critical became the goer's position. An erg of speed too much, she could easily scream blue murder, assume she was being ravished by a maniac into whose hands she'd unfairly fallen. An inch too slow, a mite too gentle, she might go fuming to the Agency's phone bank, yelling obscenities about goers who didn't know that a lady wanted good honest ribald sex of an afternoon and what the hell did they think they were playing at wasting her time sending a choirboy who treated her like she was made of porcelain, etc, etc. Posser had a hundred stories, all chagrin.

Bonn was learning as his meagre experience grew. He'd

even had one lady who'd wanted beating as a preliminary to, and while, making love. His astonished inactivity, when first the councillor's wife from the Wirral had booked him, had led to her unending phoned complaints. It had all come right, though, after a talk with Posser. Bonn's rather hesitant chastisement of her on their second meeting had led to her sending banks of flowers to the Agency. The stringers joked about the incident until Grellie put a stop to such chat in case it embarrassed Bonn.

He placed the tray on the small table before Candice with a show of relief.

'Don't blame me if it's not so good.' He grimaced. 'I've never made a good cup in my life, but I try.'

'It's all right!' she exclaimed, desperate. 'I'm like that!'

He spoke with regret. 'No. Women have the inborn knack of getting through tasks with a kind of grace. We can't do it.'

She urged, 'I know the feeling! I'm terrible, always have been. No, really. I drop things.'

'Women can carry situations off. I mean, I've been on tenterhooks waiting.' He indicated the window in proof. 'I was pacing here like on a chain, wondering how I should greet you, what I could say without giving offence.'

'You were?' she shouted, astounded, her eyes growing even larger in her bottled spectacles.

'I admit it, Candice. I thought, A new lady! How on earth should I respond? What if she's an expert on, what, the Pre-Raphaelites or something and expects me to be the same?'

'I'm not!' she cried. 'I'm not! Nothing like that! I don't think I ever could be!'

'That's what you say, Candice.' He started to arrange the crockery, let a teaspoon slip to the carpet and retrieved it with dismay. 'See? Hopeless.'

'It's all right! It's fine!'

She watched him pour, declined the biscuits, eyes on him, becoming curious as her panic abated.

'Aren't you trained?' she asked, worrying. 'Am I allowed to ask? I mean, do they teach you things?'

'Not really, Candice.' He passed her the cup, frowning, making possibly too much of it, but so far her response was safe. 'We are supposed to have a natural aptitude.'

'Do they . . .?' She probably wanted to ask about, what, about possible auditions, for the goer's training.

'I love the physical side of things, Candice,' he confessed. 'I mean, every woman has her own innate beauty. That's simply a given, isn't it? And beauty imposes inevitable responses in a man. It's why love is so thrilling, life's insistence on the enactment of beauty, once it's perceived. Not like just talking.'

'Not like what?' she asked, staring. Quieter now?

'Making conversation.' He spoke ruefully, sipped his tea, made a pleased face. 'Is it all right? Must be your influence, Candice.'

'No. I'm dreadful.'

'You talk yourself down. You're attractive. A woman's beauty puts her streets ahead. I think it's upbringing, maybe school.'

'I thought that, but—'

'It has to be, love.' Bonn waited, but Candice only sat listening. 'I mean, you are in control. Here. With me. *You* decide. It's the arrangement. You have the say. I don't.'

'That's what's . . .' She petered out, reddening, inspected the carpet.

'Unless you want to simply stay and talk, Candice. Or make love, hold hands, watch a film, anything. Everything. I'm yours for the asking.'

'I don't know what I'm doing coming,' she said, dejected. 'I knew it would be beyond me.'

He took her hands. 'No, Candice. Not beyond you. It's just that having me here, for your pleasure, is maybe too new for the moment.'

'Too new,' she said miserably, tears starting. 'That's it.'

'Then let it be less new!' he said, as if surprised that she couldn't see the obvious. 'Let's just have met, maybe in the park or coming from a film. We get talking at the bus stop. One's not come along yet, so we have a minute to talk about the film.'

'Sort of pretend?'

'No, Candice.' He shook his head, reluctant to accept such an easy foil. 'Not pretend. Because we're both here. I'm yours to do with as you wish. You have bought me. Remember?'

'What do you want me to do?'

'We are here at the bus stop. I ask you if you liked a film we've just seen. You say it was better than you expected. I say I didn't think much of the leading actress. You say . . . what do you say, Candice?'

He put his hand along the couch back.

'I don't know. What film was it?'

'Your hair's bonny. Do you always wear earrings?'

'Not usually. I've never had my ears pierced. These clips hurt.'

'Can I take them off for you?'

With painstaking care he removed them, frowning with such concentration that she had to smile. He laid them in her hand, closing her fingers on them.

'Does make-up smart when you put it on?' he asked, intently studying her features. 'I often wonder.'

She turned away. 'Don't.'

'I'm interested, Candice. You don't realize what an opportunity this is.'

'But you have so many women,' she said, coming back. 'Don't you?'

'Yes.' He made the admission, waiting on her response. Then, 'And the lady's wishes are mine. There's only one problem. It's knowing what those wishes are. I never know until they say. Even though it's her hour, her wishes.'

'It's just I had to go through with it. I despise myself.' She put in quickly, 'Do other women have doubts?'

'Some steel themselves. Some arrive with no intention of going through with being made love to. Others come and leave rejoicing in their personal triumph. To me, they are all queens, goddesses. Like you, Candice.'

'Me? *Me?*' She stared at him. Then timidly came to her crux question, the fear she had come to ask. 'Aren't you ever disappointed?'

'Heavens, no. A lady's company, for a whole hour? It's all I ever wish for.'

'What should I do?' She was almost distraught.

'Let go, darling.' He embraced her quickly, immediately released her. 'Sit and hold hands? Ask to be made love to? Just say you want us to sleep – as sleep – together and nothing happen? Everything's all yours. Say any, I shall rejoice.'

'Can I?' She seemed astounded, the words a vast speculation out there between them.

'Have the choice? Of course, love.' He paused, his eyes on her face. 'Might we lie together, Candice? I'd love it. We'll do nothing but be there, if you wish. I won't move. Honestly. I won't even reach for you, unless you insist. It'll be a beginning. For you. For us.'

'Will it count?' she asked behind her spectacles.

Gently he removed them, laid them on the coffee table. 'Yes, darling. It will count.'

He raised her and led her into the bedroom. She came, looking round the sitting room as if in farewell.

HORDERN THE BUTCHER drove out to JB's Caff which stood in the Bowton trunk road lay-by and listened to the radio until it was time. He climbed down, no need to lock his motor. JB's Caff was a ramshackle old bus that went nowhere. It served as a lorryman's nosh place. Long-haul wagons were nearby, their drivers stodging up on grease and bread, anything to stave off a halt when hitting the south where food got thinner and journeys stretched round the clock. JB's was noisy, radios on different wavebands, a record playing an extinct Houghton Weavers track. Jesus, Hordern thought, was music really once that bad?

He got a mug of tea and a plate of fried bread. JB was in good form, smoking one of his rich cigars the drivers dashed him from Holland. 'Too thin to cut, too thick to plough, eh, Hordie?' JB always bragged about his tea.

Hordern sat to look out over the neighbouring fells. Sheep there, some small Lancashire cattle in the distance, drystone walls. He was hardly into his first slice when Rack came and sat.

'Hordie.' Rack seized the man's plate and began to wolf the slices. 'Know why wagoners always have songs on loud? Stimulates their eyes. Know why?'

Hordern listened obediently, in sadness watching his tea slurped to the dregs. His breakfast was engulfed. Rack wiped his mouth with a sleeve then sat in silence until the butcher rose and brought more fried bread and tea from the counter. Rack started on them.

'Went okay, I heard, Hordie.'

'Aye. I had to statement, where I'd stopped and that.'

'Who wus it?'

'Some cow called Mzzz Payne. Everything ten times, her.'

'Newcomer. Yorkshire.' Rack sniggered, spraying the butcher with greasy crumbs. He swigged the scalding tea, Hordern marvelling. 'Day she left, the Leeds plod threw a frigging party. A right mare, she.'

'That Dr Burtonall's a cracker, eh, Rack?'

The stander looked. Hordern shrank.

'I mean, she were good at her job. That's all I meant, Rack, honest.'

Rack forgave. 'Where's your van?'

'At the shop. The wife's got the keys.'

'Don't need keys, stupid prat.' Rack finished Hordern's breakfast. 'Your money's under its front off wheel, okay?'

'Ta, Rack. Any time.' Hordern was eager to prove his loyalty. 'Don't you want to know how Stir's doing? The hospital—'

Rack paused in the act of rising. 'Don't know anybody in hospital, do I?'

Hordern paled. 'No. Sorry. My mistake. I don't either.'

'Tadda.' The stander went to the door, calling good-natured insults to JB. 'Grub's crap, JB. Know why?'

His bickering played itself out. Hordern heard Rack's motor start and pull out into the traffic. He wiped his clammy hands and waited before leaving. It was good money doing whatever Rack said, but he'd not be going to the knife fights again for some time. Let things cool. He was only a fucking butcher for God's sake, innocent and with no axe to grind. He wanted everybody to know that.

The lawyer's offices were in the most prestigious stretch of Manchester Road, where the Bowton Road began its upward climb to the moorlands. Clare had been looking forward to meeing Miss Martina. She had only had three encounters with the strikingly beautiful blonde girl before this, and they had been so cluttered with contract details that she'd been unable to form any strong impression.

Oak, mahogany, teak? Clare wondered about the panelling as she declined the secretary's offer of coffee. The morning was hazy, a watery sunshine showing the montbretias and spray off to good advantage. Marcus Atherington, elderly and massively overweight, came puffing in to give a rather distracted welcome, then left Clare to it. Odd that Miss Martina always seemed to bring her own secretary to fuss, but maybe that was how registered charities impressed.

'It's about your new premises, I think,' Margaret confided in a stage whisper. Clare noticed she was uncertain which way the filing cabinet key turned. 'They're beautiful!'

Are they really, Clare thought. First I've heard of them, except for some vague hint in the second meeting with Mr Atherington.

'There it goes!' the super-efficient Margaret said brightly as a buzzer sounded, and ushered Clare through into the small conference room.

Martina was already seated, smiling a welcome. Clare sat facing, conscious of the occasion's formality. They made inconsequential small talk.

'Just as you are fairly settled in, Dr Burtonall,' Martina said as Margaret passed Clare a thick folder, 'your new premises are available and fully operational.'

Clare was surprised but delighted. 'They are?'

'They're yours to step into.'

'Now?'

'Margaret?' Miss Martina prompted.

The older woman, who had remained standing, instantly began a summary of the transfer arrangements.

'A removals firm is on stand-by. The location is a new building in Charlestown, very nearby. It matches your requirements, as first stated, for the surgery and offices. Two additional medical secretaries are also on stand-by pro-bationary appointment, to start the minute you approve.'

'Charlestown? Isn't it rather a way out?'

'Of the city centre? Precisely one mile. Possible alternatives are at Weaste, Failsworth, Audenshawe, Hulme and Walkden. All have less desirable features. Those are listed in the summaries provided.'

'It seems a rush.' Clare was pleased at such enthusiastic backing, but was a little disconcerted. It would be ungracious to ask why the haste.

'Move as and when, Dr Burtonall,' Martina said. 'You're the doctor, after all. We will fund any reasonable request.'

'Is there a time limit, Miss Martina?'

Clare saw the charity's logo on the folder: *Parader Cares.* Its number was authentic, registered with the Charity Commissioners. Old Mr Atherington was the principal, with other lawyers from esteemed charity nominees. Clare had been firmly advised of the need for reticence, not to say secrecy, about the charity's origins. Fine by her; the less bureaucracy the better. And they did the odious admin work that she hated.

'One week, unless you require some extra assistance we haven't thought of.'

'Hardly.' Clare lightened the atmosphere by a laugh. 'Coming to work for your charity from a hospital, I've never seen anything so well organized!'

Martina smiled. She illuminated the room. For a moment Clare felt quite envious. Young, lovely, so influential that the rest of the lawyer's complex offices seemed to hush while she was interviewing, and certainly brainy. Martina had everything.

'How soon may I see the place?'

'A driver is waiting, if you are free now,' Margaret said smoothly.

'Thank you. I must say,' Clare said, rising at the hint of dismissal, 'I shall miss the city centre. It's so alive! I've always been rather on the sidelines before.'

'I don't think you'll be disappointed, Dr Burtonall.' The blonde girl was confident, and did not try to detain her visitor. 'Are you finding the medical work adequate?'

Clare hesitated. This was all so friendly, but a shade too formal. 'Adequate' seemed a trifle odd.

'Yes. I hope the people who use the charity won't be dissuaded by distance. That's my only worry.'

'I see.' Martina seemed inclined to discuss this. 'Why?'

Clare hesitated. Mentioning prostitution to a reserved, almost austere and doubtless innocent girl like Miss Martina might cause affront. Heaven knows what august finishing school the girl came from.

'In Victoria Square I'm in the thick of things. Any vagrant can come in, even individuals of loose moral character . . .' She faltered, not knowing how much plainer she could be to this genteel young lady.

'They predominate among your patients, Dr Burtonall?'

'Well, yes. In fact,' Clare enthused, 'I have several such patients willing to come for repeated health checks. It's quite rewarding. I shouldn't like to risk losing their cooperation, for their own sakes as well as the health of the community.'

'Quite so.' Martina sat back. She seemed to move with some difficulty, perhaps the lawyer's enormous leather chair? 'Then have both, doctor.'

'Both what?'

'Your new surgery at Charlestown *and* a city reception office. Margaret?'

The secretary had a ready answer.

'We have three ground-floor places suitable for use as walk-ins. Very limited, of course. We could have the office prepped, desked and functioning within two days.'

Clare blinked. 'Just like that?'

'Dr Burtonall,' Martina said with gravity. 'When you first expressed your willingness to work for Parader Cares charities, my contract lawyers were at pains to convince you of our commitment. Any patient, of whatever lifestyle, is eligible. If efficiency demands a separate reception office in Victoria Square, then you shall have it.'

'Could I see the three places you mentioned?'

'At your convenience, Dr Burtonall.'

'Thank you. I suppose now would be as good a time.'

There seemed little left to say. Clare's transparent willingness to chat a little longer with Miss Martina got her nowhere, and she was shown out by the friendly secretary. A driver was waiting. Margaret rushed to get her coat and handbag to accompany her.

Alone in the office, Martina dialled on her mobile phone. Rack was three minutes answering. Martina told him Dr Burtonall was on her way.

'Tell Grellie to clear the stringers. And Rack?'

'Yes, boss.'

'You were too slow answering. And don't call me boss.'

'Right, boss. That Magdalena Four-Nine-Two's going to be trouble.'

'Tell me details soon.'

Martina shifted in the uncomfortable chair, moving her lame leg with difficulty. It hurt far more than usual today. She hadn't wanted that Clare woman to notice. Another woman could regard it as a definite advantage. So far, Martina was ahead by reason of Clare Three-Nine-Five's ignorance of realities.

How charming, Martina thought sarcastically, that Dr Burtonall had baulked at a frank mention of prostitution. Therefore I have created the right impression. It was clearly grounds for satisfaction, though not complacency. She buzzed for her car. Mrs Houchin her housekeeper came in to see that she got downstairs safely. Everything functioning perfectly, Martina thought bitterly. Another day in paradise.

BONN'S HOUR WITH Amarice Four-One-Seven left him more tired than he felt he should have been. The reason was a sense of foreboding he was unable to dispel.

The lady was pleasant, attractive, talked incessantly before making love, during, after. He knew more about her, her family, her schizo husband, her two terrible sisters-in-law, her guilt-ridden mother's troubled business affairs, than he did about his own existence. He was drained. It was going on for six-thirty by the time he left the Vivante and decided to go for tea in the Butty Bar. He saw Zen in there, a fluke.

The caff looked an afterthought, wedged between Foundry Street and Mealhouse Lane. Its tables were covered with loud American cloth, its windows misted with condensation. The clientele was never more than a dozen folk waiting for out-of-town buses or watching the clock for trains. A few youngsters played noisy machines against the rear wall. Bonn thought the Butty Bar truly sad. He went towards a corner table, but Zen waved to invite him over. He was with Dingo, his stander.

'Good evening, Zen, Dingo.'

'Hello, Bonn. Cuppa?'

'Thank you.'

The tea was brought instantly. Zen's standing joke was, the girls always stared at Bonn, whomever they served. It happened now. Bonn saw Zen smile and reddened, knowing why. Dingo asked Bonn if he should leave.

'Please don't go on my account, Dingo, but thank you.'

'Good to be back, Bonn,' Zen joked.

Bonn didn't share his amusement. Zen meant his temporary suspension over the death threats.

'I hope I won't be thought presumptuous if I express my anxiety, Zen,' he said. 'It is possibly a far more serious matter than is generally thought.'

Dingo, listening, thought, Jesus, Bonn, you do go round the fucking houses just to say something. 'You want me to leave, Bonn?' ought to get a plain 'No', gets instead something from a Restoration play. And like 'Don't go back, Zen, wack,' would have done instead of a frigging speech. But Bonn was the man, no messing about. It was like you had to be on your best behaviour. No argument, just do it.

'I'm not worried, Bonn,' Zen was saying, talking like a bloke ought.

'What does Dingo think, if I may ask?' from Bonn.

'More risks, Dingo? Or less?' Zen asked his stander.

'I can cope,' Dingo said straight off. 'Rack says I can have two more standers. One's already on crow.'

'They are reliable, I trust,' Bonn said gravely.

'I believe so, Bonn,' Dingo said, thinking, God Almighty, it's happening to my own talk too. *I* fucking *believe so?* He'd never said anything so flowery in his whole life. 'Yeh,' he added, back to legit.

'Rack chose them, Bonn,' Zen said, which closed that issue.

'Please take care, both of you, if I may,' Bonn said quietly.

Coming from him it was outrageous persistence. Even Dingo stared. Zen felt uncomfortable.

'Look, Bonn, mate. It's good of you to be concerned. But Dingo's been my stander ever since, see? And I'm not so slow. What with the hotels being sussed – Rack's on it now with Toothie and Henno from the snooker – I'm safe as I'll ever be. Okay?'

'Very well.'

Bonn tasted the tea. It wasn't too foul tonight. He wanted to leave it but the counter girls would be upset. If he drank it, they would come hurrying over bringing more. If he said no thanks, they might be sad. If he only drank half, they'd be desolate. He didn't know what to do. In the mirror, he caught their reflections watching. He felt his face colour.

'Seen the new working house, Bonn?' Zen smiled. 'I went round with Connie and TonTon. It's superb. You wouldn't think those houses were so big inside, would you?'

'Knocked into one, with a connecting roof walk over Number Thirteen between the adjacent houses.' Bonn could carry this off. None of the goers, and especially the keys, ever referred to his lodging with Posser and Martina.

Zen was frankly curious. 'You picked Trish, eh?'

'Yes. I advised.' Bonn felt his face become hotter still at the implied question. 'I was interrogated rather, as if I had developed some special interest in the lady. She does seem to have an ideal attitude.'

'She's slow on money matters, though,' Zen said. 'Connie's narked about that. Madams are all dynamite on accounting. A chatter has to pull her weight.'

'I pointed that out early,' Bonn said ruefully. 'I was thankful it was a remediable deficiency, and not a fault in her character.'

'Took some stick from Martina?' Zen crashed in cheer-fully. 'You still look well on it, wack.'

Bonn half smiled, finished his gruesome cup.

'Thank you for the tea and your kind company. Perhaps I shall see you again soon. Good evening.'

They said their so-longs and watched him go. Zen smiled to himself, the counter girls whispering together as soon as the door closed. The caff itself seemed to sag, as if some-thing vital had just gone from the place.

'Some entertainers can do that,' Zen said to nobody in particular. 'They say Earl Mountbatten was felt in a building.'

'I don't know how to fucking talk to him, Zen,' Dingo groused. 'Like everybody's suddenly got lace hankies and ruffles. How's he get on with the tarts, then?'

'He does it right, whatever it is.' Zen checked the time. 'How long have I got before this Christina lady?'

'One hour, Zen. I'll tee up the second stander, put him on crow before we go near, okay?'

'Daft, all this,' Zen said. He felt a bit embarrassed, so cosseted.

'Not if it has to be, Zen,' Dingo said, 'unless you talk Martina down.' He went outside. A small nondescript balding man in the corner shuffled his paper and marked some horses on tomorrow's call-overs.

Zen recognized a double crow, and sighed. Like being shepherded. Kids weren't closer watched. He asked for a coffee. The smiling girl brought it across and said, 'How's Bonn, Zen? He okay?'

Before the girls could be assembled, Grellie spoke to each one separately, giving the same warnings. They were excited, but there was something to be added about pairings first.

She had them assembled in the working house. It was in the main downstairs parlour of Number Fifteen that they listened together round the luxuriously appointed coop. As a langniappe she had given Connie the choice of buying four paintings. They were predictably ghastly, and no doubt Carol would soon trot in from the Café Phryne and owff them into the nearest dustbin. All that mattered was it bought peace for a day.

'You never leave the coop – that's here, the place where the punters see you first, okay? – without a punter in tow, unless you tell the pandle. Not under any circumstances, unless the place is going up in flames.'

'Who're our pandles, then?' Grellie got immediately from Tabatha, a solid-breasted lass who'd served good time at the casino but whose failing was her short attention span. It had got her into innocent trouble, meaning a mere fine or two, no beatings or worse carnie.

'I'd like her to be the same one when I'm on,' Dilly joined in, looking round for comment.

'Me too,' Kylee added.

The others started talking all at once and didn't shut up until Grellie yelled for quiet. It was Dilly's jaunty way of smiling round at everyone that invited talk, and it really irritated Grellie. She raised a warning finger. Dilly immediately started up again, wayward and full of indignation with her interminable 'What? What'd I say? I only said—'

'Out,' Grellie said quietly, and the tall Jamaican lass dithered, staring round aghast, wanting help. The rest stayed mum in sudden shock. 'Want me to call Rack, Dilly?'

'I'm sorry, Grellie, honest. I didn't mean—'

'Door. Now.' Grellie pointed.

'You don't mean for good, Grellie? I can come back, can't I?' Dilly began to weep, still begging as she left.

Grellie gazed at the remaining five. 'Understand? Nobody here gives me a no. Not anyhow, not anywhere.' She waited until she heard the outer door close. 'If I let her back it's a double warning for the lot of you. Same if I don't. Any of you says me a no from now on gets tanked. And so will Dilly.'

She took their expressions in, nodding approval at the silence. Kylee glanced warningly at the rest. She was a slim Brummie lass who served well enough at the casino but hadn't the aptitude. She'd put in for the working house because she found the gambling boring. Tabatha was her pal. They had a couple of men in tow who worked a used-motors scam between Cheadle and Stoke-on-Trent, spent half their lives on motorways dashing stolen motors to France. It was as stable an arrangement as lives got, in the trade.

The other three girls were Fanny, a girl who never lost her smile even when crying. Her special friend was Trina from Leeds, plumper than she ought to be but a lass who would prove herself a valuable workhorse. Vacant as a brush, not a thought between her ears, forgot what she'd had for breakfast but that meant all the safer for it.

Last, sitting curled up on the carpet like a kitten, was Norma. She was interesting for her degrees. Collected them endlessly from night schools, universities, correspondence. It was like an ailment. Yet she seemed at odds with this life, until the men started coming to the Bouncing Block gym in Moor Lane wanting her to do them in the sauna. It became quite a pursuit. Her transfer would plummet the gym's takings. Thank God, though, for the Almighty always sent new girls queueing at the door once news of a vacancy got about.

'Introducing your pannies,' Grellie said. Two of the

stupid mares glanced expectantly at the door like she was compèring a TV yak show. She explained they'd meet them later.

'Trish is the spare wheel. She's new, she's your chatter, and you treat her like a Ming vase, right?'

'Is she over us?' That from Tabatha. She was used to a casino's hierarchy so Grellie didn't mind her interruption. Ignorance she could forgive. Bolshie, a girl got a good tanking. It was all necessary and they expected it.

'Yeh. She's your working house's permanent chatter. That means Trish does the housekeeping, everything from sheets to drinks. She'll second the two pannies, who cover you twelve on, twelve hours off, for the first week. After that it'll be eight hours on, sixteen off, for the three of them.'

'Can I ask, Grellie, dear?' Norma asked. Her voice was a kind of whine, hardly audible. Getting the nod, she went on, 'Can we say to be on when a particular pandle's on duty? Or is it pot luck?'

'You do as you're told, luv,' Grellie said sweetly into sudden silence. 'You needn't have asked, need you, Norma, dear?'

She waited, cocked her head as if listening.

'No, Grellie,' Norma said at last.

'There!' Grellie didn't smile, not a hint of compromise. 'Now, general rules. I'm spelling them out because you'll be twelve by next week. You all know them. No money touches a working girl's hands. No outside arrangements. A punter asks for that, you tell him talk to the pandle. Next, tell your panny if you hear anything seems the slightest bit important for the syndicate.'

'What things we lissnin' fer?' Tabatha cut in.

'Guess,' Grellie said bluntly. 'You'll never guess wrong,

Tabatha. If what you hear's superfluous, it's no loss. If it turns out vital, you'll be well bunced.'

'How much?' Kylee asked in a whimpering voice, then shrieked with amazed laughter at her own temerity.

'More than you think, girls,' Grellie said in a stony voice that pressed them back into quiet. 'Fourth, every room gets changed sheets, changed pillowcases, a quick clean between punters. If it's not, you contact your panny straight off. No taking a punter into a shop-soiled then telling after. No punter leaves this working house telling his mates he's been shagging in a fucking zoo.'

'Grellie,' Fanny asked, hand raised like a babby in class. 'Will they get mad, the pannies, if we complain, like?'

'Pointing out a room's filth isn't a complain, Fanny. It's house rule.'

'We have our own rooms, then, Grellie?'

'Days and days about.'

Fanny and Trina both groaned. Grellie smiled inwardly. The pair had more than a casual liking for each other, but that was their business.

'Until you're told otherwise, that's it.'

'Do we get told rates, Grellie dear?' Norma asked, still saccharine sweet.

Grellie thought, You have to hand it to birds like Norma. They really do bounce back, stay on course no matter what. It was either a troublesome trait, or one that would mark her for stardom and slick promotion. All those degrees, perhaps. The latest was in dramatic art, would you believe. The question was, which bits of Norma were acting and which not? She'd tell Trish to watch Norma.

'Course you do, silly cow. I'll send the pannies in once you've had a few minutes to grumble among yourselves. One is Judith, the other Nessa. Both rule. Details to them.'

She waited, but the girls had got her markers and said nothing. She said tadda. They called, 'Tadda, Grellie' after her.

Outside, Grellie breathed a long slow breath, feeling the cold air enter her lungs. She felt worn out. What she would really like now was a lovely bath, then a change of clothes into something half-decent, then a lovely meal at the Vallance Carvery, no great shakes but good enough. Then a long forgetful sleep with Bonn. Just his presence would be enough. Maybe.

Two out of three, she thought sadly. Not bad, said quick.

THE BLUE JAGUAR rolled over Snake Pass, moorland on every side. Fern tried to relax, but it proved impossible after what she'd just experienced. Gordon was an expert driver, the sort you relied on to move world past the car windows without the slightest chance of alarm. He talked on and on about House division procedures. She hardly listened, still dazed.

This feeling, Fern thought, must be the same when you win a world championship. Anthems, the cheering. And you thrilled, in the vortex. Twelve hours ago she'd been lying in a bed with a stranger.

She corrected herself. No, think it as it was. Put in those taboo words she'd never dared even let her brain utter. She had had sexual intercourse. The man, Zen, had straddled, entered her very body. He had striven, rutted, finally spending in a flailing action that had knocked her head thump thump against the selour. It had sent her breathless and light-headed. She hadn't minded. That astonished her – used, thumped, penetrated, and she *hadn't minded*. Shoves, leaps even, a battering. She felt bruised, yet was exhilarated.

'Simplification,' Gordon was saying. 'It comes down to keeping things simple. That's the secret.'

'Are you all right, Fern?' Mrs D'Lindsay asked. 'You're awfully quiet.'

Fiona D'Lindsay had been more or less ordered to come along today. TV cameras would be there, the new baby unit issue a must. The gain? A cool four per cent on the polls, money for jam. Gordon's agent Pens Pennington always lectured that, some issues were money for jam.

'Yes, thank you, Fiona. Just hoping it goes well.'

'Isn't it a routine thing?'

Every political event was a 'thing' to Fiona D'Lindsay. Smart, shapely, bright, she shouldn't be an MP's wife because of her casual attitude. Politics was no place for it. An MP needed devotion, conscientiousness.

Gordon, eyes on the road, took it up. 'Only in the long-term planning sense, Fiona.' Leaving Fern safe to dream.

Of course, she hadn't had the slightest intention of *allowing* that Zen *do* anything to her, not at first. After all, she'd made the arrangement in the way of pure research, meaning on Gordon's behalf. Somehow though it had taken a course of its own. The conversation, his calling her by that assumed name. Thoughts she'd never even imagined – well, sometimes, but not with any hope – had somehow come into being. Once she was Christina Seven-One-Two things strangely took her over. She'd felt inclined to speculate what would happen *if.* Then while that Zen had smiled and poured her a sweet sherry, her mind had started a nudging game.

So quite naturally – she was paying, after all – she'd stayed. Zen's innocent talking had masked her mind's quiet question: Shouldn't I *find out*? Wasn't it a clear plain duty? The details would help her Gordon enormously. She'd come this far. She was acquiring evidence. She ought to justify the cost. She shouldn't leave without discovering what Ellot

Shacklan's odious wife really *was* doing with this sex hireling. And on and on the reasons scurried, always ahead, always marking the path for her to follow.

In her imagination, Fern hadn't actually believed a word of the rumours. Meaning she'd assumed that bought love would be somehow unreal, sort of synthetic. A woman hiring a man surely would feel nothing but disgust, her mind inevitably becoming full of detestation and her body in neutral.

It hadn't been at all like that.

Treacherous parts of her had climbed, moved, accepted. And, she remembered guiltily, urged. She had craved, hoarsely demanded, his spillage in her. Deeply shocked afterwards, thinking over her behaviour, it had seemed just like her real lovemaking with Gordon, though that of course was true love and without shame. Yet if the two processes were indistinguishable, then what *was* real? She badly needed time to adjust, time to think. In fact, she wanted not to be here in Gordon's blue Jaguar on the way to a political photo-op.

One unexpected feeling was pity. She actually felt a mite sorry for Zen, whereas previously she'd imagined him to be some kind of stupid boor bent only on exploiting deprived women for cash. Could anything be more revolting? Now, she felt sympathy. Used, abused, by a coarse woman like Mrs Shacklan, Zen would obviously be obliged to treat that sordid cow like a genuine decent person, just because of his unfortunate position. And how typical of Dawn Shacklan, to exploit others!

Fern had heard Dawn speak on several occasions. She was nothing if not a bully, jeering from the rostrum at hesitant village-hall questioners when she spoke – shrieked, more like – in support of her wretched husband.

'Sure you're all right, Fern?'

'Yes, thank you, Fiona.' Greatly daring, she added, 'I'm just mulling over a speech Mrs Shacklan gave two months ago.'

'Euro subsidies?' Gordon immediately asked, shrewd.

'Yes, that one.'

'Is there a transcript?'

'I did one. Mr Pennington looked it over for the Manchester meeting.'

'Worth making a point about it today, you think?'

Fern wisely waited, but Fiona offered nothing. She was doing her nails. Another minute she'd be wanting the radio blaring or some mindless tape on.

'No. I shouldn't think so. It'd be best to ask Mr Pennington.'

'He'll say yes. It's what agents do, Fern.'

Fern's eyes met his in the rear-view mirror. He smiled. She looked away, thinking of the evidence she'd collected from Zen.

The notion forming within seemed outrageous at first, but the nearer the Jaguar took them to the ceremonial unveiling of the baby unit's plaque the more reasonable it felt. *Tell Gordon what she'd done!* Lately he'd been losing certainty. Her evidence would restore his convictions. He would be elated, and see his road clear to re-election. Confidence! He often said confidence was everything. In her handbag was a typed summary of her encounter with Zen. She'd kept herself anonymous, relying on descriptive minutiae. Been brilliantly careful.

Choose the moment, though. Take care. Don't be fully explicit. Give him a partial tale. Best to say that nothing sexual went on. A man could become jealous, and Gordon was a man of powerful emotions. She was his real love. He'd declared it often enough, in those intimate moments no one else could possibly share. There were rumours – weren't there always, with any MP? – about affairs, but only because an influential man soaring in politics was bound to attract gold-diggers. You never saw a bimbo enticing a poor elderly ex-miner, did you? Different if the man was rich and a born leader; then the women flocked.

Once she explained, Gordon would see how totally committed she was to him. He'd be thrilled, have all the evidence he needed. And he'd call a press conference immediately, expose Dawn Shacklan to the newspapers. Fern alone had proved that this Zen was real. Zen had told her that he couldn't reveal anything about other lady clients. But surely there would be records somewhere? Anyhow it would all come out. There were other witnesses, for Dawn Shacklan, hairdresser gossip recounted, had giggled openly to her queer hairstylist of 'my own dear Zen'. The male stylist had chirruped, 'Can I come too, dearie?' making the whole hairdressing emporium hoot with laughter. Dawn was *such* a wag.

Choose the moment, Fern thought, after they returned to the city, before the sessional meeting at the Party house near the Weavers Hall. She would tell Gordon then. *Carpe*, as some people were always quoting, *diem*.

'What is next?'

'Women's boxing, Miss Martina.'

'Women's boxing's finished,' Rack said. 'One-week wonder.'

He was feeling belligerent on account of the rumble outside the Triple Racer. He'd had to send Toothie, Henno and Drench from the snooker hall to sort it out instead of going himself, which really narked him. Rumbles were serious diss for the syndicate. Disrespect was down to him. Besides, a scrap was what he liked doing.

'Cleo?'

The pretty Malaysian girl was one of Martina's counters. Numbers needed on anything, Cleo had them. Prices, conversion factors, everything at her fingertips. If she hadn't, it was only a matter of minutes.

'Rising fast, Miss Martina,' Cleo said. 'Almost exponential in the United States. Predictions—'

'I meant our weather's too bad,' Rack put in. 'Know why?'

They sat in the sedate old Bentley, Martina's motor. Rack was itching to get back to the Triple Racer, where things might still be going on. Instead, he was having to sit here in a motionless crate looking out at a derelict mill alongside a canal clagged with dead rats and old mattresses.

'What is next, Cleo?'

'Carnie shows, Miss Martina.' She looked downcast for an instant. 'I confess I do not know precisely what they are. I have figures, however, from—'

'Carnies?' Rack cried exultantly. This was more like it. 'They're great! I go to them!' For the first time he looked optimistically out at the soot-stained mill to judge its worth. 'Say you've got a bloke who fancies himself as a slasher. Y'know, a knife fighter? Your mate has somebody better, a quicker fighter, geddit? You match one against the other! Who wins gets the purse, see? How much they want for the mill, Martina? Buy it on a Sunday, you get buildings cheaper. Know why?'

'Rack,' Martina said. Her one-word rebuke sent him into a silent sulk. He'd had a good theory going there. 'Cleo?'

'I have information on four carnies, Miss Martina.' The dark girl perused the ledger she always carried, taking time to arrange it on her lap. 'They revenued three hundred per cent for the organizers. Total and averaged, three hundred and four per cent. Costs I estimate at eighty-nine per cent.'

Martina nodded, staring out at the huge mill wall. Some city districts were like sores. Blemishes, necrotic, decaying. Architectural gangrene. Like this at Haleys Wharf, where houses had been deserted. The stagnant canals were an affront, but property was almost free. The city council would rescind all rates and property taxes for a decade, were anyone foolhardy enough to risk development.

'What do they do it for?' she asked Rack.

She could imagine Bonn wondering the same, but not wanting to offend by actually speaking. Bonn asked no questions, from some inner Jesuitical reticence. Crossly she realized that was why she had raised the question. She must stop doing it. She was her own person. Bonn was simply another, somewhere out there, making his own doubtful way.

'Money! League tables!' Rack was immediately restored. 'You've a panel fighter, see? He's welterweight, say, reckons he's better than my panel fighter. But *my* fighter's a cruiser-weight, see?'

He beamed at them, mimed a boxer's advancing shuffle. The Bentley rocked.

Martina said, 'No, Rack, I don't see. I asked why.'

'The bets!'

Rack wondered if he ought to tell Martina – Cleo didn't matter – why women's brains couldn't see the obvious. It was the way they walked, right from birth. It was their fucking *shoes*. He wanted them to ask him why.

'Please, what is a panel?' from Cleo.

'Boxers fight at weights, see? They go into the ring too heavy, the fight's called off. That's official matches, like you see on the telly, right?'

'Yes. Official.' Cleo knew official.

'Here, outside, there's no such thing. The odds get fixed.'

'Odds!' Cleo brightened, making notes.

'Fixed by the match factor. The heavier fighter stands a better chance. He's bigger, stronger punch.'

Rack mimed thumping a punchbag. Martina told him to stop it. She could not explain that the rocking motor made her leg hurt.

'So odds of, say, five-to-eight or two-to-one against gets multiplied by a match factor. Fighters can fight who the fuck – sorry – who they want. The odds get adjusted, see?'

Martina still didn't follow. She knew the panel fights went on, that Rack went to watch. Her dad connived, even allowed them. But buying a whole venue to stage such shows was a new risk. She felt worried. She merely wanted to avoid having to inspect the mill herself, exhibiting her lameness.

'This is very interesting.' The Malay girl was busy scribbling, head down. 'So the panels are simply a register of—?'

'Fighters, barefisters, knife slashers, Thai kickers, karate nutters, all them. Illegal, with special odds.'

Rack also got fed up. Wait for a bint to write things down, you were here for the generation. He reckoned women didn't drink enough. Make them move faster if they'd only drink bigger drinks. He wanted to check who'd started the Triple Racer rumble. Toothie had better have it sussed or else. He wondered if Drench was up to doing a real bludging.

'Who keeps it?' Cleo asked, pencil flying.

'That will do.' Martina sat back. Alone, she normally had cushions, never in the presence of others.

'Home, Miss Martina?'

'Yes. Please get out before we reach Victoria Square.'

'And the mill? I have its details.'

'Give me everything you have on potential profits for the major twelve panels.'

'There's only ten, Martina,' Rack said. 'Magic number. Know why?'

'Forget the mill, Cleo,' Martina said, exhausted. 'Find some other place.'

Rack tapped the security glass. The anonymous old driver hunched his pock-marked neck, and drove them out of the district.

Fern's dressing act this time seemed shoved to the middle ground, as in a painting more indistinct than was once supposed. Gordon however noticed nothing as he readied, idly speaking about a forthcoming *Daily Mirror* poll. He hoped Pens Pennington could rig it, given the opportunity. Being Gordon, Fern noticed as she drew on her stockings – never tights for Gordon – he was distracted, thinking of his old politics, using phrases like 'as every schoolboy knows'. She was surprised to find herself irritated by his mannerisms, him forever struggling with that collar of his. Why didn't he simply get a size bigger, save all that red-faced grunting before the mirror?

'I've got evidence for you, darling,' she said. 'Exactly what you wanted. Dawn Shacklan.' She'd been saving this with delight, her present to him.

He turned sharply. She was sitting on the edge of the bed, skirt now on and blouse about to be.

'You've *what*?'

'Evidence.' Just as she'd planned, she gave him her composed delivery, the Pleases Agency, Inc., the young man called Zen she'd hired. 'Under an assumed name, naturally,' she added airily. 'I was so incognito I could hardly recognize myself!'

Vital to avoid remembering the intimacy. A woman could so easily give herself away. She spoke offhandedly, just like she did when Fiona D'Lindsay was with them in the car, and told Gordon her carefully prepared tale.

Slowly he crossed the bedroom to sit beside her. He wasn't usually so concerned. She smiled inwardly. She had his attention now all right! Gratified, Fern went over it all again, then a third time. It was delightful. She glowed, thrilled he was at last taking her seriously.

'I've done well, darling, haven't I?' She reached to adjust his tie but he pushed her hands away, then amazingly wanted to hear it all over a fourth time.

'Does Pens know this?'

'No! Why on earth should he?' In fact Fern suddenly didn't want the agent to know any of these important details. She disliked the political agent profoundly. When she and Gordon were together for always, she must get rid of the odious man. Replace him with someone less oily, less sinister.

'He'll have to be told, Fern.'

The MP went to stand before the mirror, staring at his reflection. She couldn't discern his expression, but was unperturbed. The facts spoke for themselves. Preoccupied or not, he surely must be pleased. Probably working out how the immeasurably new political advantage she'd gained for him could be best used.

'Get Pens,' he said after a while, unexpectedly curt. 'Tell him to be at the local HQ in an hour.'

'Very well, darling.'

'And, Fern?' D'Lindsay's features seemed clouded over. 'Please say nothing to anyone?'

'Of course not!'

'Thank you,' he said. 'Darling.'

Fern went to ring, thrilled at the impression she'd created. Gordon was rarely silent, whatever the news. She'd produced impact! The change in him was like magic. More grave than she'd expected, but that was Gordon for you.

The news instantly made Pens sweat.

'Jesus, Gordon. Didn't she give any inkling?'

Furious, D'Lindsay rounded on him. 'Do you think I'd have let the stupid bitch do anything like that if she had?'

'No.' The agent had already had a Scotch and soda to hear the MP out. He went for a refill, swigged it down in one throw.

'It's crap creek, Gordon. Gossip gain gone, our platform of family values up in fucking smoke. The ignorant *cow*.'

'I know, I know.' D'Lindsay's features became haggard. 'What do we do, Pens? Everything's on this election. My only hope's to clip and shuffle in the next administration or I'm done.' His voice became almost a whine. 'I've not looked after my own interests, Pens. Honesty's been my thing. I should have looked out for myself more instead of worrying about others. It's rumour, Pens. Rumour can put us out in the cold. It's death.'

'Right.'

Pennington thought, Sod it, had another whisky. He let the other see. They were in it together after all. Lose this sinecure, no other MP would as much as look his way. He'd be a failed political agent. Nothing more pathetic. He'd end up running some bean-and-burger franchise in the Midlands for drunken louts to smash up Saturday nights. That'd be him finished.

'This Zen might get to link you and Fern, Gordon. The tabloids would have a field day – MP's campaign tart with a hired dickster. You'd lose all round, allegations that you'd paid for her to go shagging on the sly, a cunt's perks on campaign funds.'

'I know all this, Pens, for Christ's—'

'Shut up, Gordon. Listen.' The agent enjoyed his moment of rudeness. He felt newly in charge. About time, considering what he'd done for the pompous windbag. The dolt talked too much and never listened enough. 'Fine when we could prove a link between Ellot Shacklan's missus and this Zen character. It handed us the moral high ground. Now, we daren't use it. Anything you bring out about the Shacklans will look made up. So we do two things. Urgent.'

'Yes, Pens?' the great MP bleated obediently.

'First you tell Fern to shut her gob. Silence about her escapade, whatever happens to this Zen. Right?'

'Right, Pens. Look. What if I sack Fern?'

Pennington dismissed that with, 'A woman scorned, Gordon. No. We've got to use her.'

'How?'

'To get rid, Gordon.' The agent eyed D'Lindsay, silently measured him up. 'I'm good at selective disposals of a certain kind. Exactly how tall are you?'

26 |

THE NIGHT HAD gone cold. Dingo was handing over to Henno at the Victoria Square end of Rossini Street between the Vallance Carvery and the Royal and Grandee Hotel. Across, among the street lights, nothing was happening or out of order. Two of the stringer girls, Gina and Vee, were right there where he'd told them to be.

'Coming on to rain, bach,' Henno said.

Dingo wondered if his Welsh talk was put on. So what?

'Zen's just finished. He's talking in the foyer.'

'Who's with him, Toothie is it?'

'Nah. I put Selk because he's posh.'

'Like I'm not?' Henno waxed indignant.

'That's right, wack.' Dingo grinned, was about to start across the road when Zen showed in the hotel doorway and began to walk along the pavement. He was with someone, a gent in overcoat, dark hat, gloves, glitzy shoes, the whole shmut.

'Who's him?' Henno said, inexplicably edgy of a sudden.

'Dunno.' Dingo too worried a second, but Zen seemed casual enough, speaking and starting to raise his hand as if about to point some direction out.

'He should be on his tod.' Henno always complained when something was amiss.

Zen seemed to pause in the gloaming, bending quite as if he had stomach cramp of a sudden. The well-dressed gent abruptly turned on his heel and walked quickly back towards the bright hotel foyer. Dingo suddenly exclaimed and started running. A car squealed, the motorist shouting as he braked and swerved to avoid the stander who suddenly dashed through his headlight beams.

'What the fuck?' Henno stood, baffled.

One of the girls, Vee, Henno thought, screamed something to Gina, who began to trot, clip-clipping on her high heels, towards the central garden, traffic in Victoria Square now honking, tyres screeching. Two cars ground into each other but Dingo was bawling something to Henno, who ran after his boss towards Zen shouting what the fuck, what?

And Zen was crouched on the pavement, holding his belly somehow in an impossible position. Henno thought, *Duw!* and raced across the street. The posh gent was already into the foyer. In a way, worries were gone because now Henno knew the clean simplicity of that feeling he'd experienced only once before when the white heat of the berserker took over. He went like a racer after the gent, heeding the direction of Dingo's outstretched pointing arm, clicking his knife open as he moved and fuck the CCTV video cameras.

The sickening reality hit him as he leapt up the hotel steps because people were already running about the fucking place like ants. Only then did Henno register the most terrible sound in the world, the racket of the fire alarms discordantly sounding all over the fucking place. He thought, *Oh, na! Jesi mawr!* Great Jesus, no!

'Here, sir, outside with you,' some bloke was saying but Henno simply lifted him bodily aside, eyes all over the place.

'Where's the man just come in?' he said, throttling the uniformed commissionaire. 'Sharp, bach.'

'I didn't see—'

Henno dropped him and grabbed the woman receptionist. 'Where's the man just come back in, luv? Fast, now.'

'He's quite safe, sir.'

She didn't recognize Henno so she was new. Henno twisted her hand so she yelped and focused on him fast. People were running, the firebell clamour joined by the foyer staff calling instructions. Kitchen people were already beginning to move out of the stair exits, stained white rats, eyes staring, everybody saying what, what, stupid fucking litanies when he, sick to his belly, wanted that posh bloke, had to grab him. He thought, Zen, oh, fuck, Zen, Christ's sakes Zen, please be all right, bach.

'Where'd he go, luv?' Henno yelled into her face. 'Tell it fast.'

'Through to the dining room—'

He threw her away and shoved past two uniforms trying to direct guests into the street and ran-shoved against the tide into the restaurant. Diners were leaving in a steady drove, one or two actually laughing as they hurried out. Some security bloke tried to bar Henno's way but Henno took hard hold and repeated his question, where was the gent just come in.

'Went through looking for his woman. Henno, innit?'

'Aye. Where's he now?'

'Left, I should think.' The man yelled in a sudden foghorn voice, 'Waiters dog out now.'

'Josh, innit?' Henno did his steeliest. 'Listen, Josh, listen. Find the gent in ten minutes, your wage doubles for life.'

Josh stared. They stood there being jostled by waiters

who were shepherding the last of the diners from the restaurant sheepdog style, walking steadily in a rank among the tables, doing their traditional 'dog out', herding guests from the place.

'But the firebell, Henno.'

'There is no fucking fire, Josh. Do it now, do it now.'

Repetition was the thing, Henno knew. Back in Llanelli – Llanelly proper as used to be – you could spend a whole hour saying just one thing, just enjoying varying emphasis. Here among terrible Lancastrians you depended on words, losing enjoyment of speech that way.

Josh got it and was off, talking into his mobile, wading back across the restaurant and gesticulating to the waiters to keep going. He beckoned Henno from the far side. Henno ran after, throwing chairs aside in a bow wave.

They raced down steps, two flights. One fire door in the vacant stairwell was ajar, but Henno had more sense.

'He must have took this way, Henno.'

'Got checkers-out?'

'Car park, aye. Two on the one exit.' Josh dithered, the enormity of Henno's promise and alarmed determination striking home. 'I'll go inside, you—'

'No. I'll go in. Got them held, have you?'

'Did it straight off, Henno.'

So no cars allowed to leave. Henno thought fast. That meant no *more* motors.

'People too, men, birds, everybody, Josh. Keep them penned in. Tell them any tale.'

'Right.'

Josh raced down to the underground car park, yakking into his phone, while Henno bullied through the firedoor, emerged on the landing. A room cleaner, white pinny trailing, hurried across the intersection of the long corridor. He dashed, caught her by the lifts.

She struggled. 'There's a fire, sir!'

'I'm the city fire officer. There is no fire, false alarm. Did you see a man, gent in overcoat, come this way?'

She gaped. 'No fire? But—' He slapped her, brought her to.

'He's going to die if we don't find him in three minutes, luv. He's diabetic. Did you see—?'

'Yes.' She stared at him, frightened. 'He come in, went back down into the foyer, the end stairs. He took his coat off. Are you sure you're the fire—?'

Henno cast her, took the stairs three at a time, reaching the foyer. The last of the guests were leaving, being almost wafted out and down the steps. Sickeningly there came the wah-wah of an ambulance. He glimpsed a flashing blue light, heard people shouting to make way. Two uniformed policemen were positioning themselves by the hotel steps, urging people to move along there, move along into the dark street where anybody could vanish like fog.

The chance was small. Henno shoved through to the reception desk. The concierge was somebody he recognized, a broadish young lass with tight twenties curls and silver lapel brooches.

'Una? Henno. Gimme the day book and the reception register.'

'I think you'll find the guests are all accounted for. Who're you looking—?'

He reached over and simply took the register.

'Here, you're not allowed—'

'That computer saved the noise, has it?' Noise was records, lists, names.

'Yes.' She started to be scared, her big eyes on his face.

'It's my first time on a firebell. Tells it to save automatically. Is somebody hurt? Security should have announced where the fire is by now. I saw Josh—'

'Una, your computer records. I want them all.'

Somebody bumped against Henno. It was difficult talking to her while standing with his back to her counter and staring hard at the press of people moving in a tide towards the night. He shoved them back.

'Steady on,' somebody muttered.

'I'm not allowed to make copies, Henno.' Truly frightened now, knowing something was gravely up and wishing she was somewhere else.

Henno knew fuck all about computers except they were electric. 'If I take the whole thing, will it still know what it's got?'

'Yes. It's got a—'

'Make a copy of everything in it. Do it now, do it now. Then give me the whole computer. Do it now, do it now.'

'Henno.' She inserted something, started to click the keys.

'Do it now, do it now. Make it can't change anything. Then give it me.'

He felt retching sick, didn't dare let himself even think of the figure outside folding over in the dark of the night. He saw Toothie push in past the two ploddites, who both tried to haul him back but Toothie battled on through. The detached part of Henno's mind perceived Toothie's pallor and thought how extraordinary. So black a skin, yet white to the gills? Who the fuck would have thought that?

'Henno? Rack's here. Blood time.'

Henno was still scanning the laggards of the crowd leaving the hotel lounge. Three main exits was the fucking trouble, *three exits*. Henno felt rage stirring at the whole thing, coming up in his throat thick enough almost to choke. Fucking blood time all right, no stopping things now. Jesus, Rack would burn the fucking city.

'What else do I do, Toothie? Did Rack say?' He summarized his actions. 'The bloke went in, took the service stairwell, come back down and I think out. I got Josh on. I blocked the motors and them on foot through there.'

'Rack says security cameras.'

'*Duw!*' Henno sent Toothie to find Josh, collar the cameras and the valuable tapes they might – just might – contain. He ought to have thought of them.

'What is it, Henno?' Una was shaking, frankly terrified.

'You done what I said?'

She was almost in tears, though she kept up her concierge smile, a ghastly rictus below appalled eyes. 'Is it Zen?'

He reached over the counter, grabbed the skin on her throat and twisted.

'Is it done?'

'Nearly.'

'Do it now, do it now.'

Silently as the last guests moved into the street she handed him two small disks in an envelope. He slipped them into his pocket.

'I can't lift it, Henno.'

He went round her side the desk. 'Do its wires.'

'It's unplugged.'

'Good girl.' He hefted the console with a grunt, found it so astonishingly lightweight he almost owffed it over his shoulder. He stood telling her orders, looking his do-it-now into her. 'Write your address and home phone number. Get me every staff full name, address and phone number on one list. Mark who's on and who's been on today. Put times they're on, times off. Nicknames, livers-in, lovers, gossip, other addresses. Find me and give it me. No exceptions, no substitutes. Then get who they live with on a second sheet, okay?'

'Yes, Henno.'

'Use whoever you need. I want it bad, Una. I'll come back for you if you don't bring them quick.'

'Where will I—?'

'Do it now, do it now.'

Henno left by way of the concierge's stairs. He came into the street by the underground car park exit. Several motorists were arguing with three of Josh's security men, who were steadfastly blocking their way and refusing them permission to go. A fire engine had drawn up across the street, firemen dropping from it and hurrying closer among the crowd. Why was everybody talking, talking, with nothing to say?

Henno went to the security men, spoke to the tallest.

'I'm Henno. Josh told you?'

The big uniformed man eyed Henno and the computer. 'That your machine, is it?'

'Yes,' Henno said evenly. 'Get two things, bach. First, some camcorders, best on earth. Stand here and film every person and motor you see, security folk included. Search every one. I want names, addresses, driving licence numbers.'

'Right. What am I looking for?'

'A knife, clipper, army, shiv, any fucking knife, manicure set to a long sword. And get every bugger's fingerprints you let through.'

'What on?'

'Anything that'll take them clean, bach. Named and signed.'

'Is it legal?' the uniformed attendant asked.

'Fuck legal. Do it now, do it now.'

'Excuse me,' some motorist shouted down the queue of cars. 'Can we go now? Can somebody make a decision?'

'Second,' Henno said. 'I want every motor inside your car park fucking immobilized. Car clamp them, anything. Collect the keys yourself then give them me. Who are you, bach?'

'They call me Fally. I'm Richard Failsworth. Everybody knows me here.'

'I'm Henno. Problems, square with Josh. Don't let a bastard through different.'

'What do I do with the films, videos, lists?'

'Bring me them. Do it now, do it now. Give them Josh or me, nobody else.'

A uniformed ploddite entered, inspected the queue of cars, came over.

'What's going on here? Why aren't these motors on their way?' He weighed Henno up and the computer he carried. 'And what're you up to, lad? Opportunist looting?'

Henno said, 'You idle fuckers never ever know how fucking late you are, do you?'

'Right!' The constable pulled out a notebook, incensed. 'I'll fucking have you, mate.'

'Bert,' Fally warned, 'just leave things be, okay?'

Henno didn't even give himself the satisfaction of a reply. He simply walked on out into the street. God alone knew what was in the computer, anything or nothing. The syndicate would wring it out.

Ten minutes later he trudged into the wrong end of Waterloo Street, beginning to flag under the computer's gradually increasing weight. He heard girls sobbing even before he turned the corner in sight of the Lagoon doorway. He paused, sweating, leaning the console against the wall for a breather. Sure enough girls were weeping, catching their breath. He thought, *Arglwydd mawr, na*. Lord, no. At least let it be something less than death. They'd all failed. Himself, the aghast pale Toothie. Dingo. And, God rest him, poor Zen. And Rack. The whole fucking syndicate, Agency and all. Now, death would be everywhere. Blood time was right.

He collected himself, and started walking towards the bright end of the street. Grellie's weeping stringers watched him come then turned away.

THE WOMAN ASTRIDE Bonn laughed helplessly. Bonn's blank expression set her falling about even more and throwing the bedclothes up in the air. Bonn wondered if this was hysteria. He'd read articles in magazines about the condition. 'Hysteria' from Ancient Greek, previous to the Latin, supposedly related to terms for the uterus, as a feature of women, but such derivations lost him. He wasn't quite sure what a uterus was. And where, exactly? She was kneeling over him, head back, hair anywhere. There'd be knots tomorrow. One recent lady had hired him an extra hour to brush out her tangles, purring as he'd painstakingly worked her hair to a languorous smoothness. She'd kissed his hand, to his surprise. He hadn't known quite what to say. Who was it among the famed old writers – perhaps De Quincey of Manchester in his *Confessions of an English Opium Eater* – who used the terrible phrase, 'the burden of the incommunicable', to mean the intolerable emotional pressure on the heart that silence may cause? He had so wanted to say something, if only to express thanks, or surprise, to the hairbrush lady but was too stifled by awe at this brilliant carnal process.

'Don't you see, Bonn darling?'

This lady, Valetta, hit him with a pillow. Even that simple playful act caused her more hilarity. He lay naked, hands behind his head, smiling, not a notion what was going on. Why laugh?

'No, Valetta.'

Which caused her almost to tumble. He had to reach and clutch to keep her on him. He felt himself almost slide out of her, gasped and held her until she settled and he felt safe. Tears streamed down her cheeks, her breasts quivering.

'I've done it!' she managed to gasp eventually, having to repeat it because he couldn't tell what she was trying to say. 'Don't you understand? I've made me *me!*'

He considered this as she began to calm down. No, not hysteria, for wasn't that frantic destructiveness, throwing vases against the wall? He would have to ask Posser when Martina was out of the room, perhaps after supper one evening. He thought, in bemusement, Yet why not while Martina was actually there? Perhaps because he didn't know – had he ever speculated? – what Martina thought of the entire business, at once so commercial and intensely personal.

'Made you,' he said gravely.

Valetta knelt astride him still. She'd insisted on wearing a nightdress, mouth rucked with determination as she undressed to some plan she must have worked out and rehearsed in detail. Now she touched his chin to keep him looking, and slowly stripped her nightdress off over her head.

'See, darling?' she said in wonderment, examining her arms, watching the garment crumple to the carpet. 'Don't you recognize freedom when you see it?'

Was that it, freedom? So Bonn had to ask, 'Freedom is not absolute, Valetta. It must be *from* something.'

'Valetta!' She became reflective, sinking back so he felt her full naked weight. 'That's part, isn't it? Seeming somebody else.'

'Seem.' Distantly, Bonn heard the moan of a siren. Odd that sirens pierced the nullity of traffic noise. He'd read that a siren only penetrated in proportion to its mimicry of a bell. So why not bells on those emergency vehicles? Almost a similar problem to what seemed to be Valetta's explanation. 'But you are you, Valetta.'

She shook her head vigorously, serious now.

'No, Bonn. It's stepping outside who you are. That's exactly what I've done. Don't you see? I often wonder if I hate my husband.' She took his look for disbelief. 'No, truly. D'you know I've never called him darling since we were married?'

He considered this. Did spouses use endearments constantly? He was uncertain how to put the question.

'I have never been married, Valetta. I don't know how wives normally address their spouse.'

She wriggled, settling herself more intimately. She made a purring sound.

'You're funny, darling. I suppose you know that. Do you?' She asked it solemnly, waited, then shrugged off his silence. 'You talk odd, like from some musty old book you can't get free of. I don't think I'd have gone through with it.' She stirred, rocking, feeling him harden anew. 'If you'd been any different, I mean. Are you all different? A woman at the Institute said there are four of you who do, well, this.'

The conversation had become too complicated for Bonn. Another siren sounded, joining the first, a faint shrill susurrus audible somewhere that troubled him. No need to worry, though. Rack, best stander in the business, had never yet let him down. No client had suffered by unexpected intrusions, though Bonn had heard rumours of disturbing events with goers. Rarely there was the weirdo, as with the unbelievable death threats to Zen.

'Can it not be simple, Valetta?'

'Darling, that's *exactly* why I was glad! It's all so simple now. I'd assumed it would be hideous!'

She smiled with fondness and adjusted her position, head back as if readying to laugh again but now uttering closed-mouth grunts. Bonn watched her features and thought, how could she possibly feel fond? We've been together less than an hour. Would Posser have any answer for this query, when Bonn finally got up courage to ask? Women's responses, like Valetta's, only proposed new theorems, even parables, about behaviour. In the way of parables, they never offered answers.

Three sirens out there now? Unless it was some distant football crowd celebrating. Were United or the Wanderers at home tonight? He never knew.

'You sound so sure, Valetta.'

Her assumed name brought out her smile. She had lovely teeth. Thirty, she'd told him determinedly when she had arrived, giving a catalogue of herself almost as if attending an interview while shedding her coat. It had all come out in a few sentences, married, a child school age, some investment company's office under-manageress, husband distributing computer parts, prospects. But why her decision to become 'Valetta' if she was desperate to define her proper persona so minutely? Unless all that too was concocted. She was the customer, he the hireling. It was her right to be whoever she wished. Perhaps it was no more complex than this: Had she played at being anybody different, and so become pre-cisely what she secretly wanted? It was a possibility.

'I was set on doing it, Bonn darling, whatever the consequences.'

'Whatever!' Here it was, that familiar amazement at what they said. 'I trust you really mean it.'

Her face became grim as she moved in a slow swirl. 'I'd have killed to go through with it tonight, Bonn. If you'd been a gorilla, I made myself promise to stay, let you do whatever you had to. You know how many times I've tried, phoned, made appointments and cancelled? Fifteen. Fif*teen*! I've had to pay fortunes in cancellations. I have the cheque stubs.'

His eyelids forced themselves down. She was now rocking swiftly on him. He felt her moisture on his thighs, saw her breasts swing. She pressed the heels of her hands on his shoulders, shoving him back down when he tried to lift himself to embrace her.

'Stay down, darling.' Her breaths were quickening. 'My first one was all your doing. Now it's mine. I have seven ways I've dreamt of. This is the second. You've to stay still.'

'Killed.' She'd said killed.

'Yes, darling. Me. I mean killed me. It was either come home having done it or I'd have taken an overdose. I mean it,' she said breathlessly. 'I tried once before when I had to cancel. They found me and took me to hospital.'

He too was becoming slightly breathless as she worked, but she was telling him something vitally important. He had to discover what she was saying before the leaps to oblivion obliterated all thought.

'Tell me quickly, Valetta. Please.'

'What?' She halted, startled at his intensity.

'Why. Suicide is so . . .'

She smiled, an element of absent wistfulness in her eyes, jerking dreamily. 'This is assurance of life, darling. The only other time I wanted it so badly was when my sister died. I loved her. I wanted proof of life. I went out and stood by Rochdale railway station. Stupidly I'd thought men would simply come up and proposition me, take me somewhere, do crude things to me as a matter of course.'

'And did they?' He groaned, trying to keep track as logic shuffled to randomness.

'No.' Her eyes moistened. 'I stood there, freezing. The only man who spoke to me in the whole three hours was an elderly man who advised me to go on home. He was ever so kind. Like your grandad, the voice that always means take care, don't scrape your knee, whatever the words.'

He still couldn't follow. His mind was entering the dark umber landscape where thoughts got lost and remembrance forgot.

'This, Valetta,' he tried in a last sally. 'You know what it's for, then.'

'For me,' she said hoarsely. 'To make me who I want. Now, darling, shut up and rut.'

Her last words, before incoherence took hold of both in a great shaking, were cried aloud but they were unreasoned, abusive, crudely uttered in the language of lechery. When he came to afterwards, she was whispering street vulgarities in a steady satisfied purr, her eyes closed, his sweat on them both as she lay with him. He wondered if all sex was one syncytial anthem constantly dreamt of by everyone on earth, and slept.

He left the Hotel Vivante by the Walmsley Street exit facing the railway. Valetta had made him stand before her while she paid him, counting out notes and watching him put them into his pocket. The small ritual seemed to give her immeasurable satisfaction, but he had no time or inclination to ask why. She said huskily, 'That was beautiful, darling. The icing on the cake!' Meaning the giving of pay.

Bonn felt tired, mystified. He wanted so many answers. Where, for instance, did sperm actually *go*? Did they become an actual part of a woman's body by, what, some kind of osmotic assimilation? If so, was he now an ostensible component of Valetta Three-Four-One? Where did that leave morality, if that was so? He would ask Clare Three-Nine-Five, who being a doctor would know. Except, how on earth could he raise such a question? 'Excuse me, please. Might I ask, while I penetrate you, a couple of anatomical problems that have just occurred to me?' Like that? He admired questioners. Such bravery! And why did Valetta get such obvious pleasure from counting out money that way?

He decided to call in at the Butty Bar. Thank goodness everything in Martina's empire lay on or near Victoria Square, a short restorative walk.

No Rack, though?

It couldn't be. Bonn told himself that Rack was undoubtedly around, or had somebody else on crow lurking among the pedestrians. Yet something was wrong.

For a moment he stood there by the foot of Station Brough at the traffic lights. He let them change once or twice, the small tides of evening people crossing without him as he tried to work it out. Police lights, were they, on the square this side of the Granadee TV Studios? Crowds, as anonymous as night crowds always appeared, were on the pavements by the Vallance Carvery. A fire engine emerged slowly from Rossini Street and drove sedately off round the square, taking the Deansgate exit by the supermarket.

No fire, therefore.

He felt ill. The prospect was to discover what had hap-

pened, or continue standing there. He could not move.
People thronged past as another London express arrived
and folk crossed into the bus station, heading home to the
moorland towns.

He came to. Grellie was standing looking across at him
from the opposite side of the road, as if she had just come
from the direction of the Butty Bar. Askey the diminutive
messenger was standing beside her staring at the floor,
waiting for instructions, some message.

She made no move to come over, though the lights
changed in her favour and the signal's little green man was
illuminated. Oddest of all, Bonn saw old Osmund from the
snooker hall, without his jacket, walk with an old man's tread
past Grellie and make some signal to Askey. They went
along the pavement, turning right up Foundry Street. Probably making for the Rum Romeo, Bonn thought. Why, this
time of night? Nothing was making sense.

Some of the girls, ought to be on troll down Waterloo
Street this hour, were coming away from the central gardens
in a cluster. As if in a dream Bonn observed that they were
going the wrong way, moving to the Greygate corner.
Grellie would have something to say about that. Except
Grellie was motionless, standing there opposite him while
the traffic lights changed, red, amber, green, amber, red, on
and on.

Osmund, then, in the main city square, in a state of what
was practically for him undress. Grellie, white-faced, her
girls almost amok, and uncaring? No Rack? He felt somebody close on him, stand beside him, and looked. Gabby, an
older stander famed for chameleon tactics, was there.

'Good evening, Gabby,' Bonn said.

Gabby looked at the pavement. Bonn saw the stander's
face blur. Lights formed haloes all about the streets. Passers-

by stared at him oddly, but their features too became indistinct. He felt warmth trickle down his cheeks, and fumbled for a handkerchief to blot his face. For some reason couldn't lay his hand on one. Clients sometimes stole them, he knew, for souvenirs. He never forgot a hankie, so Valetta must have taken it. Why? A memento? There was no telling, no knowing, what clients did or why. Or what anybody on earth turned their hands to. Look at Valetta, for heaven's sake, who would have killed herself tonight if she hadn't been able to bring herself to hire him, get herself made love to by a complete stranger. And who, strangely, had kissed an embarrassing bruise he had inadvertently made on her arm and purred with pleasure at the sight of it. She had licked his hand, steadily, chin down then up with each stroke of her tongue. He ought to have asked but couldn't, didn't know how to. He lacked the ability of speech. He should have spoken out about Zen. The warmth from his eyes reached his mouth, trickled in. Salt.

The traffic lights changed. He could cross in safety. He cleared his throat to speak.

'I think I might go home,' he told Gabby. 'Good night.'

He walked over among other pedestrians, passed Grellie without a word, and went towards Bradshawgate. On Grellie's signal Gabby mournfully trailed him several paces away. Grellie watched him go. There was no sign of Rack.

HER BLEEP SOUNDED. Before she could even make half-laughing excuses to the dinner table, the mobile phone she carried in her handbag, then her separate pager, joined in cacophony. She rose, made her way to the hall.

Alone in the Rendlesons' hallway she heard Mr Fazackerley's wheezing insistences.

'I will go, of course,' she told the elderly charity auditor. 'Why exactly am I being asked to attend?' And admonished his unhelpful silence, 'It's only that the doctors at the City General will wonder the same thing and want to know.'

'The young man who was injured, Will Ladislaw, was seemingly employed once by our charity,' he said. She got the odd notion that Mr Fazackerley was inventing as he went along, but then he was an old man and the hour late.

'An ex-employee?' she cut in. 'Do we have obligations towards him now?'

'I'm not sure, Dr Burtonall. I'm trying to establish that. I'll ring you while you're on your way. I stress that it is essential you go immediately.'

'I'll leave now, Mr Fazackerley. Thank you for letting me know.'

She explained to the mixed company and found her

things. Jim Rendleson and Bernice who were hosting the supper party accompanied her to the door. Clifford tried to catch her eye as she left but she refused to exchange glances. Jim came with her to the old Humber.

'Sorry about this,' she said as the engine kicked to life. 'Lucky I finished the dessert!'

In a way she was glad to leave. Kindly meant, but reconciliation was out of the question. Clifford was now merely inert. He and some political smarmie called Pennington, thick as thieves and full of boring golf anecdotes, had been seated nearby. She would have declined the Rendlesons' invitation had she known Clifford was invited.

Out of their drive and on the road, her forced smile died. How very odd. Natural, though, wasn't it? And her terms of contract, true, specified that she would attend 'special cases' if particularly asked by the trustees. Will Ladislaw sounded a familiar name, yet she was certain she'd never had a patient so called. 'Some physical injury' was the old lawyer's description before, 'Please hurry.'

On the way her bleep went four times, her pager twice, and her mobile. She picked up as she arrived in the City General's jigsaw car park. It was her secretary Vannie, overwhelmed with relief that she answered at last. Clare snapped back, said she was already at the hospital, and quickly rang off, telling herself that she had better things to do than give supportive psychotherapy to a worried typist. She hurried inside, waved to the desk pests in the foyer, and trotted to the surgical unit in Intensive Care.

Mercifully she recognized Eric Garden the surgeon. He was standing talking with two registrars new to her. He was in bloodstained greens, slate-blue surgeon's cap on his head, was just ripping off reddened disposable gloves to bin them.

The registrars were in full operating theatre garb down to the boots.

'Dr Burtonall.' He tried to smile, eyeing her evening dress. Only then did she become conscious of her incongruous appearance. 'We've bad news and bad news.'

'Sorry to barge in, Eric. I was at a do and got called. Anything?'

Eric Garden was the consultant trauma surgeon at the City General, a London man, and for a while had been at the Farnworth District where Clare had worked when first coming to the city. She knew him as a fiercely practical man, keen on teaching. His home life had been somewhat chequered. Now he lived alone a mile or so from Clare's house after an ugly divorce that had been the talk of the Medico-Surgical Society.

The surgeon sighed, shook his head. Curtly he introduced her to his registrars and led the way into the special care unit.

'Come and see.'

Two nurses looked up as they entered. They were putting away the monitor connections. Clare was shocked at the speed of it. How long had she taken coming? Not more than ten minutes. Yet here was the body of a young male, hardly twenty-three or -four, about to be bagged and dispatched to the mortuary. Two narrow incisions showed beneath his left costal margin.

'Not a relative, sister,' the surgeon said as the senior nurse looked her consternation at Clare. 'Dr Burtonall's been called in by . . .?'

'Employers,' Clare said, determined to be vague on the subject until she herself knew for sure. 'Knifing, was it?'

'He was BID, wasn't he, Ben?'

The first surgical registrar nodded. 'Died before he was

brought in. We'd not even a trace. They'd tried the usual, ran in whole blood, MRP bugger all use I'm afraid. The crash lot claim they got a pulse, but seems to me they always do.'

Clare inspected the young man's dead form. 'Is he distended, thickened about the abdomen, or is it my imagination?'

'We thought that,' the other registrar said. 'Christ, I'm dying for a fag.' He blinked apologetically at Clare. 'Gave up smoking eighty-one days ago. Times like this I wonder if it was wise. I mean, look at him, poor sod.'

Even in the subdued lighting the figure's pallor showed with unnatural intensity.

'He bled a deal internally, then?'

'That's what we think. Not much evidence of external blood loss. Just look at the dorsum.'

The registrar glanced at the consultant for permission, and rolled the cadaver onto its side with a grunt of effort. Clare leant to see. A slightly everted wound was evident. She straightened and the registrar let the body roll back to the supine position.

'I'll bet the renal artery got severed by one stab of a large-bladed knife. Could even be the aorta. Maybe he started instant haemorrhage retroperitoneally, bled simultaneously into the peritoneum as other blood vessels were cut.'

'Blood everywhere internally,' the junior registrar added. 'I think the anterior perforating arteries were also severed.'

'God knows what damage there is to the gastrointestinal tract,' Eric Garden added.

'Savage sod, though, whoever did it. Desperate stuff.'

'Facing his attacker?' Clare turned her head, looking at the recumbent form, trying to work it out.

'Probably. Maybe some begging lout approached him, attacked him intending to rob.'

'Then not robbing him at all?' Clare put the question. 'Was his money in a hidden wallet?'

'That's another oddity,' the surgical registrar called Ben answered thoughtfully. 'It was just loose folded notes in his jacket pocket. No wallet, no money clip, nothing.'

'Easy for some hooligan to snatch,' the consultant surgeon said. 'Get the point? Maybe deliberate murder and not robbery. We were talking about that as you arrived.'

'That's allowable, though. Think of the stabber's panic if somebody happened by. That's not the real conundrum.'

Clare asked the registrar, 'What do you mean?'

The consultant grunted and took on the reply. 'He's so damned healthy. Fitter than I'll ever be. See?' He flicked the green sheet from the corpse's feet, mechanically removing a Middlesex intravenous needle that the nurses had over-looked and dropping it on their instrument trolley.

'See what?'

'Spotless, is what he is,' Eric Garden said. 'No street drinker he, no workman out on a jaunt. Scrubbed by maidens, laundered for. This chap's never done a hand's slog on the oil rigs, that's for sure. What do you think, Sister Dymond?'

'I think it's tragic.' The senior nurse spoke with asperity. 'He was lovely. Expensive clothes, everything about him cost a mint. It's like he was going to a wedding. I've never seen anyone so clean come into Casualty.'

'Expensive clothes?' The surgeon peered beneath the surgical trolley on which the body still lay. 'Them?'

'We noticed it straight away. His hair's styled, just as if he'd left the hairdresser. All his clothes are designer wear. There's not a speck of dust on him. He was a lovely young man.' She stared accusingly at Clare. 'The police ought to do something, instead of dishing out parking tickets.'

'Dr Burtonall's not police,' Garden said in Clare's defence. 'But you're right.'

'Not robbery, then? Didn't they catch anyone?'

'Not that we've heard,' the second surgical registrar said morosely. 'We've no identification. No address. We don't even have a name.'

They all looked at her expectantly.

'Will Ladislaw,' Clare said lamely. 'His former employees phoned me.'

'Literary,' Ben said.

'How did they hear?' the surgeon asked, curious. 'There were no witnesses. Didn't the crash team say so, Ben?'

'Nobody saw a thing. A paramedic said it was outside some hotel in Victoria Square. They had difficulty because some fire alarm went off. A panic, I suppose.'

'The police?' Clare prompted. Sister Dymond snorted, clashing bowl trolleys angrily.

'They're outside in the office.' The surgeon sighed. 'Ben, I'm knackered. Will you do the coroner bit?'

'Remember that case a bit ago, Eric? Knife cuts all over him, like he'd been involved in some lunatic game of slashing?' the other registrar said suddenly. 'That's where I saw your name, Dr Burtonall. I was trying to remember.'

'Yes. I sent him in,' Clare recalled. 'Lost a lot of blood. How did he get on?'

'Remind me, Matt,' Garden said. 'Was he that tough nut, slashes in an odd distribution, massive blood loss, cuts mostly superficial?'

'That's the one,' Matt said, frowning. 'Opposites, aren't they? This poor bloke out of the blue, the other's cuts seeming sort of planned and geographic.'

'You're not linking the two, are you, Matt?' Ben said in ill humour.

'Not really.' Matt almost started to say more, but glanced at Clare and said nothing.

'You attending the post mortem, Clare?' Eric Garden asked casually. He stretched, yawned. 'Sorry. See you there if you do come.'

'I'd better, perhaps,' Clare said. She told her thanks to the three surgeons. 'I'll pull together what information I can for identification records, address and whatnot.'

She left Intensive Care then, passing the office. She saw two plain clothes policemen waiting. One was Hassall, her old acquaintance. She went into the waiting area and seated herself to start phoning. Better if it had been that carping woman inspector.

The astute registrar called Matt had hit on a troubling connection between two patients. Yes, both were male, fit, young or youthful, both knifed, both from in the city centre. But *the* link was herself. Was it accidental? The first case, perhaps her involvement was simply incidental. Her office was handily right there on the city's main square, after all.

This latter case, though? There had to be some definite reason for Mr Fazackerley's urgent summons. Inevitably she would be asked by the police. It would be vitally important to volunteer information before they came calling. Their question would be blunt: Why had she arrived in evening dress, clipping into Intensive Care at her most glamorous, to check on a young man she'd never even heard of until the instant he was murdered? She badly wanted to know the answer herself.

'Mr Fazackerley, please,' she said as the number answered.

'Speaking. Is that Dr Burtonall?'

'Yes. I'm afraid the news is tragic, Mr Fazackerley.' She glanced quickly round to see that she was not being over-heard. 'Will Ladislaw, I'm afraid, didn't survive. Probable stab wounds to the abdomen causing fatal internal injuries. It will be a coroner case, probable post mortem in the new Forensics suite.'

'Thank you, Dr Burtonall. Where are you ringing from?'

'The City General. Do you have a full name and address for the deceased, please? Only, police are in attendance and will probably want to know how I came to be here.'

'Certainly, Dr Burtonall.' It was a prepared response, she felt. 'Please offer them my number. I shall be here all evening, and will be most willing to give them every assist-ance. My partner is preparing a typescript of Will Ladislaw's details for them this very minute.'

Outside Clare heard the consultant surgeon go through and greet the policeman. She recognized Hassall's voice. He introduced his assistant, Sergeant Cockle. Eric Garden's dour chuckle was audible.

'Do you want to give me the details now, Mr Fazack-erley?' Clare asked. 'I can simply hand them over.'

'No need, Dr Burtonall. It would result in unnecessary duplication and take your valuable time. They will be faxed to the hospital records desk within minutes.'

'They will also need somebody to make formal identifi-cation.'

'I already have an associate on his way to the hospital. A distant cousin.'

It was all so pat. Was Fazackerley equally efficient about all former employees? She was about to ask more, but the old lawyer was called away by his partner to check some information, and rang off with an apology.

Clare hesitated, wondering whether to stay, but finally

thought her anxious presence would be even more difficult to explain, and began the drive home. She thought of the spotless young man bleeding to death in his designer attire, one jacket pocket crammed with loose notes, no means of identification except a name given so imprecisely it was almost hearsay. Still, Mr Fazackerley had been his usual efficient self. It was reassuringly all in hand. She shelved her worry.

It came to her suddenly as she neared the Rendlesons' district. She remembered the junior surgeon's chance remark. 'Literary,' he'd muttered. Will Ladislaw was quite an unusual name even in Lancashire. She pondered it, and realized. At convent school, she'd written a dire essay on *Middlemarch*, got savagely marked down by Sister Cecilia for 'grossest inattention to narrative detail'. The hero? Will Ladislaw. Remembering, Clare felt strangely relieved. What's in a name? And after all, assumed names were common in and out of National Health Service records, and who knows what the young man had been up to?

Her misgivings returned. She was unsure why, but they were strong enough to make her pull off the main road at Gilnow to think. Bonn had once given his name as James Whitmore, after the old film actor, when first she'd met him at an accident. Two out of two? In the lay-by she rang the Pleases Agency and asked to make an immediate booking with Bonn, giving her code, Clare Three-Nine-Five. The woman said Bonn was temporarily unavailable. Clare drew breath, and asked for any other. She received the same stilted reply. No availability.

'Thank you,' she said. 'I'll ring tomorrow.'

For a time she remained in her car. *All* the goers 'temporarily not available'? However little she knew about the Agency, this was inconceivable. Could the murdered Will

Ladislaw be a goer, like Bonn? Slowly she turned the ignition and drove on. It was urgent to find Bonn. There were three places: the Café Phryne, the mogga dancing at the Palais Rocco, or via the Agency. Maybe now there'd be a fourth, the funeral of Will Ladislaw?

ARTINA WAS STRUCK by how few of
them there now seemed, when one
was missing. Except Zen didn't
merely count one. Units were different, sums in a total.
People were not numbers. Bonn appeared isolated, miles
from her yet he was seated close.

The Barn Owl was cold, though Miss Charity had placed
several fan heaters about the vast mill room. Posser was
wheeled in, covered in blankets up to his chin. Trish had
come with him, patted him comfortable then left when Miss
Charity gestured. They sat in silence.

'Good morning,' Martina said as Fret Dougal plonked
himself down, the last arrival. 'I have sent for Rack.'

'Isn't that too early?' Suntan asked. He looked ill. 'What I
mean is, he's got things to do, right?'

'They're done,' Martina said flatly. 'He's got an army.'

'Is there a result?' TonTon said outright. 'If so, what're
we doing here? Sorry, Posser.'

The old man raised his head tiredly. 'It's awreet, son.
We're all of a do. I'd rather you speak out.'

'To answer a question. What's to be done?' She gave them
a moment to take hold of the responsibility. 'Rack will pin
the mark probably no later than noon today. He's got it

down to a handful. My question is this: Do we leave it to the constabulary?'

For the first time Bonn looked at her. Martina said harshly as if in reply to an unspoken comment, 'The constabulary will take their time, due process, interview everybody, make a meal.'

'Then the bastard will get away,' Suntan said. 'Sorry, Martina. The law might not work is what I mean. He could get off on some technicality.'

'Off what?' She gave them her serious eyes in turn so they got her point. 'Off murder? Life in gaol, until such time as his friends might collect enough opinions to get a judicial review? Then he goes home, scotage free, with Exchequer gelt to compensate for "loss of liberty". We see it often enough.'

Bonn stirred, remained silent.

'Even if,' Martina went on, cold, 'he serves a full time, it will be exactly seven years, GC Rem being what it is.'

Good Conduct Remission was always in public debate, whether it should continue to be a feature of prison sentencing. Bonn cleared his throat. The other keys looked at him, but Martina angrily shook her head and continued, 'My question is, should he be sentenced by law, or by us.'

That set them shuffling, taking time to settle. Posser wheezed noisily, beckoned to Suntan to pass him some gadget from the bag hanging from his bath chair. He clicked it, inhaled noisily. They let him come to.

'You want us to vote, Martina, or what?'

'Your opinions, TonTon.' She let them stew a moment. 'It's my responsibility. I'll take it. Were the killer on syndicate strength, Rack would have cleared it away by now. As things stand, I feel obliged to ask you first. You have the right.'

Bonn spoke quietly. 'The right?'

'To be heard.'

'That is a vote, Martina.'

'Call it what you like. Stay silent if you wish.' She fixed him. 'You say little often enough, Bonn. Well?'

'It's two problems.' Fret Dougal offered, eyebrows raised inviting Bonn to go ahead of him, but Bonn declined. 'One: what we think is right. Second: what the rest think's right.'

'Explain, Fret?'

'Look at it like this.' Fret Dougal tried to work it out for clarity, gave up after a few moments and simply spoke on with a shrug. 'Suppose we think it ought to be left to the plod, and say so among ourselves, okay? But the street's boiling, Martina. We can go for Law, it'll make no difference to what happens. The street won't wear it.'

They hesitated as Posser worked up breath. 'Out with it, son,' he managed. 'No good holding back.'

'It's this. Whoever murdered Zen has had it anyway.' Fret looked round the group. 'Well, hasn't he? Can any of us see Rack taking this quietly? He'd not last ten minutes on the street if he let this diss go. So the two problems aren't. They're only one. Whoever the feller is, he's topped.'

'I can put it on hold,' Martina said.

Suntan cut in, 'For how long? I agree with Fret. We might let it slide. The street wouldn't. We might even give it to the plod. The street wouldn't. They'd read bits of the trial, go and see it. But all the time they'd be doing what we're supposedly doing here now, putting him on trial and deciding sentence.'

'It's death or not,' Bonn said, 'the way you talk of it.'

'Well, Bonn?' Martina asked, a palm out to keep the others silent. 'Questions are sometimes useful, but no good now. I want answers.'

'Very well, Martina,' he said quietly. 'We have no right to decide a man's death.'

'We have, Bonn, wack,' Fret Dougal said, his manner keeping animosity out of his comment. 'Zen's one of us.'

'Also,' Suntan said to Bonn, speaking directly across Martina and Posser, 'the pig shouldn't go round killing people, should he? Seems to me there's no mystery.'

'There is one,' Bonn said. 'Was it anything to do with the death threats or not?'

They considered this. 'It must have been,' Suntan said.

'A woman threatened repeatedly. Then a man—'

'The woman was warning Zen what her man told her he'd do. That too is possible.'

'That's the elementary explanation,' Martina interrupted abruptly. 'It's either truth or so near the truth we needn't be bothered.'

'Bonn, son?' Posser prompted. Bonn said nothing.

'All done?' Martina said. She dialled on her mobile phone. 'Rack?' She listened a minute, nodded as if to herself. 'All done. The snooker hall in five minutes.'

Bonn thought, that's what auctioneers say when they think bidding's come to an end, all done. Martina didn't look his way as she spoke.

'Rack has a clear identity. He's just told me. I'll find a means of speedy resolution of the problem.'

'The identity of the perpetrator is not to be divulged, I take it, Martina,' Bonn said slowly.

'Your supposition is correct, Bonn,' she answered with mocking pedantry. 'No further dithering? Then thank you for your frank opinions. Business as usual starting tomorrow.'

The keys left, hardly exchanging a word. Martina and Posser remained still a moment. Trish nervously peered

245245245

round the door but Martina angrily gestured her out. Martina touched the tears from her eyes.

'See, Dad? See what he's like? He's such a wimp. It's like he simply wants everything to be clean and holy, instead of—'

'Instead of hell? I know, luv.'

'I want him to take a lead!' she cried angrily, in real distress. 'And what happens? He sits there wanting problems to go away!'

'It's the way he is, luv, that's all. He's trying to adjust to us, to life out here, that's all.'

'Well, the way he is won't do!'

'No, luv. I'm beginning to think you're right.'

'I got Akker, Dobber, Henno and Cad,' Rack told Martina. 'I got plenty others, but them's up front.'

She said nothing, looked steadily into him the way he hated. He felt studied, among specimens in some mythical row of which he was only one instead of a real bloke standing in front of her. He'd been in a police ID line-up several times. It was bad, but nothing as evil as Martina's prolonged blue-eyed gaze. Analytical, he'd have thought, if his mental words ever got that far. Not for the first time he wondered how cold Martina really was. Maybe she was one of these birds who secretly loved carnie? 'Take your bird to see the birds, you'd have your bird by sunset,' was a local saying. Meaning, of course, take your girl to see the cockfights, and the creatures' bloody battle for life would so excite her that you could do anything with her on the way home and she'd love it.

'Think straight, Rack,' Martina said, cold as a frog.

'Sorry.'

That was another thing, he thought, standing there like a spare dick at a wedding. She often ballocked him for nothing. Or even just for thinking ordinary thoughts, like about whether she ever got herself fucked or not. She was weird. Even Bonn, who regretted the state of the whole world and everybody in it, didn't get mad at him for that, which showed that blokes were fair and birds weren't.

'Who did it?'

'Gordon D'Lindsay, Member of Parliament,' he recited, off pat.

Martina considered this. 'Why?'

'Dunno. The threat woman on the phone's one of his campaign workers, Fern Allbright. Coll the slider got the plod's videos and identified her. She gets out of a blue Jaguar. D'Lindsay's wheels. They shag at the First Drop, Drumhead Court, Mandoral Garden Hotel out on the moors—'

'Right.' She stared into the distance, which was fine, no direct looks was okay. 'Are you sure? It sounds unlikely.'

'The mark shags her – sorry – regular. He's got big political support, multo gelt, but he's down in the polls. He's moneyed bad with lenders. His wife doesn't care a tinker's.' Rack looked crestfallen as Martina raised her eyebrows for more. 'I don't know what campaign worker means. It doesn't sound proper, does it? I thought it was somefink army. Ask Cleo?'

'No, leave it. Where is he this minute?'

'You want him topped now?' Rack was doubtful. 'Jesus, Martina. He's talking at the Drill Hall. It'll be full of his supporters, workers and that.'

'I want to see him.'

'Wouldn't do it, Martina,' Rack said, regaining confidence now she'd stopped her fucking staring. Sometimes Martina was worse than Bonn, and that was a fact.

She ignored this. 'Tell Osmund I want the motor immediately. You go separately. Which drill hall?' The north was covered with harrier halls and drill sheds, every night crowded out with amateur athletics and whist drives.

'Halliwell. You go to Bowton along—'

She stared at him. He left immediately, filled with misgivings. This was a fine fucking time for her to go into one, just when he wanted to do things on his own, clean and trouble free. He'd already decided to use Ali as a decoy, cause the plod endless confusion if an immigrant got blamed and Ali sound as a bell. Instead, Martina going along now would bugger up the works. Was nothing straight any more?

Out in the snooker hall, quieter than he'd ever known it, he gave Toothie the bent eye, stay here until you're told. Osmund got the vibe and nodded, get the motor. Askey the diminutive messenger was already hanging about by the street door. Rack told him to go to the the Triple Racer.

'Tell Flash I've a job on, Askey.'

'Right, Rack.'

The snooker went on in virtual silence as Rack waited. Twice he looked round to see if they were all still there. It was well eerie, everybody waiting, the silent polluted city night full of accusations. He felt they were all aimed at him, all asking the same terrible question, why he'd let some burke down Zen like that when he was supposed to be out making Zen safe.

The balls clicked to a background of a few muttered bets, but nobody's heart was in anything. Worse than your team losing the Cup Final. Worse than cancer, this.

Flash came in a roar and a squeal. Rack took the offered crash helmet, strapped it on, climbed on the pillion seat.

'Halliwell,' he said. 'Calm as you like.'

THE MORTUARY AT the City General was better appointed than that at the Farnworth District Hospital. The pathologist, Dr Halesowen, was fortyish, cool, distant. His two PM technicians moved with a detachment approaching stealth.

Clare went alone onto the gallery, introduced herself through the intercom.

'I was asked to visit the patient by the deceased's former employers,' she announced to Dr Halesowen. Speaking directly at a wall of glass disconcerted her, but the pathologist was preoccupied. 'Might I watch?'

'Almost finished, Dr Burtonall,' Halesowen said. 'Massive extravasation of blood from stab wounds with a long straight knife. You saw the direction?' He peered through his varifocals at her. 'Eric Garden mentions you in the notes. You inspected the cadaver?'

'Yes, with his registrars. He was BID.'

'Hopeless. The blade pierced the aorta and the renal artery. Long-bladed, went right through. No signs of struggle. One stab would have been enough. They intended to do it, right enough.'

'They?' She picked him up on the plural.

'Whoever.' He paused, weighed the liver after cutting through the hepatic ligaments to lift the huge organ out. 'One thousand five five nine grams. Harbour suspicions, do we, Dr Burtonall?'

'Not really. Just here because I've been asked.'

'You with the police now? I heard you've gone indie.'

'Not police. I'm part-time for a charity surgery. Is anything unusual?'

'Spotlessly clean is one. The other, well, is almost as odd.' He hesitated, judging his words, shaking his head when one of the technicians asked if he should cut the recording device.

'What is it?'

'Discharge of semen. Spermatozoa in the meatus, easily expressed.'

'Inferring?' she prompted.

'Implying,' he corrected primly, 'that Will Ladislaw here had just had sexual intercourse. Spermatozoa also under his foreskin over his glans penis, suggesting he probably used a condom sheath.'

'Why is that unusual, Dr Halesowen?'

'He left his lady-love in some haste, or at least with a degree of unconcern after sexual congress. Usually a man will take his time, visit the loo, dilly-dally, idle, maybe take a bath. This young shaver didn't.'

'His general condition was good?'

'Excellent, I'd say. We don't often get them in here in anything like as fine a nick.'

'Thank you.'

She watched while he completed the autopsy. She could never attain the degree of detachment the pathologist seemed to show as he took the calvaria off, lifting the skull cap away after running the continuous saw round under the skin incision. Quite the worst part of the whole proceedings was seeing the scalp reflected forward over the handsome pale face of the lad known as Will. Wet hair straggled over his features.

'We'll take the eyes, if nobody minds,' Halesowen said, 'after the usual tests. They'll serve somebody well enough, I should think. Lovely cornea each side. We're always getting razzled by ophthalmologist surgeons for forgetting them. What's his job?'

'I'm afraid I have very little information on that.'

'Thought you said—' One of the technicians murmured something Clare didn't catch. 'Solicitor's clerk, eh? Good prospects, little pay, eh?'

Halesowen paused, both his gloved hands deep inside the cadaver's abdominal cavity, to read a clipboard offered him by a mortuary technician.

'Attire: expensive, designer labels, highest market range,' he read. He nodded the technician away and peered quizzically at her through his spectacles. 'No disposable salary, Dr Burtonall, yet wearing clothes that cost a fortune? Your solicitors pay better than most!'

'I'm not exactly sure what his present job was,' Clare replied lamely.

'Evidently doing something profitable on the side!'

She made no reply to that. She saw the whole PM through, only making her farewells when the pathologist started sewing up the abdominal cavity with the large hagedorn needles, doing the slick double overlapping sutures that took so much strength to accomplish effectively.

Driving to her new clinic, Clare was in a dream state. The motor drifted. Traffic conformed. Nobody swerved. Even the lights served her purpose. She couldn't remember having to stop for a red.

The street was deserted. The building's exterior was floodlit, however, and security cameras tracked every movement. A guard stepped out, nodded to her and stepped back. The protection was shared by three neighbouring enterprises, a small religious foundation on the corner, a peak-hours café, and a garish stationer's shop.

Though she had done nothing clinical, she bathed and changed completely. She tried to book Bonn as a matter of urgency, and failed twice, to her annoyance. She even swapped her shoes, though the muted fawn clashed horribly with the umber skirt with its kick-pleat.

Refreshed yet still deeply troubled, she went to the computer screen and her standard files. It took only a minute to find the PP sheets for the week. The office felt somehow alien tonight, probably the lateness of the hour rather than its newness. A painting she had selected, overruling Vannie's somewhat chocolate-box suggestions, looked woefully corny in the garish light. Emptiness did it, she thought.

'Prospective Patients' booked appointments days before, and were given times more or less as they asked. She steeled herself, went down the past lists examining the names of males. They were mostly examined for 'FFI' – fit and free from infection – before starting some new job. Others attended for insurance purposes, pre-medical PULHEMS examinations in the old doctors' slang. She had carefully gone down the initial letters – Physical status, Upper limbs, Lower limbs, Hearing, Eyes, Mental status, and finally the catch-all Stability. There were various translations of those routine initial letters into medical examination procedures, but the important thing was not to omit a single aspect.

Additional acronyms came from less military medical sources, some of them embarrassingly undergraduate.

She began to go through the lists of her patients.

David Garrick. Twenty-six, IWM for indigenous white male, solicitor's clerk, potential employment. She remembered him, jokey and pleasant. Was the name odd? Hardly, for both forename and surname were common enough. And somebody had to share even a famous actor's name, right?

Next, John Buchan. Insurance agent, twenty-three, IIM for indigenous male of Indian appearance, transfer of employment between offices. She remembered him, too. A week ago, worried about blood tests. Author, the original Buchan, of *The Thirty-Nine Steps* was it? Again, common enough name.

Down the list.

She could put faces to most of the names.

Moxon, Edward, twenty-one. Trainee building society clerk. She knew of no actor, artist, by that name. Was she wrong, then?

But Rupert C. Brooke cancelled that twinge of doubt. IWM, twenty-four, amused at having to come for a medical when he was only a railway engineer. Astonishingly clean engineer, though.

Richard Sheridan, IBM, shopfitter and interior designer, oncerned about how soon the blood tests would come back. What *was* it about blood tests? Such faith! And James Buckingham, IW-IM, late-entry sociology student at the university.

Arthur Doyle – missing out the Conan – she remembered for his impatience, wanting to be out in five minutes; early twenties, gave his occupation as theatre box-office clerk.

Thomas Peacock, music retailer.

Ford Madox, swimming instructor, a massive youth.

Samuel Richardson.

They went on. Jack London, Rudy Kipling, Ed Gibbon, Harry Fielding, all of assorted so-say lightweight occupations in and around the city. She vaguely remembered making some casual remark to Vannie about a particularly glaring coincidence, and forgetting the same instant. Common names, yes, but examined together an obvious façade.

Names of females, then.

They were less obvious pseudonyms. But there was one Mary – how about Moll, the English countryman's traditional diminutive of Mary? – Flanders, said to be an unemployed vagrant. And Charlotte Prunty, whose memorably rude 'put me down as librarian' had irritated Clare; eighteen, chewing gum, garish clothes; wasn't that the original spelling of the Brontë family name?

She laid the lists aside and thought. Well, drifting youth was famous for obfuscation and subterfuge. She'd probably noticed it subliminally, sort of, then put it at the back of her mind. This discrepancy, though, between the young males whom she saw, and the females. Except she had, early on, set aside one particular day for the more obvious vagrant males, the 'mumpers' in city parlance, sleepers under viaducts, who begged and smoked and drank and required delousing. Study the pattern, she'd almost instinctively used the social services for those, not for the literary phoneys.

So, males and females each fell into two subgroups. One subgroup was clearly 'slag-lag' in local jargon, the vagrants, drifters, the lost, all of no fixed abode. These were the ones she'd been so-say hired by the charity to examine and treat, refer for monetary or domicile help, to cure or admit to hospital. They took most of her time, but that was fine. Her commitment, after all.

The other gender subgroups were posher, a cut above. No vagrants here. The males were mostly years younger than herself and, with a woman's defiance, she noted that she at twenty-eight was certainly not old. Among those spotless and manicured patients, mostly expensively dressed beyond their stated means, only one had given his occupation as 'unemployed and unemployable', though smiling as he'd done so. The posher females were less obviously showy, less tarty, and less cocksure than their drifting sisters. Some seemed hard, certainly, and most registered themselves as unemployed. None stated that they had children, though Clare had detected in several the abdominal stretch lines and nipple pigmentation so characteristic after pregnancy to term.

Under the 'PP' list she found one 'Will Ladislaw', due for a first examination in a fortnight.

She laid the PP sheets aside. The one she had looked for right from the start, 'James Whitmore', was missing. That was Bonn, she knew from that first speaking encounter. He'd admitted taking the old film star's name as pretence.

Leave aside the vagrants, the cold and old, her viaduct and doorways clientele, she had accumulated clearly identifiable clusters of patients. The street prostitutes, mostly females, formed one, and with those she could group the three admitted male homosexuals she had examined and treated. Then the other group, mostly males; all were young, fashionable, expensively geared out.

It raised the question of the charity which hired her, which paid so lavishly for this premises, and which gave her such large and unchecked allowances; and which wanted her to lose her distinctive old maroon Humber SuperSnipe and buy instead – their expense – some trendy new saloon car, plus any medical equipment she deemed reasonable.

'Money will not prove a problem, Dr Burtonall, I think you'll find,' was one of Miss Martina's more memorable pronouncements.

So who exactly was Martina?

Clare had to face it. The charity paid for medical services for the goers of Pleases Agency, Inc. Yes, it gave her funds to serve the city's wandering souls, old and young, but probably merely as a mask for the real purpose, the medical super-vision of the Agency's people. She reflected on the death of Will Ladislaw. Finally she got herself together. She judged her appearance in the mirror, did the best she could with her travelling make-up, and drove into the city intending to find Bonn.

The Café Phryne was its usual tranquil self. Clare entered, seated herself at an alcove table, pretended to be somewhat abstracted, ordered tea and toasted crumpets. During the rest, she appraised the decor, superb and understated. In rare previous visits, she had gradually learned that it was a genteel outpost of the Pleases Agency, and therefore a natural place to visit and pass a quiet half-hour. She wondered how many of the women customers in today were Agency clients, and how many were there unknowingly.

The girl Carol, assured and smiling, was on the counter by the door. She gave Clare a casual greeting, attending to her notes there while the café's patrons, all women, talked or read magazines, sipped tea.

Not knowing how the Pleases Agency communicated with its personnel, Clare simply had to wait for assistance. Carol seemed to be the means, though. It certainly wasn't via the waiters, all slim young men with exaggerated mannerisms. Was that too Agency policy, insist on rather camp staff, to reassure ladies all the more?

Today she felt remote. She had been in only two or three times before, and then only when pressed to discover Bonn's whereabouts. Clare tried to speculate on why the place felt momentarily distant, but it was no use. Was it the tragedy of Will Ladislaw? She tried to look interested in the café, glanced casually about.

The motif this week was flower paintings, muted water-colours of Victorian design. There could have been no more than half-a-dozen and the flowers setting them off were dried, seeming thrown into place. Yet it was an exercise in brilliance. She caught Carol's eye. When the girl came by and paused to say a casual hello, Clare asked her outright about Bonn.

'It seems he's very busy lately,' she added lamely when Carol looked blankly back. Clare spoke quietly, making sure her voice would not carry. The nearest other lady was two tables away.

'I'm afraid he must be,' Carol said.

Clare could tell the girl recognized her from her previous visits. It seemed worth a lie.

'He told me to contact him here today,' she invented, smiling. 'I do hope he isn't indisposed or anything?'

'No.' But there was a little indecision in there. Clare's hopes rose. 'You're certain it was today, madam?'

'Absolutely.' Clare sighed, shrugged with as much affability as she could manage. 'I suppose I shall have to come back tomorrow. Unless you could pass on a message?'

'I'm afraid that's out of the question,' Carol said. She didn't quite hesitate before adding, 'Tomorrow will possibly be a better day.'

'I do hope so,' Clare said.

She had her answer. Bonn was out of circulation. He wouldn't be in the Café Phryne, or reachable. She had no idea of his other haunts, since he had never revealed any. Calamity had struck the organization.

Will Ladislaw had been murdered. If Will truly was a goer like Bonn, the Agency would have called off its firms of goers. Tomorrow they would possibly start again. Was something going to happen tonight, restore the norm?

She left the place as quickly as she could without raising eyebrows, and hurried out in the direction of the Palais Rocco. It was within walking distance, a large ornate Edwardian building lying between Waterloo and Market Streets. It was the place where she and Bonn had had that first lesson, the venue for the north's mogga dancing. She found herself almost running.

31

D'LINDSAY MADE A point of posing outside the hospital Casualty and Emergency entrance wearing his Grade Two hospital smile. This was a relatively sombre business, hardly mirth-filled. Tinge of sadness in there, a brave forbearing smile done reluctantly for the cameras while he, noble MP that he was, was clearly anxious to get inside the building and see what sort of balls-ups opposing parties were keen to make of things. He looked about to stride in, but carefully held the pose until all the photographers were done.

He toured the children's wards, then female surgical, then the obstetric unit, before buttering up the toads in Admin last of all. He hated – rightly so – photographers who did their shots as he was leaving, so had Pens Pennington drive round to the mortuary entrance and meet him there, his departure unwitnessed. He settled back in the car seat.

'Horrible,' he groaned. 'I'm weary. Got a tot?'

'Not here, Gordon.' Pens drove with care, checking oncoming traffic at every intersection. 'Don't take the risk.'

'Did you see Burtonall?'

'Yes. He'll try, he says.'

'Try?' D'Lindsay bleated. '*Try?*'

'He's divorced her, Gordon.' The agent tried to let the MP down gently. 'Ordinary divorce, six of one and half-dozen of the other. Mutual agreement.'

'But he can still ask the woman, for Christ's sake!'

'Gordon,' Pennington appeased. 'Clifford and the doctor are going to stay acquaintances. He'll find out.'

'Not too clumsy, eh?' D'Lindsay begged. 'We can't afford the slightest risk.'

The agent hated his boss in this wheedling mode. Like carting a great kid around.

They came to the Moorgate entrance to Victoria Square and halted for the traffic lights.

'It seems to be cartwheeling out of control, Pens,' D'Lindsay said.

'But not freewheeling.' The agent hated his boss in this melancholy mood. The man had everything. Chrissakes, all his filthy jobs done for him, the stupid scrapes he got himself into swept under the carpet. The burke had fucking jam on it.

'Burtonall knows the drill, Gordon. He'll be seeing her soon about division of property, who gets the sideboard and that. He'll slip it into the conversation, what post mortems you been seeing lately, what did the police say. Best leave Burtonall to get on with it.'

'You're right, Pens,' the MP said with such feeling that the agent would have felt quite touched. If a politician were able to feel any sentiment, that is. 'Everything's gone brilliantly since you put paid to that creep Dulsie. Trying to blackmail us for booking tarts for a visitor, scrounging bastard.'

'Quiet,' Pennington said. Technology got everywhere these days, including the interiors of large costly motors. The tankers knew their job, which was to tank Dulsie, accept the money, keep mum and get ready for the next. Done and dusted, if the plod kept out of it. 'I'll keep you informed.'

'Thanks, Pens,' D'Lindsay blubbered. The agent thought in horror, What, is the bloody oaf snivelling? 'I owe you, honest to God.'

Indeed you do, Pens thought, indeed you do.

Clare felt awkward meeting Clifford, quite as if they'd arrived at the restaurant from separate encampments. It was at the River Walk, where once they'd recognized themselves as lovers, as betrothed, then as newly-weds. And now as divorcees, the whole gamut. A restaurant of omens, she thought.

They had a light meal, neither wishing to prolong the encounter, while they spoke of the terrible mundanities of separation. Neither had anything to argue, Clare realized with something like astonishment.

'How often can we continue this dialogue?' she asked him, almost laughing. 'Meeting was your idea, remember!'

'No, my lawyer's.' Clifford pulled a face. 'I'm lost in the whole business. I thought the wedding was a trial, but it's been nothing like this. You don't think differently, do you?'

'Who does?' Clare deliberately kept it light. 'Every marriage is permanent.'

'Except for most!' Clifford laughed, quite at ease. Clare glimpsed for an instant the man she'd married, wondering quickly if he momentarily saw his bride in her and whether he felt any regret. 'Back into your work, I take it?'

'Yes. I like the new post.'

'Did you hear anything about that man who was killed?' Clifford saw her frown and shrugged to make little of his remark. 'Your old acquaintance Mr Hassall came asking at the office. Dulsworthy was one of our dogsbodies.'

'I saw the post mortem. He'd been savagely beaten.'

'Poor bloke. Drugs, I suppose?'

'Violence,' Clare said cryptically. 'Why, they don't know.'

'Thanks. You know what, Clare?' To her surprise he reached across the table and took her hand. 'I honestly believe nobody in the city knows anything about anybody else.'

'That's somewhat harsh, isn't it?' She disengaged her fingers.

He grimaced, admitting he might be wrong.

'Do me a favour? Let me know if you hear anything more about the tragedy. Any little thing. I might be able to help Dulsworthy's relatives. I'm looking into insurance. You never know.' He sipped his chilled water. Once, it would have been gin and tonic even at midday. 'You must have seen the autopsy on that young feller killed at the hotel round the corner from my office.'

'Yes. Poor thing.' She shivered.

'Do they know who did it?' Quickly he explained, 'Our typists were all of a do about it, imagining all sorts.'

'Not that I heard.'

'No leads, then?'

'Ask the police, Clifford. Don't ask me.'

'Sorry.' He smiled disarmingly. 'Remember Dulsworthy. It might benefit his people. Our ... being apart doesn't mean I still can't be interested in your career, does it?'

She made a mild promise and they parted amicably. Now if all their encounters had that gentle affability, she thought as she left through the revolving doors, we might still be together. Then Bonn's face swam from the recesses of her mind and she thought, no. Clifford was only for living. Bonn was for life.

The drill hall was typical of its kind, brick exterior still etched by soot and airborne industrial grime of a century, a weak double door with arty tulips and seaside emblems in stained glass. Three dozen people were inside listening to Gordon D'Lindsay, MP, speaking from the front. No stage. A panel of four union nobs sat with him, arms folded, reflected glory their big moment.

Martina was wheeled in by Margaret and positioned at the back among stacks of wooden chairs and tables. She was dressed in a thick taupe-coloured coat, wore a cloche hat of navy blue, thick woollen gloves. Her hair was concealed. Wire-rimmed spectacles and the absence of any cosmetic aged her. A faded tartan blanket covered her knees and feet. A woman could be a chameleon, given the right circumstances.

'I don't honestly know why we turn out on these cold nights, luv. Do you?'

Martina turned. An elderly lady was knitting in the last row of seats. She cast her voice into a gravelly alto.

'Makes no sense,' she said. 'Yet we still come.'

'Try telling that to my Geoffrey,' the old lady said. 'He's like a mad thing on politics. I keep saying folk are too tired, end of a hard day. Will he listen? He says it's duty.'

'It's cold,' Martina said. 'Is that Mrs Knowles?'

She had seen the blue Jaguar with D'Lindsay's personal number plate parked outside. Fern Allbright was seated to one side of the panel of dignitaries, her features matching Rack's photographs got from his slider Coll. A stout suited man was by her. They were evidently non-speakers.

'Her? No. Yon's Fern Allbright, his campaign worker. Goes everywhere with him. Takes notes, you see, for the political agent Mr Pennington. Can't be here tonight, him.' She snorted. 'Too *busy*. Why an MP needs an agent beats me. It's a waste of our money.' The old lady reached the end of her row, flopped her work over and swapped needles. 'My Geoffrey says it's the remnants of a corrupt fascist system.'

'They should get some heating in this hall.'

'That's quite right, luv. I was only saying—'

Several people looked back down the hall at the conversation, which silenced the old lady and gave Martina the excuse to listen. D'Lindsay was a practised speaker, with all the hallmarks. Catchphrases, slogans disguised as liberalisms, slick elisions when policies edged into the audience's questions. He gained bursts of scattered applause.

The woman Fern Allbright was of more interest to Martina. She was without doubt the woman in three of the videos. The first two had been possibles. The last, though, was conclusive. Coll had somehow managed to synch a grainy security camera's trace with the voice pattern dubbed from the threat phoned in to Miss Faith. Martina had no doubts.

But why threaten Zen? And why kill him? The link between the two acts was missing. Had Zen known D'Lindsay before he'd come to the Agency? The audiotapes of the threats had sounded unconvincing, for the hatred of an incensed woman was somehow missing. Fern Allbright's had been an admin voice doing a job, not a passionate viperish expectoration leading to death.

The MP concluded an answer on the need of state subsidies for local industry and got more applause. Another question was thrown, on the free National Health Service.

D'Lindsay swelled, started his usual rigmarole. 'The problem answers itself, Jacob!' and so on.

Martina studied the man and considered the evidence that would lead to retribution. There was frankly no connection between this MP and Grellie's stringers. Rack and Grellie had hunted, scoured, and found nothing. If D'Lindsay used any of her working girls, he'd been clever beyond belief. None of the girls recognized him. They'd never seen Pennington his political agent, either. Dead end. The only link was this Fern woman.

Rack had caught Una's words verbatim on a pocket tape recorder when he'd interrogated her about the man who'd caught up with Zen and walked with him out of the foyer. D'Lindsay's height, stature, him in fact. The security video too more or less confirmed it. Josh the security man said so. The one thing was some car security man Henno tangled with when removing the console from hotel reception. He'd been adamant that he'd signed out Mr D'Lindsay's blue Jaguar a good hour before Zen's murder. And the MP, certainly it had been him, had been driving. The motor security man, one Fally, was reliable and observant. His word therefore gave the politician an alibi. Rack however said he could have parked it somewhere and simply walked back.

Una was sure it was Zen. Una herself used one of Zen's goers called Boris, a boisterous ex-holiday camp Pink Coat given to tap dancing and humorous pub singing on daft nights off. She'd once wanted to rent Zen for herself, but hadn't the money. Her attempts to negotiate a special rate, on the grounds that she did many of the Grandee's bookings for Zen's and TonTon's goers, had been rejected out of hand on Martina's say so. Una knew Zen by sight like a mother duck, so no mistake there. It was coming together, sort of. Never firmly enough to sway Bonn, of course, but what was?

'Hear, hear!' the audience cried in that odd yap only heard in political assemblies.

Gordon D'Lindsay basked in the approval, warming to a new subject.

'Which brings me to the hustings that will lead inexorably to the election.' A murmur of concern grew, was quietened. 'Ellot Shacklan – one of those old-school-tie mobsters – has vowed that he will conquer this constituency! Can you see Shacklan and his posh missus chatting on *our* football ground? Is it any wonder . . .?'

A small excitement sparked in Martina. Fern Allbright had stopped writing. Her expression subtly changed as she laid her hands on her lap. The woman radiated a sudden gratification at something private, hidden. As D'Lindsay went on to damn Shacklan – who was this Shacklan? – getting roars of laughter when mocking Shacklan's 'high-bred wife Dawn the Disdainful!', Fern Allbright almost dissolved in rapture. The way she looked at D'Lindsay was no casual glance to check a boss's progress. Martina felt a spurt of anger, perhaps even something near jealousy, and gestured to Margaret. Time to leave. She had the answer.

'Going home, dear?' the old lady said in sympathy. 'Don't blame you. It's freezing here. I keep on about the heating, but will they listen?'

The Palais Rocco was hardly at its best when Clare entered. The entire place had no more than a few score people. The spectators' tables were bare and only one downstairs bar was operating. Dancers wore everyday clothes and moved to records spun by a tired DJ on the stage above the half-lit dance floor. Viewers seemed to be taking little notice.

She wisely didn't head for the balcony where she had

previously found Bonn. Instead she walked casually in and
took a vacated table on the ground floor. The dancer Lancelot whom Bonn had seemed to know was practising, this
time with a dark-skinned girl. He had a real dancer's phys-
ique, lissom. But, Clare worried as she seated herself, was
'lissom' only used of females now, or were such divisions
seen as some oblique form of abuse? Anyhow he was slender
and tall, elegant of movement, and he evidently loved
himself. As she looked, he stamped his foot petulantly,
shouting at his partner. She stormed back. Nobody took the
slightest bit of notice. Practice day blues.

It was her chance. She took it, letting her gaze go from
the couples to the balconies opposite. Bonn was there,
speaking to somebody over his shoulder, leaning with one
elbow on the gilded balcony. Her heart felt as if it rolled
over. He must have noticed her, because he always noticed
so much. As his attention returned to the dancing, she saw a
figure move behind him almost in shadow. Bonn sipped at
a cup, laid it aside, and looked directly at her.

For an instant she froze, cursing herself for stupidly not
having a plan, not knowing whether to look away. His gaze
held. She found her hand reaching for her handbag as if she
automatically intended to rise and go to him. Then common
sense returned and she sat back, tearing her eyes away to
watch the dancers. A waitress came. Clare asked for coffee.
The music slowly returned to her consciousness. She tried to
hum along, feeling more foolish than ever, couldn't prevent
herself from looking, and found Bonn still there taking in
the scene.

What now? She badly needed to speak to him. She felt a
momentary anger. If he'd been in the Café Phryne it would
have been easier, for the place was made for such social
exchanges. Here, though, what did you do? Send a waitress

with a written message? Wave and beckon? It always seemed to be up to her to make contact, never him. And she was desperate. God's sake, she needed his help.

In irritation she glared at him just as he solved the problem. He nodded and his hand appeared, patting the balcony rim twice as if in invitation for a child to be seated. The gesture's incongruity almost made her laugh of a sudden. No, she was a professional lady meeting a casual friend in a somnolent dance hall, nothing remotely romantic about the place.

With a pretence of idleness she collected her handbag and casually walked to the staircase. When she emerged at balcony level Bonn was alone. Few spectators were about. One nervous couple were making diagrams of those practising below, evidently getting nowhere from their arguments. Clare walked over and sat alongside Bonn. After all, it was his invitation.

'How do, Clare. Not as many people this time.'

'One less, Bonn.' She felt surprisingly cool now it had come to this. 'Will Ladislaw. The name is from George Eliot's *Middlemarch*, isn't it? Wasn't he its hero?'

Bonn continued to watch the dancers.

'He was my friend,' he said eventually.

'I'm so sorry. I went to the post mortem examination. It was tragic. Is there anything I can do?'

'No, thank you.' A long pause while two girls on the dance floor shouted angry demands at the DJ, who responded tiredly and refused to change the record. She heard some girl scream, 'A fucking samba. Got nothing else but a fucking samba? We're in hell here, Jerry, your poxy records!'

Then Bonn said, 'Thank you, Clare.'

'If there is . . .' She felt a wash of sympathy. Was

heartbreak always so obvious? She knew the answer, no, it wasn't. 'Can I know his name? I'll be careful.'

He thought a while. The screaming girls below finally prevailed and Merry Jerry Doakes swapped the record for a cha-cha, causing a desultory riot for a moment. It quickly settled as the dancers opted for dull routine.

'He wouldn't have minded, not now. Between us only.'

'Yes, Bonn.' She ached for him. He hadn't looked once at her.

He spoke at last. 'Zen. We called him Zen.'

'Thank you, darling.'

There. She was astonished at herself. Just listen to me, she thought, calling my hired man that, straight out and in public. Lovers in the afternoon. Lovers, perhaps, of a different afternoon? She felt a strange exhilarating pride that was even worse than astonishing. It was reckless.

She gazed at him, thinking of herself with utter amazement. Am I committing myself? Is this what it feels like? I never had this sensation with Clifford, and I went as far as marrying him. It was gliding down some unexpected ski slope, of a sudden abandoning safe hold and simply letting go. She knew that she had just cast all plans away, without actually knowing what those plans were.

'It is full of risk, Clare,' he said, as if he read her.

'I know. I don't care.'

Now he did turn, so swiftly that she almost leant back, startled. His eyes seemed afire. Her breath caught.

'Now, that may be true. In an hour, it might have cooled to a pleasant memory. Tonight, you could recollect this as a teasingly thrilling chat. Tomorrow, as even less than that.'

'You disbelieve me, darling.' She felt in combat against his scepticism, but didn't care or mind. She thought, if this is what it takes. 'I don't understand why or what, Bonn. I only know that I must commit myself.' She strove to find some analogy, quickly gave up. 'I've never done this before except in, what, physiological ways. Sex, agreeing to go out with somebody, exams, joining the hurly-burly.'

'Marriage.' His attention went back to the dancers.

'That was social. This is more.'

'I have always assumed that marriage was, is, the ultimate in union.'

Her exasperation flared and took hold. She held her next remark in to get it straight. God, the way she felt this instant she would kill for him, leave everything. It was like being drugged. His sadness was a tangible enemy. Whoever'd caused that much sorrow should *hang*.

'So had I. I was wrong. Do you want my help, Bonn?'

His nod was at her use of his name. 'No endearments in public, please. Perhaps. I myself feel lost, Clare, at Zen's death.'

Her heart ached. She ought not to have come, should have left him alone in his grief that was more than grief. Except gladness was creeping in, warming her. He accepted her presence, when he wouldn't have welcomed any other woman, would he? She was sure of it.

'You've only to ask. I'll do it.'

Then he exhaled, a protracted sigh. 'Learning is useless, isn't it? What other folk do has no meaning. The selfsame dilemma, thousands of millions of answers all at variance.'

'Tell me the dilemma. Let it be mine. I shall solve it for you, and take the consequences.'

'The only question is, would you kill.'

His look seemed to admit him to her mind, quite as if he stepped inside, noting convictions, seeing where her dreams were lodged. She didn't recoil. It became an instantaneous duty to render herself open to his enquiry.

'Yes,' she said, thinking, *Is this me?* 'For you. I'd save you the task, go where you couldn't.'

Only then did she qualify it to herself, explaining: If he'd decided such an act was necessary, it would be wrong to expect him to carry it out, for he was Bonn. Therefore it must fall on somebody else. But killers were often discovered. Who better to kill and get away with it than a doctor? Oaths aside, personal values aside, status and social conscience and all other duties aside. As humankind had evolved, the man became the explorer, the finder and bringer, sure. That was the way of things. But the woman was ultimate protectress, the true guardian, and thereby the saviour.

Some acts must fall to her.

How come, she wondered in a daze, she'd never seen this before? Now it was in her mind, with such stark clarity, she was almost incapable of speech.

'They say they have the mark, Clare.'

It was said in warning. 'Mark?'

'The mark is the one who did it.'

'Are they sure?' And who were 'they'?

Her throat was dry, her hands cold, her face hot. Yet she was now so calm.

'They want to impose a final sanction.'

No question what that would be. Another squabble broke out among the dancers. The DJ began a laboured explanation, his microphone crackling and missing.

'Listen, everybode! I've to get through sixteen rhythms a fucking half-hour. It's sodding mogga dancing rules. Jesus Christ Al*mighty*, why the fuck you agree then don't?' etc, etc.

'If you decide to go ahead, darling, come to me.'

She threw aside hesitancy, doubts, the warnings rising within. She felt a simple anger at the killer, the one who had laid such a burden on Bonn like this. The murderer had brought this on himself. Murderers did.

'No endearments in a public place, please.'

'Sorry.' Manners, now, in this mad context?

Sister Immaculata at the convent school had failed. What on earth had the prim tight-lipped nun actually taught, for heaven's sake, in those years of instruction? Certainly nothing of any use. Mind you, what a lunatic classroom session it would have been: *Pay attention, girls. When plotting the murder of an individual with your cicisbeo, that is to say the hired male you use for sordidly sinful fornication outside of the bonds of Holy Matrimony, do remember to observe all social proprieties throughout. Let's try that. Clare, please, would you go through it . . . ?*

The couples on the dance floor were booing and shouting. Meanwhile, Dr Clare Burtonall discussed the abrogation of all morality. Meanwhile, too, a stoutish middle-aged cleaning lady started vacuuming further along, flicking her trailing flex with expertise.

'Will they tell you to do it?' she asked, scared.

'It's regarded as obligatory on the street, but no.' He had difficulty going on. 'We are protected from that kind of thing.'

She knew that he meant he alone was cocooned. Everyone else would be expected to get on with it, execute Zen's killer. She quelled an insane spark of pride.

'Whatever your part is, I'll take on.'

Take on? She was talking like a navvy. 'I asked to book you urgently,' she said. It felt incongruous, this need to be somewhere she could use endearments, be even blunter. 'They refused.'

'I do apologize. The Agency has closed appointments for the whilst. Resumption is tomorrow.'

'Can I ask what's to be done?'

'I am afraid,' he said. She waited for him to go on, but he stayed silent. Did he mean physical fear, or of what was happening to his beliefs? Either way, she was with him. How strange to feel such a sense of peace.

'Don't be, darling.' She spoke the endearment recklessly, planting her flag. 'You aren't alone any more. Please remember that.'

The absurd desire to embrace him was simply a maddening nuisance in this shoddy dance hall. Her cheeks coloured at the thought of nearby strangers seeing such a display of fondness. *When in public, girls, it is quite improper to reveal by manner or speech anything that might be interpreted as transgressing decorum . . .*

'I do appreciate your stopping by,' Bonn said formally. He stood. Clare saw the stocky dark-haired youth appear from the staircase.

'Goodnight.' She too rose and stood there awkwardly, not wanting to leave him like this. 'May I see you tomorrow?' Having to ask was the insult, after what she'd said and admitted, but now she was far beyond anger or mere rage.

'Thank you,' he said. 'I shall look forward to it.'

Hard to spin on her heel and walk down the balcony as if nothing had happened. She knew she could face the clinics, emergencies, even Clifford or Hassall, any day of the week now. Was this how divorce worked? Not really. She had refereed too many of those sordid fights, the squabbling and actual fisticuffs when patients leapt at each other in her surgery, battling for money, possessions, children, the 'financial settlement'. No, she had long since passed that stage. She'd shot the stormy reef. Now she was tranquil in the lagoon.

'Always arguing,' the cleaning woman said as Clare stepped over the flex with an apologetic smile.

'I beg your—?'

'Them down there, luv.' She nodded at the dancers. 'When I were a little lass, you didn't dare open your mouth. Just hark at them girls. Make a guardsman blush with their language, they would. It's terrible, manners these days all gone to the dogs.'

'Terrible,' Clare agreed, and went past.

'AKKER, HENNO, DOBBER AND CAD.' Martina thought it through. She had to tell Posser. 'It should do.'

'The keys and goers, luv?' Posser smiled to himself. He heard one of the house women calling for the laundry list downstairs into the basement door from the yard. 'They've got to have alibis.'

'That's seen to. Football matches, greyhound racing, various assemblies.'

'The girls? They'll be all of a do.'

'Dobber's arranging a crash, two buses in Victoria Square.' She capped his sudden concern with impatience. 'There's more security videos in the city since Zen than the parson preached about, Dad. They'll all be on camera. Don't worry. We'll have alibis for everybody from front to back door.'

'All?'

'Every single one. They know they're doing it for Zen. Vengeful, they keep each other in order. They're like that.'

'Ammies?'

Already she'd let him get away with an extra tot of whisky in preparation, but she wasn't having this.

'You just stop that, Dad. I'm not going to have the

amateur prostitutes cleared out of Victoria Square. It's not a stage set, like in some silly pantomime. The city's got to look ordinary.'

He blew out his cheeks, decision brewing.

'Who'll do it?'

'They all put in to be picked. Suddenly everybody wants a stick of dynamite. Like they've all gone mad. I told Rack to decide. I don't really want Rack on cruel, Dad. You know what he's like. He'd have them in an oil vat.'

'You're right, chuckie. Keep Rack. Me, I'd set Akker alone. Who's this Cad?'

'Wigan, reads a lot, helps in some church, resigned that darts club over bad umpiring.'

'Daughter in the Salvosh? I remember. Him and Akker, then?'

'Henno's desperate.'

'Then he's out, luv. It's the road to rusty ruin, that.'

'He feels responsible, Dad.'

'No.'

Posser's wind was going, Martina saw. Dr Winnwick's routine visit was due in two hours, and he'd blame her. She got up.

'I'll be here with you. Get somebody in, Dad. Drinks after supper, that kind of thing, but nothing to do with the charity. I'll see Bonn's here.' To Posser's sudden smiling glance, she said sharply, 'They can think what they like. And so can you!'

'You sure the mark did it?'

'The security cameras, Dad.' They'd been over this. 'It looks like D'Lindsay, that MP. He was registered in the hotel. Una, Josh, that Fally, the others all say so.'

'Do they know him enough to be positive, luv?'

'They say yes, Rack says. Coll the slider says so, and Rack

says Coll's never been wrong. The only blip's that security car man, who saw D'Lindsay leave some time before. He must have come back. There are three side entrances to the hotel.'

The rest of Martina's time was spent making sure that the new session girls were in and knew the rules. Grellie did the talk-ins, but to Martina's annoyance unnecessarily took her time with each one. As soon as the last girl was done with, she said so to Grellie.

'Seshies need longer, Martina.' Grellie's tone implied that she did the work while others like Martina only laid down rules. That was Grellie's position, and she held firm. 'They leave here, go home, come back with a new notion every single time. It doesn't do.'

'So why keep on?'

Martina had had to go into Number Fifteen, and then had had to limp up a flight to find the right room. She was furious, ready for war. Who knew what Dad was swigging while she was out? The two Bowton women who looked after Posser and organized things were good, but in awe of Posser. They'd pour him boot polish if he ordered it. They'd have to learn.

Grellie was up to the argument today. Martina's outside moods were nothing to do with her. In any case Grellie was long overdue, ought to've been out on her street beat by now.

'I want them to know how far they *can't* go, Martina. Talking's no good. I tell each a different tale. They tell each other and get warned. They ask the full-time working girls if the stories are true.'

'And are they?'

Grellie met Martina's eyes. 'Some. They must still do as they're told.'

'I can't see why you must dawdle like you do. Part-timers are part-timers, in and out for a session and that's it.'

'That last girl, Martina.' Grellie deliberately seated herself on a low couch. Even with her light weight the cushions rose up on each side of her form like pudgy wings. 'Look at her. Teaches in Chequerbent by day. Husband, two children. Has always wanted to be a working girl. Very like a young Trish, I suppose.'

'So? A teacher should have enough intelligence to understand a few rules.'

'They don't see it like that.' Grellie remained patient. This argument wasn't really about session girls. 'They come with a handful of different questions. Debbie wanted to know what if her youngest fell ill, had to be taken to the doctor's that night.' Grellie shrugged. 'I'd already given her the rule – phone in soonest and predict the next three nights in order. Yet still she puts the question, what if my kiddie. See? It's like they want to hear the same rule spelt out to their own case. It's not stupidity. It's they're scared, thinking they'll get blamed.'

She smiled easily, wanting normality back, and added, 'It's no big deal, Martina. A minute now's a stitch in time. All three are willing horses.'

'With risks?'

'Hardly any that I can see. Trish liked them all. She was at the picking.'

'Was that wise?'

'I think so, Martina. And you said right from the start Trish was to come in.'

'So I did. Let me know how the seshers get on, please.'

'Okay.'

Martina felt suddenly tired. Maybe things were getting too much. Grellie's unrelenting appraisal sometimes wore her down. It was so combative. And now she would have to descend the stairs in front of the working girls waiting in their lounge. When Martina went past, they didn't all keep their eyes on the telly, she knew. They'd talk about her lameness. Bitches.

'There's truth night coming, Grellie. Rack will tell you. The signal's Dobber doing something with a couple of buses in Victoria Square. You can draw honchos from the snooker hall, but don't use Toothie. He's done too much lately. I want him playing some Round Robin eliminator for prize money, that kind of thing.'

'Good idea.' Considering it was Grellie, that was a real concession. 'Witnesses everywhere.'

'What cover'll you have for here?'

'It's their card night, Martina,' Grellie said, unsmiling. 'They'll be at the doctor's.'

'As long as it's not visiting Lady Lever's gallery in Port Sunlight taking notes on some Tiepolo.'

Grellie pretended to hear no sarcasm, just showed amusement like life is this merry jest, and belled Connie, who came instantly. She looked excited, thrilled at the coming activity.

'Sum the house for Martina, Connie.'

'Trish is doing well,' Connie said quickly, ticking on her fingers. 'It's marvellous! I'd say she's a natural.' She sat on a chair, felt round herself for a cushion and chucked it to another armchair. 'She should've been in work fifteen years gone.'

'Summarize it, I said.'

'Sorry. First night, nothing. The girls were miserable. Second night, three punters, one trying it on for gelt and losing. Third night, all of us got business and we've not looked back since.'

'The money's no problem,' Martina said. 'Forget totals

and expenditure. Tell Trish. Work's guaranteed, unless the sky falls. I want them all to know that.'

'These seshers, though.' Connie grimaced at Grellie, but friendly. 'I think the fewer the better.'

Martina's instantaneous change of expression chilled her. 'If you're thinking democracy, Connie, forget it. The working girls have no say whatsoever. If they think otherwise, aim them out. I won't have opinions from anybody except those I ask. That means only Grellie, and whoever else Grellie says.'

'Yes, yes, I know that, Martina.' Connie paused as one of the girls went past the open door, and smiled cheerfully at her. Her smile instantly faded. 'It's just that three session girls seems a bit much. Proportions, I mean.'

'Grellie?'

'I think Connie's right. A few months established is different. Then it's all hands, isn't it? The girls pulling their weight, they feel justified, doing right by the house.'

'Goers and keys don't think like that,' Martina mused. Immediately she guessed they thought the remark stupid, and coloured slightly.

Grellie sighed heavily, covering Martina's gaffe.

'It's women, see? The goers and keys are men. Like, it's work and work. Women judge work against each other. They're the first to complain if they think some bird's on idle.'

'The goers?'

'Men judge work against the job. They do it, then check they've matched what their boss laid down. That means the keys.'

'Tell me, Grellie. I keep wondering how the stringers would get on if they were divided into strict teams.'

'Not like the goers are in firms, with a key bossing each

lot.' Grellie considered it. 'We keep on about this, don't we? I've got it straight in my head, but I don't know how it would really operate.'

Martina was curious.

'You already call the stringers different colours, don't you?'

Grellie laughed self-consciously, embarrassed. She sat on her hands like a child caught out.

'Only so I can keep the girls clear in my head. Yellow, green, blue, red. It doesn't mean I don't shift them about when the clocks tick.'

This was where Martina felt her abysmal lack of experience. Grellie and the workaday Connie were the best any syndicate could wish for. They'd both encountered nights when the rush was on and punters were practically lining up at the street corners and pubs. In comparison, Martina knew nothing.

'Do you like the idea?'

'Can I think more about it?' Grellie sounded guarded. Martina wondered if she didn't want to discuss the arrangement in front of Connie. 'Some nights are different than others.'

Reassured, Martina knew she'd guessed rightly. Connie was Grellie's problem. Overpromoted, too fast? Yet Grellie was younger than Connie by a year, and just look at the territory she controlled. And the skin – numbers of working girls out on the street – that she had to keep in order.

For the first time, Martina felt a twinge of anxiety. Connie might be too ambitious for her own good, maybe wanting to take over Grellie's position. Or too ambitious for Grellie's liking? Though Martina was not wholly displeased by this rivalry.

'Well, whatever's decided, Grellie,' she concluded more easily, 'it's you that has the say. Thank you for your time.'

On the way down, Martina talked about the catering, hairdressers, laundries, cleaners, until she was out of the door, then escaped into her waiting motor with what expedition she could manage. She decided to have a light meal at the Vallance Carvery – it had a concealed rear entrance in Settle Street – then give the word to Rack to go ahead with the truth night, if all portents were auspicious. She felt the whole city waiting. You could wait too long for a thing. Look at Bonn, for instance.

AKKER LIKED QUIET, truth to tell. And solitude, because he'd a staunch hatred of company. Some folk never stopped yapping, like taking a bag of fucking puppies anywhere. This was the reason he moaned when Rack laid it down. Taking Cad was worse than advertising.

He knew Cad by reputation only, as a quiet refugee. On the way to do Rack's job, Cad had twice started singing gentle hymns that meant nothing to Akker.

'Lead kindly light,' Cad carolled under his breath, 'amid the encircling gloom,' and chuckled to himself. That was when Akker got out his flashlight to find the car keys.

'Would you fucking cut that out?' Akker had to tell him. 'You're getting on my fucking nerves.'

'God's harmony is heard in mighty silence.'

Akker almost chucked the sponge in there and then and went back to ballock Rack. Except he'd got the ask, and anyway you didn't ballock Rack.

'Look.' The rule was, no names when on pike. 'We say nowt unless urgent. Follow?'

'Righto, wack.'

'Then let's off.'

They were dressed as legit electricity repair men, overalls, gadgets, a van. The two genuine electricians were watching TV in some dosser Rack had arranged, getting shagged with all the booze they could blot. Coll the slider would have photographs of them on the nest, taking bribes, God knows what else. They didn't know it yet, but they were in hock for life, would say anything on demand. Rack was brilliant at that sort of fix. Rumour said that Rack'd done his first ask when he'd been fifteen, never went wrong. Except, Akker remembered uneasily, for Zen.

'We're tracing underground cables,' Akker told Cad, surly. 'There's Phillips machines, audios, flexes, awreet?'

'I don't know how to.'

Akker started the van and pulled away, thinking God give me fucking strength.

'We're not *really* tracing underground cables,' he said, weary. 'We're pretending.'

Cad said doubtfully, 'As long as the real pair don't get in trouble for not doing their job.' He met Akker's incredulous stare with defiance. 'Well, that's problems, innit? I'm always very careful, me.'

Akker thought, I don't honestly fucking believe this. Had the cretin never heard of doctored worksheets, phoney time boxes? He'd have a word with Rack after tonight's frigging game was over, straight up he would. Better to let this loony holy roller sing his barmy hymns somewhere else and have done.

He drove to the political meeting. Only once did Cad draw breath, pleased when Akker nearly missed the turning in the dark night, but Akker raised a finger in warning. Cad sulked in silence the rest of the way. Akker hoped it was prayer.

*

'They're always hustings,' Gordon D'Lindsay corrected Fern. 'Electioneering's nothing but. As long as the voters come good. It's all that matters.'

She snuggled into the passenger seat beside him. The Jaguar's interior seemed so vast. Her own car was so small. She gave fervent thanks heavenward. Fiona had been unavoidably detained, and of course had leapt at the chance to default, some unexpected phone call from London. Which meant that Fern had Gordon all to herself.

They drove north from Bowton through the moorland dark, the Preston road showing up as a distant string of orange lights. The MP knew the area fairly well. He was meticulous at avoiding congested streets, for gossip could grow from nothing. The spectacle of a well-known Member of Parliament driving some woman would be tabloid fodder. Cabinet members had been ruined by less.

'You're so marvellous at them, darling.'

'I felt great tonight, Fern.'

'Standing ovation!'

'Let Shacklan pick the bones out of that,' D'Lindsay growled, coming to the moorland junction. Here, he would turn right and make the Blackrod intersection, catch the great motorway. They'd be resting at a friend's house in less than an hour. Pens had fixed it, one of his regular places. It all came from campaign funds, a trick he'd learned from Tory bastards like Ellot Shacklan.

'That's four out of four, applause like that!' Fern was remembering, when Gordon slowed and signalled he was pulling in.

'What it is, Constable?'

A police motorcyclist had cut in front. Another was behind. One approached, pulling off his crash helmet. Gordon wound the window down.

'Sir? Are you the Right Honourable Gordon D'Lindsay, MP?'

'Yes. There's nothing wrong, is there?'

'No, sir. We have an urgent request, sir. The Home Secretary asks you to come to the town hall, Blackburn. It's nine miles, sir.'

'The Home Secretary?' D'Lindsay glanced at Fern. 'I didn't know he was in Blackburn tonight.'

'Two MPs of other parties are there, sir. The Chief Constable sent us specially. We nearly missed you. We have patrolmen looking out on the M6 motorway and the A triple-six. Excuse me a second, sir?'

He spoke energetically into his communicator. D'Lindsay and Fern heard clicks, hisses, indistinguishable talkback. The rider leant in.

'Have you got identification, sir? Only, the lieutenant says you were expected on the M6. Sorry, sir.' He dictated the Jaguar's registration number into his com, and explained to it, 'Thought that would be sufficient, sir.'

'Can't be too careful, Constable. I quite understand.'

The MP surrendered his House of Commons pass and waited as the policeman slowly read out the number code before returning it.

'Fine, sir. Would you please follow me?'

'Certainly.'

They reversed, started back up the moorland road, one policeman ahead, the other following the blue saloon car.

'Their lights aren't flashing,' Fern said.

'Security.' D'Lindsay mused, 'What the hell's old Kinseller doing talking with MPs of other parties?'

She felt a vague misgiving. 'Why didn't they phone the local lobby group? They knew you were there tonight.'

'Edward's up to something. He must be. Other parties means the fucking wets. That's *all* we need!'

He swore. The road had dwindled. It was now nothing more than a cart track between drystone walls, moorland climbing each side into black.

'Parties, plural?' Fern asked. 'Not some national thing?'

'Christ knows. Unless the Prime Minister's for it.'

Fern twisted herself, her seat belt cutting tightly between her breasts. She said excitedly, 'It's the Party, Gordon! They're going to oust the Prime Minister!'

'And letting the other sods know ahead of the move?'

She reached for her handbag. 'Should I phone?'

'Pens should have some news.'

It was then that they were almost sideswiped by an electricity van that loomed at them from the darkness to the right.

Fern screamed as Gordon cursed and wrestled the car to a halt. The police motorcyclist kept going, Fern saw dazedly through the windscreen, but by then Gordon was out and yelling in fury at the two overalled men who clambered out of the van.

'What the hell do you think you're doing?' the MP bawled, shaking with mixed alarm and rage. He looked about for the police. 'I want these men taken in charge and—'

One of the two men shoved him aside so Gordon staggered and almost fell. The electricity men opened the rear door, reached in, took Fern's mobile phone from her and lobbed it into the night. It plopped. Fern saw he wore thick gauntlet gloves.

'That accident was your fault,' she said shakily, looking round for the second police rider. 'It wasn't Mr D'Lindsay's.'

The other electricity worker clubbed D'Lindsay, who

would have fallen but was caught under the arms by his partner. Together they bundled him back in the driving seat.

'What is it?' Fern asked, her voice a crescendo.

They said nothing. One fumbled about her clothes. She screamed, fighting him off. He fisted her head with one savage blow so her head swam. She couldn't focus for a moment. The engine started, the car moving gently. Somebody was pushing it, grunting with effort and giving commands to his mate, left with the wheel, left, more left. The car lights were off.

Were they turning the Jaguar round, so they could get back to the main road? Or were they trying to somehow clear the track so they could drive back down to Dunscar? They'd want to pretend they weren't involved in any accident, she could see that. The man had *hit* her.

'Mr D'Lindsay's a Member of Parliament,' she called out, frightened. She was still dizzy. 'I'm calling the police.'

'That'll do, mate,' she heard one man say. 'Okay?'

'About right.'

The Jaguar rolled, began to bump downhill into the night. Fern screamed, struggled to reach over and switch the engine off. Frantically she tried pulling the handbrake, desperately pushing herself against Gordon's bulk as he slumped over onto her lap. His head felt sticky.

She screamed as a low drystone wall slammed against the driver's side, smashing windows so the glass flew in and cut her face. She screamed again, got the handbrake locked but the car started to slide, slithering left to right and back, lashing itself downhill on muddy bogland, windows cracking and shattering, glass everywhere.

Then it all stopped in one slow impact. The Jaguar buried its radiator in something soft and muddy in a nosedive. She tried to undo her seat belt but couldn't find the clip. It came free after a series of desperate fumbles.

Torchlight shone for an instant. She screeched at the horror of the sight. The motor was in some sort of bog, the mud oozing in through the broken windscreen, coming cold on her knees and feet, onto her lap, covering her Gordon's reclining head.

She shook the door but it wouldn't give. She tried to move but the only way she could escape was through the windscreen and that was already pushing itself under the mud surface. The passenger window was broken and mud was coming in there too.

The light went. Abruptly, she was in total darkness. Gordon, her Gordon, was gagging, retching, unconscious, trying to inhale in the tide of mud. She screamed for help, promises, threats, trying to brush the horrible mud away from his nose and mouth so he could keep breathing but it was no good. She tried freeing him so she could escape that way, possibly pull him free and then call out to the electricity men that they'd made a ghastly mistake and pushed the motor the wrong way, and get them to climb down the moors and help get her and Gordon out, save them both.

The mud swelled, gave a plopping rush, and engulfed her. At the last, she kept trying to keep it away from Gordon's face. Her final thought was one of astonishment: What's this for?

34

THAT NIGHT WAS one of the best Rack could remember, better even than when Mama had got ill when he was seventeen and he'd had the house to himself. Back then he'd drunk himself stupid, had three different girls, two he didn't know.

Winnie tonight was on song, meek, laughing, doing what he hadn't even to ask. Playing some manky record, though, so he smashed that. He had her doggo, her kneeling and growling. He ripped her nape hair, but that was okay because it wasn't his fault. Blokes forgot what was going on. Lasses never did. Odd, that.

He'd once told Bonn his theory. 'Bints shag like answering,' he'd explained. 'Know why? Coz blokes shag like asking them summert. See?'

'Thank you,' was all Rack got. 'I shall try to remember.'

He'd once made Winnie tell him what she was thinking, why she was moving like she did when being fucked. She'd tried, but Rack saw she didn't understand. He'd kept asking, 'Whatcher pushing back fer?' and pulled her hair so her head turned and he could hear what she said. Instead, she was just licking her lips and making noises, 'Ooh, ooh.' Where was the answer in that?

Still, right from coming in, three in the morning after the D'Lindsay Jag repped missing, he'd wanted to celebrate, which was only natural. Martina would be relieved, which meant the known world would be over the fucking moon. The girls would say serve them right. The blokes would say fair's fair. And Rack could relax, Winnie for afters.

This was where Bonn went wrong. He should be doggoing Martina like this routine – well, if her lameness let him, otherwise do it different, but get on with it. Any road led right on the right night. Not having his own bird worried a bloke deep inside his mind. Rack reckoned that was half Bonn's trouble, caused all his sorrow, all that silence stuff. And maybe most of Martina's, because Bonn at least shagged his clients stupid whereas Martina didn't get shagged at all, at least as far as Rack knew.

He spent into Winnie, flailing to a final chug, collapsed.

Winnie said almost immediately, 'Can I tell you now, Rack?'

'Christ Almighty.' He clouted her and they sprawled alongside each other, him gasping, heart thumping, sweating. 'I said shtum, silly bitch.'

'It's urgent, Rack.'

That called for another thump. He was still near dead, like always after sex. Winnie was crying. She'd been desperate to tell him some crap soon as he came in running and stripped off, yowling. He'd had to straighten her with a clip so she got him on fast, and he'd said keep your rabbiting until after. He'd had to tell her three times before she shut up and got to work. Women were un-fucking-believable.

Weeping, Winnie still went for it. Rack, dozing, felt dead twice over, being hauled out of his slump.

'I've got to tell you, Rack,' she blubbered, sniffling. He thought, I don't believe this. I'll kill her. 'Fast Len said come to the car park. I'm sorry, Rack. Honest. I wouldn't wake you after fucking, not for all the—'

'What?' Rack came to, cold. The light was off, only advertising words flashing and blinking all colours in the lace-striped bedroom. 'Fast Len what?'

'Said come straight off, Rack. I'm so sorry, love, only—'

He sat up, head pounding, the world going wrong. 'Tell me.'

'Fast Len come by. Said is Rack here. I said no. He said tell him come to the car park in George Street.'

'He give you a number?'

'Twelve. He said twelve. Come to the car park in George Street because he had some clothes.'

Clothes? *Clothes?* Rack swiftly dressed in silence, Winnie weeping because she thought she was going to get a real pasting this time.

'I tried to tell you the minute you came but you were like a mad thing and clouted me for speaking so I just did—'

Rack turned to face her in the bizarre on-off colours. His eyes were afire, his face chalk white.

'Winnie,' he said in a whisper. 'Shhh.'

She sat, bedclothes at her chin, as he left without a word. She shivered the rest of the night, freezing cold, though she put the heating on max.

Fast Len was still there when Rack jogged up. The night was sky-lit only. Street lights didn't reach as far as the small car park. It was only cinder.

Fast Len was a manifest cripple, crutches that really worked and one and a half legs that didn't. He did a bit of busking to justify his position as trad man for the Greygate corner of the city square. Trad meant getting paid, in kind or gelt, for stray news the syndicate gossips would otherwise miss. He held a parcel.

'Got something, son.' He was older than Rack's missing dad, but far more welcome. Except when bringing bad mother, as now. Mother was news.

'Just tell.'

'Clothes. They're shoes, banked up like clowns wear, make you tall.'

'And?' Rack's heart sank. Jesus, had he told his lads to kill the wrong bloke?

'Wig, loose and floppy, pale hairs sort of.'

'You got them in there?' Rack peered in the gloaming at the brown paper wrapping.

'Overcoat, like what somebody else wears.'

'Knife?'

'Nar, son. I asked. Una said some hotel maid found them on the fifth floor where—'

'Shhh.' Everybody wanted to spell out when it was already too late. What the fuck was the matter with everybody? 'And?'

'Shirt, bow tie, suit. Six-footer. Bloodstained.'

'Were you seen, Len?'

Fast Len spat in disgust. 'Give order, lad. Seen? Me?'

Rack knew when to be gracious and tactful. 'Just thought your gammy legs got noticed, you being a cripple and not like normal.'

'What do I do?'

Despite the calamity of possibly having killed the wrong bloke, including that Fern woman, Zen's murderer away scot free, Rack was moved. This old sweat had stood, eeled, hidden his parcel for hour upon cold hour, until Rack had come. That was loyalty.

'Give it to Osmund. Back window, Shot Pot snooker hall.'

'What if he's not there?'

'Lob it through.'

Unbelievably, the silly old soak started limping off. Rack said, 'Hang on. Be at the Rum Romeo, the casino. Give in an empty envelope to Petra. She'll be by that computer. Just say me.'

'Right, Rack. Hope peace comes, eh? Night, son.'

'Night, Len.'

Rack stood there, thinking how somebody had taken Gordon D'Lindsay's clothes after the MP had driven out of the hotel's underground car park. How that someone must have walked, looking tall in built-up shoes, dressed and done like the politician. And knifed Zen. Thus giving D'Lindsay an alibi, should he need one.

He groaned. There'd been him rutting in little Winnie, her arse sweet as a nut and tits crushed in his hands, her trying to tell him the grim news but getting clouted if she opened her mouth. He'd thought it was Derby Night. Instead, he faced the worst, which was Martina hearing serious evil news. You couldn't get badder than that.

A long breath, and he went to examine the parcel that soon would be falling through the lavatory window of the snooker hall. He'd have enough light there. Ten minutes to examine it for the full story, then the long walk to Bradshawgate and knock on the door of Number Thirteen. He'd phone first, as ever, try to tell her what. All he needed now was for Bonn to hear this.

35

RACK ENTERED. MARTINA was fully dressed, Bonn also. Hadn't they been to bed? He almost blurted the question out. They were seated beside the parlour fireplace, definitely not Darby and Joan. Bonn brought Rack an armchair before the fire embers. One standard lamp gave light.

'Rack.' Martina had not let him say anything over the phone.

'We wus wrong, Martina. I think.'

'*Why* do you *think*?'

Her calm was worse than fury. Rack wondered if he ought to tell her his theory why, except he felt ill. That Winnie had worked him too hard when he should have been thinking. He'd blam the silly cunt, getting him in this state. He could have spewed on Martina's carpet. He wondered if this was what fear felt like.

'We got clothes. Long suit, tall enough for D'Lindsay. Wig. Built-up shoes, shirt, overcoat, bow tie. Bloodstains. No knife.'

'So?'

'From the waste disposal, fifth floor where D'Lindsay wus staying. He scarpered before Zen got topped. We know he left the hotel, got clocked out in that blue Jaguar. Zen come out. The killer come along with him, talking, knifed him, went back in. No wonder he wasn't seen. He come out looking all different after he'd pressed the fire bell.'

'Who is he?'

'My guess?'

Rack shrank from Martina's stare. He could have sworn the embers dulled from her cold. He blamed Bonn. She needed shagging so she could talk rational instead of all this bloody eye business. He wondered why his cheeks felt prickly.

'No. Your proof.'

'Pennington. It couldn't have been that Fern woman, because we got her on the videos several places, the foyer—'

'That's enough.' Martina held the quiet for an age, nearly quarter of an hour. Rack heard the hall clock chime. 'Bonn?' she said at last.

'I trust this is factual, Rack.'

'Cert, Bonn.'

'Then similar questions apply as to D'Lindsay.'

Rack shifted uncomfortably. 'Look, Bonn, Martina. I reckon D'Lindsay's got done. It's not on the news yet,' he said feebly, seeing Bonn's look of infinite sorrow. 'Soon it'll be on that printing the telly does all night.'

He prayed Bonn wouldn't leap to try it.

'Rumour is it were some accident on the moors.' Rack added piously, 'He oughtn't have let that bird of his drive, Fern. She was the one who—'

'That will do.' Martina said it like to a kid, delays between each word. That . . . will . . . *do*. Other circumstances, he'd have told her off. Maybe.

'I've to see Fast Len gets dashed from the Rum Romeo.' Dash was illicit pay, oil for wheels.

'Pennington is the political agent?' Martina remembered

the old lady knitting in the cold drill hall. Mr Pennington, who couldn't be there that night. It could only be him in different clothes, knifing Zen.

'Yih. He oughter've got rid of his stuff. The maid closed the rubbish chutes when she heard the fire alarm. Henno thought of it, got the hotel rubbish collected separate. It wus good work.'

'Dash her too.' Martina swivelled slowly, looking at Rack. 'They were all in on it, then? The woman with the thick ankles, Fern Allbright, D'Lindsay, Pennington?'

Bonn avoided looking Martina's way. How did she know Fern Allbright had podgy legs? She'd never seen her. You couldn't tell such details from a security videotape, or maybe you could.

'Yih.'

'Then you've been lucky. Two out of three.'

'That's what I thought.' Rack swelled. 'See, it's like luck's in the eye of the beholder, Martina. Know why?'

Martina raised a hand. Rack stilled.

'Find Pennington. Know where he is constantly.'

Bonn stirred. The heat of a fire was hard to bear. He failed to comprehend how ladies found such comfort at a fireside. Martina, now, could sit close enough to roast. Enquire of her, when the time was right of course, she would almost certainly deplore the passing of the inglenook. There had been a two-bar gas fire in Bonn's seminary sitting room, never lit until the first mass of Michaelmas, and never again after Easter Sunday.

'Right, Martina.' Rack very nearly hesitated, an alltime first in Bonn's experience. 'Do I set it?'

'Mend it, Rack.'

'It wus done proper, Martina!' Rack shot out, an explosive grumble, seething at the hint of criticism.

'It fell short, Rack. One too few means he's escaped laughing. What would the girls say? The goers? Your standers? Who'd look them in the eye and say it'd been squared?'

'Morning, then?'

'Sooner the better, Rack. Use Akker. The stringers and Grellie'd all like that.'

'If I may,' Bonn said. He moved his legs to one side, sat obliquely. The embers were still hot.

'No pleas, Bonn. Rack's on his way.'

The stander rose, waiting for Bonn to get to the fucking verb. Like some professor finding his way among dusty books, this page, that phrase. It got Rack mad, but what could you do with a key like Bonn? Too much reading must have changed his brain. It happened, but teachers were too thick to see. A few solid pints, getting drunk with the football lads, would do him a power of good, clear paths in his brain, make him talk proper.

'I think this is compounding the crime,' Bonn said after like a century.

'Not our crime. Theirs.'

'We are glorifying their crime.'

'Punishment isn't glory. We've already had this out, Bonn.'

Rack thought, What the fuck's Bonn saying? Topping them for killing your best pal's not bleeding fair? Even if Martina didn't want him to talk any more, he saw he had to step in. Her bird's brain wasn't up to it, and Bonn's mind was a fucking tangle. This needed real brain power and tact, like what he had.

'Bonn, mate,' he said. 'You're off your fucking trolley. Pennington's not getting away with it.'

'Thank you, Rack,' Martina said. 'Go now. No limit on the wadge.'

Rack saw Martina was pleased at how he'd solved the problem. His respect for her soared. She had more brains than he'd thought.

'Don't worry, Bonn,' he said. 'I'll see it's clean. Henno'll love it, being Welsh. Know why?'

'Rack,' Martina said.

Bonn rose, accompanied Rack to the front door in silence, and closed it behind him. He went to Martina's chair and stood before her, wanting to speak but not knowing how.

She looked up, full of sadness.

'It has to be, Bonn,' she said. 'I'm so sorry. Everything falls apart unless it's correctly finished. It's what the city sees as decency.'

He saw then that her eyes were moist, glistening in the glow from the grate. He raised her from her armchair, her hands in his.

'Shall we rest here a while?' he suggested, and conducted her to the couch.

They sat in silence. After a few minutes he went for a blanket, drew it round her shoulders, and brought a footstool from the other sitting room.

'I had an aunt,' he said eventually. 'She used to sit so close to the fire her legs became mottled. I tried it, with the same degree of proximity. My legs smouldered.'

'You must have been very little.'

'No. I was four.'

She sniffed, felt for a handkerchief. He had never mentioned even having a childhood, as if he'd been suddenly born midway through his nineteenth year. She knew it was a difficult step for him, speaking so.

'I'm grateful that you are here, Bonn,' she said. 'I worry for you in all this.'

Instantly she cursed herself. What on earth way was that to speak? She had never been close to him before, physically or mentally, and now says a stilted I'm-grateful.

'Thank you. I am content.'

Now what did that mean? She gave up. She was so tired.

'Please don't warn Pennington, Bonn.' In a whisper, 'You do promise?'

'I do,' he said.

He put his arm round her shoulders and let its weight press on her as if they were familiar with each other's ways. They remained like that, until the sky made the dark blue velvet curtains pale and the fire in the hearth died.

THE NEWSPAPERS WERE filled with the missing MP. Tabloids speculated on whether Mr Gordon D'Lindsay had left for the Continent on the Harwich Ferry or through the Channel Tunnel. He was reported at international airports. Differing TV stations suggested he'd vanished with some woman, a tale hotly denied by his political agent Pennington, who was featured in several dailies and on *News At Dawn*. Terrorists were blamed. The Socialist Party headquarters in Salford had no comment, but a spokesman 'expressed anxiety'. Mrs Fiona D'Lindsay was filmed by TV reclining in her fashionable parlour, saying she was devastated. 'There is some perfectly mundane explanation,' she said as convincingly as possible. 'I confidently expect a phone call any minute to say Gordon has been delayed somewhere...'

Twenty past ten that morning, two lads and a girl on the moors beyond Dunscar saw the rear bumper of a motor shining below the surface of a quag moss. They noticed paint scratches on nearby stones, indentations of tyres. At home they told their father, who phoned the constabulary.

The moorlands soon swarmed with reporters, TV cameras, police. The news hit the evening editions.

*

That same afternoon, Clare was surprised to receive a personal call from some man purporting to be seeking an appointment for a Mr James Whitmore, twenty years of age. 'Routine PEM,' the man said offhandedly. 'Three o'clock all right, Dr Burtonall?' And rang off before she could ask for further details. She entered it for Vannie in the Pre-Employment Medicals record book, with reservations.

When Bonn came – it was he – she greeted him as a stranger, sat him down and asked routine questions of family, siblings, past illnesses, while Vannie preoccupied herself with entering the laboratory deliveries for the evening. Clare felt herself redden when Bonn leant forward, having checked that Vannie was out of earshot and the nurse in the clinic room.

'I wish to ask you to do something.'

'What?' she heard herself whisper, all complicity.

'Get a message to Mr Pennington, the political agent of Mr D'Lindsay. Tonight at seven-thirty he's going to hold a press conference in the Lord Mayor's office, City Hall.'

His expression was composed.

'Why can't you just—?'

He said simply, 'I can ask no one else.'

'You want me to post something?'

'No.' He glanced towards the door. The secretary's hatch remained closed. 'I wish to warn.'

'Can't you tell the police?'

He stood then. 'Thank you, Dr Burtonall. I'll do exactly as you say.'

And left her. As if mesmerized she saw the door close, felt panic arise, wanted to run after him and cry out, What was all that, tell me more about what you want me to do. Vannie tapped and put her head round the door, smiling.

'Who on earth was that, Dr Burtonall?' She fluttered her eyelashes. 'Any chance he wants a dedicated secretary?'

Clare forced a smile. 'He came to the wrong surgery,' she said lightly. 'He shouldn't be our patient at all. Isn't. I'm referring him.'

'If he books in again, let me know.'

'Can you get me the phone number of the City Hall, please, Vannie?' Clare asked smoothly. 'I might have to get down there this evening.' She smiled disarmingly. 'Another chore I don't really want.'

The girls were satisfied by the news, Ava told Trish. She had to explain when Trish asked about what. The older woman frankly disbelieved everything the newly arrived working girl told her.

'The bloke that did Zen,' Ava said, always at her face with more potions than any High Street chemist's. 'He got done.'

'Deliberately?' Trish exclaimed in horror.

'Serve the bleeder right.' Ava claimed to be eastern, but it was only make-up. She made her eyes slanty. 'The girls were going mental out there.'

'Why?'

Trish couldn't see it. And she hadn't time to gossip. She'd never have believed that running a brothel was half this hard, had she ever thought, but didn't dare let on. She'd imagined it was all reclining and being, well, hired. Connie and now Lorna were always around, and she, Trish, was supposed to keep tabs on everything. Martina hadn't yet come by while the place was operating. Trish had nightmares, because what if Martina did come and the catering was to pot and the laundry late like it had been yesterday?

She thought Martina quite sharp but nice. Now, with

even Grellie blanching whenever Martina's name was mentioned, Trish was practically paranoid about the pale beautiful girl with the lovely features and fire-ice eyes and the limp you hadn't to notice.

Seven punters were in, nobody watching the clock because tonight wasn't much of a rush. But there'd been the phone calls. Trish had been landed with them, and hadn't a clue how to answer.

'It's the way the city is, luv.' Ava was still doing esoteric magic with her mirror and cosmetics. The other girls joked about Ava's handbag, what did she keep in it, a parachute, all that. 'Zen got downed, bless him. Somebody has to get topped back, see?'

Trish didn't see. 'No. Who did it?'

'Don't matter. And not our business, is it?'

First it was, now it wasn't?

'Who told you?'

Ava turned her head, pursing her lips and smiling at her image.

'Everybody just knows, luv. Toodle-oo. I'm on go in thirty minutes, that right?'

Trish told her yes, then went to find Connie for advice. A woman had phoned to know if the house did conducted tours of the premises, a group of interested city ladies.

'It's social welfare that we're concerned about,' the caller gushed. 'We're all highly qualified in sociology. It might become a regular event, if it went as well as we hope. You would gain, because we'd be able to reassure those with influence—'

Trish had blustered, said she'd get back to her as soon as possible with an answer. Connie the rising star was one of Grellie's seconders. She heard Trish out, listened to the taped conversation and shook her head.

'Listen, Trish.' She wasn't unkind, just exasperated by the other's rawness. 'This won't be the last. Nutters, queers, idiots, social workers interested in "analysing the general responsiveness" of our girls. It's all gunge.' Connie ticked on her fingers. 'People who contact us are only two sorts. They're either punters and are welcome. Or they're cling-ons, wanting vicarious thrills, and get the elbow.'

'But she said it would benefit—'

Connie closed her eyes until Trish went silent.

'Cling-ons have three excuses to snoop. One, they say they want to help us by writing, visiting, suffering along with us, defending our fucking rights. It's balderdash. It means snooping, all of them nosy for gossip. They seem to have the gift of the gab, until you listen. Then you know it's simply crapology.'

'I see,' Trish said doubtfully.

'You don't,' Connie said rudely, 'so fucking listen when I'm talking. There's two other sorts. One claims to be invest-igating us for the plod, Department of Health, drains, warts, God-knows-what. They're phoney, because all that's taken care of, see? The other comes wanting to be taken on, part-timer like you did.'

'How do we tell who's who?'

Connie laughed suddenly, seeing Trish's stricken face. 'You come and ask, silly cow! Unless you want to walk into Martina's office and ask her instead!'

That made Lorna laugh out loud. She was a taller, rangy girl, Connie's friend, who was always listening, having a rum punch in the coop.

'What do I tell her? She'll ring again.'

Connie smiled, raised her eyebrows to Lorna. 'Get her name and address, Trish. If she won't give it, ring off. If she does, say we'll be in touch.'

'What then?'

Lorna smiled. 'We tell Rack. And the problem vanishes like snow off a duck.'

'Why? What does Rack do?'

'Too many questions spoil the broth.'

Which was as far as Trish got. She thought it over later the same evening, and wondered if Rack was the one who'd solved the street girls' anger about Zen the key goer by carrying out a crime. She watched the late BBC for news, but the police were guardedly taciturn and the media more concerned with politics. Grainy pictures of a Jaguar being winched from the quag were indistinct. It was supposedly an accident, a night drive across a moorland always dangerous.

The phone went. Some hotel receptionist had given some advertising people the number, and could some travelling businessmen obtain personal all-night entertainment? Four, possibly five. Trish marshalled her reply, conscious that Connie could overhear.

'Fine, luv,' Connie told her as the call ended. 'Always think how it'd sound if it was taped.' She smiled at Lorna. 'One thing. You've not really got going yourself, have you?'

'Got going?' Trish felt her cheeks drain. 'You mean . . .?'

'Done your turns. Isn't it time?'

'Me?'

'That's why you come, innit? Get your own jumps in?'

'My own what?' Trish's hands chilled with something like excitement, but she wasn't sure.

'Sessions, luv.' They were both amused at her anxiety. 'Unless you want to be a housekeeper all your life.'

'I hadn't thought to—'

'Tonight, Trish,' Connie said with finality. 'Take on a quick-timer or a nighter, but do one. Okay? Hearing what the girls do for the punters, how they do it, is all very well.

It's like swimming, luv. No good just watching from the sides. You got to do it.'

Lorna laughed. 'No time like the present!' she said. 'Anybody fancy another of these?' She waggled her glass.

Connie took it off her.

'No. And you've had enough. Personal all-night entertainment, you. Don't want you dozing on the job.'

Trish wanted to ask about how to behave, what to do. So far she'd only listened to the girls talking over punters' behaviour, saying how they'd coped with the demands for this or that sex. She felt green.

37

THE PAVEMENT OUTSIDE the City Hall was fairly crowded when Clare arrived. She was able to park her maroon motor in the adjacent street near the law courts without much difficulty, and walked round to enter the front. A constable prevented her.

'No admissions this evening, missus.'

'I have an urgent message for somebody, Constable.'

'You the press?' He refused to admit her.

It threw her somewhat. She smarted, being used to unimpeded access. To her chagrin she saw two newspapermen allowed through. It was then that she saw the security trucks arrive, and decided to be more devious. She went across the road to a bank of public phones with the Hall number. To her relief they answered immediately.

'Please. I have an urgent message for Mr Pennington,' she said. 'He's being interviewed tonight for television in the mayoral offices.'

'Who is calling?'

'Ah, his political party's central offices. Please be quick.'

'Hold on, please.'

Night had fallen. Two police cars drew up, uniformed

officers alighting. Clare thought she saw Hassall walking, head down and hands in his pockets, up the stone steps into the building.

'Pens here. That you, Belle?' He sounded tired, worried.

'No. Mr Pennington?'

Now she'd got through she didn't quite know how to phrase the warning. She was reminded of the evening she'd confessed to Clifford about wanting a divorce.

'I've been asked to pass on an urgent message concerning your safety. Please be careful. It is in your very best interests.' She dithered helplessly, wondering how to end. What on earth did one say? 'Do ask for extra protection,' she concluded lamely, and rang off.

Was that enough, or had Bonn wanted her to do more? If so, what was it? He'd not specified any particular threat, not told her exactly what to say. Thinking back, what *had* he said? That he'd nobody else to ask but her. She smiled at that, warmed by his dependence. And when she'd demurred he'd risen and left the surgery. They were definitely becoming a couple, paired off. That meant – didn't it? – he knew she'd help him without question.

It was only when she reached her motor and started the engine that she realized she'd used her mobile phone. She hadn't touched the public phones at all, though she'd made the call from one of the booths. Security cameras would only show her indistinct dark form making a phone call. Trace how they might, they couldn't link her with the records of the public call box. Cleverer than she supposed. Like all criminals, she thought guiltily, and drove away.

What she wanted was to reach Bonn, see his face light up when she told him how she'd helped. He'd be so pleased. Ridiculous, she chided herself as she started away, and you a grown woman. But smiling, thrilled she'd done right.

The broadcast went predictably well enough, with a few hitches. Pennington spoke second, after a fellow MP from the city's rival electoral ward. Both were pressed by the interviewer to speculate on the reasons for Mr D'Lindsay's detour across a remote moorland road. Short cut, yes, but not well marked and known to be dangerous in adverse weather. Pennington stoutly denied any suggestion of wrong-doing by the campaign worker Fern Allbright and the MP.

It was as he was leaving that Pennington came up to Hassall and told him of the anonymous warning. Hassall wanted details, standing in the ornate foyer where words echoed and shouts of the media made ordinary speech almost impossible.

'A woman, Mr Pennington?'

'No name. I thought she was from the Party's central office at first. She said I was to be careful. "Take extra precautions," she told me.'

'Anything more?'

'I started asking what she meant, who she was, just got the dial tone.'

Hassall got Cockle to arrange for the political agent to have police protection all the way home, and alert the local police in Halifax where he was due to stay that night. That was the end of it. Hassall also made enquiries about possible threats to the campaign agent from any other source, but there was none. Weirdos always fringed politics.

It seemed fair enough to leave it at that.

*

'It were reasonable.'

Rack told Toothie how kind he'd been about the carnie. They talked almost in a kind of code, Beth at the snooker hall serving them and not following.

'Good on you, man,' Toothie said, sarcastic, wishing Rack would sometimes be a bit fairer. After all, Toothie'd been dissed as much as anybody by what'd happened to Zen, and he was left out.

'Don't start,' Rack almost shouted, pointing a finger.

'Rack, maan. Yo' no' bein' lev-vel givin' it to eve'bode but me.' Toothie was from some unknowable island in the Caribbean where they wrote best English to each other but had to do their doh-dee-doh talk or they weren't manly. Rack couldn't understand it. He thought it just showing off. He thought them stupid, for instance they'd never listen to a theory.

'How the fuck?' Rack demanded reasonably. 'You stand out like a lamp in a fucking mine. You dress like a fucking tart.'

Toothie rolled in the aisles at that, slapping his thigh and swigging Beth's ale. Rack had talk in him, was a fact.

'It true Bonn got three goes tonight, Rack?' Toothie wanted another pint, but Rack wagged a warning. City snooker championships were first-leg tonight. Rack had money on Toothie, twelve-to-one. 'Phew-ee. Bonn lucky-yess man alive.'

'I'll be busy,' Rack said. 'So you stay where folk can see you, Toothie. Be with them two goojers from St Helens even when you go for a pee. Nobody can miss them noisy sods.'

'Right, Rack.'

But Toothie felt terrible disappointment. Lately Rack was always sending somebody else. Toothie reckoned he did the cleanest job in the whole black north, no messing. Look how fast he'd done that Belfast carnie, in-out like a fiddler's elbow, no trace. It wasn't fair. Maybe he'd speak to Bonn, get a chance? Ask Bonn to remind Posser he'd got the slickest carnie man on his doorstep, no need to send out like was happening all the fucking time.

Rack patted Toothie's hand. 'Next time, Toothie. Promise. Given the right night.'

'Ta, Rack,' Toothie said, relieved.

'Tonight, just stay in view of everybody.'

Rack drank the ale, called abuse to Beth who came and silently cleared their table with raised eyebrows. Rack looked at his watch, grinning up at her.

'Know why women don't play snooker?' he asked. 'Because they cook. Know why?'

'Ten times you've looked at the time in less'n ten minutes,' she said. 'Waiting for a train?'

Rack laughed and laughed at that with tears in his eyes, because he really was.

The train left the station almost on the hour. In view of the dicey nature of the warning, not repeated, Cockle told Hassall the political agent could be put on the train, local constabulary to meet it and check Pennington was okay as it went the few stations across into Yorkshire. Hassall agreed. He was due to see the SOCO, the Scene of Crime Officer, soon after nine.

Pennington boarded the train. It wasn't crowded, just the usual scattering of late-nighters and families, a few students. It wasn't an Intercity. That meant no special central locking devices on the external doors. Good news for some.

Akker sat in his overalls reading the *Sporting Chronicle*. The entire journey to Halifax wouldn't take long, seven or so stations to stop at and gawk out at the darkness while a few got off, a few got on. He was stained by metal dust, wore impossibly thick bottle lenses to his specs. Jesus, try seeing in them, let alone read a fucking thing. Just imagine, some folk had to use these glasses all their lives. Un-fucking-believable.

The political agent seated himself in the next compartment. Akker made to get up at the first stop, corrected himself by checking the signs on the platform, went and sat near the interconnecting door to Pennington's compartment. He could have seen along its length but for the frigging spectacles. Rack's idea, Carruthers of fucking MI5. Have them all in false beards and staining their skins brown next, Rack would. Akker reckoned Rack was a prat. He never said this.

Two stations came and went. At one, Akker actually saw a uniformed ploddite walk along the train looking in. He didn't board, just nodded when Pennington got up, went to the end window and leaned out to exchange a word. Fair enough. That's how they were doing it. SDA they called it, the plod. Akker almost sniggered. A lady opposite looked at him. He turned his laugh into a cough, thumped his chest. Her expression cleared. They understood silicosis coughs in the north. Serial Destination Appraisal, meaning you check along a journey. It was so the plod could booze theirselves stupid in their sports clubs instead of getting outside and doing a proper job.

Taxpayers ought to hear about it. Akker almost smiled, but didn't on account of the old crone vigilante opposite. The taxpayers'd hear about the flaw in the plod's system soon enough.

He saw Pennington move to the loo about half an hour into the journey. That helped. Akker rose too, idly made his way to the end of the compartment, stood swaying outside the lavatory door. ENGAGED, it said. He opened the side door, pulled it to so the noise wasn't too obvious, and stood there reading his paper. In his gloved palm he held a one-inch iron cylinder, brass knuckledusters inside the shortened leather fingers of the gloves. Made special. He was proud of this foresight.

The loo door clicked, opened. Nobody near, nobody peering. Half the travellers asleep, just one babby keening a bit, getting itself breastfed, lucky little sod, and every woman within reach naturally giving the mother advice because they knew best for the little barn. Could you believe it? That's people for you, everybody's notions better than everyone else's all the bloody time. Crazy.

The political agent stepped out, made to close the door, saw Akker waiting, and helpfully left the door ajar. Akker glanced quickly about, drove his fist low into the man's belly. Swiftly he did it again and hauled Pennington round to the side door. A dozen things flitted through his mind as he shoved the political agent out into the darkness of the track – one click of the door, the window open. Easy, but not yet done.

Akker caught and held the agent's ankle as he fell out into the black roaring night. Too many films made people careless. He honestly believed that. He knelt by the open door, clutching Pennington's ankle so the man swung, swung fast, slow, caught on something so the whole body shuddered once, repeated the prolonged flailing. Akker let go, quickly stood, pulled the door to. No blood, no nothing.

One of the hardest things in the world is to close a train's window when it's travelling. Honest to God, Akker thought in disgust, you'd think engineers'd do something useful for a bloody change. He took so long about it that he had to check twice nobody was coming down the train, moving from compartment to compartment.

It had gone really well. The knack was to hold the body by the ankle so it came against the wheels underneath, got caught, dragged in to join all that stainless-steel motion happening down there. Sort of thing you couldn't teach. He checked himself for spats of blood. None.

He moved to another compartment, sat reading through his baffling specs until the next station. As it slowed to pull in, he went to the rear of the train, alighted and walked into the night. No ticket collector this hour. He went over two fields and found a road. From there he phoned Lav, gave directions, and remained sitting in the drizzling rain by a drystone wall until the idle sod came on his motorbike, picked him up.

They reached an alley off Raglan Road behind the Barn Owl mill in under an hour. Lav, a bronzed Greek biker from the Triple Racer, told Akker his alibi.

'Your straw's Mrs Dolly Horrocks from Westerfram. Don't ring her.'

'I know her. Where were I?'

'You stayed at her home, shagged her while her husband were at a darts. Okay?'

'Aye. I got her address. Tara.'

A straw was a woman who spouted perjury on demand, for a paid alibi. They learned it parrot fashion, easy gelt. Martina's syndicate had a dirty thirty of such trusty house-wives, faces like angels, tongues of lies.

Akker was stiff. He stretched, and went towards the square.

He wasn't sure, but thought he'd grazed his finger, really annoying. After those flaming specs he could hardly see a damned thing. He'd tell Rack he wanted danger money. The things he went through for the sake of the job. Still, a pro was a pro.

38

Cushy, cushti – profitable, easy (*Romany*)

NOT TO PUT too fine a point on it, the man was fat. Trish had steeled herself for the occasion, did what she thought were all the right things. She even remembered to work away, moving her hips and trying to thrust up against him as he thrutched to a finish. Afterwards he lay there breathing heavily while her left leg under him went quite dead. She was worn out.

Half the trouble was, she'd only ever had Harry before this. (Leave aside two sexual goings-on in youth and one fling at night school with a bored, boring, panel beater building some new internal combustion engine, like Ford hadn't already got the hang of it.) She'd really craved sex with them, though she hadn't really known what on earth she was up to with those earlier two sweaty encounters. In the same park, remarkably, though different benches, different months. This time she knew most of it. Same actions, different bed, was that it? Anyhow, she felt triumphant, dead leg and all. She thought, astonished, I've behaved like a whore! Maybe I *am* one! Am I? Should I feel different? Do I now know more than all those others, the upright women of the parish?

The man had wanted her to bestride him, *and she'd done*

it! She'd pretended to come, breathed hard, screeched a little, heaved about on him when he'd spent. Terribly, she'd enjoyed most of it. She'd even felt herself leak, getting wet just like the best of Harry. The problem for her was where did she, Trish, end and her sell, Trish the tart, take over?

'Working girls don't kiss, stupid cow,' she'd overheard Martha telling one of the Brummie girls. So Trish had primly averted her head when the punter made to. 'That's for your bloke, not for punters.'

Flo the Brummie lass had said, 'What about gobbers, then?'

'That's different,' Martha told her, offhand. 'Work is punters.'

It hadn't been a complete explanation. Trish wanted to ask more, but daren't, seeing she was the house chatter. This, her first paid-for sex, was a revelation. The punter had had a hard time keeping his eyes open. He'd wanted to see Trish spreading herself. He'd lain there, huge and tubby, admiring. She hadn't known what to do, whether to stay there feeling stupid, pose somehow, walk about.

'I'm done for,' he'd told her. 'You do most of the work.'

'Right.'

The trick was to sound casual to the point of indolence, to hear the girls. Connie and Lorna had 'talked in', as they called it, the new house girls. Trish made it her business to earwig. She'd practised what they'd told the others in front of her mirror but didn't do it well. Really, Trish fretted, there ought to be one-way mirrors so she could actually see what the girls *did* for the customers. The amazing thing was the matter-of-fact way the new girls worked themselves in. Hardly any of the established lasses called out, 'How d'you get on, then?' when they came back into the cow parlour, the coop, which Trish thought really nothing less than callous.

She made a point of taking a new girl to one side and saying, 'Did it go all right?' The most she ever got was, 'Yih, ta, Trish.' Or, 'Why shouldn't it?' And one sharp, sour Oxford lass Trish really didn't like shot back, 'Think I'm stupid or summink?'

It was a nighter. The question was, how does a working girl leave, after being used and having to lie beside the sleeping bloke until morning? This was another problem. Did it mean that she was simply to stay there until he woke, and offer him another? Or not? Troubled, she lay awake listening to his breathing, straightened the bedclothes so he was covered.

Eventually she heard the house stirring. It was getting on for four o'clock. And, Godsakes, the front door bell already going at this unholy hour! Some commuter nigging the day off work and making an early start? She couldn't simply lie here all the next day as well. Surely there was some rule about this? Maybe she'd missed it.

Nothing for it. She rose, leaving the punter sleeping. Heavens, but he was enormous, sumo fat. The whole bed sank under him, rose at each side. Quickly she dressed in the same clothes as she'd worn before taking him to bed. Shouldn't she have had a change with her? What if he woke, wanted her to be in the bath with him? Was it right to pretend that she'd tried hard to rouse him, maybe claim that she'd had to give up because dawn was getting on? There'd be time to bath and change as soon as she was out of it.

Payment would be downstairs, Lorna on the counter this morning. Trish tidied the punter's clothes, put his trousers in the trouser press. Some punters actually brought a complete change of clothes with them. Honor, twenty-three-year-old from Stourbridge with a stunning figure, had replied when asked, 'No, Trish, no trouble. Except for his bloody razor.

Took an age plugging it in and adjusting it on the mantel. Men are funny buggers.' That was all Trish had learnt so far about parting from a punter.

This punter had something on at ten this morning, Trish had heard him say. He'd wanted fondling, which was all right, then astonished her by the urgency with which he'd demanded her breasts. She'd offered them tentatively, the light still on by his insistence. He'd sucked and slurped, grunting with relish like having a good meal. She'd watched in amazement. Harry had never shown much interest in them, certainly not like this. It was the strangest thing. Was this extraordinary eagerness the punter's hallmark, or were they each different again?

She determined to find out from, who, Connie maybe? Men liked shapes, she knew from magazines and smutty comedians sailing close to the wind after the nine o'clock TV watershed that marked permissiveness. It was only after he seemed satiated with her breasts that he began to reach down. She was still sore, though, everywhere. Of course, she'd been sensible about actual intercourse, made sure of a condom – that was one thing the girls did talk about. He'd not demurred, by then wanted her simply to get a move on. And for all his sloth and weight he'd been frantic for release.

Oddly, this new whoredom actually seemed more personal than with Harry. There had been times at home when she'd gone along with Harry's need though she'd been fed up with it. Other times, she'd been mildly excited. Only once or twice had she shared his frenetic craving for sex. And she didn't always know when the mood would come on her and take over. Was it a fault in, with, of marriage, the acceptance that dulled sexual interest simply because you'd made it, contracted a husband for life? Stranger still, her passive willingness had almost become desire with this anonymous, obese stranger.

As she moved to the door he tried to open his eyes. He said, 'Mhhh?' She went over to the bed and looked down at him.

'Shhh,' she said. 'I'll send breakfast up, shall I?'

She closed the door, walked downstairs on air.

The offices of the one lawyer she'd used since coming to the city were depressingly ancient. Creaking oak, gleaming but musty staircase, worn carpets that ought to have been replaced three generations gone. Even the lampshades looked pre-nouveau, with dulled brass and copper chains for switches. She had wisely decided not to use Martina's charity solicitors. Mr Winstanley was unchanged since her first encounter over two years since, desiccated, waistcoated, almost skeletally thin. His greetings were professionally sorrowful. He would have been as doleful, she was sure, had she come to announce that she'd won the National Lottery. Now, the final settlement assessment from the divorce was in.

'I have given it serious thought, Mr Winstanley,' she countered after he'd given her a homily on loyalty, values, propriety, social stigmata. She was determined not to shock the elderly gentleman. 'I am not running amok. It is simply a change in position.'

'I shall ensure it is "simple", Dr Burtonall,' he sighed. 'I do hope you won't regret this step. The process of separation can be extremely damaging to each spouse.'

'I'm well aware of that, Mr Winstanley. Clifford will keep his house.' They had gone through it. 'I shall make no demands on his future income. He will provide me with a severance amount equal to our joint savings over one year, and that will be it.'

'So frugal, Dr Burtonall?'

'I appreciate your concern, Mr Winstanley. But I've seen possibly as many divorces among my patients as you have among your clients. They have been horrid battles, with appalling scenes involving children, money, greed. Detestable. I'm sufficiently warned. The house has been his home all his life.'

'Despite your medical career, Dr Burtonall, do you not feel at all vulnerable?'

'Not in the slightest. I have an excellent part-time position with a city charity, and my hospital work. I'm guaranteed employment. I have separate savings, not immense but—'

'It is in your interests to make more of a contest,' he huffed, polishing his spectacles, 'even at this late stage.'

'Thank you for your advice, Mr Winstanley,' she said firmly. 'If I am to stay in the city, my way is best.'

'Where will you live?'

'I have a new flat by my medical centre in Charlestown,' she said. 'In two years it will become my freehold. The only problem will be my actual moving. I have many belongings at home – I mean, still at Clifford's house. There's just one more thing.'

'Yes?'

'I don't want the term "pay" in any settlement documents. Nor do I want the term "husband" or "wife" to appear.'

The old lawyer was unfazed. 'Very well. How will you be addressed in future, Dr Burtonall?'

'As that, please.' She felt no loyalty to the name. 'Let convenience serve.'

'As you wish. Now, about the time this will take . . .'

She was conscious of a sense of completion, but none of loss. It was fulfilment, she realized with satisfaction. No heartbreak, only a breaking free. Strangely – she hardly listened to the old man as he went on – it was not liberty but duty to herself that she was embracing. Would Sister Immaculata have accused her of utter selfishness, plus certain sin? Then so be it, she told the faded black-garbed ghost in her mind.

'Now I would like you to sign, Dr Burtonall, if you would . . .'

It took less than an hour, and she walked down the staircase into the rain.

I T WAS LATE. Bonn was already home. Martina was met by Mrs Endacott as she threw off her shoes and found her slippers.

'Your father has had not too bad a day, Martina,' the nurse announced. 'Dr Winnwick will be here first thing tomorrow.'

'Thank you. The instruments?'

'They were delivered. I got the mechanics back to the oxygen piping. They saw to it.'

Martina heaved a sigh and leant back in the armchair. While the other woman was in the room she wouldn't rub her lame limb the way it needed.

'How are you two settling in, Mrs Endacott?'

'Joanne is fine. So far, we've done well.'

'Let me know if anything is needed. About tonight.' And Martina paused. How to say that her father was to be excluded from the evening meal?

'Yes?'

'I have a series of business commitments to discuss with Bonn. It might prove too much for Dad. I'll see him in a minute. I think he ought to have supper in his room.'

Mrs Endacott pursed her lips. 'He won't welcome that,' she said carefully. 'Might I suggest we give it him in the conservatory? He likes being out there. And the television might have a night match.'

Martina didn't like the nurse's familiarity with her father's likes and dislikes, but didn't contradict. She forced a show of agreement.

'Good idea, Mrs Endacott. I'll need to have some ledgers out on the table, so please have Mrs Houchin lay the places at the far end, give me room.'

'Right. Will they be brought in later?'

'With computer disks and a console. Have it set away from the hearth, please. Bonn can't stand heat.'

'Very well.'

Mrs Endacott left, pleased, to bring some tea for the tired girl. Secretly she liked the other lads to come, so full of wit and cocksure ribbing. Joanne would have been pleased too, though they were never allowed to stay long.

Alone, Martina rubbed her calf, so deplorably thin. Once, she had approached one of these cosmetic surgery clinics to see what could be done, but the orthopaedic surgeon had been pessimistic. Nothing remedial, it amounted to, after a week of tests and measurements. Surgery was just not worth it. Minimal and possibly transient gain, for maximum trauma.

The two nurses, Joanne and Mrs Endacott, were both related Bowtonians. They had been told of the situation, the house sandwiched between linked establishments which were houses engaged in somewhat disreputable commercial practices. Almost by accident, Martina had painstakingly explained to the older women, Posser's ownership of this whole side of Bradshawgate had made him and his daughter partners in those commercial enterprises. Thus by a fluke, as it were, they had unexpectedly come into enough funding to provide Posser with home nurses. Wasn't that fortuitous?

'Providential!' Mrs Endacott had exclaimed, while promising herself a private thrill at working respectably between houses of ill fame. She spent a deal of time at her chintz curtains until rebuked by Mrs Houchin, who still retained ultimate housekeeper's power.

Martina went through to see Posser and report on events. He was in the small conservatory. She never knew if he would be sleeping. This time, he was watching blackbirds turning leaves.

'See them, Martina? Still at it! You used to laugh so much when you were a little girl. "They're reading, Daddy!" you used to say. I can see you now!'

He did look rested. Pleased, she bussed him, acknowledging the tea tray Mrs Endacott brought.

'They don't mind the house lights,' she observed.

'Not they! It's others that hate them. Blue tits, even owls.'

She poured for herself, checked Posser's chart, and poured him a cup. No sugar. She had to be firm for him as well as herself.

'Dad?'

'Bonn, is it, luv?' He gave a friendly grimace at her raised eyebrows. 'Close that door.'

She obeyed, sat on the stool beside his chair nursing her tea.

'It's high time, Martina,' Posser said. 'Don't mind my talking like this, luv. It's a different world today than it used to be.'

'High time for what? Don't give me reminiscences, Dad.'

'Look, chuckie.' Posser trod with care, knowing Martina could fly off the handle at the slightest thing. 'When I were young and the mills were all on the go, everybody was in work. Nobody lacked a job. And what jobs! Dirty, hard, hard. Yet we were rough-not-rough, as they would say back then. You know this city alone had forty choirs in it, performing regularly? Bands of every description, societies, debates, all life on the go.'

'And these were all fields when you were a boy?' she chided, smiling.

'Mock away, but it was true. We had tea dances, six to seven o'clock of a late afternoon. Crowded. Ballroom, not just jigging about any old how. Rough as we were, we danced properly, with girls we grew up with.'

'And now?'

'You know what it's like, luv. The world dances at random. Alone, or with anybody who happens to be jigging by. Either gender. And any old dance, too. The whole world's mogga dancing, but wanton.'

'I told them to serve your supper in here, Dad.'

He smiled. She'd always been one thought ahead of him.

'Good girl. I've always liked Bonn.'

'I'm glad. I'm . . .' She hesitated, didn't say anything more until he nudged her with his knee, then finished, 'I'm scared, Dad.'

'It's the same with everybody, luv. One thing, though.' He smiled, his rheumy old eyes watering as he suppressed his mirth, 'Bonn'll be a damned sight more scared than you'll ever be!'

They watched the light fade and the night lamps take over out in the garden, until Mrs Houchin came to say Bonn had just arrived home and would Martina want his tea served in the conservatory.

'No, thank you,' Martina said, suddenly decided. 'Ask him if he'd be down for supper about half-seven, please. He can have his tea wherever.'

'Good idea,' Posser said after the housekeeper had gone. 'Give us a kiss, luv. Go and get ready.' His generation, it was wrong to wish a girl 'good luck' in affairs of the heart. And never congratulations to her. They were correctly reserved to the man.

Bonn came down just as two of Askey's messengers delivered the last of the ledgers. Seven, stacked on a sofa table with a computer nearby.

'They look ominous, Martina.'

She was already there, looking particularly lovely in a close-fitted velvet dress, powder green, with a new pendant necklace Bonn had never seen before. The fire was low, the room darkly lit by only two standard lamps.

'We can take our time,' she said. 'I had your bookings declined for this evening. And Dad won't be in tonight.'

'Out on the razz-dazz!'

She smiled, shy. Bonn concealed his surprise.

'He's very tired, wants to stay in the conservatory. Secretly I think he's bribing the nurses to give him an extra tot. He threatened as much when you proposed the working house arrangement.'

'He bribes me, actually.'

She really smiled then, gaining a near-smile in return from Bonn. His smile warms me, she realized. Does mine soothe him the same? He never gave her a clue of her importance to him. Anything he said could be routine politeness. He'd be a great spy.

'I have to thank you, Bonn. It was all your idea, after all. This is by way of it.'

'Er, thanks.' He considered thanks, frowning as he took the chair she indicated. 'Now I'm lost, Martina. It seems to me the thanks is due from me to you.'

'You thought up this whole arrangement, remember?

The working house. And Trish has proved herself, improving leaps and bounds by the day. The house girls are doing a bomb.'

'I thought you meant—'

He poured her a glass of sherry as she spoke on. 'The benefits to Dad? They're the crux, aren't they?'

'If you say.' Gravely he took her the glass, set it down on the table for her.

'I do. It seems, Bonn, that we ought to make the position more firm.'

Position? he wondered. Whose position? Where? 'Your health, Martina.'

'And yours, Bonn.'

She saw his doubt, and let Mrs Houchin knock and enter with the first course. As if by unspoken agreement both restricted the conversation to generalities. These included deploring the terrible accidents to the city's MP, his campaign worker, and some political agent who'd thrown himself from a train on account of depression. The menu was the meal she had prepared herself the day Bonn had arrived from Mrs Corrigan's digs in Waterloo Street. He wasn't aware of this until Martina shyly pointed it out: mushrooms, tomatoes, black olives, pine nuts and hot bread rolls; then supreme of salmon and vegetables.

They dined with an austerity made agreeable by mutual hesitancy. Martina let the housekeeper clear away, explaining that she needed the space for the ledgers. Mrs Houchin made a great to-do of banking up the fire, prattling how badly the traffic coped now the by-pass had opened. When they were alone, Bonn eyed the stack warily.

'I'm afraid we are really going to go through those, Martina.'

'Of course we're not. Please sit here.'

The couch was drawn up to one side of the hearth. He left his wine glass and moved to comply. She said, 'Firmer, Bonn.'

'Firmer.' Position, he remembered.

'Let me, Bonn.' She took some time starting, then spoke looking into the fire. 'It's not easy to say this. I am inexperienced. I want to know if you . . .' She ran out of impetus. 'Can I begin again?'

He was uncomfortable. If he offered to help he would make a mess of it, tangle her up in his terrifying anxieties. Had he lived a normal life before, or even after, those mute and introspective seminary days, talk would come easier. As it was, he felt gagged, bound even. He felt such sympathy for this exquisite girl with the glittering drop earrings and the perfect features, so composed yet so much at variance.

'Incongruity's hopeless,' she resumed. She looked at the grate, firelight gleamingly outlining her face. 'Is that why we laugh at it? This seems laughable, doesn't it, in a way?'

'I can't see how.' Nor could he. Incongruity implied a world of congruence known and understood. He had never dwelt in such a place, except once, and it had vanished without warning leaving him out on the pavement.

'Me. My syndicate doing what it does is one existence. You, what you do, is another. Nominally I'm in authority. You could be made to do my bidding, always assuming.'

'Assuming.'

He thought over 'assuming', turning it this way and that, getting nowhere. For him to make assumptions in this verbal minefield might be his ruin, provoke her to fury. He had in his time been close to tears. The same feeling was incipiently close now, in view of what he dreaded was coming. Could a man say no to a proposal, for example? To uppers, his regular clients, who wanted to whisk him away on a cruise, a prolonged holiday, or a life of indolence abroad, he'd always been able to plead his way out behind the syndicate's rules, 'defence of superior orders', perhaps. Now, here was Martina, the font of all authority, leading up to exactly that proposition. He felt quite ill.

She spoke levelly into the flamelight, using prepared words.

'You've been here three months or so, Bonn. I want us to be closer. I mean to relate more than we have so far.'

Slowly she turned and looked at him. The firelight gave a glow to her countenance, made a halo of her blonde hair. He thought, one of the girls said curls and wavy hair were out these days, gone for good. Wrong. Dare he tell them?

'There is one difficulty, Bonn. I'm quite inexperienced, as I said. New, so to speak. You're aware of my upbringing, the difficulties Dad and I underwent when I was a little girl. I suppose that partly explains my position.'

'I'm lost, Martina.' He was so worried, not following, scared he would get her meaning wrong. 'You'll have to tell me.'

'I'm your absolute beginner, Bonn.' Her voice was shaking. Reaching to him, she pulled his face close and pressed her mouth on his, her eyes looking anxiously into his. She was trembling, her fingers quivering uncontrollably. Now she had her lips on his she didn't know what else to do, whether to withdraw or stay there and hope he would move, knowing more of the consequences of this kind of action.

She found her lips parting. Her breath seemed to have halted of its own accord. Dizziness made her lean forward. He caught her and they separated, she looking at him, shocked.

'Bonn, I don't know if—'

He said, 'I'm the same, Martina. I don't know either. I never do.'

'What do you mean?' Tears started. 'I'm so—'

He gave his rueful smile, eyes wrinkled as if against smoke.

'Shhh. We can become used to one another. If it takes a little time, it needn't matter if we don't let it.'

He saw the almost imperceptible nod, put his arm round her. It was only when she stirred some minutes later that he moved at last and bent to her. The thought came unbidden: What is this for? Is purpose implied somewhere in this coming together? And if it is . . .

The mental process gave him up and he surrendered. Sagan's reluctance to apply the term '*tristesse*', pure sadness as such, to the sense of ineffable melancholy that came with love, was almost his last thought before oblivion made its sweet onrush and eliminated choice.

'AMICABLE' WAS THE word that kept recurring to Clare as she'd dozed.

During breakfast – cereal, tea, one slice of toast – she thought of possessions. Pictures? She had two only. Wall hangings? None. Special cushions? One. Sheets, nothing too personal, and in any case how personal could bedsheets be? No duvet other than one she had already packed. No major pieces of furniture to speak of. Clothes were a different matter. She'd gone over with four suitcase loads. The two today would be her last from this marital home.

Not that she'd been unhappy in the house because she hadn't. It was the erosion of trust, Clifford's use of her for alibis and his involvement in criminal activities in the city. It was too perilous. All were sufficiently valid reasons for divorce even without taking Bonn into account. As she finished her bath and dressed, she wondered exactly how Clifford's life differed from Bonn's. Well for one thing, she told herself before the mirror, she wasn't married to Bonn. She had been to Clifford. Past tense, and ended now.

Ten minutes to load up the car, take her night emergency bag and notes, a box of reference manuals, and that was it. She had one last look around, locked up. Goodbye house, goodbye Clifford. The end trellis was doomed, never going to be finished as she'd planned.

Churlish to leave only a note, so Clare called in at Clifford's office. It was there that she told him how she had left the place.

'I'll be to and fro, doing it piecemeal,' she said, awkward. 'I'll keep the key a while, if that's all right?'

Clifford's own office was a glazed enclosure set back from a main open-plan area where several secretaries and assistants worked. He was alone, and she sat facing him very like a client.

'Fine,' he said. He could do a smile under duress any time. 'Isn't it now we say no hard feelings and suchlike?'

'No need,' she said feebly, wanting to leave on a note of agreement.

'Likewise, Clare. The parents'll be inviting you up just the same.'

'Please say thanks.' Clare couldn't stand his mother at any price, and his sister Josephine was a trial. 'You have my new number. About the motor.' The old maroon Humber was the one chattel they hadn't discussed. 'I'll use it until I get another, shall I?'

'Keep it, Clare. Hang the expense.'

They both smiled at the quip. She stood, took her handbag, moved to the door.

She said, having prepared the sentence, 'I registered with the General Medical Council as Mrs Burtonall, so I'll retain the name for simplicity's sake. I told the lawyer so.'

'Right. I do think it's best to start as we mean to go on, don't you?'

They parted with a show of amicability. The girls in Clifford's outer office watched her go. The news must have already reached them.

In her motor she felt something of a stranger. In view of the journeys she'd already made to the new place, this would be her last real run between house and flat. At the flat, she had deliberately spread things about to show she had taken possession. Now, the sense of finality overwhelmed her. She sat with the engine running a while, then slowly drove to Charlestown.

The flat would easily be big enough. Two bedrooms, a parlour, kitchen, bathroom, separate loo, and a study big enough to swing a cat. It was abysmally decorated, but she could change that. Her two small pictures would please her, bring a little comfort for the while. One was of Farne Island, where she had once worked.

It was here she would soon invite Bonn for supper, maybe to stay a while. She could book him out, fine. It would go on from there. She looked at the walls of her flat, and felt close to tears but it was only tiredness. And the awful news about that political agent Pennington, who'd died by falling under the train so soon after his MP had also died so tragically. So very soon after she had warned him, in fact, on Bonn's insistence. And the campaign helper, Fern somebody.

There was a television set in the main room. She sat on a hard chair and watched a comedy show. With great presence of mind she restrained herself from phoning the Agency and booking Bonn tonight. It would be too hard, for him and for herself. What Bonn had to do with the political man was beyond her. His warning had failed. Her caution had got through, but that too had been no use. She'd done her best. Surely no moral blame could lie on her, or on Bonn? He must have overheard something among his street acquaintances, tried to save Pennington by getting her to pass on the message. It had been an honest attempt to save life.

Were they simply accidents? They so easily could have

been. Moorland accidents did happen. Train deaths, well, there'd been that public inquiry about hazardous doors, hadn't there? And depression could easily take hold, enough to prompt suicide.

For herself, she and Bonn would start anew tomorrow. From here. She need say nothing about the political agent's accident. And she knew Bonn well enough by now. He would never refer to it.

Their union, so tenuous now, must inevitably become stronger with time. She rejoiced at the thought. It would be a marvellous growth, of passion, friendship, of loving together. He would choose paintings for her, maybe help to decide carpets, the colours. Had he strong views on such things? Discovering him would be brilliant. Then still more wonder to come in finding each other.

Provisions would be a small problem, until she could get to the shops, make a planned foray and stock up. For now, she made do with a tin of tomato soup, bread, a mince pie. She smiled at the image of Bonn, seating himself at her table, looking with his slow half-smile, hesitating as he did, over things she regarded as utterly trivial but which caused him such problems.

Commitment? She was already there. Bonn's certainty about her would come along in due time. Slow, like his smile, but come it would. Was there some rule against goers, key goers like Bonn, getting married? She couldn't see why there had to be. She was still young. Time was on her – on *their* – side.

Whatever happened, Bonn must be with her for ever and ever. That new conviction made it the simplest problem she ever had to face.

*

'See, love,' Henno explained to Rani, 'you and me, we've got a good thing going here.'

He regretted not being allowed to use her when she was beyond caring what the hell went on. She was dosed to the nines. The clag Rack had let her keep was all gone. Her head lolled. Bonny, she was, would have been really superb sober, unstoned, doing a bit of Eton rowing while he rammed in. Still, it was good of Rack to give him this job after the way they'd all let Zen down.

'Henno?' She tried to focus. Her eyes found him after a few seconds.

'Tell me, love, tell me,' he crooned.

'You're the one I've always want...' Her voice petered out. She snored.

She was a serious temptation.

Half the trouble was, Henno liked mouths – his on a girl, hers on him, sixty-nine, a routine he had off to a real art if the girl was any good. But Rack said not to dick her; his rule was no dicking at any price when you were out on a pike. And Rack was like a criminal God, every-bloody-where, as ubiquitous as the God of Henno's boyhood who loured threateningly over Capel Sardis and the posher, more affluent Bethel down Ammanford Road of an Easter. No, Rack said no shagging so it's keep off the bint until the carnie's done. Agony was not being allowed when the girl was blotto and all evidence about to be crisped.

Henno waited, left the gadgets of her addiction all about: the needles, blood-stained syringes, the foil, sachets. Obscenities all. He almost puked, despite the terrible temptation of the desirably inert Rani, snoring into coma though still round and alluring, sprawled on the bed of her one cramped fifth-floor garret.

Twenty minutes later he decided to do it.

'Should've done as you were told,' he told her, 'and got gone.'

The petrol was hardly adequate, didn't seem much. Maybe that was part of the plan? He didn't dare go out for more. He poured the bottle over the bed, saving about a quarter for Rani as Rack had instructed, then dragged her to the open window. Why not the other way round – splash her by the sill – God alone knows, but Rack had ordained it so.

He tried to lift Rani's eyelid and peer in. No good. She was flat out. Was her breathing shallower? It had better be. He checked his mental list: light left on, her shoes on, her hands pressed briefly to the window-pane.

She was heavy. He heaved, got her kneeling on the windowsill, and reached for the bottle of petrol. He poured it over her dress, keeping his gloved hands away. Then he struck the match – not a lighter, Rack's orders – touched it to her and flicked it onto the bed behind, in that order. He let her go as the flames licked up her. She fell without a sound. He stepped instantly behind the curtain, terrified at the sudden whoosh of flame on the bed. The heat almost singed him. Thank Christ he hadn't gone for more petrol, and done exactly as Rack said.

Listen for the crunch, was Rack's instruction, *before leaving*.

There was a thump below in the courtyard. Henno slipped out, wincing at the heat.

Two doors along the landing he slipped into another flat, not needing to knock. The woman was watching television with a babb on her tit. Henno walked on through and ran a bath, discarding his clothes. The woman took no notice, except after a bit she called out asking would he be much longer.

'I'll be as long as I like, love,' he answered. 'I'm here until breakfast.'

'Only, my barn's to bed soon.'

'So'll I be,' Henno gave back. 'So will you. We've got ten hours in here before I can go. Where the fuck's a towel? You not got me a towel?'

The woman stifled a laugh. 'Top rail above you. Want me to scrub your back?'

'My front, you lazy cow. And get me some fish and chips. I'm fucking starving.'

41

O FF TO LEARN dancing, Clare thought, leaving brightly from the hospital's main entrance when one of the reception staff pointed remindingly to the indicator board. That's the answer I should call out, let everybody hear. With my hired lover, my booking phoned in and confirmed. Two hours, one dance lesson and one better not even thought about until she pushed open that hotel bedroom door.

Instead, she said as if tired, 'I'll be on my clinic number until nine o'clock,' saw the clerk entered it in the display screen behind the desk, and left, acknowledging the wave from the man at the League of Hospital Friends papers-and-flowers shop. She felt on top of the world now her plan was finally made. She unlocked the driver door of the old Humber and threw her handbag onto the back seat.

Leaving the house as she had was the catalyst, she knew, severing all marital ties. She was transformed. For a moment, adjusting her position in the driver's seat, she inspected her face in the courtesy mirror. Bright, alert, youngish, not at all bad.

Smiling, she keyed the ignition, looked up and saw Hassall standing there. He came to the passenger door, waited for her to reach across and click the handle.

'Not at all bad, Doctor,' he said. 'Makes me wish I were half a century younger. Give me a lift?'

'Where to? I'm not going past—'

'Drop me anywhere. Ta.' He doffed his hat to enter, sat heavily. 'Had a good day? I haven't.'

'I'm sorry to hear that, Mr Hassall. Yes, not bad.'

All the better when you get out, she thought candidly, trying not to focus on her coming interlude with Bonn in case some clues of her anticipation leaked out to the unwelcome passenger.

'Hear the sad news about Mr Pennington?' When she nodded, pulling out of the car park and gauging the stream of traffic in Cardington Road, he sighed and said, 'I'm taking a risk, being here with you, eh?'

'Risk? Is my driving that grim?'

'Mr D'Lindsay, Fern Allbright, that Dulsworthy, and now Mr Pennington, all deceased. Like an epidemic, statistically speaking. All acquaintances of yours.'

'Not mine, Mr Hassall.' She spotted a gap before a Stobart lorry and accelerated into it, taking station behind the series of red tail lights. 'My ex-husband's, yes.'

'Harbour political ambitions, does he?' Hassall enquired mildly.

'Clifford? Not that I know.' She smiled, perceiving his tack. 'I see. Clifford had everybody eliminated to become the city's MP?'

'No, Doctor. We police aren't that thick. Besides,' he added, embarrassed, 'I've already looked into it. He's not even offered candidature. And he'd need a fund-raising agent, a free devotee like Fern Allbright, and a fixer like Dulsie. Daft to rub out his support team.'

'Clifford hasn't the nerve for Parliament.'

'I think you'll find he has, Dr Burtonall.' In the shocked pause he added, 'Had.'

She glanced at him. 'You surely—?'

'Eyes on the road at all times when in control of the vehicle, please.'

He said it smiling, still avuncular. She was worried. She had intended to go straight to the car park behind the Station Brough. Her route was taking her that way, but she had to get rid of him. He was more purposeful than he looked.

'Clifford?' she shot back. 'We're talking of Clifford?'

'I came to ask why you phoned him at the City Hall. Pennington, I mean. The deceased, the alleged suicide. Why did you?'

She felt her cheeks warm. 'It was a confidential source. Something I overheard in a doctoral capacity.'

'And like a kind doctor citizen you tried to warn him?'

'Yes, Mr Hassall. I felt foolish, really wasting my time. I didn't ever properly meet the man. I'd no idea he was suicidal.'

'The poor bloke maybe regretted his action at the last minute. He seems to have been dragged quite a distance dangling from the train, maybe as if he'd made a grab for the open door.'

'How terrible.'

'Have *you* any regrets, Doctor?'

He pointed warningly to a motorbike overtaking at speed. She nodded that she'd already spotted him.

'About marriage, divorce. What?'

'Say about leaving your full-time hospital post and looking after a load of tarts and dossers.'

'Certainly not. I feel I'm really doing some good.'

'Taking your labour into the market place, eh?' He said

nothing more until the Humber rolled into Victoria Square. 'Here will do, if that's all right.'

She checked the mirrors, signalled and pulled over, earning a couple of irate shouts from taxi drivers. Clare avoided looking out as Hassall made to alight. It was unfortunate that he'd asked to be put down at the junction with Quaker Street, near the Conquistador Bed and Grill, close to where the girls touted at Waterloo Street. It was almost as if he'd chosen the most embarrassing spot, the pavements where many of her new patients strolled.

'Ta, Doctor.' He made to open the door, half-turned in the seat. 'Just one thing. I'll be bringing Mr Burtonall in tonight, questioning. Help us with our inquiries, sort of thing.'

'Clifford? You're arresting him?'

She thought, *Why am I not shocked, alarmed, afraid?* Not too long ago, she would have been all those, and flown to the police station to insist on Clifford's innocence and make a fuss about legal representation. Now, it felt strangely distant, like news of a possible change in the weather, rain before midnight.

'It might come to an arrest. He's skated close to the edge quite a number of times in the past. People have always rallied, given him alibis. In the way of relatives and allies.'

'What has he done?'

'You mean what charges will I bring,' Hassall corrected pedantically. 'Somebody had Dulsie topped. The same people stabbed the young man known as Will Ladislaw to death across the road there. I'll be asking your Clifford about the former. I believe he knew the perpetrator of the latter.'

She remained silent. Her cheeks now felt so cold they almost tingled.

'My question, Dr Burtonall, is whether you know of

anyone who might provide your ex-husband with an alibi, should our evidence come to that.'

'Alibi?' She realized what he was asking.

'Yes.' He shrugged, looking over his shoulder at her. 'See, I remember when your Clifford badly needed an alibi. You were able to provide him with one pat, just like that.'

'That was—'

'Back then, wasn't it?' He examined the inside rim of his hat. 'These bloody things always sweat. It's a wonder I've any hair left.'

Clare thought of Zen, so clean, so young. An innocent, really. Her only encounter with him was seeing those strands of wet hair draggling over his handsome dead face when the pathologist reflected the scalp to begin the examination of the meninges covering his brain. It could have been Bonn lying there.

She could provide Clifford with an alibi. She had done it before, frankly, 'back then' as Hassall had said, when she'd believed that Clifford's only transgressions were financial. Rationalizing, she'd convinced herself that it was only city funds being filched, and that very little was involved. But could she now? Everybody listens to a doctor. Her evidence would carry a weight of conviction that witness from others might not. What did she feel for Clifford, if he'd somehow been complicit in the killing of poor Zen, maybe known that D'Lindsay and Pennington were going to arrange for the goer to die?

The image of Bonn's expression came to her, from the time when he'd asked her to warn Pennington. No explanation. No accounting for his presence in her surgery. But she had sensed his profound sorrow at the unwonted death of a friend.

A policeman walked over, tapped on Clare's windscreen.

'Have to move you on, lady.' He stooped, came face to face with Hassall.

'Won't be a minute, Constable. Just one or two things to clear up.'

'Sorry, mate. Move on, lady please. This traffic—'

'You uniformed branch get on my wick, lad,' Hassall said, rummaging. 'I can never find my bloody card when I—'

'Oh, right. Sorry.' The policeman understood and walked off.

'Not a good advert, some of them,' Hassall apologized. 'I might be on the verge of a breakthrough, interrogation-wise.' He smiled. 'I keep trying to talk like them Yank cop shows. Pathetic, at my age.'

'No, Mr Hassall,' Clare said evenly. 'I'm afraid there's nothing I could possibly help you with about Clifford.'

'Nothing you might remember later and come up with?'

'Afraid not.'

'Nothing to help Mr Burtonall, if charges are brought?'

'Not a thing. I'm so sorry.'

'Best get out,' he said after a protracted pause. 'Or that plod'll have you taken in.' He struggled out, puffing, held the door ajar and stood looking in. 'Thank you, Dr Burtonall. Enjoy your dancing.'

'Thank you, Mr Hassall.'

She would have reached across to pull the door to but he pushed it to. She drove off, heading for the Station Brough. She'd be a few minutes late now because of all that, but it had helped her come to terms with her new life. How on earth had Hassall known she was going dancing?

In a sudden pique she decided to meet up with Bonn at

the Palais Rocco as arranged and then insist that they go straight to the hotel instead. It was what she really wanted.

She could dance any time. Chained to Bonn for life, she'd never before felt freedom.